CU00829271

Heavy Metals

Wandering Blacksmith 2

Copyright 2020 Mark B. Gilgam
All rights reserved, including the right of reproduction in whole
or in part in any form.

Cover Art: Kobri
All rights reserved

This is a work of fiction. Names, characters, places and incidents are
the product of the author's imagination. All situations in this
publication are fictitious and any resemblance to actual persons,
living or dead, business establishments, events or locales is purely
coincidental.

1

Table of Contents

The Bronze Crown

Chapter 1
Wandering Stars

A time has come when the sun does not stand among the five Wandering Stars, drowning their light in his golden glare. Two years before, King Tirnmas was still a ruler; now he has grown weak, and the Wandering Stars make their play in the night sky, undisturbed by the moon which has moved up and beyond their arc. The number of the moon is two, the crown-Prince, and who? Srad the satellite watches, standing in the afterglow of its lord, the sun. The number of Srad is five, five spies, but soon Srad will sink below the horizon. For now, attention. Mavors? You'll never know what he'll do.

Prince Ardri's Star Observation Journal

It was the seventeenth day of the month Merzeh when Ardri, the youngest Prince of Rilante, left the Castle of Iwerdonn and rode into the town of the same name.

Despite his youth, he was twenty years old, his shoulder-long, straight, black hair was shot through with white strands. His eyes were of a startling, vivid blue, the features of his face straight and the skin very pale, with the pallor that comes from staying indoors, underground even, for a whole year.

He was dressed for travel in brown wool cloth of simple cut and leather belt and boots. Riding came easily to him despite not having done it for a year. The big, black gelding, though spirited, seemed to remember his rider.

Where the paved road branched, Ardri turned around in the saddle to look back to where the one hundred slim, light-grey stone towers of the royal castle of Iwerdonn crowned the hill of Kaisil. High-flung, pointed stone arcs described a weightless pattern before the grey sky, surrounded by a massive stone wall. It was strange how nothing showed of the octagonal dark heart – the tower Brontigern,

4

the remains of a far older, colossal edifice, the last remnant of ancient Mechanon.

At the end of the road that led to Cape Long, stood thirteen pillars arranged in the shape of a ship, one plated with gold at the prow, and twelve with silver; the Gold Pillar faced east. The two times of the year when day and night had the same duration, and the evening sun stood precisely between the two last silver pillars, her golden light struck the golden pillar and drove the boat east, forever. Ardri remembered how strangely the people of Iwerdonn had looked at him, the ten-year-old boy, as he watched the sunset of equinox with his brothers. They looked strangely at him now as he rode down to Iwerdonn town. They didn't know who he was, but they knew him to be different from them.

The past year now seemed like one long day to him, spent in the tower Brontigern - a whole year of learning about the metals, and the stars, the blood, the sacrifice and the mountain. Alchemy was a hard discipline, and it did not become easier the more one learned. Often one hated his master - a pupil learned more through hating him, his uncle Angkou said. He underwent many probes to prove that his blood was pure, his brain cool, and his heart still.

The consequence of failure is suffering -always.

His mother was there also, but she wouldn't help. 'Don't fail me,' she'd said every time Angkou made him go through the trials. Always he failed at least once. The tainted blood was in the way of passing any probe at the first try -or the second. There were never more than three attempts.

Ardri was the only one left of Queen Serenaiba's sons, as she kept reminding him; if he failed, the last chance for Cryssumha to rise would be lost for a long time, even forever. He was her last die to cast, so she had said, and for an uneasy moment, Ardri had thought that his mother would cry. But no, there had been no softening in Queen Serenaiba. That was a relief. What Ardri needed were allies who were hard and cold and reliable always. He was his own one and only die to cast, so he told himself. This time he had to succeed at the first try. This time failure meant death.

His mother's words kept ringing in his ears: "Don't fail me!"

Ardri had not seen the town of Iwerdonn for a whole year, but it seemed far longer than that.

Now, he remembered not one specific building, knew none of the inhabitants, fair- or redhaired sturdy people. He rode through the main street as a stranger from a world lying in Rilante's past, and the place appeared to him all wrong shaped, peopled by invaders. Two and three-storey houses lined the road. They were built of cut stone, with rectangular lines unpleasing to his eye, and their basements were taken up with workshops which sold clothes, shoes, and furs; there were a goldsmith and a silversmith side by side, and inns where people sat eating and drinking beer. Farmers sold foodstuffs from their ox wagons in the squares.

All of this formed a dirt layer obscuring the old Cryssumha, which was still there, shining through the filth as a rosy glow of bronze. Before an armourer's shop, Ardri dismounted to finger the slick, heavy metal of the knives and mail; there were also some brooches with patterns delicate as lace.

The shop owner was a Rilante man. "This is genuine Dundingin bronze," he said, staring at Ardri with undisguised puzzlement. "I buy from Master Gobin himself. He is..."

"I know who he is." Ardri picked up a bronze knife to weigh in his hand, and laid it down again with regret; this was metal that originated from his own hereditary realm. The Prince had no money to buy it, had never once thought of money for more than a year. Where he was going now, he wouldn't need the Rilante coin.

A troop of riders came past, led by a tall, broad-shouldered warrior with red-golden hair and beard cut short. His cold blue eyes swept over Ardri without saluting the prince. He knew who that was. Lord Gasda, who was called the Dog of Rilante for his unquestioning devotion to King Tirnmas, whom he had served his whole life, first as an arms-bearer, then as a general. His ruthlessness against the realm's enemies was legendary. Gasda had worshipped King Tirnmas' first wife, the Queen Murine, Beloved by All, as much as he hated Queen Serenaiba, whose sons he referred to as the Cryssumha-Brood. Like all the soldiers Lord Gasda was devoted to Queen Murine's only son, the Crown Prince Nolan Ri, nicknamed Flannan for his wild red hair and hot head.

6

The troop swung left into the Harbour Road that wound around the foot of Kaisil Hill, and at the end of which stood our big warehouses silhouetted darkly, a forest of ship masts visible between them.

Suddenly people began to run and call out: "The prince!" Girls smoothed down their skirts, and a market woman quickly passed a comb through tousled strawberry blonde curls. They couldn't mean prince Ardri, being only the Cryssumha brat, so it had to be the crown prince whom Gasda was coming down to meet.

It was Ardri's older brother. Flannan came in sight up the street from the harbour, escorted by a swarm of soldiers like the effigy of a young god, with lord Gasda leading his horse beside him, and sailors and townspeople following in procession.

The crown prince was tall and rangy, unusually powerful across the chest; he had a suntanned, freckled face pleasantly ugly with a hook nose, a strong cleft chin and a long, humorous mouth. His cornflower-blue eyes were the only things beautiful about him, and the dark-red mass of curls caught back in his neck in a gold clasp, the glorious red hair that had given him the nickname Flannan. He wore grey-blue silk above his mail tunic, oblivious of the fabric being slowly shredded by the bronze, high sailors' boots, and at his side a long bronze sword with a golden hilt in a sheath inlaid with gold and silver.

A stout publican in a stained leather apron offered the crown prince a great mug. Flannan accepted and emptied the beer in one long draught to the cheers of the crowd. Never a thought of poison. Flannan's mother Murine, Beloved by All, never had a thought of poison either. Ardri thought that Flannan was just another in the line of brave, bighearted fools, heroes like the mythic Torin Daraval, like King Tirnmas, before Serenaiba and Prince Angkou got to work on him.

Flannan caught sight of his brother sitting his horse alone at the crossroads, and his face lit up. He changed the direction of his triumphal progress, thereby leaving a reluctant lord Gasda a few paces behind him. He laid a hand on Ardri's saddlebow and looked up at him with an affectionate smile. "Riding out, little brother? Do you good to get those noxious fumes of your alchemy out of your head!"

"Yes, big brother. One of the caretakers came to the castle today with a tale of a white stag in Killinibenji forest, eighteen ends."

"Eighteen and white?" Flannan looked keenly interested.

"So they said. Seems wonderful, doesn't it? I want to see." It was at least true that there were two caretakers, who so firmly believed in having seen such an animal in Killinibenji forest, that they had raced each other to the palace, to provide the pretext for Ardri's expedition.

"Did you hear that, Gasda?" Flannan called out.

"Who were those gamekeepers?" the Dog of Rilante wanted to know. He was no fool.

"I don't know."

"How like you, little brother!" Flannan shook his head. Of course, he knew every gamekeeper and caretaker, how many children they had, and the names and age of the brats.

"And you, had a good haul?"

Flannan brightened. "You can say that. The infamous Long Hashtee caught in the attempt of running a cargo of Tolosan wine past the royal tax."

Twenty men in chains were brought through the crowd, headed by a broad man of medium height, whose face was hardly visible under the wild tangle of red hair and beard that clashed abominably with the scarlet silk he wore above the mail tunic, complemented by leather belts and high boots. Following Flannan's signal, the soldiers brought him before the two Princes.

"Meet the redoubtable Lynch, of a reputation richly deserved. Gave us many a merry chase, he did." Flannan smiled affectionately at his captive. "Don't you look so glum, skipper, tonight we'll sample your wine together. That will cheer you up."

"The Kraken take you, royal beachcomber!" Lynch's green eyes glittered furiously. "May all your masts break, may you be becalmed for a year!"

"One or the other would be your only chance to run illicit cargo through my waters, now that I have the Golden Hind." Flannan turned back to his brother. "You should have come, Ardri. When was the last time we went hunting together in the seas or the woods? It must be much longer than a year." He looked wistful. "You have neglected me, little brother."

"So I have." Ardri returned his brother's smile. "How about coming now? I wasn't going to share that stag with anyone. Let's go just you and me."

Flannan's ugly face lit up. "That's an idea! Does anyone have a spear for me? Gasda, lend me your horse!"

With malicious pleasure, Ardri noted the suspicion on Lord Gasda's face. Flannan, of course, didn't think twice about going to the hunt alone with the one next in line for the throne -after a ludicrous thing like a white stag.

The Dog of Rilante dared make no protest. Flannan's affection for his half-brothers was known by all and shared by none. Lord Gasda called five names, and five men stepped forward. "You will accompany Prince Nolan Ri! And...er...Prince Ardri."

"You are right to be careful, Lord Gasda," Ardri said, laying thick approval into his voice. "That story about the white stag does seem a bit incredible, now I think about it. The pirates might attempt to free this Lynch. Taking a hostage would serve admirably for that purpose. I wonder now, will five men be sufficient under these circumstances, maybe double the number would be better? Not that I'd presume to interfere in your command!" He savoured the puzzled look on Gasda's face as the Dog called five more names. They could all come along as far as Ardri was concerned. It was not the throne of Rilante which he was after.

Flannan swung himself into the saddle of Gasda's dark brown stallion. It snapped at Ardri's black mount which bared great yellow teeth. Their riders reined the beasts in and forced them to trot side by side along the road that led inland. They passed the eastern gate in the city wall, and the guards stood to attention and greeted Flannan.

The green expanse of the countryside lay before them, the royal domains, pastures dotted with neat farmsteads built of wood and thatch. Away from the sea, the air was soft, the trees about to bud. Under the grey sky, the green of the land had a luminosity of its own. Ardri drank it in; he had forgotten this saturated green in his year in the tower Brontigern.

"If the wind doesn't change, and I don't think it will, I must go out to sea again tomorrow, after the Birlinn Yehan, the other pirate ship. Lodemar, Lynch's associate captains it. Not half as flashy as Lynch, but double as intelligent. He's by far the more dangerous of the two."

"Birlinn Yehan? What a strange name for a Rilante ship?" Ardri said with distaste. "It cannot really be built of iron?"

"The Birlinn Yehan is a new ship. Reports are contradictory, nobody is really talking. I don't know what Lodemar is thinking, calling it a name like that, even if it has some iron. I mean to ask him." Flannan's eyes had a suddenly absent look.

Ardri's thoughts were racing. The name of the ship was significant. The Red Wandering Star, Mavors, signified war and iron. He wished he knew everything about this Captain Lodemar. The Star Pattern would rise in the sky invisibly at sunset. As the sinking sun stood for the king, King Tirnmas was indeed going down, a splendid ruin of a man, jumped every time Serenaiba looked at him. Flannan was standing for the moon in the Star Pattern. Tomorrow night, the waxing moon would stand by Mavors, its light drowning that of the Red Wanderer. It was almost as if Ardri felt the great wheel of the Star Pattern beginning to move.

"If it comes to a battle in the next days you'll surely win, brother! The stars are right, and a man like you can't lose when the stars are in his favour."

"Those stars of yours!" Flannan shook his head in exasperation. "Ingaly, the Pole Star, to sail by, that is all the need I have of stars! But as you are so sure, come tomorrow. Early, because the tide..."

"Er...Flannan, I may not be able to make it." Ardri blushed fiercely. "You see, when we have the stag," *or find out that those gamekeepers dreamt it up*, but he didn't say that aloud, "I want you to go back alone. There is somewhere I have to go."

"Oh, don't tell me you want to gaze into a girl's warm eyes for a change, rather than your cold stars?" Flannan laughed. "Who is it, a caretaker's daughter? When did you take time away from your alchemy?"

"I promised to keep the secret!"

"Of course, you did!" Flannan hesitated. "You are aware that Queen Serenaiba will want you to take a bride from the old Cryssumha nobility? So be kind, little brother. Don't go breaking hearts too much!"

Just as Ardri had counted on, Flannan swallowed the fiction easily and would make the excuses for his brother's absence.

"Come to think of it, you can't come tomorrow," Flannan said. "We mustn't risk both remaining Princes of Rilante at sea. If I go west, you are the last arrow in the quiver, brother." His face darkened. "Why, oh why did Ridevin and Kuranori disappear like that? To hunt in the Great Wood Bacenis? Killinibenji forest not big enough? It all seems so utterly senseless!"

"Ridevin, and then Kuranori, were on the quest for Torin Daraval's ship, the Kione Lonnir," Ardri said deliberately, looking straight ahead.

"What?" Flannan gripped the rein of Ardri's horse, bringing it to a standstill. "What is that you are saying there, little brother?"

"You see, people were calling them, us, the Cryssumha Brood. Bad blood. Degenerate. You know they do." Ardri's painful swallow and the heat welling up in his face were genuine. "Ridevin, and then Kuranori wanted to prove...don't you see...if they had found Kione Lonnir...but they failed."

"So that was it?" Flannan roared. "If I'd heard anyone saying that hateful word, I'd have bashed his spiteful teeth through his neck! So that was why they started behaving so oddly towards me." He looked sad. "I wish they had told me. Though I can understand why they didn't. But to think how they must have hated me, before, before...I hope they died quickly, but I'll never know, and I can't bear thinking about it." Flannan let go of Ardri's reins, and the brothers rode on silently.

Ardri knew that Flannan was mistaken about Ridevin and Kuranori hating him. They had merely grown up. How they all used to admire their big brother when they were little, he thought. Flannan was always there for them, for weapon training and making mischief, and to protect them from those who hated Serenaiba's sons. It was only that they knew, as he knew, that Flannan would have to go with the rest of Rilante; that was all. But Ardri had always liked their big brother, for no logical reason, and he would prefer if nothing bad happened to him. Who wanted a good heart that brought you nothing but pain, he thought and glanced at Flannan's deeply preoccupied face. "You mustn't think that I would ever hate you, brother."

11

"Listen Ardri, don't you waste another thought on Kione Lonnir! I forbid it absolutely! I couldn't stand to lose my last little brother. Promise me that you are not planning any such suicidal adventure!"

"Of course not, Flannan," Ardri's eyes met his brother's candidly.

"Let Torin Daraval's ship be wherever it is, for now. One day brother, you and I will lead an army into the Bacenis, wipe out the Woodstalkers, skin the Murder Bear, take back Kione Lonnir and the mines, and stuff the mouths of all the spite mongers! I promise!"

Ardri was content with his morning's work. When it became known that the younger Prince had gone to Dundingin, Flannan would draw all the wrong conclusions, and mislead King Tirnmas, the court, and most importantly, Lord Gasda. With a little luck, it might even result in a split between Flannan and Gasda if the Dog of Rilante was careless in what he said.

The dark trees of the Killinibenji forest appeared before them, and the brothers edged their horses on, side by side they galloped towards the forest, leaning towards each other their faces touched for a moment.

*

The tower Brontigern stuck in the heart of Castle of Iwerdonn like a stake. The octagonal tower had been there long before Iwerdonn, had been part of a greater structure, more than a thousand years ago, when the city of Mechanon had stood here. Of that ancient place, only Brontigern remained, and the subterranean passages that tunnelled Kaisil Hill.

In the times of the old Cryssumha, four hexagonal towers had been added and four round staircases inserted in the spaces, thereby converting the tower into a keep. Much later, the builders of ascending Rilante had built the hundred towers of Iwerdonn Castle around that keep. Differing wall thickness and slightly oblique angles conspired to convert all hexagonal shapes into rectangles; doorways and windows had been hidden by tapestries and furniture. The central octagon was forgotten by all but four people, three of them now gathered in the windowless uppermost chamber.

The light from pale green bronze lamps shone on a woman, wrapped in purple silk. Long black hair streamed down her back in a heavy, slick flood. Her wide, black eyes held a silvery shimmer and were fringed by lashes so long that they threw a shadow on cheeks white as curdled milk. Queen Serenaiba resembled a blossom that opens only at night. She was descended in a direct line from the kings of Cryssumha and was the second wife of King Tirnmas of Rilante.

Opposite Queen Serenaiba stood a tall mirror made of glass so clear that the figure in it showed to the smallest detail, a tall, thin, slightly stooping man, in a cloak of threadbare red velvet, with black eyes burning in a bone-white face and unusually long straight hair of a faded, dusty black. Glic Tusil of Ulud was the ninth Master of Mirrors of the ancient Cryssumha, alchemist and astrologer. Few people knew that he still lived.

Beside the queen, a man clad in wine coloured silk sat in a great armchair which had two yard-high bronze wheels. A little of the lamp light fell upon the big wheels that were adorned by bronze gargoyles, which resembled small scaly jungle creatures with huge, round eyes clinging to the spokes with all four feet, each toe ending in a tiny suction cup. Serenaiba's twin brother had been born a cripple.

Angkou's features were sharp, where Serenaiba's face was soft; both had the same full beautiful lips, and the man's long black hair was as thick and glossy as his sister's. Very few people even knew of Angkou's existence and much less about his presence in the Castle of Iwerdonn.

The only other furniture in the room were an intricate bronze trolley beside the wheeled chair, and an eight-legged bronze table in the centre; on the latter stood a shining bronze disc suspended from a tripod.

There had been a long silence between the siblings. It was broken by Glic Tusil's voice, which reverberated in the shining bronze disc on the table and jingled in the bronze wind chimes hanging from the candelabra and on long copper wires from the ceiling. All the bronze sounds joined in a harmony that modulated the voice of the Master of Mirrors.

"The Queen Star Vasara has entered the arena, and opened the heavenly battle. On earth, the figures take their place on the gaming board. Vasara, Mavors, Lute, Dilo stand above the sunset in an arc of power. By the time when the Queen Star, Vasara, and the King Star,

Dilo, marry to stand in the sky as the Star of Cryssumha, then the time will have come to crown the king with the white bronze crown Fenifindrune in the old capital Minit Claghini, to forge the sword Slatynrigan and then...ah then! Ancient Cryssumha will rise again after nine times eighty-one lost generations."

Angkou stirred in his chair. "As you can't resist repeating all over again quite unnecessarily what we all three know by heart, you might as well be thorough about it," he said in a deep melodious voice. "Every three or four years that the Star Pattern repeats itself, you say the same thing. What you mean is, that the last pure-blooded Prince of Cryssumha must sit in this chair, because these my useless legs won't carry me to Minit Claghini to win the crown Fenifindrune. That the last Princess of Cryssumha, my sister Serenaiba, shares the bed of a redhaired barbarian sailor, and tainted blood spewed from her belly."

The corners of Queen Serenaiba's pale, full lips turned upward. "The Wandering Stars pass without consequence in futile repetition over and over again because Cryssumha has been unable to regain her strength, just like you can't gain your feet." Her voice was clear and sweet and merciless. "Cryssumha is a cripple like you, my brother, but I have given it feet."

Angkou's face was expressionless, the long white hands with the oval glassy nails lay motionless on the black velvet, impotent rage emanating from every fibre, and at the same time, there was a strange and perfect understanding between the twins.

"If you could have married Morrik," Angkou muttered. "Younger line but least he's of the blood. Of sorts."

"Ah Morrik," she murmured. "He is strong, but it is I who protects him."

Even coming from the bronze, Glic Tusil's voice contrived to sound acidulated. "The Red Wandering Star is blazing in the sky, his brightness grows day by day. The influence of Mavors has grown over a long time. Some say that an iron age is looming on the horizon of time. A mistake now, and Cryssumha will never rise again, with the Star Pattern rising and falling, meaningless forever."

Neither the queen nor her brother paid any attention to Glic Tusil's words; they knew the stars as well as he did, and this was between them.

"Tainted blood. The thought of a pale-eyed mongrel to wear the ancient crown of Cryssumha does not bear thinking." Angkou's voice was colourless, his figure remained immobile. "And yet, there is no other way." He reached out to a wine cup standing on the bronze trolley beside him.

Serenaiba stretched out a lazy hand and pushed the trolley so that it rolled slightly out of Angkou's reach. "There is enough Cryssumha blood in Ardri for him to pass all your tests, Angkou. Even pure blood has been known to fail under probes less heavy than those you imposed on the prince."

"And why not?" Angkou made no attempt to wheel his chair within reach of the trolley. "I had to be sure."

"Is there so much material to choose from?" Queen Serenaiba purred and leaned over the back of Angkou's chair so that it rolled back a little, and forth again, back and forth. "Or is it impotent jealousy? Did you want to kill Ardri rather than see Fenifindrune on his head?"

Angkou hissed, and the creatures inside the wide bronze wheels tensed and blocked the movement of the chair. As Serenaiba laughed, she looked like a mischievous young girl.

"You speak as if it was already an accomplished fact that Ardri will sit on the throne of Cryssumha," the bronze chimes of Glic Tusil's voice interjected. "But the prince may yet fail, like the princes Ridevin and Kuranori failed before him. And when the stars come right again in two years, there will be no more royal Cryssumha blood left to be crowned with Fenifindrune, not even such as is tainted with the blood of the redhaired sailors."

Slowly, deliberately brother and sister turned their heads towards the mirror from where Glic Tusil calmly met the joint onslaught of two pairs of silver-black eyes. There had been a thousand descendants of the royal house of Cryssumha, but there had always been only nine Masters of Mirrors. Now there was only one of them left, in the far-away city of Ulud.

"What can we do but wait," Angkou said. "Since you, Glic Tusil, in all your indecently long existence still found no Ledrithud magic to put up against the primitive Maldryg sorcery of the Wood Savages."

15

For the first time, the white face in the mirror showed emotion. "You don't understand Prince Angkou. Maldryg, the woods sorcery is the very power which destroyed Cryssumha, no less. Cryssumha did not fall under the stone axes of savages, as each chronicler keeps parroting after his ignorant predecessors for want of accurate knowledge."

"You know. You were there. You failed. Maybe you will never know any kind of Ledrithud that is powerful enough to overcome Maldryg, not then, not now."

"The Maldryg magic belongs to a different world. But for small enclaves, it has replaced Cryssumha's Ledrithud magic in all the worlds. Once Ardri is inside this alien realm beneath the trees, none of us can reach him. The best way to go into another world is to take as much from your own world as you can with you, allowing nothing of the other world near you. Just like a diver, who prepares to go down into the underwater kingdom, he breathes deep to take as much air as he can and takes a knife for defence against the predators of the sea. That is precisely why I have opposed this idea that Ardri should go alone into the great wood called Bacenis, but nothing I said could dissuade him. You, Prince Angkou, instead of taking my side, chose to keep silence when the King in Waiting came with this idea." The eyes of Angkou and the Master of Mirrors locked in a black, cold fire, with the suspicion which Queen Serenaiba had voiced maliciously hanging in the air, that Angkou's jealousy of a cripple wanted Ardri to fail in his quest for the crown Fenifindrune. Glic Tusil addressed the queen. "And you, Queen Serenaiba, who exert the most influence over King Adri, your son, you should have used it, you still can. He can't have gone far, a rider dispatched with a summons..."

Queen Serenaiba met the Master of Mirror's basilisk stare placidly, pale lips curving upward. "Ah Glic Tusil, but I concord with Ardri, the King in Waiting, not with you."

"And so, do I." Angkou's lips curved in a mirror image smile to his sister. "You are old, Glic Tusil, you hide in Castle Marrak, and you are beginning to think only in terms of the safety which lances and soldiers can ensure. You seem to have forgotten the essence of Ledrithud, the Magic of Cryssumha. Sacrifice. As Ardri pointed out rightly, the King in Waiting Ridevin went into the Bacenis with the most experienced Woodsrunners as guides, and none of them was seen again. King Kuranori took three hundred elite soldiers with him, at the added risk and inconvenience of having to silence all these men later on. They will never speak now. I believe it is indeed as Ardri suggested, that a King of Cryssumha must come to Minit Claghini in a different way, by putting himself into the power of the stars, and offer himself as a sacrifice, promising to pay more, and then pay more than he promised." An animated flush crossed Angkou's pale cheeks as he was speaking of the sacrifice.

"What if your pride has just thrown away the last chance for the rise of Cryssumha, my Prince Angkou, my Queen Serenaiba?" Not looking at brother and sister, Glic Tusil brushed an invisible speck from the red velvet of his sleeve.

"What if two Kings of Cryssumha were the sacrifice Minit Claghini required, and the third will succeed, no matter what we do? What if Minit Claghini demands a third sacrifice? What if the sacrifices are not pure enough and nothing we do does matter? Ardri asked you this, and you could not answer him. Can you now tell me yes or no to any of these questions, Glic Tusil?" Serenaiba hissed.

With burning, terrible eyes, the Master of Mirrors stared at the royal twins, but they just smiled coldly that double smile of theirs, and then Serenaiba whispered: "After these many years you still just do not know enough."

Glic Tusil slid his long white hands into the sleeves of his dark-red cloak and bowed his head so that the long straight hair fell forward to hide his livid features.

After a moment of silence, Angkou coughed a little. "In a departure from tradition, the marriage of Ardri, King in Waiting, must take place in Castle Marrak before he crosses the river Struenfoly."

Glic Tusil's white face had settled into an expressionless mask. "That will be a most wise precaution, Prince Angkou," he said in a colourless voice. "Who did you have in mind as the bride?"

"Neelam, lord Morrik's daughter. Her mother was of the most exalted, purest blood, and lord Morrik himself is of royal birth, albeit from a somewhat inferior lineage, but there isn't much choice any more. Later, the blood of Cryssumha must be purified further. See to everything in Dundingin, Master of Mirrors. Everything, do you understand."

"You may rest assured that I understand best of all, my prince."

Prince Angkou answered Glic Tusil's thin smile with an equally thin one. He took a bronze bell and rang it violently, and at the first sound of the high metallic tone the door opened, and a boy came in on his knees, from time to time using his hands to steady himself. He crawled to where Angkou sat in his chair and looked up to the Cryssumha Prince with twitching lips and eyelids.

Angkou pointed to the bronze trolley.

*

On his way east, under the Wandering Stars, Ardri rode across meadows, to avoid the farmsteads and the manors of the Rilante lords, and used the road proper only after dark.

He rode faster than any royal courier could. If two hoofs of his steed pounded the ground then the other two stepped upon a different level. Whether the animal was aware of this trick or not, it moved with total indifference.

His eyes on the Wandering stars, Ardri paid no attention to the stiffness of riding after a year indoors, the discomfort of brief rests in barns that this time of year held only a few dusty haulms of hay and straw.

In the first night, the moon waxed beside the Queen Star, Vasara.

In the second night, the moon stood beside the Red Star, Mavors.

In the third night, the moon had not yet reached perfection and stood beside the Dark Star, Lute, who was called dark for magical reasons.

The next night, the moon stood alone, and Ardri came upon an old copper mine and a honeycomb cluster of six-cornered stone houses. Mine and houses were deserted except for one old couple. They received Ardri with abject recognition and served him on their knees, and their dark eyes glowed with passion.

The night after that, the full moon stood beside the King Star, Lord of Lightning, Dilo.

When the waning moon exited the Star Pattern, Ardri wondered what this might purport for Flannan's life. Riding ahead of all notice, he had outrun news of the possible capture of the Birlinn Yehan, and what her Captain Lodemar had said about iron.

***

The two cannons were silent; the western wind blew steadily, and the waves were blue.

In the iron ship's wake, the Golden Hind limped under emergency rigging. With her elegant lines, one hundred and fifty-five feet overall length, two masts and two and a half decks, she looked like a mackerel beside a bull shark. The Birlinn Yehan measured three hundred sixteen feet, including her battering ram and beam; she had three and a half decks. The three-mast-ship had a hundred-and-fifty-foot mainmast.

Captain Lodemar was a lithe, broad-shouldered man, not quite as tall as Prince Flannan. He was in his early thirties, wore his blond hair in a clubbed braid and had the beardless face of a scholar. His attire was simple, consisting of brown cloth breeches, a blue shirt under a brown brocade waistcoat and over-knee boots. From his belt on the left side hung the sword which he had surrendered to Flannan, who had given it right back, after appreciating the Aurora Steel.

The Captain of the Birlinn Yehan was taking the Crown Prince of Rilante on a tour of the ship. He was calling attention to the masts in their movable shoes and the iron-plated hull.

"This ship even smells of iron," the prince remarked.

"Rust," Lodemar said ruefully.

"Bronze doesn't deteriorate."

"Can't use bronze for the steam kettle. Gets too hot."

"Your steam didn't help you to outrun my Golden Hind."

"Nothing helps against infernal good luck," Captain Lodemar said with feeling. "It was your day, Prince Nolan-Ri. As if the universe worked in your favour. Could make a man believe in the mumblings of the star-mongers."

"Call me Flannan. Everyone does. Sea room and weather gage. You're too heavy. And you didn't get the best out of those things." He pointed to the cannon.

"We didn't have enough practice yet."

"Don't know what I think of these. It's taking fortress breaking to the sea."

"Whatever gets the job done."

19

"There I don't agree with you, Captain Lodemar. What if you had hit our waterline instead of our top-mast and we were all floundering in the water, what would you have done then? Couldn't leave us to drown, couldn't let us all climb onto your decks."

"That question naturally occurred to me, and I couldn't make up my mind, not if I'd had more than the little time you left me, hauling up fist over fist as you did," Lodemar admitted.

"I say you aimed too high on purpose. It's a matter of principle."

"If we are to talk about principles, then we better have a glass of wine in my cabin, to wash them down. Strictly speaking, it is now your wine and your cabin, so you should invite me."

"Not so, Captain Lodemar. You are the best man to do justice to this ship. You know her in and out while I'm just flabbergasted that such a big iron thing should float. Do justice to me also, and we will both profit."

"So you ran after me all sails set just to tell me that?"

"That, and to explain that I really must insist on those quayside taxes. In compensation, what do you think about a Royal Commission to the Lands under the Sunset? Your ship is uncommonly suitable to cross against the western winds, and the Northern Circle can't have it all their own way. So much to discuss. If you had just waited for me, my dear Lodemar, then my poor Hind wouldn't be in the state she's in!"

***

The farther Ardri approached West Cryssumha, the remnant of his ancient land, the more Cryssumha people came crawling out of dark workshops and mine shafts to greet him. They were small people, and almost misshapen, with dark hair, black eyes, pale faces, furtive movements; their hands and mouths and eyes had a curious tick of twitching. They knelt to Ardri, served him on their knees, as he looked into their steady, glowing eyes.

In his year in the tower Brontigern, his uncle Angkou and his mother Serenaiba had taught him that the Cryssumha people were passionate slaves, obliging their king to assume ownership of their bodies and souls. Ardri now realised that if anyone ever proposed to cut their chains, they would swarm over him like ants and tear him limb from limb with those twitching, shaking hands.

Chapter 2
The Marriage in Ulud

Ardri saw Dundingin from afar, lying on a mound which rose above the floodplain of the river Struenfoly, and crowned with the eighty-one towers of Castle Marrak. Beyond that skyline, and darkening the eastern horizon, stretched the unbroken tree line of the great wood called Bacenis.

The prince rode towards Dundingin openly; it didn't matter anymore if he was spotted. A message to Iwerdonn needed ten days to convey by courier, and ten more back for the answer. By that time, he would wear the crown Fenifindrune, or be dead.

Once this place had been the city of Ulud; translated into Rilante the name meant a treasury. The second meaning was a meat locker, a stone tomb. The ancient ring-wall retained an atmosphere of monumental size, the tumbled cut granite stones were each the size of a peasant's hut. Ardri knew that once it had been eighty feet high, in places still was, and so wide that two chariots could pass each other on the crown. Even after more than two thousand years, the wall's stone mass remained so great an obstacle that it could only be passed where the gates had been.

Ardri entered Ulud through a gap that had been the west gate, on a carriage path that ran along the old street. The stone slabs of the pavement were still lying firm, and only partly dislodged and broken. To both sides of the road, lay a ruin-field resembling a honeycomb of six-cornered houses; the street junctions and squares had been eight-cornered.

Present-day Dundingin took up less than a quarter of the size of Ulud and a wall had been built around this inhabited space with stones from the ancient buildings, topped by wooden towers. The wooden gate stood open, manned by four red-haired Rilante soldiers, who had laid aside their lances and helmets and were dicing on a stone with tiny faces carved on each of the six sides, that two thousand years ago had been the capital of a forty-foot column.

Oblivious of history, the soldiers were not so of their surroundings. "And who may you be? Sir?" The watchful eyes of the guards took in the contrast of the dark hair and blue eyes, noting the well-made clothes and the big, black, elegant mount.

"Prince Ardri of Rilante, watchman."

Surprised, the guards muttered among themselves, reluctant to let him pass, but evenly reluctant to continue challenging him.

"Fetch your commanding officer!"

Ardri's peremptory tone had the expected effect; it brought out in the soldiers the reflex to obey. One guard went into the wooden barrack inside the gate.

The brief waiting time passed silently.

The officer came at a quick pace, another Rilante man, with the distinguishing mark of a thick, white scar that divided his face diagonally from the right cheekbone down to the left side of the neck.

"Captain Warmond, at your Royal Highness' service." He bowed, but not very deep. "Your presence was not announced, my Lord Prince. We had no idea that you were on your way. Where are your attendants?"

Ardri waved a negligent gloved hand. "They couldn't keep up. I left them somewhere back."

"I see you are just as impatient as your brother, my Lord Prince. I've never seen Flannan checking his stride to wait for anyone." He paused embarrassed, "I mean, of course, the Crown Prince Nolan Ri."

"Warmond," Ardri repeated slowly. "I remember my brother mentioning that name. More than once." This was a lie, of course. Flannan always mentioned some name or other, but Ardri had not bothered to remember them.

The guard captain's face lit up, showing Ardri that here was another soldier besotted with the crown prince, who had a habit of calling every man his friend, and meant it too, and so they were his friends.

Warmond tipped at the scar dividing his face. "You may know then that it was your brother who saved what was left of my head in

22

the battle of Cobhe. I was flat on my back half-blind with blood and the Culuris invader who'd sliced apart my face proposed to also slice my gullet, as he was at it. The prince cut the bastard down personally and then stood over me until somebody dragged me out of the fray. After the battle Flannan, I meant to say the crown prince, had his own physician patch me up well enough that a woman could like my face again. So now I am even married."

"My sincerest congratulations, Captain Warmond. Well, you may like to hear about Flannan's latest." Ardri regaled the guards with Flannan's capture of the Long Hashtee, concluding: "And Captain Lynch was shouting all over the market place, wishing mast break and becalming, and my brother said that any of that happening would be Lynch's only chance to run an illicit cargo through his waters."

Roaring with laughter, the guards slapped their thighs, and Ardri laughed with them. "And would you believe it, but the next day he was at sea again, hunting that fellow Lodemar, Lynch's associate," he closed. "Rumour has it that he has an iron ship, but that can't be true?"

"Hard to say with Lodemar, I know him for a strange one. Where did you think of staying, my lord?" Warmond hesitated a little. "My wife keeps a decent inn, the Mocking Bird, and she would make you very comfortable indeed."

"Thank you, my dear Warmond, but I believe my mother's people have a place somewhere here, and they expect me to put up with them, of course."

"Of course. That would be Castle Marrak." The captain stepped back, the friendliness gone. Ardri was sure that this was not on behalf of Warmond's wife missing out on royal business. It was because he had just reminded everyone that besides being Flannan's brother, he was Serenaiba's son.

As Ardri nudged his horse to pass through the gate, the guard's captain addressed him again. "Since you elected to leave your entourage behind, I will escort you to Castle Marrak myself, Prince."

"If you consider that necessary, captain."

Warmond frowned. "Not because of any dangers to your Royal Highness. Not in my town. I merely consider it owing to the entrance of a Prince of Rilante into Dundingin."

"Thank you, Captain. I appreciate it," Ardri replied, carefully laying some of the said appreciation into his voice, although at this stage he couldn't care less.

Warmond mounted a white and black mare and reined it in slightly behind Ardri's black gelding, with ten men of the Rilante guards following on foot.

To ride up the main street of Dundingin was almost like coming through Iwerdonn, passing the same square fronts of workshops and inns, and most of the people he saw in the main street, vendors or customers, were Rilante people. They mustered the dark-haired pale prince just as the people had in Iwerdonn.

A glimpse into the narrow alleys showed different contours and colours, dark and oblique. The smell of sulphur hung all over the town, and underneath the busy noise of the main street was a stratum of incessant ringing and chiming of many bronze bells. Somewhere behind Dundingin, another city existed, a world apart. Somewhere nearby, ancient Ulud was alive. Castle Marrak lay ahead, a brooding mass lowering above the town like a thunderstorm cloud.

They passed a house with a wooden gallery on which men in leather garb sat drinking, some of them Rilantemen who wore their red hair long and open, but many of the men did not belong to any specific race. One huge brute caught Ardri's eye; he had squarely cut black hair and ice-blue eyes, his face and thick upper arms were sunburnt and scarred, and he held his hands near the hilt of a long iron sword. Iron, here in West Cryssumha.

Ardri noticed dark eyes without the white showing, which belonged to men with long blue-black hair clad in an odd mixture of Rilante clothing, and leather, feathers and bones.

"Woodsrunners, fur hunters," Warmond explained, following Ardri's look. "Some of them are pureblood Amhas. They are tame, not like the wild Woodstalkers of the Bacenis."

Woodstalkers -the same race that had choked Cryssumha in her blood and two of Ardri's brothers. The Prince looked at them carefully, as he rode past, and they stared back at him out of their animal eyes. "Flannan told me about a Woodstalker, some incredibly primitive name. I forget what it was." But he had not forgotten, and his heart was burning with deadly hatred.

24

"That will be the Murder Bear. One vicious son of a wood's bitch, begging your pardon, my lord. So, the Murder Bear's infamy has reached Iwerdonn, and well it might."

"Murder Bear, that was the name. Crude!"

"The Murder Bear first stopped the East Cryssumha ore and metal trade, and then he also ruined the fur trade for us. About thirty hunters were killed since last summer. The prices for skins and furs have gone up, and from time to time that entices some woodsrunners to take the risk, but for the last year none of them has ever returned across the Struenfoly."

"And you trust these tame Woodstalkers? Might it not have been they who betrayed the hunters to the Murder Bear?"

"The Amhas are a different Woodstalker tribe; they wouldn't give the Murder Bear anything. The wild Woodstalkers hate our tame ones and more than once the Murder Bear came after the Amhas for selling skins to us, and after each raid, many more come to us for protection. And drink. They can't resist it. Well, I'm not the one to blame them for that." Warmond winked. "But my wife doesn't like to serve them as they can't stop drinking once they start."

They passed another inn, a two-storey stone building with customers looking out of the window with lively curiosity. A stately woman with long cinnamon coloured hair and merry blue eyes stood on the porch. Warmond exchanged a smile with her. "And that, my Lord Prince, is my wife, Beibini."

"Your servant, mistress!" Ardri bowed in the saddle down to the horse's mane.

The colour of her face heightened, Beibini curtseyed. A girl with a mass of red curls spilling down her back came running out of the door behind her, with both her hands holding an overflowing silver beaker. A smell of beer filled the air.

"And my daughter Blaitisin," Warmond said, with his face softened.

Blaitisin's hair was like Flannan's, perhaps a shade more golden, Ardri thought. Thick, pale lashes framed her blue-green eyes that looked at him with frank curiosity, as she offered him the beaker. He made a show of drinking, but let the beer run out and down his horse's side, satisfied that nobody noticed his sleight of hand.

As they continued along the main street past a fur trader's shop, Ardri saw yet another who was not a Rilante man. He was standing in the door of a smithy, and his shoulders were so broad that he filled the doorframe; a bushy black beard concealed half of his face. At the sight of the prince, he bowed to the floor.

The greeting between the Rilante and the Cryssumha man was brief and cordial. "Master Gobin," Warmond introduced. "If ever you want a sword or armour made, Master Gobin is your man."

"Show me one of your swords!"

Without straightening up or moving from his doorstep, the smith reached inside his smithy and brought out a hilt to Ardri.

The Prince turned the short stabbing sword in his hand, looked the edges up and down, nodded and returned the blade to Gobin, who let it disappear behind his back again.

As they continued the ride uphill, Warmond looked at the Prince curiously. "Good blade?"

"The best. His wares sell in Iwerdonn."

"Some say Master Gobin is a wizard. However that may be, Dredorocht-born or not, he is the best bronze-smith in all of Dundingin, and a good man. He equips the guards and we are highly appreciative of his work."

Past Gobin's smithy the houses were empty and tumbled down except for an eight-cornered tower which rose to the left of the road; its massive bronze door was secured with a big padlock. There, the soldiers on foot stayed back, while Warmond continued to ride with Ardri, until they came to a waterfilled moat, with a draw bridge leading to a high bronze gate.

Warmond halted in the shadow of the towering walls. "Castle Marrak," he said unnecessarily.

There was a door in the bronze gate high enough to let a rider through, but it remained shut. Instead, both tall wings began to open silently.

Warmond turned his horse. "My Lord Prince, before I leave you, allow me to remind you that this is a border town. Although there haven't been any Woodstalker outrages lately, as we haven't given them a single chance, it is not advisable to feel too comfortable. I advise you to go about the countryside only with a sizeable escort, which I will consider my duty to provide, whenever you require it.

And most of all, remember that it is certain death to cross the Struenfoly."

"You know Captain that my brothers crossed the river. They never returned."

"That was before my time, Prince Ardri. I should never allow such a thing. Flannan...I mean to say the Crown Prince Nolan Ri would never forgive me if I let anything happen to you."

"He would take that very badly indeed, Captain Warmond. Flannan loves me. He is the best brother I could wish to have."

Ardri drove his horse onto the drawbridge, leaving the guards captain standing in the road with a pensive expression. The hoofbeat sounded hollow on the wooden planks, and the dark waters of the moat rippled as if the attention of something big had been woken. He noted that the chains that drew up the bridge were new, the pulley in order, the wheels greased. This bridge could be drawn up any time. Looking back, he saw that Warmond had reached his waiting foot soldiers.

Although the sun had not yet set over Dundingin, it was evening already within the towering walls of the castle Marrak. The light of hundreds of torches played over the magnificent façade of petrified gargoyles, while the tower tops were still lit by the sun. The courtyard thronged with people -Cryssumha people. Not a red or fair head in sight, and all the eyes looking at him were dark, which made Ardri very much aware of the blueness of his eyes. Pages came running to take the reins of his horse.

A big, squarely-built, black-bearded man in heavy bronze armour that seemed to be growing on him like the shell of a centipede, fell to both his knees with a crash and kissed Ardri's foot. "I am Slachlan, my king, steward of your castle Marrak. My family has served yours from the old days of Cryssumha." Still kneeling he looked up at Ardri with large, dark, moist eyes.

"How would I not know that, Slachlan." Ardri dismounted, stepping on the big man's shoulder.

A tall, heavy man with haughty black eyes and a carefully groomed black beard stepped forward. Ardri knew him too, lord Morrik, from a younger branch of the ancient royal family of Cryssumha and governor of Dundingin -Ulud. He bowed deeply, motioning behind him and the people stepped aside. "My daughter Neelam."

There she stood, her eyes black with a silvery shimmer, and cold, so cold. Her mouth was red as a wound, and her skin as pale as the white silk of her dress. She wore her long, black hair piled up on her head in a glistening mound.

Neelam came towards him, floating, more than walking, it seemed, lowering her eyes, and the shadow of her long lashes fell on her white cheeks. She curtseyed deeply.

Gazing upon her fragile white neck weighed down by the heavy black hair, Ardri felt Rilante sinking behind him.

*

It was midnight and the mists from the Struenfoly River branded against the wall of Dundingin, when the more awake of the Rilante guards at the gate poked his dozing comrade in the ribs.

They stared at a disembodied greenish-white face with burning dark eyes at the height of eight feet that floated towards them in the haze. The guards pushed their torches into the coal fire which burned in the bronze basket beside the gate. The flames leapt up, and the white face showed on top of a thin body of average height, that shivered and twitched inside a green cloak.

The white hands that held two mirrors were rock-steady. "Look!"

Compelled, the guards looked into the mirrors. Several minutes later, they still stood looking straight ahead, although the mirrors had gone and their captain stood in front of them with his fists stemmed into his sides. "What did you open the whole gate for? Why are you gaping like cows at thunder?"

"We didn't open the gate," one guard said at the same time as the other said: "There was a green man."

"And he needed the whole damn gate to get through?"

"He had two mirrors."

"Aha, you were admiring yourselves?"

All of a sudden, the first guard began to cry while the second continued to look dazed. Warmond cursed and ran back inside to scan the deserted main street. In the distance, a tall shadowy figure approached the deserted zone before the castle. On Marrak, all the windows were lit and in their distant light, Warmond saw something

28

moving very unlike a man, swaying, bobbing, and flinging out thin arms. Then he disappeared -to the guard's captain, it looked as if the figure sank into the ground. Then, he was gone, and Warmond couldn't see that anyone was crossing the drawbridge.

"So, is that the Prince's missing entourage?" he muttered.

*

Long past midnight the celebration was still in progress on Castle Marrak, as Ardri of Cryssumha, the King in Waiting, wedded Neelam of Ulud.

The hundreds of guests sitting at the long bronze tables had arrived on subterranean roads unobserved by the authorities of what was called Dundingin on the surface, and each one declared as a subject of Cryssumha. All those present were aware that the last die was about to be cast.

When the newlywed retired to the marriage chamber full of mirrors, they were accompanied by eight witnesses of the oldest nobility.

Neelam, pale and dark, wore the golden dress with the skirt split in front. Before Ardri left the tower Brontigern, Queen Serenaiba had explained how on the occasion of the marriage consummation, the wedding dress did not come off. Laughter rose in his throat as he remembered not knowing where to look, as his mother spoke of these honeymoon matters.

Neelam briefly stayed his hand that undid the first of the hundred gold buttons, and then she let him proceed. After the stiff gold-brocade, he also slipped the white silk shift off her shoulders, so that she stood bare in her golden heeled slippers. His hand went up to pull out a gold-tipped needle, and released the heavy mass of her hair, seven hands full, which dropped onto her fragile shoulders and down her back in a dark wave. As he ran his hands over her sleek, white curves, her skin sparked under his fingertips.

The eight witnesses didn't know where to look, while love sighed among the mirrors and out of each stared a white, disembodied face.

Chapter 3
Children in the Woods

Fourteenth day of the month Ebrel. The moon begins his passage down the Star Defile led by the Queen Star Vasara, attended by the imperfect mirror of the waning moon. Day Atenu of the month Ebrel. Moon stands beside Red Mavors. Sixteenth day of Ebrel. Moon meets Dark Lute. The Courtier Star Srad makes his appearance, and is moving in the splendour of the Sun.

Star Chronicles of Cryssumha

The oak trees crowded like wary observers of a catastrophe, unwilling to cross a danger line. Two young men were standing under their gnarled boughs with the young leaves budding. They looked like brothers; both were fair-haired, very tall and wide in the shoulders. One was slim in the hips, while the other was more squarely built. One wore leather breeches and tunic and was armed with steel knives, sword and lance. The other was naked, with light hair all over his body, and bore a wooden lance.

From the cover of the trees they looked out over ruins, broken floors and low murals, six-cornered like giant honeycombs. Sparse, stunted bushes lodged in crevices, and there was very little grass.

"No trees no good," the naked young man said. "No go more. Go back Mothers. Liunblunhier and Liuwhier name brothers both go back Hilde. Bring five pigs. Hilde glad."

"I can't go back," the other said, sadly. "There will be trouble with Bear Mountain. Because of my Sheen. You take the pigs back to Hilde. Tell Hilde to give you my cookie."

The naked youth brightened a little. "Liuwhier tell her." He set off in an easy trot without looking back.

In the centre of the ruin field lay a perfectly circular crater, three hundred feet wide.

Kitt wondered how deep this hole bore into the earth, hundreds of feet, a thousand even beneath the brown mirror of water, it was impossible to judge. Tunnels and shafts opened in the crater walls. He would have liked to see closer, but there was not enough cover unless he went down on his belly and approached like a snake. Which he was unwilling to do, not knowing what prevented the growth of trees and grass.

Keeping under the oaks, Kitt circled the perimeter of the pit. Halfway around, he caught sight of gigantic trees, with red trunks glowing with their own light in the shadows cast by their boughs which were fringed with thick, deep-green needles. These were called Tini trees, a friendly Woodstalker had once told Kitt. He hated the sight of them.

The grove held a circular stone pavement with a charred stake in the darkly discoloured centre, and hanging from it was a bundle of old bones which was wrapped about with light coloured leather-bands with red and black characters, bright and sharp as if these had been painted the day before. Feeling the hair stir in the nape of his neck, he wondered why the victim hadn't been taken down. Why Woodstalkers did the things they did - Kitt now knew a little more about that, but he couldn't begin to understand. He retreated, but it was too late.

Kitt retreated, but it was too late.

Among the red tree trunks, a Woodstalker warrior materialised. His skin and also his loincloth and the girdles wrapped around his body were painted red, white and black in patterns so glaring that he could not be a hunter. In the red and white face, the eyes blazed black. Kitt was surprised that he only saw this Woodstalker so late.

The warrior ran at him frontally, swinging a spear in one hand and a club in the other. Kitt drew his sword, struck aside the spear and impaled the warrior on his lance.

The warrior pushed himself farther onto the spear and Kitt heard bone scraping along the shaft. For a split second, the shock threw him off balance, and the attacker nearly brained him with the club.

Kitt released the lance, stepped back and swung the sword in a high arc, and smashed through the warrior's wrist holding the club and into the shoulder with a blow that would cut the man in two. It sounded like the cracking of dry wood. There was no blood. A bundle of bones and leather stuck on Kitt's sword. Loose bones fell to the ground with the spears, the club and the cut girdles.

Another warrior appeared as suddenly, painted like the first, so near that Kitt had no time to disengage his lance or sword. He also ran straight at Kitt with lance and club. Kitt gripped both his wrists and wrenched. The arms sprang out of their sockets, the elbows cracked, but the warrior did not release his weapons. The white face with the dark animal eyes was inches from Kitt's and showed only fury. Kitt jerked the captive arms a full turn. They tore out, and he held two dry arm bones. By the fraction of an inch, he saved himself from the gnashing teeth about to tear off his face.

Kitt pushed the armless fiend away and ran for his sword, to disengage it just in time from the bones of the first warrior as two more closed in. He swung his sword in a double ark, connected twice, and spun out of reach. A bundle of bones and cut girdles hit the ground.

Two halves of a body began crawling towards him, and the armless warrior came towards him. Kitt stepped back to avoid the crawling thing, and the tip of his sword missed the painted head of the armless warrior and sliced through girdle and loincloth. The painted leather bits fell to the ground, and the warrior dropped to his knees, of which only the joint and kneecap were left when he hit the ground. Kitt cut the girdle of the halved warrior, who ceased moving, the teeth of his skull an inch away from Kitt's foot.

He was surrounded by the bones of four Woodstalker warriors, who had been dead a time. *Surely nobody can blame me for killing them again? Can they?* But if they had been living men, he would have slain them just the same. When they had attacked, his mind had felt clear, without a hint of the doubts assailing him now.

Doubt and die. Doubts cost moments that decide life or death in battle.

It was the cold, hard voice that a chisel wouldn't cut, and that sometimes spoke to Kitt from somewhere. He had said the exactly same thing about doubt once before.

***

Sixteen round grass houses surrounded a circular place paved with ancient cut stones, the Feen village Mukine-Kad-Nidyas.

In the centre of the village stood a high wooden pole, carved with the figures of a bear, a tree cat, two eagles and topped by a crown of nine rearing serpents. A little off-centre was a second pole, this one plain and charred by fire.

A Feen warrior appeared, tall and rangy, his naturally fair skin tanned deeply by the sun, and long black hair hung loosely down his muscular back; his eyes were black without the white showing. He was naked except for a leather loincloth, and his only adornment was a hand-long curved tooth hanging on a loop of leather around his neck. He was the Feen war leader, and his name was Mangan Sorkera, that meant Singing Bear.

Beside him, holding back a little, shambled former Munitera, the Ludoshini of the vanquished Zoyamizoyi Feen, who had brought Shangar Shaark Ayen's summons. Mangan Sorkera crossed the stone place and approached a hut standing by itself, before it a stake with a bundle of serpent skins.

Munitera sank down beside the serpent stake. He was not allowed to enter. When the Wise Man of the Kra-Tini Feen died, he had a faint chance of again becoming the Ludoshini he had once been. Until then, he was Shangar's servant. Mangan Sorkera did not believe that Munitera would ever have enough power or even brains to take Shangar's place. Without acknowledging him, he entered the hut.

In the centre burned a fire, and its light threw into stark relief the hooknose and hollow cheeks of the man sitting on the skin covered floor facing the entrance. His back was straight, and his shoulders broad; long white hair framed the deeply lined, gaunt face. Shangar Shaark Ayen, Nine Serpents, the Ludoshini, the wise man of the Kra-Tini Feen, resembled an ancient Tini tree, the great trunk hollowed out by the years, spare and light. His eyes, sharp and ageless like serpent's eyes saw into the innermost of the young war leader. When he spoke, it was like the nine serpents hissing.

"Liba Ri Cryssumha cross Skailibashural?"

"Yesterday." The corners of Mangan Sorkera's mouth dropped. "Clumsy Dshooka."

"Liba Ri Cryssumha go Gliyet-Sotal."

The war leader raised his head in surprise to look at the Ludoshini, but as Shangar Shaark Ayen did not add any explanation, he shrugged indifferently. "Guard kill Dshooka."

"Gita destroy Guard Beingil," Shangar Shaark Ayen whispered.

Gita. It meant the dangerous race, extinct except for one youth who for the last five Sun Squares came and went in the Sreedok as he liked. The Feen had different names for him. Mangan Sorkera had hunted him all this time without ever catching him, and for that accomplishment, the war leader called him Gawthrin lye, meaning a clever cub. Whenever Gawthrin lye made a stand, the best warriors went down under his fist. To alleviate their shame, they called him Djanadir Thomiat, hard hammerer. He had bested and killed Agetool-A-Shushei, Mangan Sorkera's blood-brother, and had saved Mangan's life in the Sharkro Shork, the Black Thorn.

Now Gawthrin lye had destroyed the four Guards on Beingil, the Lost Mountain, who had been put there to slay the Dshooka intruders who searched for the green metal they called bronze. Now the Kra-Tini Feen warriors would need to watch that area so that no Dshooka would return from the Sreedok, because if one did, then many would come.

"Call warriors." Mangan Sorkera rose.

***

Ardri had learned everything about the towns and mines of Cryssumha; he knew the distinctive architecture by heart.

There was a detailed map in his head of the places that had to be near now, the Lightning Towers Meltirau, Gwinminit Meingloud, the White Mountain Mine, and Minit Claghini. But nothing had prepared him for the Bacenis wood, so unlike the stands of beeches and light undergrowth, the grass and flower clearings of the Killinibenji forest. Here, oaks towered darkly, their thick boughs twining above, unbroken for miles. The sunlight filtered green through the young foliage like an emerald haze above the rough bark. The rare clearings were overgrown with young trees, bushes and brambles. He couldn't see what lay ahead, could be passing a great ruin without ever noticing. His progress among the thick tree trunks was meandering, and he had no idea how far he had come.

Now that Ardri stood beneath the crowns of the enormous trees, and heard noises that he could not connect to anything he knew, the

34

dark dream he had dreamed in the catacombs of Brontigern lost its meaning. How he hated the Bacenis wood, he thought with sudden passion; he hated the way these trees clawed the earth with their roots like beasts, the way they closed a man in, grabbed for him with thorns. What monsters it was hiding and if he would see what killed him – that moment could be just a breath away. Here man was not the lord.

The only consolation was his knowledge that the Wandering Stars were revolving above in their calculated positions, unmoved whether it was day or night under these trees, whether Ardri saw them or not. The stellar mathematics appealed to him for their logic and precision. He liked to know about the secret wheels and levers that guided peoples' actions without their knowledge, the irresistible forces that drove them.

Down in the catacombs under the octagonal tower Brontigern he had been overcome by a revelation -suddenly he understood the spirit of the sacrifice. Two had gone to Minit Claghini and not returned - Adris's brothers. He thought that Queen Serenaiba, his mother, had known that her first two sons would die in the sacrifice for Minit Claghini. Ardri was the third. He would return. Therefore he would find the way. Now, he realised that despite all his learning, he had not really believed and lost his little faith under the trees. The landmarks would reveal themselves to him if he stood still and waited that they did. *Think calmly!* he admonished himself.

Suddenly, Ardri saw towering rock columns, at the foot of which ran a creek. Time had made them look like a natural rock formation, but Ardri recognised Meltirau, the Lightning Towers. He was standing right in front of them.

When he looked into the water, he saw heavy, grey silvery grains swirling over the bottom. Where the creek had washed out the shore, brown and grey layers had been formed by the shining crystals. The whole creek-bed consisted of tin sand, the first ingredient for the sword Slatynrigan. Ardri unhitched the shallow bronze bowl from his girdle and knelt down by the water.

There was a growl, very near him, a noise such as he had never before heard, hungry, cruel. Quickly, he looked up and into a mask of nightmare, which was looking down on him from the high shore, a triangular, tawny face with wide green eyes filled with intelligent malevolence. Two long, sharp, white tusks protruded from its upper jaw. He felt a sense of doom as he never had at the third try of the probes. This was the Bethrek of the legends. Was there really such an animal, or had Maldryg wood's magic conjured this terror? Hulking tawny shoulders rippled with muscles, and Ardri knew the beast was about to spring. He dropped the washing bowl and sprang up, reached for his bronze spear, and planted it against his foot.

The Bethrek inclined its massive head, and it seemed to grin. Then it began slinking slowly, deliberately down the steep shore towards Ardri.

Kitt heard a splashing noise coming from the creek, then scraping, and another splash.

What it could be that did so little care if it announced its presence to the wood at large - only something dangerous, Kitt thought and glided onto a boulder with a movement so fluid that a lizard, which was sunning itself on the flat top, did not stir. Cautiously he raised his head to look down into the creek valley. Or extremely foolish, he amended his speculations.

He saw a man kneeling on a flat rock, who passed a bowl through the creek water, tilting it back and forward. Beside him lay a lance with a broad, gleaming bronze blade, two hands long. He wore an embossed leather tunic and trousers under a thick jacket made of sheepskin with the wool turned inside and showing at the seams. Kitt couldn't see the face hidden under a hood of marten fur but judging by his movements, the stranger was a young man.

As immobile as the lizard beside him, Kitt watched the stranger. With a quick practised movement, he swirled the contents of the bowl, then decanted the turbid water with a splash and emptied the sediment onto a cloth lying beside him. It seemed to be sand, layers of black and brown, with a crystalline glitter. The young man used the bowl as a shovel to scoop up more sand from the bank beside him, which accounted for the scraping noise Kitt had heard, and dipped the filled bowl into the creek again.

Suddenly, there was a different splash in the water, a fish or a frog, and the man's head jerked up. The hood fell to his shoulder and revealed shoulder-long, square-cut black hair, shot through with white strands. As he turned around, Kitt saw the stranger's face, it was finely cut with high cheekbones and blue eyes, a young, brave, intelligent face. What made this creek-sand so valuable that this man would go into Feen territory to collect it? And also, Dodlak, Death-Smile Cat, territory.

From the corner of his eye, Kitt caught sight of a tawny back, ten feet long at least, worming his way among the boulders. Kitt felt his scalp prickle. The Dodlak had been on his track, and he hadn't had the least idea of that.

The Dodlak approached the boulder that was Kitt's perch.

Kitt froze and held his breath. The lizard shot away.

The Death-Smile Cat raised his head with baleful emerald eyes, and the two hand long white teeth gleamed.

Another scrape and splash came from the creek. The Dodlak turned towards the noise. Now the predator was directly below Kitt's perch. It stood more than four feet high, and he looked upon the rolling muscles of the massive shoulders and sloping back. The tawny fur with lighter spots gave it a sun-dappled appearance. The Dodlak slid by the boulder, not noticing the youth squatting above him.

It was quite clear to Kitt what was happening. The Dodlak had followed him. Kitt knew that he did not leave very much of a scent for a predator's nose, due to his habit of rolling on the earth among herbs and fallen leaves. Now the beast's attention was diverted by the astoundingly clumsy behaviour of the unwary stranger by the creek. It need never notice him. Kitt could just wait until the beast was feeding and then retreat. He remembered too well when three years ago he first had come face to face with a Dodlak, a moment in which his own death had seemed very likely. Kitt had fought the beast and killed it, and had never kidded himself, knowing that if he had made one wrong move, he would have died that day. The powerful shoulders tensed as the Dodlak edged towards the precipice.

The squatting man's attention was taken up with his work; he did not look up to see the Death-Smile Cat above him on the rim of the steep slope.

The Dodlak growled, a low, and almost purring sound.

The stranger looked up to the high shore and Kitt could see his suddenly chalky face, blue eyes widening. At first, he seemed paralysed at the sight of the enormous predator above him on the ridge. Then he dropped the washing bowl and sprang up. With a practised movement he gripped the spear and planted it against his foot. Kitt knew that would not answer. A Dodlak did nobody the favour of jumping into a planted spear. Secure in his strength, he had warned the doomed prey, to play with it. The Dodlak was as intelligent as a Woodstalker, and as cruel, it was the only animal Kitt knew that killed for pleasure.

The Dodlak Death-Smile Cat stood staring down until the knowledge that he was lost settled on the stranger's face like a death mask. Then, it began to move deliberately down towards the creek.

Kitt sprang. His feet hit the ground to both sides of the Dodlak, and his legs clamped its sides, his left arm fastened around the muscular neck. He drove the long knife into the beast's upper chest. The Dodlak roared; together they tumbled over the edge in a shower of gravel. Turning over and over they continued rolling down the steep slope, the Dodlak screeching and Kitt driving in the knife. It seemed not to have the least effect; the Dodlak continued thrashing about with unabated fury.

They rolled into the creek, and Kitt came to lie under the massive, writhing animal, his head pushed under the ice-cold water. Holding on to the knife hilt with both hands, he pressed the blade in farther, the muscles of his arms and shoulders locking in an iron-hard ring.

At last, the Dodlak spasmed, and lay still, the dead weight pressing Kitt down. He felt the rocks of the creek sharply in his back. The cold water sloshed under his leather clothing, and he shivered violently. He pushed with his mouth and nostrils full with soft fur.

Suddenly the beast's weight slipped from Kitt and left him free to come up out of the water, to gulp air in big draughts.

Ardri watched as his sudden rescuer extricated himself from under the Bethrek and straightening up.

He was well over six feet tall, shoulders made to scale, the hard muscles of his arms sprang out in cords. He wore a sleeveless leather tunic and leggings, both of indefinite brown and green colours, and soft leather shoes without soles. On his belt were several leather pouches and bags, the sheath for the long knife that now stuck in the monster's heart, and two smaller blades. All hilts seemed to be iron. No adornment was visible but he had something on a loop of leather around his neck, hidden under the tunic. His mouth was firm, chiselled, and the grey eyes slanted very slightly above broad cheekbones. Long fair hair dripped with water, fine hairs gleamed on arms and legs. A barbarian. No beard, he had not yet started growing one. This was a youth, no more than maybe fifteen or sixteen years old, as Ardri realised with amazement.

The young giant stooped and dragged the Bethrek carcass out of the water. Ardri noted the ease with which he handled the dead beast that must weigh as much as an ox. He wrenched his knife from the tawny chest, and Ardri saw that it was indeed an iron knife that had killed the monster.

Thoughts began racing through his head: if here was a manifestation of Mavors, with the iron in his hand, the iron of the great muscles, the quiet iron-grey eyes, and if so, what it meant in the present constellation of the Wandering Stars.

The big youth used the knife to break out the dagger-like ivory teeth and then began skinning the carcass, apparently forgetting the presence of Ardri, who was watching him from under lowered lids.

"What is your name and where do you come from?" the young King of Cryssumha asked in a sharp tone that invariably extracted answers from the lower orders. "Is your village near?"

The big youth stopped his skinning work for a moment to consider Ardri carefully.

"No village near here," he finally answered in the language of Rilante. That was a nasty shock.

"You don't look like a Rilante man?" Ardri demanded.

"What are you doing here this deep in the wood?"

"I can ask you the same question."

"You don't belong here. I do," the young giant said, appraising Ardri with his light-grey eyes that overlooked nothing. He bent down again to continue skinning the paws and extracting the Bethrek's claws one by one.

"My name is Tagard," Ardri lied. "I am a liegeman of King Tirnmas of Rilante. He sent me into the Bacenis to search for his lost sons, Ridevin, Kuranori and Ardri."

The Prince noted with relief that this revelation did not produce any reaction from the young giant, who turned over the carcass to get at the other side of the monster. Blood swirled down the creek. "You found something?"

"No. I don't even know where to look. And almost was I lost also. I thank you for saving my life from the Bethrek. Whenever you come to Iwerdonn, the king will reward you well."

"My name is Kitt. Of Isenkliff. I've never been to Rilante."

Isenkliff. Minit Houarn. A solitary island in the Northern sea, a centre of steel, where a temple of Mavors stood. Mavors, the Red Star, whose metal was iron in his aspect as the Destroyer, was the obstacle in the way of Vasara and Dilo in their approach to each other. The Destroyer had entered the Star Pattern, on the sixteenth day of the month Ebrel.

If the young barbarian calling himself Kitt was the manifestation of Mavors in the Star Pattern, he did not seem aware of it though. He tugged energetically, and the Dodlak's dripping skin came off the carcass like a coat. So that was left when one lost the battle, just a nasty heap of bloody meat and white bones, Ardri thought with fascinated horror, looking at the remains of the stalking death. "In Rilante this beast is called a Bethrek. It is also called a myth. And the myth nearly killed me."

"You call this beast Bethrek, I know it as Dodlak," Kitt remarked. "Here in the great wood Murkowidyr animals survive, that have died out in other places."

"We call this wood the Bacenis."

"Do you? Interesting," the youth said with a satisfaction this remark hardly deserved. "I always wondered if it was the same wood." He knelt down again and drove the long knife into the chest of the Bethrek, parting the breast bone with a sharp crack, and then pulled apart the ribcage. He thrust in his hand, tugged, and then he held the Bethreks's heart in his red hand. The bleeding organ was the size of the young giant's fist, and they could see that each thrust of the long knife had hit. One stab had pierced it through. The two young men exchanged a thoughtful look.

"What a lot of killing that Bethrek took," Ardri said. "What damage an animal like that could inflict with those claws and teeth in the long time it takes it to die."

Kitt cut himself a piece from the heart and ate it raw; then he cut a second piece. The barbarian was obviously hungry. "I haven't eaten today," he explained, and cut another piece of the heart to hold out to the Ardri, who waved away the bloody chunk with ill-concealed disgust.

"Do you always eat your meat raw?"

"Not the place to make a fire." Kitt ate the rejected piece himself. "And not the time, either."

Ardri watched his saviour with distaste, as he was sitting there on his haunches, and bit the red, raw flesh with strong, white teeth, tearing off bits with a determined movement of the head like a wolf. He chewed with dark clotting blood running down his chin and hands, and his calm, grey eyes roamed the rim of the valley.

What monsters this wood held! Ardri could not tear his eyes away; with morbid fascination he watched until the last shred of the bloody heart had gone, and again he felt so very lonely in these terrible woods, with this young wolf sitting there and devouring his bloody fare.

When he was finished, the barbarian washed his hands and face in the creek. The wolf reverted to man. "Let's go!" he said. "Fast. The fight with the Dodlak has made a lot of noise. Somebody will come soon."

Ardri looked about him. All he saw and heard was spring awakening. "I see nothing," he said.

"That's what you see if it is the Woodstalkers who come. Or the Hunters in the Mist."

"Woodstalkers, we too call them that. I don't know the Hunters in the Mist. Who are they?"

"Dangerous. We must go. Fast!" Kitt repeated.

Ardri could not see at all what had caused this sudden agitation in the young barbarian, and his old distrust of everybody began to assert itself anew. But he didn't argue, and just started to pass his bowl through the water again. "I am not finished here."

"You are finished. One way or the other."

"Kitt, I thank you again for saving my life. Remember, there is a reward waiting for you in Iwerdonn."

"Not if you die now."

"Listen, I am all grown up, more than you are. I'm a man, not a boy. Hasn't your mother taught you to mind your own business?" It seemed reckless to talk in this manner to a being like this Kitt, but Ardri wanted desperately to offend him enough so that he would take off in a huff. For what he had come to do in the Bacenis, Ardri needed no witnesses.

Finally, he seemed to get through the barbarian's thick skin; he did not look offended, but as if he thought Ardri an incredible fool. He didn't care what the youth thought, only wanted him away.

Kitt shouldered the Bethrek skin, climbed the riverbank and was gone. Ardri was surprised how fast he had lost sight of that big youth. He passed the wooden bowl through the water a few more times, all the while looking up to the high shore, asking himself, if this Kitt was watching him hidden among the ruins of the Lightning Towers, and would he see him, when he hadn't seen him before, any more than the Bethrek. Ardri's time was running out, the dance of the wandering stars did not wait for anybody. He took up the cloth with the tin ore, tied the ends and stowed it into his bundle. It was not far now. The gate from which this water was streaming had to be near. He wondered if one of his brothers had ever come this far, at what point he might have passed their remains, bones strewn about and chewed.

Keep your mind on the landmarks! he told himself, and followed the creek. The ground began to rise, and he almost ran, feeling that he was on the right way, Meltirau the Lightning Towers behind him, Minit Claghini had to be ahead.

A grey mountain wall rose before him and from a perfectly round opening above the creek gushed, jumping over the stone threshold and running down the stone steps, carrying the tin ore into the valley. This was Tungiat, the Tin Gate. Ardri had pored over pictures of it, painted on old vellum, to recognise it instantly, even with the cut stone withered and forced apart by roots, making it to look almost like a natural cave.

A winding stair climbed up further past the Tin Gate Tungiat, the steps smoothed with rain and overgrown with grass. Fearful of failure at the last moment, Ardri looked around him, and his heart missed a beat. *Was that a Woodstalker I just saw?*

But where he thought to have seen the tall naked figure looking at him with those black animal eyes, there was nothing now. Fear must have played him a trick Ardri decided, but his exhilaration was gone, as he set his foot on the first step of Minit Claghini.

Chapter 4
The Queen in the Mountain

Halfway up Minit Claghini, Ardri came to another opening in the mountain. Here also time had dislodged the cut stone, smoothed the ornaments, and erased the façade in more than a thousand years.

Gyatorlowinel, West Gate. He stepped across the threshold, into a long high hall formed by mining. The grey rock walls still held traces of glittering copper ore. The tunnel widened, narrowed again to take a sharp left turn and ended abruptly before a white stone veil. Without hesitation, Ardri slid behind it into the hidden opening.

He took nine steps and stood in absolute darkness. On the wall above his head, his hand touched a metal projection. It was an indescribable feeling to find a thing that was as he had learned about it, in his year in the tower Brontigern. For the first time since he had crossed the Struenfoly, he dared hope that he would succeed. Now for the decisive test, Ardri spoke a word: "Lugom Lun Gawaru!"

Here, inside Minit Claghini, this word carried power. The metal piece clamped at the tip of the copper rod ignited with a blinding white flame. It lit a corridor ten feet high with a vaulted ceiling. Not all the ore had been extracted, and the polished walls were striped with white, grey and brown layers glittering with golden speckles. In the centre, the floor deepened, ground by the passage of many feet for a thousand years, the last passing more than a thousand years ago. The inside of this mountain had nothing to do with the wood outside. This was another world, this was Cryssumha.

*

Kitt picked up his sword which he had left on top of the rock and slung it on his back.

The Dodlak skin he rubbed with a mixture of bitter-salt and herbs disagreeable to meat-eaters, using up all he had with him for the purpose, and folded it, so that the raw side was outside. He selected an oak tree and tied the skin to a thick bough, safe from animals, but

44

for the Woodstalkers to find, should they set out on the man Tagard's track. Kitt did hope it wouldn't come to that, as he had rather set his heart on owning the soft, tawny pelt. But it would serve as a distraction.

He picked up his lance and returned quietly to the creek. It did not surprise him to find Tagard gone. The young man was careful, what they might call careful in Rilante, deeming it cunning to walk in the water for a while. It was easy for Kitt to pick up the trail where Tagard had left the creek, easy for him to follow the spoor along the valley. It would be equally easy for a Woodstalker. By himself, Tagard would never get out of the Murkowydir alive. It was a wonder that he had come this deep into the wood.

Kitt realised that again it was his decision if Tagard lived or died. He did not want that decision, but he had to make it. Life was the right choice, always, that was what his mother had taught him. Perhaps this life saved would weigh in the balance with those of the Yeheoeinee, the Hunters in the Mist, who he had slain at Bear Mountain. He never wanted his mother to know, but since he had learned that there was a thing like the Sheen, which all people possessed, and some could perceive, he realised there was little chance of that. That he'd barely escaped being roasted over a fire and eaten made no difference.

Kitt spent some time removing crushed grass blades, restoring disturbed leaves and upturned pebbles to their former place on the ground.

The young man from Rilante appeared to know exactly where he went. Getting tired of scrambling along the creek his track became glaring, and it took Kitt ever more time to alter the tell-tale signs of Tagard's clumsy progress, to convince the Woodstalker warriors that they were dealing with just the one familiar intruder. Too much time. Another ruse was indicated. He returned to the place by the creek and laid some false trails originating from where the dead Dodlak lay, all petering out at some distance in the woods.

Just as he was about to follow Tagard again, he stopped dead. Three Woodstalker warriors stood by the bloody remains beside the creek. Two of them were splendid with necklaces of bear's teeth and claws, feathers in their long blue-black hair, and ornaments of human skin and hair on leggings and arms. They had long spears with leaf-shaped blades made of dark grey stone with white bands, transparent and razor-sharp edges.

The third man wore a Dodlak fang as the only ornament and clearly was in command, the Feen war leader, Mangan Sorkera. He was armed with a short lance that had a bronze blade, and a broad bronze knife stuck in his girdle. The Singing Bear had hunted Kitt more than once before, at Latunsrigo, at Bear Mountain. He wondered disgruntled if he was everywhere in the Murkowydir, if he was out for Kitt's heart again - or for Tagard's.

From his vantage point, Kitt saw several warriors in the woods, hunting for tracks and finding too many. He grinned to himself. But soon the war leader frowned, set the whistle to his lips and blew an impatient tone. He didn't believe in those tracks. Kitt had had little hope that he would. The Woodstalker warriors abandoned their search. At Mangan Sorkera's command, two of them set off along the creek. With luck, they would mistake Tagard's genuine trail for a fake now.

The war leader seemed not in a hurry to leave, and while he stood still by the Dodlak carcass, his warriors in unquestioning attendance, Kitt did not dare to make the slightest move. The blue-black eyes scanned the rocks and the treetops, a faint smile twitching the clear-cut mouth.

Kitt stood still, so still that he became stone among the rocks that lined the rim of the little valley. For a moment, the war leader's eyes seemed to look right into his, and he even stopped blinking, and did not so much as exhale when those eyes continued their search.

The two warriors dispatched along the creek returned; one had his arms full. Kitt cursed inwardly. That was the second Dodlak skin gone.

The Woodstalker warriors gathered around the tawny pelt; they touched it hesitantly, traced the light spots, scrutinised the paws and the knife marks.

At last, the war leader gave the sign to leave the creek valley; he passed not far from Kitt's hiding place at the head of his men. There was a faintly dissatisfied air about the way he slightly turned his head to the right and left.

As soon as the Woodstalkers were out of sight, Kitt threw himself silently into the shelter of the trees.

Mangan Sorkera took a wrong step and stumbled slightly, suddenly remembering grey eyes looking into his, grey eyes that had been upon his every move -until now.

"Gawthrin Lye!" he muttered.

His warriors looked at him, surprised. With quick movements of his hands, he commanded them to spread out among the rock columns by the creek. One after the other returned and shrugged in answer to Mangan Sorkera's questioning glance. With hanging heads, they all stood around their beloved and feared war leader, whose sharp, brief comments on ineptness they dreaded.

Mangan Sorkera said nothing.
*

Ardri followed the passage, which after about four-hundred paces widened into a dome with glittering walls and columns of copper ore. From where three tunnels opened, and he chose the left one, which after two-hundred paces lead to a second dome from which again three tunnels opened. Here, Ardri chose the middle tunnel leading down. The air became dank, but he was not afraid for a moment; inside the mountain, he felt safe.

Another cave like the first, and a fourth - after that, the tunnels Ardri took were going up. Each time he made his choices without having to stop and think; he had studied the outlay of the ancient palace of Minit Claghini for so long.

The last tunnel was a high pointed arch which ended in a bronze portal green with patina, on which a king and a queen were depicted standing, between them a flower as tall as they. In the centre of the petals was a mask, and in the mouth of the mask was a lock. Ardri reached to the velvet band around his neck, drew out the key he had been carrying next to his skin, and inserted it into the open mouth of the mask.

Both door wings swung inwards.

As Ardri went in, he remembered not to step on the threshold formed by a bronze snake with a chain of small holes running along the back, which were not ornamental. The slightest pressure would bring out a row of sharp needles steeped in venom. He wondered if the venom was still toxic after more than a thousand years, and thought that is must be.

The evening sun lit the mountainside, and a cave mouth opened before Kitt, the creek waters running down from it. The track he followed so easily led past the cave, and ascended on something that looked almost like stairs.

Further up, another cave mouth opened like a gate, high and narrow, and Tagard's spoor ended there on the smooth cave floor. The cave was not a natural one; the stone bore traces of sharp, heavy tools that had shaped the rock walls and in places, golden-sparkling quartz remained. Some kind of ore had been mined here long ago; the tunnel penetrated into the mountain, to take a sharp turn and end in the twilight before a veil of glistening white stone like a petrified waterfall.

Tagard was nowhere to be seen. Kitt wondered if he had underestimated the Rilanteman and overestimated himself, and thought not. He ran his hands over the stone veil which closed off the cave end, and was sure that it could not have been formed by the action of water. It was not the right stone. When he looked closely, he saw that there was an opening behind it, disguised by an optic trick. What seemed one sheet of stone were two. A narrow turn to the left led behind the veil, another turn to the right led further into the mountain. After he slipped through, Kitt saw a bright white light disappear around another bend ahead. Silently, invisible in the shadows, he followed, guided by the faint sound of Tagard's secretive progress into the cave and the glare of his light.

The tunnel widened into a dome again. The walls glittered white and golden and columns of golden speckled stone carried the roof, too regular in shape to be natural formations. Several passages opened from that dome. Tagard disappeared into one of them.

Kitt followed the light, taking cover in the shadows thrown black by the stone columns that the miners' pickaxes had left to support the tunnel roof.

This cave was very different from Bear Mountain; the walls were high enough to allow Kitt to walk upright, the floor was smooth and level, feeling more like the inside of a building and tempting him to go in farther, with the only light coming from the device which Tagard carried.

Ruined places abounded in the Dark Wood Murkowydir, but this was stranger than anything Kitt had seen. If at first he had wondered about what was man-made in the cave and what was not, the artificial character became clearer with every step. The atmosphere remained fresh; from somewhere came air.

More corridors opened from the next dome. Somehow the Rilanteman made his choices, but Kitt could see no markings, and he hoped that, if Tagard had memorised a chart, he had a good memory. He followed as closely as he dared. Tagard was still unaware of this shadow just outside the circle of blinding light.

They passed another dome, and another until Tagard stopped in front of a green door. The light showed the images of a king and a queen, clear and sharp, and between them a mask surrounded by flower petals.

Tagard inserted something into the open mouth of the mask, and both door wings swung inwards. He entered, and stepping over the threshold, he lifted his feet high.

Kitt neared the door which had not closed completely. A dim light shone through the crack. The threshold that Tagard had avoided to step on was fashioned from bronze, in the shape of a serpent. A closer look revealed a row of holes running alongside the serpent's back.

Behind the door a high gallery opened; pale daylight shone, like sunlight changed by passage through water, reflected from a double row of polished metal mirrors. The hard, grainy stone was entirely shaped by tools, the ceiling was vaulted, and the columns channelled, with round capitals. Every surface carried ornaments. Lengths of dull, metallic brocade hung from the walls, partly ripped by its own weight.

At the end of the gallery, Kitt saw Tagard open another door, and followed him through a flight of three rooms which contained bronze furniture, tables with small wheels at the legs, cluttered with mirrors, candelabra, bowls and suspended discs the purpose of which he couldn't see.

*

After Ardri had passed the bronze door, every room was lighted with daylight that was channelled down through a complicated system of mirrors and lenses.

49

He went from room to room, until he came to a hall tiled with pale blue stone slabs and lined with columns made of malachite and azurite ore, which met high up in a pattern like cobwebs, the stonework delicate and unchanged as if no time had passed at all. Shimmering red lights were caught in it.

The pale light was reflected from nuggets, cubes and octahedrons of pure copper and blood red crystals; heaps of polished malachite, lapis lazuli and turquoise gems reposed in big, pale-green copper bowls which stood on the floor.

In the centre of the room the Malachite Flower stood. It was taller than Ardri, and had the shape of a tulip with the petals opening and bending outward. Beside the flower a double tripod stood, six feet high. From the upper tier nine small bells were suspended and from the lower a shining bronze disk was hanging.

From the walls hung nine tall bronze mirrors that did not reflect anything in the room. Each one belonged to a high-priest of Minit Claghini, a Master of Mirrors. Ardri knew that only one had survived, Glic Tusil of Ulud.

"Izvara Monedorigan Rigantona!" Ardri called the Queen of the Mountain. This word also was heard. The bronze disk hummed, and the bells chimed.

*

"Izvara Monedorigan Rigantona!" Tagard spoke in a clear ringing voice that was echoed in bronze throughout the chamber.

And then Kitt nearly made an involuntary movement or even cried out, for in that strange, unaccountable room in the middle of the Dark Wood Murkowydir, something even more incredible happened: The stone flower opened. The malachite petals moved apart and inside the blossom a woman appeared. Dripping with red and green and blue gems reflecting the pale light, her outlines were diffuse. The white face under a crown of silvery metal encrusted with green and blue gemstones was perfectly regular and devoid of human emotions.

The woman, the Queen, rose from the calyx onto a petal, and glided over the curve like a rolling dewdrop. She was growing, and when she floated to the ground, she had reached the size of a tall woman, who walked towards Tagard, bearing in her hands a crown the twin to the one she wore.

Tagard knelt before her, and she bent down and set the crown on his head. Then she spoke, in a language that Kitt did not understand except for the word "Cryssumha."

So that's who the young man was, Kitt thought, a king out of a fairy tale.

*

The Queen of the Mountain approached with the crown in both her hands, a nine-pointed ring of white bronze that was studded with malachite and azurite gems of unsurpassed colour.

Ardri stared up at her with a feeling of unreality.

"I greet you, King of Cryssumha!" Izvara Monedorigan Rigantona spoke in the old language.

She set the crown on his head - it fitted, and was heavy. Her white face bent over his for a moment, and then she disappeared.

With the same feeling of unreality, Ardri saw her float up to the Malachite Flower, diminishing in size, and saw the petals closing over her head. He remained kneeling on the floor for a long time, the crown Fenifindrune on his head. Finally, he rose, swaying a little.

Next, he confronted the mirrors, one by one. Eight of the polished copper ovals did not show him anything, not even his own reflection, but in the ninth, an image appeared. Ardri saw the Master of Mirrors, Glic Tusil. The outlines of his long robes were dim and fading, and his face was a white mask out of which burned black eyes.

"I greet you, King of Cryssumha," the voice of the Master of Mirrors vibrated in the suspended disk and jangled in the bells. The mirror showed his thin smile, which was repeated in the disc.

"Nice of you to congratulate first."

"I consider that my greatest pleasure." The thin mouth curved impossibly in the chalk-white face. "Yours are the first footsteps to sound in Minit Claghini for more than a thousand years."

"So, my brothers never came this far."

"No matter now." The mirror image waved a long white hand. "You are the new King of Cryssumha after the Fall."

"Still purely nominally, as the whole way back through the Great Wood lies before me."

"That, alas, cannot be helped. And I don't even have the smallest word of advice for you, King Ardri of Cryssumha. Under the trees,

51

you are on your own. And worse, if you were to lose the Crown Fenifindrune there, it may be lost forever. Bring back your crown! Don't fail now!" Glic Tusil's image faded, the white face disappeared, like the moon behind a cloud. The mirror still showed the room in castle Marrak.

And then a slight figure appeared, pale like moonlight, her neck weighed down by her raven-black hair.

"Neelam!"

Neelam his wife, whom he had known only six days and six delirious nights, was looking at him from her black, lovely, cold eyes with the silvery shine of hematite. She held out her thin, white hand, and Ardri touched the mirror from his side. His fingertips felt nothing, not even the smooth bronze surface. That nothing began to ripple like water beneath their hands, and they both drew back.

Suddenly, the mirror was empty.

Ardri knew then that he had to return, through that horrible wood, to her. He took off the crown, wrapped it into a cloth and put it into a bag with long straps which he tied doubly around his body.

From the bowls on the floor he collected copper nuggets into another bag he had brought for the purpose, and then selected malachite, lapis lazuli and turquoise stones. It took a long time to pick out the gems with the right weight, dimensions and colouring. When all was done, and he was ready to go, he felt extreme reluctance to leave this enclave, where he was safe, to go back into the Bacenis, this world where he did not understand the rules.

When the newly crowned king of whatever left the temple cave, his shadow was waiting for him outside the serpent door of the gallery.

In the last cave, Kitt noiselessly overtook Tagard - was that even his name, to pass first through the hidden entrance.

Outside it was morning. Kitt sat down just inside the entrance of the outer cave and waited.

*

Ardri returned through the tunnels and slipped out from behind the stone curtain, and as he rounded the last bend, he stiffened.

Just inside the entrance of the outer cave sat his saviour, the giant, wild youth named Kitt. With his back to Ardri, he did not seem to be aware of him, but somehow, Ardri knew at once that Kitt had seen everything that had happened in the temple of the Malachite Flower. He could not say why he was so sure about that, as there was nothing to indicate that the barbarian had ever moved far from the cave entrance. Indeed, it seemed as if he had spent the night in the outer cave and just woken up. But Ardri didn't believe that for a moment. Staring at the broad back before him, he hefted his spear, knowing that he had just one cast, and he would not miss an aim like that. *Could I?*

The spear wavered, and Ardri balanced it out. Those broad shoulders intimidated him. If his spear missed the heart by an inch, and if this young giant did not die at once - Ardri remembered the heart of the Bethrek, riddled with knife cuts, and he was not so sure that this barbarian would need less killing than the beast. It was too risky.

He lowered the spear and proceeded towards Kitt. "Why did you follow me?" he demanded.

"Tagard." Kitt looked at Ardri over his shoulder. "Your trail was plain enough for a Woodstalker baby to read. The Woodstalkers are searching."

"That is not a good reason."

"No?" Kitt stood up, his eye on Ardri's spear. "The Dodlak, Bethrek would be better for you than they."

"So, you think that makes it your business?"

"Yes."

"Nonsense!"

"What are you really looking for?"

As if you didn't know. Fine, let's continue this charade. "I told you, I have to find the princes, King Tirnmas' sons. Ridevin went four years ago and Kuranori two -Prince Ardri only a few days ago. I could save him, at least."

"You don't know how to look. You can't save yourself. What did you wash in the creek?" When Ardri didn't answer: "It wasn't gold."

"Tin ore," Ardri said with an air of sudden frankness.

The big youth cocked his head, looking very interested. "Is there no tin ore in Rilante?"

"Very little. Tin does not grow everywhere. The richest mines lie here, in the Great Wood called the Bacenis. The Woodstalkers will kill anyone who tries to mine it. But now that I know where the tin lies, the king can send an army to secure it. So now you know my whole mission. The tin and find out what happened to the Princes."

"They are dead or wishing to be. So will you, on your own."

"Well, since you insist on saving my life, what would you advise?"

"Stay here, lay low, very low. We can defend ourselves better here than in the wood."

"How long should we lay low?" Ardri asked, thinking of the Star Pattern, the inexorable, complicated movements of the Wandering Stars above. If he did not go with them, he would be left behind. "I have no time!"

"You have time till tomorrow?"

"Well, yes, I suppose so," Ardri said with some surprise.

"Fine. Then we'll decide tomorrow. I hunt now." Kitt took up a short lance and walked towards the cave entrance.

"Hunt? You said Woodstalkers were combing the area!" Ardri objected.

"If I missed out on food each time I see a Woodstalker, I would never eat. Soon, I would be too weak to fight and run. And then I would die. Therefore, food is necessary."

Ardri saw a faint smile in the corner of Kitt's eye. The big boy thought that Ardri was afraid to be left alone. That would be humiliating if he still wasted his time with unprofitable emotions like that. As much as he had wanted to get rid of Kitt before he was crowned with Fenifindrune, he now wanted to keep with him the witness to the secret of Minit Claghini.

"What if the Woodstalkers catch you?"

"They take the torture of enemies very seriously. Your chance to get clear, if you do nothing too stupid."

"But if you tell them about me?"

Kitt shrugged. "They wouldn't ask."

"But you might tell them all the same."

Again Kitt shrugged. "It wouldn't save me."

The boy couldn't know much about torture yet, Ardri thought, and that it might be the best solution if he did die at a Woodstalker stake.

Mavors had become the centre of the Star Pattern, in the skies and on earth, in Kitt's person, through the immense secret he had found out -a secret that he must never be allowed to tell, even if it meant that Ardri had to die and Cryssumha would wait again, until another of the Cryssumha Blood would come after him. If all went to plan, there would be one. He was surprised at how coolly he could consider that possibility.

If Cryssumha ever was to break the tree roots holding her down to the earth, her king had to master the Red Star, embodied by this Kitt. There was no other explanation possible, when he considered the broad shoulders, the long limbs packed with muscles like living metal, the assured carriage of a strong animal. But it was the firm set of the mouth, and the quiet grey eyes missing nothing, that made this man-boy into a terrifying adversary, the perfect avatar of Mavors.

Kitt glided out of the cave with an incredible fluidity of movement and disappeared with quickness that defied the eye.

Ardri looked around the leaves, broken wood and bones covering the cave floor. He found three fist-sized rocks. Better than nothing.

*

When Kitt left the cave, he became like the animals, hunter and hunted at the same time.

He descended the path down the mountain, careful of every scant cover the budding bushes and trees could give him, and likewise to any other stalking predator, man or beast.

A slight movement caught his eye; sitting under a bush was a hare, with its grey-brown fur nearly invisible against the bare rock, it was nibbling the first green shoots, oblivious to the hungry shadow that glided through the awakening wood. Kitt's hand shot out, there was a faint dry sound, and with a broken neck, the hare hung in the big hand, the open eyes peaceful. That was good luck so near the cave. Kitt ran his hand along the hare's back and found it thin. The animal had not had time to grow fat on the fresh green.

Kitt was about to go further in the search for more and bigger prey, when he became aware of what was not quite a movement, but rather the idea of one, something that had come between him and the cave. Then he saw two Woodstalker warriors, not twenty paces away. They wore leggings and leather shoes and their upper bodies were naked and painted with black lines and dots, that made them nearly invisible on the sun-dappled ground. They were armed with spears and arrows. One had a broken nose, across which three black lines ran; he wore three eagle feathers in his blue-black hair. The other had two vertical red lines painted from forehead to chin and a broad black stripe across the eyes; he wore a necklace of bear teeth and claws.

To judge by the way they moved, they were not on a track, just nosing about. Their course was uphill, and Kitt followed them, wondering what he should do when they came upon the second cave and decided to enter it. Should he have to kill two Woodstalkers he did not know, for the sake of the man from Rilante, whom he did not know either?

He still had not solved that question when the Woodstalkers came in sight of the first cave from which the creek ran. With a muted exclamation, the eagle feather warrior spread his arms as if to prevent the other from proceeding.

Suddenly they both came directly towards Kitt, fast, almost running, and he did the only thing there was to do, keeping stock-still. They did not see him, although they passed him within five feet. It was fortunate that Kitt had killed the hare with bare hands, because in the short distance they could not have failed to smell blood. On seeing the warriors so near, he decided that the one meagre hare would have to suffice for the evening meal.

He went to the creek to cut a willow branch, carefully disguising where he had taken it. Once, Mangan Sorkera had tracked him by just one injudicious cut.

Upon entering the cave, Kitt ducked immediately, and a rock intended to brain him whistled overhead and clattered against the wall. Another followed, and a third.

A shadow glided into the cave, and Ardri took his chance to throw his rocks in quick succession.

"No noise!" Kitt reproved.

"Why didn't you call out?" Ardri accused, his voice shaking a little. "I thought it was a Woodstalker."

"They are near," Kitt said, almost inaudibly. He took up station by the cave mouth.

"Where?"

"Shut up!" the command was no more than a soft breath, but with the force of a blow.

After a long time of tense silence, Kitt lowered his spear. "They are not coming," he murmured. "Not yet. Keep quiet!" He carried the hare to the back of the cave and freed it from the skin with a few practised cuts; thus naked, it looked like very little meat. He broke it up and placed it together with the innards on the inside of the animal's skin.

"Do we have to eat that hare raw?" Ardri knew that the same distaste was on his face that it had shown when he had seen Kitt eating the Bethrek heart.

"The smoke will go inside the cave."

Kitt collected dry wood and leaves from the cave entrance and brought them to the back together with the three rocks Ardri had tried to brain him with. With a piece of steel and flint, he kindled the leaves and fed the small flames with small twigs, carefully avoiding to look directly into the fire.

Firelight and shadows began playing over the cave wall, and Kitt ceased feeding the fire and only as the flames subsided did he continue, until he had a small heap of glowing boughs. As Kitt had predicted, the smoke was drawn behind the veil. Ardri followed it with his eyes and looked sharply at Kitt.

From a fresh branch, Kitt cut two spits, stuck the heart and liver onto one and handed it to Ardri. "Turn!"

Ardri obeyed. A mouth-watering roast smell filled the cave. They both burned their tongues on the singed, half-cooked chunks.

Kitt cut the rest of the hare into pieces and stuck them on the second spit. From his belt he took a leather bag and rummaged through it for a mixture of salt and dry herbs to season the meat.

Leaving the man who called himself Tagard to the cooking, Kitt went back to the outer part of the cave, to make sure that no visitors were arriving. When he returned, Tagard had divided the rest of the scarce food exactly, waiting for Kitt before starting to eat.

The hare took little more than the edge off the appetites of two young men who had run through the woods all day.

Chapter 5
The Watch that Ended

In the World beyond the Fire, Nyedasya-Dyarve, the real world, the guard stood painted and armed, facing the mountain Gliyet-Sotal.

Nine times seven sun squares had passed in the Shadow World Nyedasya-Aurayskahan-Ashyalish, the dream world of illusions and lies he stood guard over this nexus of Dshooka Mirril magic. The mountain Gliyet-Sotal shook as if something was tearing it from its socket, turning it, all outlines were blurred and there was smoke as if the Sreedok wood was burning. The mountain snapped back, standing unchanged. Then the tearing began again.

Nine tracks appeared as from nine serpents that whipped through the high bluegrass. Where they converged into one, an old man stood. The guard knew him well. They had been young together.

"Shangar Shaark Ayen."

"Griaran."

Griaran, Cricket, was the boy's name which the warrior had kept. Shangar Shaark Ayen, Nine Serpents, the Wise Man of the Kra-Tini Feen was an old man now, while Griaran was still young and strong, as he had been when the sacrificial stone knife in the Ludoshini's hand had carved his arms and legs and belly. Because his heart did not die on that day, Griaran's eyes had seen the World Behind the Fire, and he had been able to pass into it, and return. Now his feet stood in both worlds.

Side by side, the two old friends watched how the mountain Gliyet-Sotal shook, watched a gleam of bronze metal flare up like a flame, and fade again, and blood running down the bare mountainside from a shadowy temple.

"Beingil watch end."

The warrior nodded; he had felt the four guards pass the Nedye-Muni World divide. They all had been young together.

"Griaran watch end."

"Who?"

"Gita."

"Griaran see Gita come Land Behind Fire. Gita hearts never die."

"One Gita stay behind."

Griaran looked west where another Four guarded the stone ship Skobu-Kasha. Twelve were in it, and their king.

"Watch Skobu-Kasha end," Nine Serpents said, following Griaran's look. "All watch end."

"Gita," Griaran spoke softly.

*

"Better be sure," Kitt said in a tone that seemed deliberate to Ardri and rose.

"The Woodstalkers haven't come. What are you looking for?"

"Hidden entrances, signs of bears or Archantel lion or Bethrek."

Look at him, Ardri thought with the now familiar feeling of admiration and dread, *he seems like a lion himself with that flowing mane of blonde hair, and he moves like one, all power and grace and danger*. He also knew, now, what it was that Kitt wore on a loop of leather around his neck – it was a Bethrek tooth. So obviously the manifestation on earth of Mavors, the Red Destroyer, the breaker of patterns, that there was no room for a different interpretation. Aloud he said, "There can be nothing here. I didn't notice a thing. Do stop pacing around!" He managed to ban the shaking from his voice and sound impatient. "I tell you, I looked, and there is nothing. Sit down. I have wine from Tolosa." Invitingly, he shook a leather flagon. "Drink and tell me about the Bethreks you've known." His friendliness sounded a little strained even to himself. He took a swig from the wine flagon and handed it to Kitt, who shook his head.

"You drink. I'll keep watch."

Ardri laid the wineskin aside. "You are right. Better not befuddle the senses here, much as I wish to forget this terrible wood for a while." He shuddered. "Tell me, what do you know about Woodstalkers? The war leader you spoke about, might he be the infamous Murder Bear?"

Kitt shrugged. "I don't know much about them, only what other people told me. I had to run away from them a lot. The Woodstalker war leader wears a Dodlak...a Bethrek tooth."

"So do you. How many Woodstalkers have you killed?"

"One." The giant youth looked so very uncomfortable that Ardri could not mistake it. "Three years ago. He attacked me. I had no choice but to fight. I had one chance, and I took it." There was a catch in his voice.

"Why would that bother you? It's not like killing a human being. They are just murderous savages. The less of them there are, the better."

"They don't like strangers trespassing on their area."

"This is not their area," Ardri said with heat. "This savage wood was once the bronze heart of Cryssumha. Once, towns full of people stood here and temples where Alchemists read the Wandering Stars, and all that was built upon the copper and tin from the mines. A rich land, until these animals broke out of the woods, and drowned Cryssumha in its own blood, nine times eighty-one generations ago. When I saw you first, I thought that you were seeking the bronze treasure of Minit Claghini. Did that never occur to you, Kitt?" He tried to gauge Kitt's reaction in the red glow of the burnt down fire.

"Bronze?" Kitt said, with surprise evident in his voice. "Ancient iron blades, or armour, that would interest me."

"Iron? Compared to bronze, iron is what an ox is compared to a battle horse. Iron is good for nothing but ploughs. For weapons, bronze," Ardri insisted.

"In the old times. Now the best blades are iron." Kitt spoke as if that was self-understood.

"Iron cannot compare with the splendour and Ledrithud magic of bronze!"

"There is good steel and lesser. But the best steel beats the best bronze at any time. No need of any magic, either."

Ardri shrugged, it did not interest him if steel was good or bad. "Your best steel won't beat a blade of Findrun bronze."

"I never heard of Findrun bronze," Kitt admitted. "I grant you that a good bronze blade may be superior to ordinary steel."

"You have no idea," Ardri said. He threw a handful of twigs on the fire.

Kitt pushed them away before they could catch fire. "It will be seen!"

"I want to show you this!" Ardri reached for his sword, and half drew it, aware of grey eyes on his hands, although he couldn't see them.

He stopped, unhooked the sheath from his belt, and very slowly held the hilt towards Kitt.

Kitt drew the blade from the sheath entirely, to assess the weight and the balance; he probed the edge and the tip, and then held it near the dying fire, to bring out all shades of the silvery rosy shimmer.

"This is a beautiful metal," he conceded. "I never thought much about bronze. Is it difficult to forge? How is it hardened?"

"How would I know, I'm not a smith."

"I am."

"You are a smith?"

"I told you I came from Isenkliff."

Yes, he had. Isenkliff, Minit Houarn -the Forge of Mavors. There seemed to be no escape from Mavors. "So I have to thank my life to an ironsmith?"

"You are not saved yet." Kitt yawned. "Would you stake your life on that there is no other entrance to this cave?"

"Certainly."

"Then sleep right here. I guard the entrance." Kitt went away around the bend with his noiseless tread of a great cat.

The nearness of the stone veil was a consolation in the darkness. He could go back to the Queen's Hall, and stay there, the King in the Mountain, in magical stasis, like Izvara Monedorigan Rigantona. If it was not for Neelam, his queen...perhaps he would just slip behind the veil again.

This far into Gyatorlowinel, the West Gate, Ardri could not see the stars, but he could feel them above him, taking their position for the dance, weaving the pattern. From the beginning, the Destroyer was also there, first outside the Star Pattern, now moving through it and playing out baleful conjunctions with the Queen Star Vasara and Dilo, Lord of Lightning. Mavors seemed invincible.

As he felt himself falling asleep, images swam up before Ardri's inner eye, of the bronze gates and spires of Cryssumha, of blood running over rocks, the sacrifice. There had not been enough sacrifices. The land spasmed and the mines fell in, the walls of the cities crumbled, and through the broken walls, the savages of the woods came, to ram their blood-spattered wooden poles into the old pavements.

And now, at last, the stars were right again, on the eighteenth day of the fourth month the moon stood beside Dilo, the Lightning Star, and it was the day when Ardri was crowned with Fenifindrune. The pattern spread out wide, the sacrifices to infuse it with power had been brought, and that was only the beginning.

First, his brothers had been sacrificed. *Where did they die, has a Bethrek devoured Ridevin by the Lightning Towers Meltirau, has an arrow found Kuranori just in sight of Minit Claghini? Did the Woodstalkers drag them to their stakes among the trees to perpetuate the reign of the wood with malicious rites full of blood and pain?*

There must be more sacrifices because there had been so many already. Stopping now was impossible. His older brother Flannan, who was still alive, was also a sacrifice, a sacrifice that Ardri himself would have to bring. *Will these sacrifices finally be sufficient for Cryssumha to rise again?*

And on the cusp of the preparations for Cryssumha Rising the Red Destroyer Mavors entered the scene in the person of a blacksmith from Minit Houarn - his mind always went back to that, and did not let him sleep. The crowned King of Cryssumha must not give in to sentiment, gratitude, sympathy, even friendship, nothing must sway him.

Ardri rose to his knees and hands and reached for his lance. The noise as the blade scraped over the stone sounded like a screech to him. He froze and stayed motionless until his knees began to hurt.

It took him a long time to cross the cave. Everything felt distorted in the darkness.

The fox does not sleep; he merely reposes, was a saying of the Nordmann warriors. Thus, Kitt always slept, like the animals of the woods; in his dream, he heard the noises of the night, water gurgling from the lower cave, a deer coughed in the valley, a dreaming bird beat its wings in a tree. In the darkest hour after midnight, there was a faint scraping sound coming from the inside the cave. Awake instantly, he lay still, listening, each muscle in his body tense.

He heard a brief clatter as one of the stones by the fire was dislodged by a stealthy foot. For a while, it was quiet, before the next stealthy step came. Then Kitt could distinguish a deeper blackness before the cave wall, and a pale shimmer, the short bronze blade of Tagard's lance. The Rilanteman had come to remove the witness. For a moment Kitt felt keen resentment. But his conscience was not altogether clear. It was natural to want to know what was in a cave, particularly if somebody was so secretive about it. He admitted his own curiosity and the considerable stealth he had employed to discover Tagard's secret. Breathing deep and regularly, making more noise than he usually would, Kitt watched from under lowered lids, so that no gleam from his eyes betrayed that he was awake.

Here by the entrance Ardri could see a little better.

At the sight of the long shape on the cave floor, his heart gave a sudden leap. He listened to the young barbarian's breath, light and even, as he crept as near as he dared.

Twice he raised his lance, and twice he lowered it again. He knew not whether he hesitated from a feeling of repugnance to thrust his spear into the sleeping breast, or from fear, because with this young barbarian, he had only one chance. Maybe less than that. Would a sword attack be more effective - the blade would make a characteristic noise when drawn from the sheath. And he would need to get at least three feet nearer to Kitt.

After standing undecided for a long while Ardri crept back into the cave, where the darkness was impenetrable. He had to feel his way along the wall. It seemed a very long way. Finally, he huddled up on his sleeping place again noticing with detached interest that he shivered, and that his teeth chattered. It was bitter cold.

He could not sleep. He had to make another attempt, but this time, he thought each step through beforehand.

Run his hand over the lance, and take it up, this time without any noise.

Feel each step with the hands, before letting the feet follow.

The wall, it was easier now.

When Ardri reached the outer cave for the second time, he had lost count of the time. Through the Gate Gyatorlowinel, he could see the grey western sky. The Wandering Stars had set, not there to help or hinder now. He listened for Kitt's breathing, but all he heard was the thumping of his own heart. He stood silently, immobile, for another long while. The dark figure on the ground did not move.

Ardri took two steps towards the sleeping form, the lance arm raised. The barbarian still did not stir. Ardri sighed almost audibly and lowered the lance again.

"Can't make up your mind?" Kitt said out of the darkness.

Ardri started and swung round. "I thought you were asleep."

"Why I wasn't."

Ardri bent down to the dark shape; it was the leather tunic, draped over a tree branch.

"The oldest trick," Kitt chuckled.

"You saw what you shouldn't have seen."

"Yes, I saw it."

"And you know that my name is not Tagard...that is if you haven't known all along?"

"Means nothing to me."

"You lie."

With a movement too fast to follow in the uncertain light, Kitt held his sword under Ardri's nose, the steel tip inches from his face. Ardri felt rather than saw the steel grey eyes looking into his along the dimly shimmering length of the blade.

"Why would I lie?"

"If only you hadn't followed me here."

"You would be dead now."

"You know too much!"

Clutching the lance in his right, suddenly, Ardri started towards Kitt, brushing at the blade before his face with his bare left hand.

Kitt lowered the sword just a little. He thrust the blade under Ardri's chin that his head jerked back. His left hand went up towards it, but he did not step back, and he did not drop the lance. "You must swear that you will never divulge the secret to anyone. You must!"

"This is my sword at your neck."

"Swear! Or you must kill me!"

"I can just leave you alone."

"Leave me then. How many times did I ask you to? Just do it!"

Shaking his head, Kitt withdrew the blade. The sudden disappearance of the sharp edge from his neck caused Ardri to stumble forward. Kitt stepped back to maintain his distance. "I didn't understand what was spoken in that...hall; it was a language I never heard before. And I swear I won't talk."

Ardri stared at Kitt for several moments. "Why would you swear anything? I can't make you. You speak Rilante so why would I believe that you are not speaking Cryssumha as well? And how do I know what oath binds you? How do I know what your idea of honour is? If I believed in such a thing."

"Think about what you can believe in. Then tell me, and I'll swear it. Do your thinking back at your sleeping place. Now go!"

There was a new hardness in the young barbarian's voice which brought home to Ardri that if he ever had the glimmer of a chance at all to kill Kitt, it was gone now. There was nothing left to do for him. He turned to obey without further objection.

"Leave your lance here," Kitt said in the same flat, hard tone.

Surrendering completely, Ardri laid down his lance and went back into the corridor.

"And whatever you name is! Don't come here again before sunrise!"

"You know perfectly well that my name is Ardri of Cryssumha," he said bitterly.

Back at his place in the darkness, Ardri could not sleep. *Failure!*

It was not so much the negligent ease with which that barbarian boy had thwarted him, that was so infuriating. No, that was not it. It was his own hesitation. He hadn't had the least inkling that an empty tunic was lying there, *so why didn't I drive my lance into it as hard as I could? Am I a broken tool that couldn't do what was necessary?*

Or - Ardri's breath caught as another thought struck him with sudden illumination. *What if it was an instinct, an inner knowledge that held back my hand?* All his life he had lived and breathed the Star Pattern but had never understood it completely. *What makes me so sure that Mavors was an obstacle? Because both Angkou and Glic Tusil said so? Because iron had recently become a threat to bronze, like a rebellious slave? But it had not always been thus. Iron once even had a place in the bronze-making process. What an epiphany!* Ardri stared into the blackness of the cave.

After some time, he fell asleep, and he dreamed.

After some time, he fell asleep, and he dreamed.

The morning sun shone onto Minit Claghini, and it was as if the rock walls had become transparent. At the foot of the palace mountain lay lakes bluer than the sky, winding around the mountain like a poisonous turquoise necklace.

Miners, small bent men with pale faces and twitching eyelids, drove tunnels into the rock, great wooden wheels turned on bronze axles, driven by naked men with chains on their feet, who would not see the light again until they died. The wheels were winding up bronze chains to draw up baskets filled with ore and buckets filled with water.

The Great Wood, called the Bacenis, had receded to a green line on the horizon, pursued by the charcoal burners. Cities with towering walls were sitting on the bare hilltops. Whole mountains became reversed, made into their own mirror image under the surface of the earth.

Women bedecked in jewellery of bronze, inset with small splinters of malachite and lapis lazuli, small and pale like the miners, sat at the foot of long walls. With round hammerstones they pounded ore, their hands and bodies shaking, eyelids twitching, but the hammerstones hit true every time.

Children carried baskets full of broken ore pieces to fill into the space between two walls. When the ore was heaped high, the charcoal bed under it was fired by men whose faces and hands were black with the coal dust, and from the ashes. Days after days followed. The enormous wooden wheels turned, the men raked the roasted ore, and the wood receded beyond the horizon.

Once a thick cloud of smoke rolled into the valley, surprised workers and left a barren track where nothing would grow for years, a scar on the face of the hill.

A column of chained captives hove into view with the clanking of metal, whip cracks, sighs and curses; they were drawing wagons piled high with iron swords, spears, mail, and they were all fair-haired with light coloured eyes, driven along by armoured guards, big, square black-bearded men armed with bronze lances and swords. The train stopped at the foot of the mountain. The captives unloaded the wagons and threw the weapons into the blue lakes.

Time passed in a blur, as a red-brown copper sponge formed around the iron, which grew until all the iron had disintegrated into yellow slush.

The captives disappeared into the mountain, where the great wheel waited for them, and the wheel turned, bringing up from the depth ore and water and blood, and new iron was thrown into the blue lakes, and new captives were chained to the wheel.

A stream of liquid metal poured into a mould, the mould's halves opened like a shell, and a tree that bore knives for leaves glittered red-gold in the sunlight, six blades, three on each side on a stalk of bronze, like metallic pods, and the smith harvested them with a chisel.

Suddenly all work ceased, and workers and guards alike looked up to the top of the mountain, crowned with Cyclopean walls over which copper red and patina green spires and arcs could be seen wrought with the images of copper dragons and brass gryphons. A man and a woman appeared under a gate high in the mountain; they were a king and a queen. On their black hair rested crowns, silver white and green and blue. The queen wore a white dress and heavy jewellery of malachite, gold-speckled lapis lazuli, and turquoise. Her black hair reached down to her golden belt.

The king's cloak was a coal-black fur cloak that shimmered like moonlight, in its folds was darkness, and silver spots shone in the sunlight. From his side hung a sword with a gleaming bronze hilt in a bronze sheath with a pale green patina, both thickly ornamented.

The king drew the sword, the blade glittered white, and a man was kneeling at the feet of the couple. The sword cut across the man's throat. He sprawled out from under the gate, hands and feet drumming onto the floor. He had not been bound. The blood gushed from the severed throat, and where it ran down the mountainside in many bright red rivulets, the rock became opaque again. A dark figure bent over the body to open it with one slash of a bronze knife. A white masklike face studied the spilled entrails where it saw the future written.

Far on the horizon was the sea, and ships lay in the harbour side by side; pulleys on cranes were swinging from quay to ships belly, loading bronze, unloading every necessity of life.

And then the earth trembled, the titanic walls crumbled, and men with dark animal eyes, adorned with skins and teeth and feathers, with their faces and bodies painted in red, white and black colours, streamed through the gaps, swinging stone axes and spears.

His mind still caught in the dream web of an ancient land, Kitt catapulted himself across the cave floor and came up on all fours, to see a spear blade strike sparks from the place where he had just lain and dreamed of the bronze spired mountain.

This time the assailant was not Ardri. It was a Woodstalker warrior, face and body thickly covered with red and white paint, eyes blazing with a black light. The warrior struck again, and in rolling out of the way for the second time Kitt got hold of Ardri's lance and blocked the third stroke; he sprang to his feet, drawing his long knife with the left.

They fought by the light of the sun of Cryssumha, Kitt and the painted warrior. All around them black-haired, pale-faced men and women died under spears and axes. Then they fought in the darkness of the wood, lances feinting and stabbing, knives lunging for the slightest opening. Kitt saw the leather band around the warrior's waist with red, white and black symbols painted on it, but couldn't reach it. It was as if his adversary had learned from the defeat of the other four bone warriors.

Finally, Kitt's blade found the warrior's right shoulder, and the arm fell off, weighed down by the lance. No blood splashed onto the floor, and there was no outcry, no wound. The arm was just not there anymore and a dry bone clattered to the ground.

Kitt slashed at the knee joint, and the warrior fell. A mere touch with the knife and the head rolled away. At every revolution Kitt stared into the black eyes blazing at him. At last, he cut through the leather band around the warrior's waist. The black light faded from the severed head. A weathered bundle of human bones and weapons of hammered copper lay before Kitt.

The ancient mines had also disappeared, and in the paleness of the morning, familiar rock contours appeared, and at the back of the cave Ardri's white face.

"That is the foul black Maldryg magic of the woods!" Ardri came nearer, slowly, his face distorted in revulsion as he kicked at the bundle that had been the ghost warrior, so that bones, amulets and copper blades rolled apart. "It's a guard. The filthy Woodstalkers have done that to other places of the old Cryssumha. These savages of the Bacenis are a survival from a darker age of the world, and the Maldryg magic that has survived with them is unimaginably alien and evil. I have talked to some wretches who witnessed the foul rites of their dark worship and have come away haunted by a lifetime of nightmares and strange visions, that darken their daylight forever. They have told me that the Woodstalkers know torture rites to create undead slaves, who have to do the witchman's bidding after death."

"No slave. This is - has been - a high ranking warrior." Kitt considered the necklace of human teeth and the fingerbones tied into the dull strands of black hair.

Ardri pointed to the cut leather band with the red symbols that had been tying the whole bundle together. "That's the Maldryg magic that gave this ghost warrior his unholy life. How did you know to go for it?"

"There were four others," Kitt said, "in another place. They attacked me on sight. Why did this one attack now, and not earlier?"

All magic, be it Ledrithud or Maldryg, had its time and depended on how the spell was cast. It seemed that this barbarian didn't know much about these things, which was a relief. This incident did much to confirm Ardri's novel ideas about Mavors. The guard had been after him, the King of Cryssumha. Kitt destroying him, and apparently, four others, confirmed that there had been a mistake in the interpretation of the role of Mavors in the Star Pattern, an error that could have cost his life, and that might still cost his life today. In his dream of Cryssumha, iron was used for the precipitation of copper, being dissolved in the process. That was how it must work, that was the right interpretation. On their own ground, Ardri had absolutely nothing to put up against the Woodstalkers. He needed Kitt, desperately, to help him cross the wood.

After last night there was only one course left, and that was to bribe Kitt if he could find what to offer him, and until he did -to beg. "Listen, Kitt, you think me ungrateful. I'm not," Ardri said with twisted white lips. This was more humiliating than he'd anticipated. "It's just that I couldn't see your motivation. I'm still not sure that I see it. I feel more comfortable playing by the usual rules of self-interest and power. But I need your help if you will still give it. Only name a price. Any price. If you get me out of this wood, then King Tirnmas of Rilante and my brother, the Crown Prince Nolan Ri, will give you anything you ask. Apart from that, I can reward you in my own right, once we have reached Cryssumha."

Kitt did not answer at once. "I won't speak about what I saw in the mountain," he finally said.

Ardri had not expected this answer. What was Kitt saying, was he going to help, or not - better take it to mean he would not and empty the bitter chalice of humiliation to the bottom. It tasted unexpectedly bitter; he had thought himself over that sort of useless emotion. *Do what you must do.* "Without your help, I won't get out of here alive."

Their eyes met.

"You realise your situation. Good." Kitt fixed Ardri with a hard stare. "That makes it easier to help you."

Eventually, Kitt would have to be eliminated from the Star Pattern, as happened to iron at the end of the old forgotten process of refining copper, Ardri thought. And that would feel good, after this abasement. Aloud he said. "Your price, name it!"

"Later. You couldn't refuse me now."

That was true delicacy, but of course a King of Cryssumha could not accept gifts, and anyway it meant nothing but beautiful manners on both sides. Ardri shook his head. "No Kitt, not so. Don't you see that later I could refuse even less! Besides, I can trust any man whose price I know. Quick, tell me yours! Now!"

"I never thought about that," Kitt said slowly. "What is my price, and what is it supposed to buy?"

Ardri looked at him curiously. "I'd really like to know what your price is. Could it be paid with the usual coin of gold, honours, and maybe women? Are you aware that knowing all the prices of the different men is what gives kings their power over the souls of their subjects? Yes, I would like to know your price Kitt, and give it to you. For now, what do you want if you bring me across the Struenfoly?"

"I want a seagoing boat, to go home."

"That is self-understood and not really a price. The life of a King of Cryssumha, even a Prince of Rilante, is certainly worth more than a boat. Or even a ship. So don't insult me and name a substantial reward."

"I want to learn all about the making and working of bronze."

"But didn't you tell me that you think bronze old fashioned?" Ardri was surprised.

"I will always prefer iron. But I'm a smith, and I want the knowledge of metal."

"Is knowledge worth that much to you, Kitt?"

"For me, it is a considerable price. I'm asking for smiths' secrets."

"As you are so unworldly, Kitt, I shall have to see to it myself, that you do alright from a worldly point of view as well."

"Give me only what I ask when I deliver," Kitt said absently, surveying the surroundings of the cave. "This guard, who will know about his destruction?"

Ardri paled. "The source of the spell, the witchman, is sure to have a connection."

"We move now. Fast."

When Ardri stepped out of the West Gate of Minit Claghini, it was as if he left a safe haven to enter a world of danger and peril. He couldn't see the foot of the mountain because of the trees; he heard the water rushing but didn't see it. Immediately he felt lost, worse than when he had crossed the River Struenfoly because then he had not known what an utterly alien world the Bacenis was, and how vast it was. When he had seen it on a map, he had had no idea of the distances and dangers every inch on the paper meant in the reality of the woods. Now he knew.

As he descended on the stairs, he saw Kitt below him, the fair hair, the broad leather-clad shoulders. He did not seem to move fast, but Ardri had to climb quickly, not to lose sight of him. When he caught up, he saw Kitt's dismayed look. The young barbarian was quiet as a shadow, and how he managed that when the ground was covered with loose rocks, dry rustling leaves and rotten branches, and those damn brambles reaching for one's legs, was more than Ardri understood, but he knew it was something he could never learn.

"If you hole up in your mountain? I go for help."

71

What will you tell my father, the king of Rilante? Or my brother, the crown prince? The very thing you promised not to tell? "That would take half a month. What would I eat?"

"Forget about quiet. Don't mind the tracks," Kitt said. "We just move fast. Better be very fast."

He began to run, and although Ardri gave his best, this resulted in another humiliation for him, who was used to riding. He tried to keep up with Kitt, but soon, he was panting. The long legs of the big barbarian carried him out of sight in a moment. It looked as if the newly crowned King of Cryssumha was lost after all.

Chapter 6
The Ship in the Forest

The Kra-Tini Feen war leader ducked into the grass hut.

Shangar Shaark Ayen, the whitehaired Ludoshini, motioned to sit opposite him by the fire that never went out. Mangan Sorkera sat and waited until Shangar Shaark Ayen would tell him why he had called him.

"Liba Ri Cryssumha finish rite. Gita destroy guard Gliyet-Sotal."

"Dead Graykhol Rere." Mangan Sorkera had found the remains of the dead predator. Shangar had his own ways to know that Gawthrin Lye was in the area of old Cryssumha.

"Gita protect Liba Ri Cryssumha."

"Dshooka slow, stupid." The war leader shook his head. Gawthrin Lye's only weakness was the weak. Mangan Sorkera had seen that before and could not understand it. He felt troubled by this strange vulnerability of his enemy -an enemy he had come to regard like a younger brother. He wanted him to fight the best fight and die the best death.

"Cryssumha rise," Shangar Shaark Ayen said.

The war leader looked up sharply. "Mangan spill Cryssumha blood. Set Gawthrin Lye guard Gliyet-Sotal. No Dshooka pass Gawthrin Lye. Cryssumha never rise."

The old Ludoshini shook his head. "Aglorim, afraid." He used the lesser word for fear, aglo, not gita.

That was a surprise for the war leader, that Shangar Shaark Ayen should fear anything. He was a wise man who had set nine of his own blood-brothers as guards over the places of Dshooka Mirril magic, the lost mountain Beingil, Gliyet-Sotal, and Skobu-Kasha, the stone ship. He waited to hear what such a powerful Ludoshini feared.

"Shangar fear Skobu-Kasha. Feen weak defeat Rilante." The old, cold eyes fixed the war leader.

Mangan Sorkera did not protest Shangar's words, as his warriors would have. He was aware that Rilante had warriors armed with metal -each one might be inferior to a Feen warrior, but there were many more of them. The Rilante had great fortified places, and they kept down the trees and forced the land to yield an endless supply of food. The Feen were too few to overthrow Rilante and extend the Sreedok to the western shore of the Great Water Skai. Some Sreedok people had forgotten how once the sea washed the feet of the Great Wood in all directions. Sreedok people such as the Amhas, seduced by Dshooka things, had forgotten how to manufacture stone weapons, didn't count the animals, whose skins and fur they exchanged for the bronze and dream-water of Rilante, and hunted too many. They thought that the Dshooka ways, that were but the ways of the illusory world Nyedasya-Aurayskahan-Ashyalish, were better. They made people weak that they did not know how to die any more, and in death became trapped behind the Ska-Muni Shadow wall. Their footprints were not seen any more in Nyedasya-Dyarve, the Land Beyond Fire, the real world. If the Sreedok was kept away from Skai under the horizon of the sinking sun, then in time, the Feen would become like the Amhas. He understood that that was what Shangar Shaark Ayen saw in the future.

The Ludoshini had never allowed the art of stone weapons to be lost, had never let the feud with the Dshooka be forgotten. The war leader accepted that only Shangar Shaark Ayen could prevent the Stone Ship Skobu-Kasha from breaking free to continue its run towards the sea Skai under the rising sun.

"Liba Ri Cryssumha go Skobu-Kasha. Cryssumha rise. Cryssumha destroy Rilante like weasel eat inside wisent. Feen destroy Cryssumha. Shangar see."

Mangan Sorkera nodded. The Feen had destroyed Cryssumha once, long ago. They would destroy it again after it had wounded Rilante to the death. Shangar Shaark Ayen saw far ahead.

"Gita die," Shangar continued. That had not changed. The Ludoshini always said that when Gawthrin Lye was mentioned. "Gita die after Liba Ri Cryssumha go Skobu-Kasha."

The war leader was sure that his warriors could herd the Dshooka to the Stone Ship like a stag because Gautsrin Lye would go along with that to avoid a fight as it was only a slight detour from going straight west. Not only did Mangan Sorkera feel no anger at thus being prevented from using the enemy's momentary disadvantage against him -he was glad. Gawthrin Lye had not used his advantage after Mangan had been caught by the Shakro-Shork, the Black Thorn, and he now thought that he understood the why. Given his wounds and extreme exhaustion then, it would have been no kind of a good fight. They understood each other, Mangan Sorkera and Gawthrin Lye. Their feud wasn't about exploiting temporary advantages. It would find its conclusion one day when Mangan Sorkera and Gawthrin Lye would meet, alone, each with all his strength and cunning, and that day would be a good day. Mangan could wait for it.

The Ludoshini spoke again. "Mangan hunt Sheh Ri. Dshooka give Aremenn lances Sheh Ri skin. Dshooka fight Dshooka."

"Mangan understand." The rare Sheh Ri cat was as dangerous as a Graykhol Rere, and its pelt was one of the insignia of the Kings of Cryssumha, and symbolised the victory over the Sreedok Wood. Mangan Sorkera knew as well as Shangar Shaark Ayen that a Sheh Ri pelt brought across the Red River Skailibashural would cause bloodshed among the Dshooka.

Shangar Shaark Ayen laid back and relaxed. Mangan Sorkera was a wilful war leader, but he always understood. Never had the Ludoshini needed to explain to him. Mangan Sorkera was about to leave the old Ludoshini's hut when Shangar called out to him. "Mangan Sorkera!"

The war leader turned around.

Shangar sat up erect again, and his old face was a red and black mask in the firelight. "Bear not fight Graykhol Rere, Mooankayit same Sun Circle!"

Mangan Sorkera, a black bear in the real world, was in no doubt that the Ludoshini foresaw such a day when he would meet both Graykhol Rere and Gawthrin Lye, who in the real world was a lion Mooankayit. He wondered himself, if he could fight both these enemies on the same day, and win. Shangar Shaark Ayen said that he could not. But to try was something he wanted to do.

"Kra-Tini stand shadow Mangan Sorkera," the Ludoshini said, almost gently. Too many people depended on the war leader.

*

75

Ardri circumvented a crater that was several hundred feet deep, a thousand even, under the mirror of water, surrounded by a field of six-cornered ruins, the worker's houses, overgrown with stunted bushes. On a circular perimeter of a hundred yards from the old mine stood the giant oaks like warriors afraid to advance, as if there was a magical power about it still strong enough to hold the Bacenis aloof. To think that this deep hole had once been a mountain, the White Mountain Minit Meltigan of the legend, full of tin -consisting of tin. In the crater walls, tunnels and shafts of the Gwinminit Meingloud mine were visible and tall water wheels on bronze axles once driven by slaves who were long dead now, to lift the water from pits where sweating workers dug for tin ore. Ardri had always thought of Cryssumha as of a land of Ledrithud magic and enchantment, but now he could see the vast mechanism of brute power. These tunnels and pits and wheels had once been the substance of the shadow. And now he was wandering among these remains of what had been, deriving deceptive consolation from being near the old Cryssumha, but conscious that the shadow could not sustain him.

Gwinminit Meingloud had been one of the places where woods-runners had come to scavenge the prized Findrun bronze. Lately, none of them had returned, and Ardri could see no evidence of their searches, no trace of them. There was no other way; he had to leave behind the remains of Cryssumha and re-enter the Bacenis Wood. The oaks were a shadow that had become substance again. The trees that once provided the charcoal to drive the bronze mechanism of Cryssumha had been resurrected. Now the King of Cryssumha wandered among trunks so thick that six men could not span them, under boughs big as trees in their own right, clad in the young golden-green spring foliage.

He came to a grove of gigantic conifers; their needles were so thick that they let no light through to the ground, and the red trunks glowed in the gloom. These were the trees the Woodstalkers nourished with the hot blood of captives screaming with pain. His foot slipped on a thigh bone, and a faint tremor began stirring inside Ardri, it was the beginning of panic. He attempted to force it down before it overwhelmed him.

Then, he glimpsed a circular stone-paved place and a charred pole with a bundle of bones at the foot like sticks fallen from white and red bindings. He fled, treading on splintered bones.

Ardri almost welcomed to be among the oaks again. He didn't blame Kitt for leaving him. In his place, he would have done the same, because it was the only logical thing to do. He'd have done it much earlier. The young barbarian had already saved his life twice at least, and he could not expect more. Five years ago, when Ardri was Kitt's age, he had been quite full of things like honour and chivalry, but it was really his brother Flannan to blame for that. Now all his actions followed a strict logic, and there was no room for sentiment. Perhaps the barbarian had just learned this too.

Ardri desperately wanted to believe Kitt's word to never reveal the secret of Minit Claghini. If only he could be certain of that, he would be glad to leave his fate to the stars alone once more. To see himself so vastly inferior to another man, a barbarian boy at that, was another new and bitter experience. It had taken more out of Ardri than he had thought possible. If he had to die, he'd rather do it alone, away from those clear, impassive eyes.

Suddenly, everything happened fast. Ardri heard a rushing noise as from a strong wind and saw Kitt coming towards him in full run. The King of Cryssumha was lifted by his girdle and the scruff of his neck like a puppy from the palace kennel and pushed up into the next oak tree. He had just managed to draw himself up to the thick bough and hold on to the trunk, when the first Woodstalkers appeared.

Pressed to the rough oak bark, Ardri kept still. With almost detached interest, he felt his hair rise and sweat breaking out. So that was what fear did to a man, the reaction of his body in the sight of death. Soon, his knees hurt from crouching on the thick bough, and he did not dare to shift his position, though the pain quickly became excruciating.

Their eyes fixed on the ground, the Woodstalkers did not look up. Then they disappeared, and the wood appeared deceptively peaceful again in the sunlight filtering through the bridal green of the leaves. Ardri hesitated to come down from his high seat, and merely changed his position. The relief was immense.

A few moments later, two more Woodstalker warriors appeared; like shadows, they materialised -he had not seen them come. One looked directly at Ardri, and he froze. *This is it*, he thought.

Unaccountably, the Woodstalker didn't seem to see him. They stopped not far from the oak and started jabbering in their savage idiom, leaning on their spears, sweeping their surroundings with cursory glances, as if they intended to spend the whole day there. Again, one of them seemed to look directly at Ardri for a moment. Fighting down his rising panic, he tried to assess his situation coolly. His new position was becoming uncomfortable again, and if he had to stay in it much longer, he'd either make some movement that would be detected or be so stiff that he'd simply fall out of the tree.

He wondered if the Woodstalkers did laugh at all under that war-paint. It was rather risible, the last King of Cryssumha treed in an oak, his first high seat after he had been crowned with Fenifindrune. For that also the Woodstalkers should pay, Ardri promised himself. Could he get one man with his lance and then spring down and finish the other with the sword?

Just as Ardri gripped his lance faster, a hand clapped across his mouth, and his arms were pinned to his side by muscles as hard, strong and immobile as massive metal. He was held motionless in that vise until he accepted that he was unable to move a limb, let alone free himself. Finding himself thus completely dominated, his panic subsided. He was trapped, and there was no way out, and that was that. Almost detached, he rolled his eyes sideways and still saw nothing.

Ardri tried to turn his head, and he could, but only because the hand on his mouth let him do it, slowly. He saw a tan shoulder and a strand of fair hair, and then the grip on his arms slowly loosened and disappeared. He was free, but stayed immobile, as this was what Kitt seemed to want. The young barbarian glided higher into the oak without the rustling of a single leaf. Halfway up, he stemmed his feet onto a thick bough, and with his back to the trunk, knocked an arrow. Ardri knew that Kitt had had no bow earlier.

The slight shift of position had brought temporary relief to Ardri, but now his knees hurt once again, and his muscles trembled with the effort of staying motionless. One Woodstalker stepped towards the trunk of the oak. Looking down on the blue-black hair that fell over tanned shoulders, Ardri forgot his aching body at the sight of what had to be human fingerbones tied into the smooth, straight strands. The Woodstalker appeared to do some Woodstalker thing to the tree, Ardri couldn't see what it was, and then he went back to his companion. The warriors dawdled away at last, and Ardri looked up to Kitt, a question on his face.

"Get down and run!" Kitt's lips formed the words without sound, and he pointed in the direction he wished Ardri to run. He obeyed, still looking up at Kitt, who made no move to follow him.

Kitt climbed higher into the oak to follow Ardri's awkward progress through the wood.

The Prince of Rilante, King of Cryssumha, did try his best to move quietly, but he was just slow. Kitt saw a Woodstalker glide through the underbrush. Another came from the other side, just like wolves hunting an elk. For a split moment, one warrior deliberately showed himself to Ardri, and he began running in earnest. He didn't have the ghost of a chance.

Kitt raised his bow, and sighted, with the idea of wounding the warriors with two long shots and to draw their companions onto himself in the resulting confusion. It was a desperate plan, but he had no other. He was not sure how long he could still protect Ardri or wanted to.

Just when he was about to shoot, both warriors veered off. Puzzled, Kitt lowered his bow. He climbed down from the oak and contemplated the raven feather the Woodstalker had wedged into the deep ridge of oak bark, the two cuts in it, and specks of white lime, Kitt counted twelve and one of red ochre. Ardri hadn't noticed it, any more than the bundle of bear hairs placed beside him this morning.

Any passing Woodstalker could read the message of that feather. This confirmed a suspicion Kitt had for days. The Woodstalkers knew where Ardri was, they had known his every move for days and were having their cruel little game with him. But those warriors hadn't known that Kitt was right above them, with the bow he had taken from a hapless pursuer, whose head was hurting him now. Had they known of his presence, they wouldn't have stood there so coolly, teasing Ardri. He was pleased to have secured a small advantage over his formidable adversaries.

After a little thought, he removed the feather and followed the trail Ardri was blazing through the wood, the crushed young grass, the overturned brown leaves, broken branches. When the Woodstalkers decided that they'd had enough sport with the defenceless man, Kitt would be on hand.

*

Ardri had run for miles, at every step expecting an arrow or a lance to hit him in the back.

Whenever he caught a glimpse of painted skin, he changed direction like a hare, until he didn't see the Woodstalkers anymore and thought that he must have shaken them off somehow. If he lived a little longer, he'd turn into a woodsman yet.

To both sides of him rose brown slopes covered with the leaves of last year. Oaks grew in this valley, their trunks so thick that twelve men could not span them, and these trees did not grow in the way that the oaks in the Killinibenji forest did, standing near together, striving away from each other for space. Here, their great boughs were thickly intertwined so that they darkened the ground into an atmosphere of evening.

It was so quiet. Then Ardri saw a human skull. Further on, the ground among the oaks was strewn with bones and skulls, until they lay so thickly that the ground was greenish white with them. And there ahead, caught between the roots, hemmed in by the thick tree trunks, was a ship. It stood as if the trees had stepped into its way to halt its progress and to the side and then closed in behind so that it could not manoeuvre. The prow had the shape of the Serpent Murdris. Thirteen were in the ship, twelve men of silver at the oars, in scale mail and helmet, and one in the prow.

Ardri had an impression of a rich cloak, a sword, a flowing mane, shimmering red-gold in the deep shadow of the trees. For a moment he thought that he saw the hull straining and heard the oak trees groan in their effort to halt the progress of the ship.

"The Shining Heads of Kione Lonnir!" Ardri said aloud in surprise. "All who looked for it, they all found it. They just never left." Mad laughter bubbled in his throat, irresistibly, twisting his mouth into a sneer. "Many more heads for Kione Lonnir." He sniggered, appalled at the sound of his own voice, but unable to stop.

"Why are you laughing?"

Ardri gave a start, choking on his unholy mirth. Kitt had appeared at his side once again in his customary sudden manner, without the faintest sound announcing his approach.

Kitt's eyes followed Ardri's stare. "A ship! In the woods?"

"I thought you had left me."

"Been near all the time."

"All the time?" Ardri looked incredulous. "I didn't see you!"

"You don't see much of anything." Kitt turned his head towards Ardri with a smile of good-natured mockery.

The young king laughed; he was so relieved that he was not alone. After days of fearful flight, it was so good to see the young barbarian standing there with his unconscious arrogance of strength. Ardri might survive after all. The hiss, as Kitt drew the sword from his back cut coldly into Ardri's newly found hope.

"I did not see them come," Kitt murmured.

From among the trees, four Woodstalker warriors had materialised; they were painted red, white and black in the same way that the guard of Minit Claghini had been, and bore weapons of hammered copper, and leather girdles with painted symbols around their waists.

The four warriors encircled the two young men methodically. Spinning away from Ardri's side Kitt slashed at the girdle of the first, and he fell and hit the ground as a bundle of dry bones and copper. Kitt reached the second warrior, but here he could not repeat his rapid success; sword and lance engaged, and the third warrior was in Kitt's back. "Cut their girdles!" he called to Ardri, parrying thrusts with sword and dirk. "Nothing else will stop them."

The knowledge of the guard's weak point was of no immediate use to Ardri. All he could do was to defend himself from the lightning-quick attacks of the fourth warrior. From the corner of his eye, he saw Kitt stalked from two sides, but had to keep himself alive.

At last, Ardri's sword reached the girdle and parted it. He sprang across the crumbling bones towards where Kitt still battled one guard and severed the girdle from behind. The last guard disintegrated into dust and bones, and the two young men stood panting in midst the unbloody remains of the battle.

"You are a good swordfighter," Kitt remarked, and Ardri felt ridiculously pleased with this praise.

Over the carpet of old bones and fragments of bronze from armour and weapons, they walked towards the stone ship. There were no bones inside the ring of the oaks. Nobody living had set foot here since the ship had come to a stand-still.

From near, it looked nothing like a ship and crew. There were upright stones arranged in the form of a ship, and inside stood two rows of six monoliths roughly hewn in the shape of men. The stern had sunken in the earth, and the monoliths standing at that end were buried up to the knees. Scale mail, shields, helmets, all seemed chance likeness caused by the play of light on the rough stone, except for the faces, which were carefully crafted and overlaid with silver.

The prow was the height of two men and from near had lost its likeness with a sea serpent. In it stood a monolith higher and broader than the other twelve, his features clear cut, the sharp nose and high cheekbones overlaid with gold, the eyes stared ahead indomitably.

Except for the faint rustle of the young oak leaves in the wind, it was very quiet at this place of stone and broken bones. Kitt felt that something was lacking, but it came to him only after a time what it was. "The Woodstalkers. They aren't anywhere near."

"Last time I saw them was three days ago." Ardri saw Kitt's mouth twitching and laughed ruefully. "Oh well. When did you see them last, Kitt?"

"This morning. I was watching one watching you. He noticed me, I must have been careless, and he attacked me. I think his head hurts him still." Kitt grinned.

"You killed him, I hope?"

"No. He wasn't that good."

"But now he knows where we are."

"The Woodstalkers have known where you are all the time. There is no way you can hide from them. So why didn't they try to kill you?"

"Not try to kill me?" Ardri almost shouted. "The dirty savages have chased me for days!"

"If they really wanted to kill you, I would have been forced to fight every single one of them to protect you. No less."

"Then, why am I still alive?"

"Why would the Woodstalkers want you to come here?"

"To let those guards have me?"

Kitt looked dissatisfied. "I think the Woodstalkers shun this place. I'll make sure. Stay here." With that, he disappeared among the shadows of the trees.

Ardri followed him with the eyes, and although the young barbarian did not seem to move fast, again he lost sight of him within moments. *What an assassin this boy would make.*

The faces of the ship's crew shimmered in the fading light, the twelve and the one. The young king sat down with his back against one of the stones that formed the ship's hull, and although he didn't see them anymore, he felt the faces above him, felt the look of their eyes as from something living. Felt their loathing.

"Tainted blood," Ardri muttered. "I hear that often."

Kione Lonnir. The Shining Heads, gold and silver. That would appeal to the Rilante traders, and pirates, lure them like moths to the light, to leave their heads here. There was space for many more heads in this valley, all the heads in Rilante, men, women and children, would not fill it to the rim. Ardri resolved that he'd make a very good attempt and add the Woodstalkers' to make full the measure.

"And then I'll see to it that you'll stay stuck here forever, Torin Daraval!" he said aloud.

Darkness filled the valley like black water, and the noises of the night began. Ardri listened to the rustling, a stealthy step, a gust of wind blowing through the branches above his head. How different the night air was from that of the day, wet, cold, with its own smell. He shivered, raised his head, and between the oak boughs black against the evening twilight he saw the triumphant light of Dilo high in the west, and in the faintly rosy aftermath of sunset stood Vasara.

As the darkness deepened, the light of Dilo and Vasara became brighter. Lute and Mavors also appeared, almost humble between the Royal Stars, but Ardri knew their weight. He could not see the low western horizon, but he knew the mercurial Srad to be there for a little while. The stone of the ship pressed hard into his back. He shifted his position a little.

A heavy body thudded and lay dark on the ground, a tooth gleamed white. Another dark thing was moving about nearby. Ardri brought his shock under control. "I didn't hear you coming, Kitt, but I never hear you, or see you, until you are suddenly there."

A red flame sprang up. Ardri saw that Kitt had scraped away dead leaves and twigs and dug out a shallow hole which he had lined with the abundant stones, apparently all by touch.

He fed the little flame with dry branches, and the fire leapt high and picked the golden face of Torin Daraval from the darkness. In its flickering light, the face of the young giant looked older, strange and stern. The dark shape lying on the ground was revealed to be a wild pig, as big as a yearling lamb.

"Seems the pig didn't hear or see you either."

"They like oak woods."

"Glad as I shall be not to have to eat the meat raw, but won't the fire betray us?"

"No Woodstalkers," Kitt said. "We are alone."

He began skinning the pig. As he knelt there with his bloody hands, he looked up at the ship's serpent head, just touched by the firelight. "What is this place?"

Ardri knew the answer to this question. "This is the Kione Lonnir of the Rilante, the Stone Ship, the Shining Heads. There are many legends about it."

"Tell me."

"Now?"

"Yes. Maybe the legend gives us an explanation for the Woodstalkers' behaviour."

"I don't think so," Ardri said doubtfully. "They should want to keep Kione Lonnir hidden for all times. You see the dead all around. The Woodstalkers have murdered hundreds, thousands of people who searched for copper or tin or the treasure of the lost cities of Cryssumha...and as it appears, for Kione Lonnir."

"And now they want it found?"

"I can't think why they would. You see, the legends never agreed how far into the wood Torin Daraval sailed, but they do agree that Kione Lonnir marks the eastern border of Rilante. If the Rilante people hear how near their Stone Ship is, they'll cross the Struenfoly with an army."

Kitt spread the pig's skin on the ground and began to cut the animal up on it. "Who is Torin Daraval? The first King of Rilante?"

84

"Yes. And a sea rover and maniac. It was after the fall of Cryssumha that Torin Daraval came across the sea in his ship Murdris, sailing on the wings of the west wind, as the poem goes. When the shore of what today is Rilante came in sight, Torin Daraval did not strike the sails; to the contrary, with full sails he drove his ship up the shore and into the Great Wood called Bacenis. Kione Lonnir is the place where the ship Murdris came to a stand-still, thus marking the true eastern border of Rilante. That is the legend of the hero, or the crazy loon, Torin Daraval and his stone ship Murdris. Many have sought for Kione Lonnir, and nobody came back. It was thought that they perished in the woods without ever finding their goal. But that's not true. They all found it, but they did not live to tell."

"Feed the fire!"

Ardri tended the fire and scrambled around for more dry wood, feeling strangely enclosed under the oaks and watched by the thirteen stone men. "While you were away I was looking at the dance of the stars. Can't see them now, for the fire light. When I was born, the stars were just like today. And when my brothers were born, they were also just like today. But my brothers are dead, and I am alive. I will never know if they ever saw Minit Claghini. Or if they died in that grove of Blood Trees. Or if their bones lie here around us."

Busy with the meat, Kitt did not respond.

"Do you know the constellation of the stars you were born under, Kitt?" Ardri pursued. "It must have been an extraordinary one."

"I never thought about it." Kitt sliced up the pig's liver and heart. "Cut some spits! Green wood," he added as Ardri reached for a dry branch lying next to him.

Ardri cast around in the circle of firelight, spotted some thin saplings at the base of the stone ship, and cut them. It wouldn't make a difference, as the Murdris was anchored well – he hoped.

"What month were you born in?" he insisted, whittling away at the spits.

Kitt looked up from his bloody work in surprise. "What month?" The question seemed to startle him.

"What time of year was it when you were born?"

Frowning, Kitt placed the spits laden with bits of the liver and heart on the stones encircling the fire. He had always assumed that he had been born in spring when all the young animals were born. His sister Swantje Birla had been born in spring. But humans could be born at any time of the year, couldn't they - how strange, that he had never thought about it. He didn't know but didn't like to say so. "Winnimanod," he hazarded. "The fifth moon. What you call Zeitein." He sliced up the meat of a hind leg. "Cut some more spits!"

"Yes, Zeitein, or Baldin. What day?"

"That changes," Kitt said. "Our year begins on the first full moon after the Longest Night." He was pleased with the evasion - *let him calculate this without a lunar table and a calendar*.

"How unsatisfactory," Ardri said. "Do you know the Star Patterns, Kitt? To know the dance of the stars means to know the ways of men. If I knew the exact day when you were born, I could tell many things about you - including your future."

"I think the stars are too big and distant to concern the small circles of men."

"You think wrong. The ancient Cryssumha stood under the rule of Vasara, who governs copper, and Dilo, who governs tin. Ships came from Cladith Culuris, from Tolosa; they came from as far as the River Meira to trade for bronze long before Cryssumha fell under the stone axes of the savages, the ancestors of the Woodstalkers who have hunted me for so many days."

"Hand me the spits!"

"After the fall of Cryssumha, there were only a few places left as beleaguered islands in the great wood called Bacenis, that reached to the western ocean shore again. The bronze traders came no more, only ships from Cladith Culuris, who traded for hides and pelts with the Woodstalkers, and they built coastal settlements, which had not been allowed to them when this was Cryssumha."

Kitt held out the meat-laden spits to Ardri. "Turn!"

"With the greatest pleasure. These settlements were the cradle of Rilante, and from that time comes the legend of the ship Kione Lonnir and the hero Torin Daraval. As the settlers of Rilante spread east, and cut down the woods, they came upon the last stronghold of Cryssumha, the ancient city of Ulud, which is now called Dundingin. But the old heart of Cryssumha with the richest copper and tin mines sleeps beyond the Struenfoly by the Mount Minit Claghini, and Vasara and Dilo weave their eternal dance above, and between them is a void where once shone the star of Cryssumha."

"What about the other wandering stars? What about the fixed stars, and the sun and the moon? Where do all these fit in your pattern?"

"Ah, but here, my dear Kitt, you stab to the heart of the problem in that unerring, and unnerving, way you have with you. Where do they stand, Srad, and Lute? And most of all, Mavors? Oho, what a smell!"

"The liver is almost ready."

"It is ready as far as I'm concerned! A bit longer in your company, Kitt, and I'll eat it raw."

"Needs to be cooked well or it can make you sick." Kitt took the spits he had placed first and considered them critically. "Fine." He took salt from a pouch and put some grains of it on each bit of meat.

"Lots of things you have in that belt," Ardri remarked.

For a while, nothing more was said until the liver and heart were eaten, taking the edge off their appetite. Kitt began loading the spits again with meat slices cut from the filet. He turned the spits with the bits of the right hind leg and set the left above the fire entirely, suspending it by the bone ends.

Ardri tended to the fire and rose to collect more wood. Not finding much more nearby, he ventured into the darker regions. Kitt had said it was safe. Away from the fire, his eyes adapted, and he could see well enough to locate more dry wood. He was quite proud of himself; he had the task of tending the fire and was discharging it well. Detached, he noted how simple things could console him now, when he was used to worry about a whole realm.

As he turned back to the fire, he was struck anew by the strangeness of his preserver. The planes of his face, strong rather than handsome, and the corded muscles of his arms under a net of thick veins standing out in stark reliefs, made him look far older -like the man he would become one day, and it was a terrifying vision. Those light coloured eyes shone in the firelight like water in a granite bowl. *Still, nothing but flesh and blood and bone, mortal like everyone else*, Ardri reminded himself.

87

After stacking his pile of firewood, he sat down with righteous joy to the meat that had become ready to eat in the meantime. They both ate their fill. Kitt was used to eating when he could. Ardri, used to regular meals, had eaten nothing since the meagre hare days ago. He forced himself to eat slowly, chew every bite. He had heard that hungry people were in danger to overeat, but he felt just fine. Sated, he leaned back looking up at the serpent head above. His eyes were closing. "Do you know about a steel ship?" he asked sleepily, "The Birlinn Yehan. A Rilanteman name of Lodemar is supposed to have it. They say it's the greatest man-made thing on the oceans."

"More than twice as long as any ship I ever saw. Has steel ribs and a steel plate bottom. I don't have any idea how anyone forged those ribs, let alone the keel. They're composite, but even so, it must have been a huge smithy. Lodemar says he found the ship skeleton on an island, gave it a wooden hull. But the inside is steel and so is the plating up to the waterline."

"I knew you must know about it. Do you know that your sentences are longer when talking about steel and you say much more? If the Birlinn Yehan is twice as long as the biggest ship, then it carries twice as many men? Or four times? I'm not knowledgeable."

"It could, but it needn't. There's steel rigging, and the masts move in sockets, and there are a water wheel and a steam kettle. It can go any way it likes."

Ardri smiled. "You took a really good look, it seems."

"I did. You couldn't do a thing like that with bronze I don't think."

"I think I will," Ardri said.

"You could cast the cannons of bronze," Kitt conceded.

"What are cannons?"

"Hollow metal cylinders that throw stone or metal balls with the directed power of a fire dust explosion."

"You amaze me with possibilities," Ardri murmured, half asleep.

*

Ardri woke in the morning and shivered in the thick white fog that filled the valley; the stone ship seemed to float.

Kitt lay still, his eyes open. The oaks creaked as the fog eddied and flowed around the ship and the few rays of the morning sun that penetrated the thick roof of the tree crowns made the face of Torin Daraval glow.

They breakfasted on cold meat. It was the first time for many days that Ardri did not feel hungry. He soon was warm again, and his face wore a contented expression, he could feel it. This was the day when everything would change, he thought.

He took an almost affectionate leave from Torin Daraval. Nothing the old hero could do about the things to come. Soon the power of the Wandering Stars would bind him more final than the Maldryg sorcery did now.

Chapter 7
Across the Struenfoly

New moon of the Month Ebrel. Vasara, Lute, Mavors join Srad near the sun.

Star Chronicles of Cryssumha

After leaving Kione Lonnir, the valley of the Stone Ship, they saw no more Woodstalker warriors. For that, Kitt was glad. To stay hidden from them in an unfamiliar area of the Murkowydir taxed all his faculties.

By midday, they came to a river. It was more than fifty yards wide and ran swiftly between high banks. On the shore stood a village or rather a camp of huts that were makeshift affairs of young trees tied together at the top with skins thrown over them, but there did not seem to be enough skins, and so the huts were only shelters open to the winds on all four sides.

"No Jays," Kitt muttered, moving with extreme caution. "What are you doing?"

The last was directed at Ardri, who had straightened up and squared his shoulders. "These are only miserable Amhas. Tame Woodstalkers. Supposed to be allies of Rilante. Not that they'd be worth anything against the accursed Murder Bear and his wild Woodstalkers." He stared down onto the swollen brown water flowing through the valley. "This must be Trout River, a tributary of the Struenfoly. The Dundingin city guards mentioned an Amhas camp near. The accursed Woodstalkers pushed us farther south than I thought. But I am sure this water flows into the Struenfoly."

"Boats." Kitt pointed to the shore where three long wooden canoes lay. These were not the Kra-Tini Feen who didn't use boats.

When the two strangers were noticed, the women and children ran to the flimsy shelters, where Kitt could see them huddling. The people looked like Woodstalkers, tall, light-skinned, raven-haired and deer-eyed. Their clothes were a mixture of leather garb, bronze armour parts, linen and wool. Their faces were thin and deeply lined, even those of the young people, and there was an atmosphere of hunger, terror and resignation. In front of the camp, they encountered the solid line of the men.

"No go more!" one of them said in so heavy an accent that Kitt at first did not realise that the man spoke Rilante. "No go!" the man repeated.

"Is that the way the Amhas keep their oath to the King of Rilante?" Ardri snapped.

"Rilante come sunset. Sunrise come enemy."

"Rilante come from wherever we want. Do you deny that you worthless Amhas cur?"

The manner of address, harsh as it was, seemed to assure the Amhas. "No, lord. Rilante go where want, lord."

"Are these all your warriors?" Ardri asked in the same authoritative tone.

"All. Kra-Tini Feen, Canaras Muntrer, Murder Bear come in winter. Take food. Kill warriors. Rob women, children. Amhas run here."

"Tell your warriors that if I have any more nonsense from you mangy dogs, I will come in summer at the head of an army and wipe out the sorry lot of you to the last cub," Ardri said with icy authority, his face a rigid mask of distaste, as if he had an army standing there behind him this moment.

The man who spoke Rilante translated his words. For a breathless moment, all talk, and movement ceased. Kitt marked the position and arms of every warrior. But the rush did not come. These were vanquished people.

Ardri smiled. That was the way to deal with these curs, give way not the fraction of an inch, lash out at the least sign of resistance. The Amhas understood strength, and they had been taught about the might of Rilante. One day, he would have the pleasure of seeing the wild Woodstalkers stand before him like this, including the infamous Murder Bear whom he had never seen, but feared enough to hate with a passion. That would be a day of punishment. "You have boats. Bring us to Dundingin!" Ardri demanded.

The translator turned to the men and began to speak, and then he turned back to Ardri and nodded, his face completely expressionless. "Amhas bring Rilante lord Dundingin."

"They are finished, crushed between us and that devil the Murder Bear." Ardri did not bother to lower his voice. "Their only chance to survive a little bit longer is the protection of the Rilante. And yet, they keep going back into the woods with all their people, and then the wild Woodstalkers attack them, like this sorry lot here."

Kitt turned his head uneasily at the Amhas surrounding them. The man who spoke some Rilante was near them. He would surely have heard.

Ardri continued to speak with the same contemptuous unconcern as they walked down to the river shore. "They'd cut our throats fast enough if they dared. But they hate their wild cousins more even than us. I too hate the wild Woodstalkers more than these wretched Amhas. They are useless in the mines, useless in the fields or with the cattle herds, they are generally not much use for anything. But I don't want them dead particularly, and if they behave, serve as scouts against the wild Woodstalkers, and hunt skins for us, I'll even protect them, like my father, King Tirnmas does." He stepped into the boat which the Amhas steadied for him. "But they remind me too much of their wild cousins, the same animal eyes, and if they give me the slightest cause I shall smash them utterly." He sat down on the middle seat of the boat with the air of one who expected his will done, and see it well done.

The boat was the smallest of the three. It had a length of twenty feet and been hollowed out of a single Linden tree. Kitt wondered if it had been shaped with heat to flatten the bottom and widen the beam to four feet. He saw a charred boat keel caught in a root downriver. The Amhas didn't have sufficient boats left to move all their people, didn't have enough warriors to protect their camp. But they did not dare to refuse Ardri's demand.

The translator and another Amhas took their place in front, and two in the back, each with a paddle. Their tanned faces were without expression, the black eyes without the white showing, what Ardri called animal eyes, looked straight ahead.

The canoe swung into the current.

92

The boat passed into a broad valley, where the river widened to flow more calmly, and the blue sky of spring was visible above.

Now, Ardri had the opportunity for a leisurely look at the Amhas. It was not through their skin colour in which they differed from many people of the north, swarthy by nature it was tanned to a deep brown. The dark colour of their hair was not so very unusual either, except for the texture; it was thick and smooth and had a blue, green or purple shimmer like raven feathers. They wore it very long; the men in the boat had theirs down to their waists. Their features were finely cut, even handsome, but what set them apart most from other human races were their eyes, shaped like a cat's, dark like a deer's, the unusually wide iris crowded out the white, and the pupils had a steel blue shimmer. These strange eyes gave the Woodstalkers a gentleness of expression that Ardri knew from experience to be deceiving.

He noticed that Kitt also observed the Amhas with curiosity. The translator left the oars to his companions, and raised his deer's eyes towards the young giant who submitted good-naturedly to the reverse scrutiny.

Suddenly the translator paled, and his tanned skin looked a sick yellow. Averting his eyes, he reached for the paddle like a blind man, and missed it the first time.

"What is it that he has seen about you, Kitt?" Ardri asked softly.

Kitt shrugged. "I don't know."

Ardri didn't think that was quite the truth. "Hey, what have you seen?"

The translator hunched over his paddle as if he had not heard.

"What...have...you...seen?" Ardri repeated in a deadly voice that spoke of the massacre of entire villages.

The Amhas translator pointed to the hand-long tooth hanging around Kitt's neck. "Graykhol Rere."

"Oh yes," Ardri said casually. "He's got two more of those in his pocket. Show them to him, Kitt."

Kitt dug the teeth of the Dodlak Death-Smile Cat out of his leather pouch and presented them to the Amhas for inspection. The other three men also stopped their paddling to stare at the white, curved tusks which lay on the broad calloused palm.

"There I thought it was my diplomatic skill that got us the boat so easily," Ardri remarked. "But it now seems to me that the Amhas really were afraid of you, Kitt." He knew that the Amhas was lying. He had seen the Bethrek tooth the moment they arrived in the village. No, that terrified look had another reason. He looked like he'd seen the devil. But Ardri realised that the damn Amhas wouldn't tell.

The trees of the Bacenis flew by, and then, suddenly, the woods ended, and they looked out over a wide river and a green plain beyond it with only a few isolated groups of trees. On a hill stood a stone tower, surrounded by wooden palisades, and brown cattle were grazing near the water. The canoe was now swimming on a broad expanse of reddish, muddy water.

"The Struenfoly!" Ardri breathed deeply and took the wine flask from his girdle. "Nearly home. I still have this. Let's drink it now, come!"

Kitt shook his head. "You are nearly home. I am far from mine."

"You are with the man who owes everything to you."

"Is that a good thing?"

"Ah, cynical." Ardri wagged his head. "My dear Kitt, I can do anything for you, if you allow me, give you everything, if you will take it."

Kitt still declined the wine, so Ardri drank alone. The taste had not improved by being carried through the woods for so many days. It was vile but soothing to his nerves, so Ardri took another sip. It still didn't taste any better.

The Amhas translator said something in his thick accent, and held out his hand.

"I will give you the whole bottle once we arrive. Now, not a drop." Ardri pushed the cork back in.

The current of the Struenfoly carried them north in a long loop that turned sharply west in the distance. On the right-hand shore, the trees of the Bacenis stood starkly down to the water, while on the left the meadows rolled, an expanse of vividly green grass such as Kitt had never seen before. They passed homesteads, log houses which lay on wharves, and stone towers, fortified with palisades. There were fields, and ploughing oxen going back and forth. On the horizon, an elevation came in sight, topped with a fringe of walls and towers.

"The towers of castle Marrak!" Ardri exclaimed. A nightmare dropped away behind him.

Ahead, a channel ran into the river, and within the fork lay a cluster of wooden houses with a palisade around them. There were three long piers on one of which a longboat was being loaded.

As the Amhas began to take the canoe gradually out of the main current, people came running onto the first pier. Foremost was a big, squarely built, black-bearded man in heavy bronze armour; Ardri at once recognised Slachlan, the Dog of Cryssumha. Five more soldiers followed him; they wore bronze breastplates and helmets, and they too were dark-haired and bearded. Hands reached for the boat to bring it alongside.

Slachlan knelt and behind him knelt all the others, right on the pier. "My King! King Ardri! My...my king!" Slachlan's voice cracked with emotion, and he stretched out both arms to the sky. "We watched the river, watched it these days and nights! So we heard about your coming, and we raced to pull you from the river!"

Ardri took Slachlan's arm and jumped out of the boat. He turned around and waved to Kitt. "Come on, Kitt. The secret of bronze is awaiting you."

Kitt stepped onto the pier.

"This is Kitt of Minit Houarn," Ardri said in a loud voice. "It is thanks to him that you see me here again. Over and over, he saved my life in the Bacenis."

Slachlan fastened dark bloodshot eyes on Kitt, while the soldiers stared with frank astonishment.

The great black mount was led onto the pier, the same who had brought Ardri to Dundingin only little over a month ago which now seemed like a year.

Kitt nodded his thanks to the four Amhas, who did not acknowledge it. The translator met his eyes as if he were about to speak. Just then Ardri returned to the boat to toss the wine flask to the Amhas with casual contempt. They caught at it eagerly.

"Come along Kitt, you won't regret it!"

They walked along the pier towards the shore. With one hand on Kitt's arm, the Prince sketched a jaunty wave into the air with his free hand.

Before he stepped off the pier, Kitt looked back to the river. The four Amhas were sitting in their boat like statues, their dark faces blank. When he looked back a second time, they were passing the wine flask among them while beginning the slow row upstream.

Chapter 8
The Return of the King

Ardri stepped on the kneeling Slachlan's cupped hands and shoulder to mount a big black horse with red and gold trappings.

Slachlan and the other five soldiers followed on dark brown horses. Upon Ardri's order, a soldier approached Kitt leading his horse and invited him to mount. Kitt refused the offer, and insisted that he preferred to walk. He had never seen a live horse before but did not wish to admit as much or make a fool of himself. How different the real thing was from a picture in a book. Riding looked easy enough, he thought, but so did sword fighting after many years of practice. Besides, if he had accepted, the soldier would have been on foot, and Kitt doubted that the man could keep up with a horse, even without armour. He also wondered whether a horse could carry his weight over any distance, well aware that he was taller and heavier than all the men he had so far seen here. But Ardri did not seem to consider any of that. Maybe you didn't have to consider many things when you were a Prince of Rilante and King of Cryssumha.

So Kitt trotted beside the horses, looked into their great dark eyes, gentle and wilful at the same time, the rectangular pupils shining metallic blue, listening to the thud of the hoofs on the ground, and watched the great muscles rolling under the glossy skins, admiring the flowing manes and tails. He would lay his hands on them at the first chance when nobody looked, to see how they felt to the touch. He watched how the riders held their balance, assessed the saddles, the function of the stirrups, the use of the spurs, and riding crops. The riders, in turn, watched him from the corners of their eyes.

"Not tired yet, Kitt? Won't you ride now?" Ardri inquired for the third time.

Kitt shook his head as he had twice before. After three miles, he was still running beside the horses in the same easy, distance-eating trot.

Behind Ardri lay the dark line of the Great Wood Bacenis like the remnant of a bad dream; the river cut it off like a knife from the land of fields and pastures, dotted with villages and single farmsteads, all palisaded.

Farmers walked behind oxen, guiding the ploughs with their hands, or with a sack slung over their shoulders, reaching in and flinging the grains over the ploughed soil. Their shields, bows and spears leaned on the stone walls which surrounded the fields. Out of their calculating blue eyes, they looked at the cavalcade which passed them, and they did not salute. Ardri would remember that; he had a good memory for slights. His eye met Slachlan's. There was fierce anticipation in the steward's eye, reflective of Ardri's feeling.

The land had been rising since they left the Struenfoly. Now the slope was becoming steeper. The riders overtook heavy oxcarts that struggled up the road. The waggon drivers also didn't salute. Neither did they seem to calculate the sheer mass of food which was pouring into Dundingin - Ulud, really. Ardri knew that this palpable indifference was not entirely due to stupidity or greed, although this time of year prime prices were being paid in the town for viands. He readily gave credit to the Master of Mirrors' unique ability to lay cobwebs over people's collective eyes and minds.

He looked where Kitt was. The young giant was still running beside the trotting horses, looking as if he could keep that up all day. Ardri knew that he could, uphill, too. Before them, the dark, compact mass of walls and towers of castle Marrak loomed above the plain and city like a squatting dragon.

"Your capital, my king," Slachlan said.

A long curving mound rose from the landscape, a crumbled ring wall of great stones, which had been dislodged by the roots of the trees, forced apart by the gentle insistence of grass and earth.

The road ran through a gap, where once a gate must have been, and into an area of stone heaps, with grass growing over them, and brambles and elderberry bushes. Arches lead into thickets, and columns pointed into the cloudy sky; a wall was standing beside the road, with a solitary window through which Kitt could see the dark wood beyond the river. Once he realised that the original structures, reduced by wind and water, had been six-cornered, some eight-cornered, he could discern the same floor plans as the field of ruins he had seen in the Murkowydir wood.

"The city of Ulud," Ardri said. He had fallen back to ride beside Kitt.

The cavalcade rode in among the ruins on carriage paths that once had been paved streets, with deep ridges grated into the stone by the wheels of heavy wagons, now filled with earth and moss.

They crossed a cleared space and halted before a high wooden gate in a wall that was comparatively new, built with cut stones from the older fortification. The man named Slachlan raised a bronze horn and blew a deep tone, like the bellow of a reptilian monster of long ago.

Both sides of the high gate swung open with a creak sounding like an echo to the horn. Mailed guards thronged by the gate. The long hair that escaped from under their helmets was blond or bright red. Their blue eyes under the round bronze helmets were suspicious.

A soldier with bronze armour more ornate than that of the other men stepped forward. "We were worried about you, Prince Ardri."

"So was I, my good Captain Warmond, so was I."

"In fact, my lord, when you had gone for five days, and I was not able to extract any useful information from your steward here," the guards' captain glowered at Slachlan, who scowled back at him, "I have seen no other way open to me, but to send a courier to Iwerdonn. I've asked for reinforcements so that I could send out an armed detachment to look for you. Glad to see it won't be necessary."

"Why should my steward be required to give you any information as to my whereabouts, Captain Warmond?" Ardri's voice had an edge to it.

"Because I have to answer to your brother for your wellbeing," Captain Warmond said stoutly. "And to your father the king," he added. "As I explained to you earlier, my prince, this is a border area. I only wish you had allowed me to provide your escort so I could have been certain..."

"Truth to tell, I didn't mean to stay away as long as I did." Ardri's smile was friendly and open again. "I don't reproach you, Captain Warmond, I know you meant well, and I'm sure you acted according to your regulations. And I also know that Flannan will be absolutely livid when he gets your message."

"So he will, my lord," the captain said with feeling.

"Well, well, best send another message to him."

"At once, my lord." Warmond's eyes rested on Kitt. "May I ask …?"

"This is Kitt of Minit Houarn, whom I recommend to you most warmly, Captain Warmond. He did me one invaluable service after the other, but that is a long story, fit to tell you over a goblet of wine or two. I hope we may see you and your excellent wife the lady Beibini at dinner in Castle Marrak. I will have the invitation written first thing."

The guards' captain would have liked to ask more questions, but apparently had no wish no irritate royalty a second time. Instead, he stepped back and nodded the train through the gate.

Kitt had the undivided attention of the soldiery as he passed through the gate and heard mutters of "What is that?" and "Fucking big." and "Got a sword." He found the guards' captain walking by his side, leading a saddled white and black horse patterned as if the animal wore a second blanket. The mane was long, streaming in white and black hanks; the tail was white.

"From Minit Houarn, the prince says?" the captain inquired.

"Isenkliff," Kitt replied.

"My dear Warmond, do ride beside me!" the prince requested. "I wish for your company." Again, the guards' captain was deprived of a chance to ask questions.

Dundingin was the first city Kitt saw, and he found it another thing that was different from pictures in books. The pages of descriptions hadn't conveyed the smell, or the noise of many voices speaking at once. All over the town lay the jingling sound of many bells. Bringing into perspective what he had read in books and imagined and what he saw now formed new images in his busy mind. At last, he was seeing the world of the men who visited Isenkliff. Then, he saw where the melody came from that he had heard from the moment they had entered the city, the bronze bells of

100

hundreds of wind chimes, hanging in windows, swaying in doorways, and under roof beams.

Behind the gate ran the main street, an ancient paved road, lined with square stone houses that had small windows and massive doors. Red-haired, blue-eyed people stood in front of these houses, like the ones who had worked the farmsteads, and watched the Ardri's entry into the city with the same curious detachment. Ardri looked back at them from the height of his black mount. Kitt's impression that the prince was not universally beloved was confirmed. He wondered what this meant for him, and how much he would need to watch his back.

On the left, they passed a long, low house with a wooden gallery in front, where rough-looking men sat on benches. They were all armed. These must be the woodsrunners and hunters Ardri had told him about. There were Rilante-men and men clad in attires of linen garbs and amulets of feathers, teeth and bones -Amhas, tame Woodstalkers, such as those who had brought him and Ardri over the Struenfoly in their canoe. Except these men were smiling, so Kitt wondered if they were the same kind of people. Most of the woodsrunners seemed the result of a mixture of races. Predominant about them all was a big, dark-haired man with ice-blue eyes and muscular, sunburned limbs who sprawled there as if he owned the place.

Suddenly the street filled with a crowd of dark-haired people, who spilled into the main thoroughfare out of the side alleys. They surged forward to touch Ardri, the foremost trying to kiss his hands and feet, dark eyes with twitching lids unwaveringly on Ardri's upright figure. Secure in the saddle, he swam on a wave of shaking, grasping, adoring hands, and bent, gnarled frames. More and more of the main street filled with them and the red-haired people retreated towards their houses, to watch the spectacle with careful attention. Captain Warmond tried to hold off the crowd but was headed off himself. He did not look a happy man.

"These are the descendants of the old Cryssumha," Ardri said to Kitt, his blue eyes blazing.

They had as much in common, the newly crowned King of Cryssumha, and those whom he called his people, as a dragonfly had with worshipping ants.

On the right, they went past a long, two-storey house where several men leaned out of the windows, soldiers in leather clothing with various regulation items of bronze armour. On the wooden porch stood two women with hair flaming red in the evening sun; the older one had generous proportions, a laughing mouth and eyes that had seen it all. The other was still a girl, and she looked at Ardri with shiny cornflower eyes, her pretty mouth slightly open. Captain Warmond reigned in his horse, to put himself between the crowd and the veranda. Smiling, Ardri bowed to the two women.

The girl caught sight of Kitt. "But he is big!" she said into a sudden lull of the noise.

"Hush!" the woman beside her said reprovingly.

The girl blushed to the roots of her fiery hair and giggled. Kitt heard her words, the girlish giggle, saw the girl, her sidelong glance, and he also blushed.

"But is he big in every aspect, is what you want to know, my girl," an old woman with a basket chuckled.

"Hush!" the red-haired woman reproved again, "At your age!" She turned away her head and coughed.

"Long live Prince Ardri!" one of the soldiers leaning from the window shouted, trying in vain to control a damp lock of hair from falling into his eyes. There was the noise of a scuffle. The soldier disappeared from the window suddenly as if somebody had pulled out his legs. "Long live Crown Prince Flannan!"

With a sharp exclamation of annoyance, the woman went inside.

When Kitt looked back, the girl had gone, and the woman had taken her place on the porch again, both hands stemmed onto her ample hips. She was talking to Captain Warmond.

"Where music is, there good people live." A high clear tenor rose over the noise of the crowd, followed by a violent storm of sweet tingling bells.

The source of the noise was a tall, thin man; everything about him was of a pale green colour, his clothes, the pallor of his emaciated face, even the hair. He had no other colour of his own than that of copper patina, except for his red eyes. Small bronze bells hung all over his clothes, and each emitted a different tone as the man's thin body trembled and shook. From his belt, polished bronze mirrors were suspended, some the size of the palm of a hand, others so small that only an eye or a mouth could be seen in it at the time; one was big enough for a rich bride to admire all of her headdress at once.

"Where music is there I belong, for evil people have no song." A shaking fit sized the green man's body, and the bells jingled a tune. "Mirror, mirror in your hand, sweetest woman in the land." His clear, strong voice stood in strange contrast to the flying limbs.

All the while that Ardri's entourage cleaved its way past him through the adoring crowd, the man performed his shaking, twitching dance of rhyme and jingle. In the brief pauses between the shaking fits, he sold his bells and mirrors. Falling under his spell, the people crowded around to buy, but however much he sold, the mirrors and bells shining and jingling about his emaciated frame never grew less.

They came past a stall before a house where a fur trader displayed his wares on a trestle table and lines from which deer skins hung. A wiry, red-haired man of indeterminate age and sharp blue eyes paused in his voluble haggling over marten pelts with a silent Amhas, to size up Ardri and his train.

The next house from the fur trader was a smithy with an anvil in front. In the door stood a massive man who wore the scorched leather apron of his trade, with muscular arms folded over a broad chest, and a keen, ugly face framed by shoulder-long, black hair and a beard that looked as if he cut it with a saw. He bowed deeply, and as he straightened up, he and Ardri exchanged a look over the heads of the crowd.

As the group continued uphill towards the castle, past houses tumbled down and empty, the crowd thinned out behind them. They passed an eight-sided tower, and a vast shadow fell upon them. The sinking sun had disappeared behind Castle Marrak.

When they came to the drawbridge, the city guards had fallen back. From the hill, Kitt could see Captain Warmond's white and black horse in the street below. The land surrounding the city was bathed in the light of the evening sun, while the shadow of castle Marrak continued to creep over Dundingin. Lights sprang up in the windows as it spread. At the foot of the hill, the fire of the smithy burned like an orange star.

Slachlan blew his horn and silently, the bronze gate in the towering walls swung open. Behind the widening crack shone saw torchlight, and the shadows of people moved about. Two sombre black-bearded men encased in bronze armour bowed stiffly in the waist on both sides of the gate.

"Hail King Ardri!" they saluted.

Their adoring voices drowned in the deep bellow of eight black hounds who strained on chains until their growls were choked to a snarling gurgle by their broad leather collars. With a deep bronze clang, the gate fell close behind the mounted group. To Kitt, it sounded like a trap falling shut.

Two gate guards took up position with their eight growling dogs. These animals were bigger than any dogs Kitt had seen before; they stood above three feet at the shoulder, and seemed far worse tempered too, as if nobody had ever petted them. That they were a pack of eight made Kitt all the warier and he made sure to keep them in sight at all times. His instincts prompted him to remain in the shadows and not step into the torchlight. *Why have I come this far? Curiosity.* He had no experience with cities and no idea how far he should go into one. Now he felt like a child in the woods, surrounded by unknown predators and hunters and a set of rules not made for him.

A disembodied face appeared in the gloom under a doorway in the castle façade. Nothing lived in that white mask but the eyes, deep-set, shining in a cold black light, remote. The face belonged to an old man. The back of the nose was thin, the pale lips pressed together to a slit, and a close look at his skin revealed a net of lines like fine cracks in porcelain. He was tall, erect, from the bony frame hung a dark red, very shabby velvet cloak with ornaments coloured the delicate green of old bronze. Long black hair fell straight over the shoulders. It was the face Kitt had seen appear in one of the bronze mirrors inside the Mountain Minit Claghini. Had the face seen him too, he wondered, and stepped back even farther until he felt the stones of the castle wall in his back.

"I watched the stars all night until I saw that Dilo, the Lord of Lightning was rising to meet Vasara the Morning star. Then I announced that the king was near. The stars never lie." The voice that came out of the white face was brittle, but it carried into the last corner of the courtyard, and the crowd fell silent.

As the old man advanced upon Ardri, he pulled a rustling document out of his robe and pointed with a finger shaking with excitement. "See here your Majesty, Vasara and the Lord of Lightning are nearing each other now, bringing the white lead of the Lord of the skies is into perfect balance with the black lead of the Lord of Ledrithud. Only Mavors, the Red Star of blood and iron still preoccupies me at this crucial moment of the passage of the bride." The cold black eyes roamed over the courtyard as if looking for the Red Star there, and not in the sky.

"Later, Glic Tusil, show it to me later," Ardri said, and walked up the stairs of the palace.

"Too soon may be too late already," Glic Tusil murmured enigmatically.

"And too late will be soon enough, so we shall be in time admirably," Ardri retorted. As if he didn't know the positions of the Wandering Stars just as well as Glic Tusil did, with his air of omniscience. As if it was any surprise to find them in the sky. The Master of Mirrors had been beyond useless when Ardri had run for his life in the woods, and now the young king had no patience with him.

The old alchemist fell in behind Ardri, clutching the parchment and shaking his head.

Both wings of the tall bronze door opened onto the throne room of Castle Marrak. The blue and green mosaic of the floor and the columns that carried the high vaulted ceiling were being revealed with the progress of the servants hurrying to light the double row of tall bronze candelabras. At the end of the hall, four chandeliers with seventy-two candles flamed up, and flooded with light a six-cornered dais of wrought bronze on which stood the a huge armchair with a six-cornered back and elaborately wrought legs and armrests of massive bronze, pale green with patina.

This gradual revelation of the ancient Throne of Chryssumha was a beautiful spectacle, and Ardri appreciated that it had been left to the last moment.

The crown in his hand, Ardri walked across the length of the hall towards the Throne of Cryssumha. As he did walk, along the avenue of candlelight, he was alone with himself. He had come through. The odds for that had been really incalculable, because all who had tried before him, had perished, a chain of dead princes, that stretched back from Ardri through time to the fall of Cryssumha. The last links in that bloody chain had been his brothers Ridevin and Kuranori. And except for those two, all had possessed the pure royal blood of Cryssumha, not tainted, like his. He felt sure now that there were those who wished to straighten out the asymmetry, saw him only as the stepping stone for another, true-blooded king to come.

Ardri reached the dais, ascended the nine steps and turned to stand above the Cryssumha people who crowded before him. All present in the hall knelt down, except for Glic Tusil, who walked towards the throne.

Ardri did not wait for him. He placed the crown Fenifindrune on his head with his own hands. Sitting down on the throne as his rightful property, he took possession of a long-vanished kingdom, to rule the last remains of what once had been the bronze empire of Cryssumha.

The old alchemist and Master of Mirrors stopped to stand still for a moment, while he and Ardri measured each other. Then Glic Tusil also knelt.

Over the heads of the kneeling crowd of Cryssumha subjects, Ardri looked for Kitt and didn't see him. That would never do. "Slachlan!"

The Dog of Cryssumha shambled towards him almost on all fours. He didn't straighten up until he had left the throne room.

Kitt had remained in the shadow by the gate, so motionless that even the hounds forgot about him. He was alone; the guards had gone to attend what was happening in the castle hall. They had not forgotten to lock the outer gate with a key; Kitt had tried. He could climb the smooth wall of well-fitting big blocks, provided he had enough time. The question was how long the crowd's attention would be taken up.

The hall portal opened wide, and over the heads of the kneeling people, Kitt could see Ardri sitting on a high chair, the crown from the mountain Minit Claghini on his head, and thought that it was remarkable that the prince, the king, hadn't lost it on his flight through the woods.

He saw the black-bearded steward come down the palace stairs, remembered the name, Slachlan; he pushed past the kneeling guards, his massive head turning like a bull's in search of the red rag.

Kitt kept still.

All began craning their necks, however, and he couldn't stay invisible any longer. A quiet escape was out of the question.

Slachlan seemed to read his mind. "Oh no, you don't big boy!" he grated. "The king wants you, whatever for, and so you come!"

For lack of choices, Kitt ascended the palace stairs. He heard the man breathing behind him. Stepping over the threshold, he felt a push in the small of his back. He stopped and rounded on Slachlan who scowled at him.

"Go on big boy!"

"Don't touch me!" Kitt warned quietly.

The big man held his ground and grinned.

"Advance, Kitt!" Ardri called.

Kitt turned his back on Slachlan and faced Ardri across a sea of bent brocade backs and bowed dark heads.

Slachlan dropped to his hands and knees beside him. Was Kitt expected to kneel too, he wondered? That was what one did in the presence of kings; he had read about it often enough, and also how particular most kings could feel about such matters. The difference between Ardri's bearing in the woods and the one he displayed on his own ground was marked; the haunted air had left him, and he even seemed taller. He wouldn't appreciate what might seem a challenge to his new kinghood.

"Kneel, wolf!" Slachlan grated.

Kitt just could not even consider to perform this simple movement. Several kings had come to Isenkliff for his father Eckehart's Aurora-Steel and been treated no better nor worse than any other warrior. He wasn't going to start kneeling now. Slachlan couldn't do anything about that, down on all fours in his abject position which he seemed to enjoy.

Somebody brushed past Kitt, a woman. He felt the draft of her purple veils, caught sight of black lowered lashes fluttering on a white cheek, smelled a cloud of heavy, sweet, perfume. He didn't need to see the woman's face to recognise her -she had appeared in the mirror of Minit Claghini.

Neelam!

The Queen of Cryssumha. How good it was not to be a rotting corpse in the woods. With quick steps that hardly seemed to touch the ground, she came past Kitt and Slachlan through the kneeling courtiers and up the nine steps to sink to her knees gracefully on the dais.

At once, Ardri lifted her up to him. She stood beside the throne, with her head bowed, as if her black hair weighed heavy for her slender neck. He kept hold of her white hand, to never let go again.

The kneeling courtiers and soldiers were rising. There were a few grim looks in Kitt's direction.

"Come nearer, Kitt!" Ardri called.

Now all the attention in the throne room was bent on the big youth. The courtiers drew aside to clear a path for him to the throne, eyeing the tall figure from the long blond mane to the stained leather shoes, the ladies hiding behind fans of whale-bone and gold-lace, as he walked towards the throne through the crossfire of glances and whimsical smiles.

Strangely enough, Kitt did not look like something dragged in from the wood. All to the contrary, the brown leaf colours of his leather clothes enhanced the fairness of hair and skin, and the way he moved and carried himself left the haughtiest courtier floundering in his wake. Adri couldn't put his finger on it how Kitt's aspect differed from the Rilante, if it was the sheer size, taller than Flannan and Morrik, the biggest men Ardri knew, or if it was the wildness.

Kitt didn't kneel, didn't acknowledge the king. Ardri would see about that, in his own time.

Kitt came to stand beside the white-faced old man in the red robe, Glic Tusil. The black, merciless eyes homed in as if seeing him only now and seeing him completely. The woman beside Ardri raised her head to look at Kitt; her dark eyes stood wide apart and were nearly obscured by the fringe of thick dark lashes, iris and pupil had a silvery shimmer, like haematite.

The steward Slachlan crawled on the ground beside him. "Kneel, wolf!" he muttered again.

He might at least bow or something, Kitt thought, but he didn't give so much as a nod.

Ardri waved a hand, and the murmur of the crowd ceased.

"If it had not been for Kitt, the throne of Cryssumha would stand empty today, and the crown Fenifindrune would still sleep in Minit Claghini. Or worse, be taken by the bloodstained hands of Woodstalkers and lost forever in the Great Wood called the Bacenis. Kitt saved me from a Bethrek, and from foul Maldryg witchcraft; he protected me from Woodstalker persecution all the way to the river Struenfoly."

"Where was Slachlan?" a tall, broad, black-bearded noble in black gold inlaid armour with ill-tempered eyes demanded.

Slachlan's massive head jerked around as if stung, opening his mouth angrily.

"The only way to approach Minit Claghini was for King Ardri to go alone, Lord Morrik," Glic Tusil said. "We thought it best not to discuss that, knowing your objections which stem from your loyalty to the king."

"I wanted to go. I would have died willingly." Slachlan's eyes fastened on Kitt with renewed resentment.

"I trust Kitt to keep the secrets he has gained knowledge about," Ardri said. "Forever."

"Very well, your Majesty," Glic Tusil said in a colourless voice. He turned to Kitt. "We will always be indebted to you, young man, indeed, indebted to you eternally. We all would die for the King of Cryssumha, just like you."

"Hm," Kitt said.

"Then rejoice, Glic Tusil, because you shall have the first opportunity to pay your debt of gratitude to this excellent young man."

"Eh?" Glic Tusil looked at Ardri as if he had suddenly grown a second head.

Ardri grinned. "But yes! Kitt wants to learn about bronze. He deserves it, and apart from that, the King of Cryssumha can hardly owe his life to a blacksmith. Yes, just imagine, Kitt is an ironworker."

Murmuring and laughter rippled through the court; it did not sound appreciative.

109

Ardri raised a hand. "Silence!" he snapped, and the noise stopped as if cut off with an executioner's sword. "As I was saying, naturally, Kitt of Minit Houarn wants to improve himself, and I have granted his wish. Who better than the Master of Mirrors, to elevate this brave young man from the slavish iron to the nobility of bronze."

Glic Tusil eyed the young giant doubtfully, and Kitt looked back in puzzlement. The alchemist did not look like a smith to him.

"My task, the task of the Master of Mirrors, is to teach the Blood of Cryssumha. Since your noble uncle the High Prince Angkou I have taken no new apprentices. I did not intend to do so again, your Majesty, until the tutor of your own son was chosen."

"Be sure that your king knows exactly what the responsibilities of the Master of Mirrors are. I am merely asking you a favour, most excellent Glic Tusil, and I would esteem it very great favour indeed if you humoured me in this little matter."

Glic Tusil bowed mutely, with pinched lips.

Ardri turned to Kitt again. "You once mentioned that you would like to learn Ledrithud, higher magic. Glic Tusil is the most skilful alchemist in all of Cryssumha. He will not merely teach you the lowly tricks of a trade; he will teach you the very essence of bronze."

"I have to begin somewhere," Kitt said. He would have been content to start with the lowly tricks of the trade. But that could surely be arranged later, he thought, remembering the smith in the main street. If this Glic Tusil could, would, really teach him about Seidar and Zaubar, the magic knowledge his mother Aslaug refused to impart, then that was something not to be refused prematurely.

"He'll never leave us!" Slachlan's face suddenly creased into a smile, which did not suit his face. "There is so much to learn about bronze." He slapped Kitt's shoulder.

What was wrong with this man that he kept touching him, Kitt wondered, checking his instinct to lash out. One of these days he would, he was suddenly sure. This must show on his face, because he saw Ardri watching him with a slight smile.

Glic Tusil looked disapproving. He addressed Ardri formally. "Will your Majesty grant his humble servant an audience under the rose. It is a matter of the Star Pattern."

"Slachlan, get Kitt something to eat, a place to sleep!" Ardri ordered, giving Kitt a smile and a nod, no doubt meant to be

110

encouraging and welcoming, with the effect of making Kitt aware even more that he was now on Ardri's ground.

"Yes, my king!" Slachlan said and bowed as deeply as his armour allowed. "Come along, big boy, lots of food and drink waiting for you."

"Go with Slachlan Kitt, he will look after you." That was clearly a dismissal. The tone in which Ardri spoke to Kitt had changed very much from that of the Bacenis.

Kitt shrugged and turned his back. He almost fell over Slachlan, who was crabbing backwards again. Kitt had never seen anyone behave in such an abject manner. Of the courtiers, none was standing up quite straight except for the Lord in the black armour.

As the steward led Kitt through the stone corridors of Castle Marrak, his forced geniality dropped from him like a dead fish.

Yellow beeswax candles burned in bronze holders along the corridors, their golden light shining on faded wall paintings, and floor mosaics with missing stones. Once they passed an open bronze door, and Kitt saw into a room filled with cobwebs, lighted by a single candle shining on threadbare velvet, dulled cloth of gold and a translucent face; pale pink lips smiled at nothing. An old, old world was looking at the young smith out of dark, empty eyes.

The guards' hall was a high vaulted room with tapestries hanging from the walls, the hunting motives alive in the dancing torchlight. Regulation items of uniform and weapons hung from pegs. There was a fireplace as big as a farmer's hut, in which a whole ox revolved on a spit. Twenty men, all of large built, dark-haired and dark-eyed, some with beards, sat on benches in their shirt sleeves, eating and drinking, and talking in a language unknown to Kitt. It smelt of roasted meat, spilt beer, dirty clothes and the wax candles standing on the long table. A dozen of the big, black hounds sat and waited for something to be thrown to them. Others lay on the floor as they gnawed on bones with zest and a lot of cracking noise, to growl deeply each time another dog came near.

Slachlan barked a command to a couple of page boys clad in dusty black velvet and dull gold lace and they darted away as if kicked. Then he settled down in an armchair at the top of the table by the grand fireplace, and ignored Kitt. As nobody else seemed to pay any attention to him either, Kitt selected a place on a bench near the door and sat down with his back to the wall. From under lowered lids, he looked around. The room was six-cornered, and there were three doors, the one through which he had come and one who was just being opened by a man who lugged in firewood; it led outside, into a courtyard lit by oil lanterns. The third door hadn't yet opened. There was a rack for bows and arrows beside the door leading outside which held eight strung longbows, and sheaves of bronze tipped arrows.

A pageboy brought Kitt an enormous piece cut from the steer roasting in the fireplace and a tall clay beaker filled with beer.

Kitt bit into the roasted meat with all the relish of a young man who had eaten too much cold, raw food for the last days. While he ate, he was aware of many covert glances directed at him.

"Those pale eyes put me off my food." This was said in the language of Rilante, spoken in a strange accent, meant for Kitt's benefit. "What's that damned Rilante peasant doing in here?"

"No, no, that's no Rilante-man, that's a wolf straight out of the Bacenis," another man responded, whom Kitt recognised as one of the soldiers of Ardri's escort.

"I can easily believe that when I see him feed." Somebody laughed, it was not a merry laugh and fell into a sudden quiet.

Kitt looked up from his food. All the faces were turned towards him, an uninterrupted wall of hostility. The great hounds rose from the floor to snarl and expose white fangs. Young and old, men and hounds, at this moment they all looked the same, and the shadows were on their side, as darkness knotted beneath the vaulted ceiling, and shadowy faces hovered there with an implacable hatred of the stranger, the outsider.

"Have a bone, wolf!" Something came flying in Kitt's direction.

As if that was the signal for attack, all the men sprang up.

Kitt caught the missile, identified it as a pig's thigh-bone, while he already returned it in the same fluent movement. The bone whizzed through the gap between the heads of two soldiers, who ducked. A sharp cry of pain sounded from the back of the hall.

A deep growl broke from Kitt's throat.

The forward surge of bodies halted in a poised wave.

Then, one of the hounds ducked and retreated slowly backwards, its belly dragging on the floor. The others laid down where they

112

stood. One after the other, each man looked aside before the grey eyes that shone so brightly in the candlelight. The tension broke, and a shuffling noise signalled general retreat.

"Peace in the hall!" Slachlan admonished from his place. "You damned yellow-bellied curs!"

Avoiding looking at each other, the men sat down again to return to their food, drink and gaming. A man moaned, his left hand cradling a broken collarbone. Nobody paid him any attention.

Kitt relaxed and sat back firmly onto the bench to continue his meal. He took an experimental sip of the beer to wet his mouth and didn't like the bitter taste or the mellowing effect. This wasn't the time for it. When the last shred of meat had gone, he drew his long knife and opened the thick bone with one lengthways cut and a twist to get at the marrow. The crack of the splintering bone echoed in the dead silence and heads turned. Kitt looked up again to see if there were any more comments upon his eating manners. None of the men met his eye. The page boy brought Kitt another helping of food.

"Bring me water!" Kitt demanded, and pushed the beer-filled beaker back at the page boy, who looked at him fascinated from limpid black eyes, and fled.

Eating more slowly, Kitt managed to put away every crumb of the food; he was used to eating when he could. The water the boy brought from the table was cold and had a lifeless taste and Kitt didn't like it any better than the beer. He leaned his back to the wall and sat so motionless that soon everybody in the hall had forgotten about him. Once or twice, a soldier would glance in his direction by chance and give a start of surprise to see him there.

113

Chapter 9
The Red Star

The young King of Cryssumha and the old Master of Mirrors met in the observatory of the east tower of castle Marrak, also called Tirdrich, the Mirror Tower. Few knew of its existence. It was octagonal outside and hexagonal inside. What the space between octagon and hexagon contained, that was the greatest secret of Tirdich; few knew to even ask the right questions about it. Ardri knew. Both his mother and his uncle had made a point of instructing him, to spite Glic Tusil.

The observatory was triangular inside the hexagon, with the three sides the same length. The triple door, only access to Tirdich, opened in this room. The chamber contained a round bronze table, which gleamed rosy red and the position of the fixed stars was marked on it with white, blue, yellow and orange gems. In shallow curved grooves seven metal balls moved, brass, copper, iron, lead, pewter, silver and gold. On another table stood a two feet high double copper arch, a bronze disk polished to a blinding silvery shimmer suspended from it. A bronze bell hung from the top arch and shone like the disk.

Beyond the two tables, taking up an entire wall, stood a tall bronze mirror. It resembled the nine mirrors Ardri had seen in Minit Claghini. He stepped before it, and as he had expected, it did not reflect his image.

There was a word that could bring the last image the mirror had shown. Ardri stared into the cloudy oval, and spoke that word. A picture began to take shape, columns, more bronze mirrors, a malachite flower as high as a man. It was like looking into the next room, yet Ardri knew that this chamber was inside a mountain lying at a distance he could not number in miles, but in dangers.

As he turned away from the mirror, Ardri faced Glic Tusil across the bronze table. "So here you stood, Glic Tusil, in perfect safety, while I had the second half of the gauntlet still to run in the Great Wood called Bacenis."

The old priest's black eyes met the challenge from the young king's blue eyes. "Yes, here I was standing, powerless to interfere. The Maldryg woods sorcery belongs to a different world, so alien that if I so much as touched it in an attempt to comprehend, I would be lost for this world, and become part of theirs. All I could do was to grant you a glimpse of your Queen."

"Kindness, or exquisite cruelty, Glic Tusil? Whichever it was, you are keeping me from her now, and that does not please me. What is so important about the Star Pattern that could not wait until tomorrow? I saw little enough of it through the tree crowns, while I ran for my life, but I felt the stars turn above me. You may assume that I know their positions and revolutions as well as you do."

"It is about the Red Star, your Majesty, Mavors, the Destroyer, the Renegade."

"Ah yes, Mavors. What a fraud you are, Glic Tusil, you act just as if the Red Star had popped up unexpectedly in the pattern, instead of running the courses that we calculated years ahead. Be assured that I have thought about Mavors as much as you have. Or more. And I have come to the conclusion that you were wrong in your interpretation of Mavors in the Star Pattern, and that error of yours nearly cost my life. Did you consider at all that the number of Mavors is nine, just like that of bronze?"

"Because you know, your Majesty, that Mavors was the star of copper once and ruled together with Vasara. But he was corrupted and became the star of iron, and his red colour degenerated to the colour of the corrupt metal. He may fool those who do not know into thinking that his colour is still the red of copper. I can only continue to warn you of him."

Ardri fiddled with the iron ball representing Mavors. "Oh, don't. Tell me something you haven't rehashed a thousand times."

Glic Tusil continued unperturbed. "Therefore, nine alone is an unpredictable number, and it can be trusted only as a combination of three and six, Dilo and Vasara. That is the reason why iron can be corrupted, but bronze cannot be corrupted. Will you deny that, your Majesty?"

115

Ardri lifted the iron ball to look at it with distaste, let it drop with a bang and wiped his hand on his cloak. "Will you explain to me then, why it was Kitt who saved my life over and over when you couldn't – interfere?" *Perhaps you preferred to wait for purer blood than mine, perhaps you are sure that I will have a son?* As he looked into the mirrors of Minit Claghini, seeing Neelam and not being able to touch, that horrible suspicion had begun to gnaw at the back of his mind like a rat. Ardri decided against voicing it. Not yet. "Your words about Mavors in mind, I attempted to get rid of him, even after he saved me from the Bethrek. I did not succeed, and that was my luck, or I would be dead, killed by the Maldryg guards the Woodstalkers set over Minit Claghini and the Shining Heads."

"If there ever was an incarnation of Mavors, here you have it; I concur with you there, absolutely. Yes, I see that there can be no doubt that the focus of Mavors' influence in the Star Pattern is this barbarian blacksmith."

"Kitt."

"Of Minit Houarn."

"So how come that the interference of Mavors was instrumental in the coronation of the King of Cryssumha if Mavor's role is what you say?"

"You may rightly reproach me, your Majesty, that I did not foresee this aspect of Mavors, but I must point out that I never claimed knowledge of the Bacenis. If I may say so, your majesty's making the necessary deductions by yourself is a great credit to your teacher, the most revered High Prince Angkou. But I beg you to divest yourself of the notion that character and influence of a Wandering Star invariably must be one or the other, and remain so at all times. Because of the fickle nature of Mavors, his role in the Star Pattern is bound to change. The barbarian was useful to you in the woods, but what will he be here or even in Rilante? Nothing but an embarrassment, even a danger. Yes, a danger. What if he brought the Star Pattern to fruition just to cut through it when it does not regrow? That is what I wanted to talk to you about."

"Very well then, I will give him the ship he asked for so that he can return to his home, an obscure island in the Northern Sea, and that is then the end of the matter."

116

"Pardon me, my King, I would hardly call Minit Houarn obscure, this ancient centre of the corruptible steel where Mavor's temple stands?"

"Why not. Even Mavors must have a temple somewhere, and Minit Houarn is far."

"Too far for your half-brother's ships to sail? Prince Nolan Ri, whom they call Flannan, I have heard rumours that he entertains the idea to have an iron sword made for him in the temple of Mavors?"

"That is a lie! He may search for ways to reduce dependency on the Cryssumha provinces of Rilante. It is only logical. Some bad advice may have mentioned iron." Ardri made a distasteful face. "It's so uncouth. When he thinks about it in earnest, Flannan won't lower himself thus."

"You have not heard of an iron ship called the Birlinn Yehan?"

"Yes, Flannan planned to capture her."

"The Birlinn Yehan escaped."

"Oh?"

"Prince Nolan Ri claimed that he hadn't even seen her, and his men back him up, naturally. But there is the rumour that he spoke long to her captain Lodemar on the high seas - a man who went to Minit Houarn before. Just as Mavors, Prince Nolan Ri is turning from bronze to iron. He is called Flannan for his red hair, but it is not the red of copper."

"That is a lie," Ardri said again, with little conviction. He didn't need the parallels pointed out, he wasn't colour-blind. Flannan too would have to go, he had known that long. "Kitt wants to learn about bronze. If Mavors was the star of copper once, Kitt could turn to the side of bronze."

"The only way iron can serve copper, you know what that is, my King," Glic Tusil pointed out.

Yes, the iron must dissolve in the process, Ardri thought. Somehow he was with the back to the wall again, as usual, and Glic Tusil knew it.

"I hope your majesty will not let yourself be blinded by, ah, sentiment, I beg your pardon."

"I merely don't want to make another near-fatal mistake by listening to your advice, Master of Mirrors. Bring Kitt over to my side, Glic Tusil! He wants to learn about bronze, that is how we will

117

win him over! And now excuse me, my Queen awaits, and I would not leave her pining longer."

A clear sound reverberated in the room from the bronze bells standing on the table. Ardri, already on his way to the door, turned around in a flash. "What now?"

A woman's face appeared in the smooth surface of the bronze disk, with eyes so black that they seemed violet burned into Ardri's for a moment. Queen Serenaiba. There was no way Ardri could gainsay his mother, or turn his back upon her.

The tall mirror on the wall duplicated the images in the bronze, and showed much clearer the queen's regular white features, framed with raven hair that lay around her head like a velvet wave, and over her shoulder, they could see a big, red-haired man sit in a high chair, a plain wool cloak wrapped around him tightly as if he felt cold. They recognised King Tirnmas of Rilante. Another clear tone came from the bronze bell as if somebody had struck it with a fingernail, and then a voice vibrated in the metal.

"He has gone to seek Kione Lonnir?" King Tirnmas groaned. "Not Ardri too! Hunting a mirage of past times. I have already lost two sons to Torin Daraval's ship. Ridevin! Kuranori! What death did they find in the Bacenis? And now Ardri, Ardri!"

The king of Rilante, in his distressed state, did not realise that the images in the gleaming bronze surfaces did not match the room he was in. Both Ardri and Glic Tusil didn't speak; so that the identical bells should not begin to ring in Iwerdonn. The image in the mirror was clear enough to show that there was nothing in the Queen's smooth face as the king moaned in anguish. "They were your sons also."

She did not answer, and the king averted his eyes and sat brooding.

When Tirnmas looked at his wife again, his eyes were full of pain. "It is not about Kione Lonnir. It is because of Cryssumha, isn't it?"

The Queen still did not answer.

"Why can't you forget Cryssumha?" the king whispered. "You have Rilante. Body and soul."

The queen's eyes blazed in their queer silvery light, and again she said nothing, just watched as the old man drew the cloak around him more tightly and shivered, despite the fire roaring in the grate. King Tirnmas shook his head as if trying to get rid of cobwebs. "I'll send Gasda with a thousand men. If they ride today, they can reach Dundingin in ten days. It may not be too late yet."

At last, the Queen spoke. "I will send a message to Lord Morrik." The cold sweetness of her voice reverberated in the bronze bell. "Lord Morrik has campaigned against the Woodstalkers and piled their heads in heaps."

"Lord Morrik of Cryssumha. Yes, send to Lord Morrik. He will help." The king sighed. "All the same, Lord Gasda will ride to Dundingin at once. He is the best I have, and he will bring order to this serpent's lair," he added with something of his old fire.

Queen Serenaiba's full lips curved upwards. "Yes, send Gasda." Her white hand with transparent nails waved casually, the images faded from the mirror and the disk, and the bells hung quietly.

Seeing King Tirnmas, after returning from the Bacenis, stirred up warring emotions inside Ardri. The shame of his mother married to that red-haired barbarian; each time Ardri looked into a mirror, he saw his father's blue eyes. When his subjects looked at him, they saw his blue Rilante eyes. Neelam's eyes were coal-black, and she never looked into her husband's eyes, when her white, long hands touched him, her head weighed down by the mass of her black hair. His son and heir would have her eyes and be the first true King of Cryssumha. That was the plan, conceived by his mother Queen Serenaiba and the Master of Mirrors. Ardri had done the part expected of him. He resolved that the outcome wouldn't be quite like they expected it. Ardri planned to cut out that part of him that was Rilante, and so he would be the first true king of the reborn Cryssumha himself, followed on the throne by his son when he was ready to give the hilt of Slatynrigan into his hands - the sword that was not yet re-forged.

"What do you think will be the result of a meeting of the blacksmith Kitt and Lord Gasda, Dog of Rilante? Your Majesty?" Glic Tusil's voice broke into Ardri's revery.

His father, King Tirnmas, would like Kitt, Ardri thought. His brother Flannan would like him. His own tainted blood liked and admired him too.

119

"We feel deep gratitude to this young man, owe him a great debt, as you said. But do you want to undo all he did for you? Don't we owe it to him not to let that happen?" Glic Tusil murmured, and flicked an imaginary speck of dust from his red velvet sleeve.

Ardri laughed. "So, to thank Kitt properly for my preservation, I must slay him? You are terrible hypocrite!"

"There have been such constellations before, your Majesty. Then and now, only Cryssumha is what matters. It is all very tragic, of course and we will preserve him a heroic memory."

"Ten days is more than ample," Ardri said. "From what that fool Warmond said, I thought I had less time."

"If we resolve the question of Mavors' role in the Star Pattern tonight." Their eyes met briefly, Glic Tusil's dark, hard and merciless, Ardri's blue, expressionless. "Are you ready, your Majesty?"

"As ever I'll be." Ardri weighed a heavy cloth-of-gold purse in his hand. "And here is the reward for saving the life of the King of Cryssumha. You will add your own token of gratitude."

The Master of Mirrors looked at the Prince curiously, and after hesitating just a little, Ardri placed the purse into Glic Tusil's outstretched hand. Gratitude, friendship, trust, they all must retreat when the rise of Cryssumha was at stake. "Perhaps you wish to leave what is to follow to me," Glic Tusil murmured. "You don't need to be involved at all. Go to your queen; you have much to talk about."

"Don't be ridiculous!" Ardri snapped. "I wouldn't miss that spectacle for the world."

"By your leave, your Majesty!" Glic Tusil preceded Ardri down the spiralling staircase, which led directly into the room below.

This room was much larger than the observatory and six-cornered. Here, hundreds of mirrors were suspended from the ceiling and hung on three walls. Another wall was taken up with ropes which led up through the ceiling past the observatory above into the tower roof where six bells were suspended.

The fifth wall contained a door that connected the tower with the staircase that ran between the outer octagon and the inner hexagon. That way, the lower chambers of the Mirror Tower Tirdrich could not be accessed directly.

Below the Mirror Chamber was a study filled with books, parchments, stuffed animals and crystal balls. Again, mirrors hung on the wall, and from the ceiling were suspended clusters of bronze bells. Another stairway led down from the study into an alchemist's laboratory, with work tables, shelves that held hundreds of glass bottles and devices of copper, brass and bronze the purpose of which was not clear at first sight.

In the middle of the workroom stood a stone basin filled with glowing coals, beside it lay fire tongs. In a corner crouched a boy; he had been tending the coal basin, and scurried away upon hearing footsteps on the stair. The whites of his eyes were gleaming in the dusk. Ardri took it without asking that the boy was a deaf-mute.

Glic Tusil added to the purse what Ardri had called his token of appreciation, and sent the crippled page boy on his errant. The first step was taken- only the first. Ardri could still stop what was about to happen. He didn't fool himself, though. The first step was the important one.

*

The lamps were burning low, the pages had stopped to serve wine and beer, and the soldiers began to settle down for the night on the long benches. Some went to sleep on the ground, wrapped in blankets. A page boy with a crooked back arrived with his arms full of thick, fur-trimmed wool blankets, and deposited them on the bench beside Kitt. On top of the bundle lay a fat purse, which fell to the floor with a heavy clank.

The soldiers turned around and stared.

The page picked up the purse, with the coins inside clinking, and under the crossfire of looks he held it out to Kitt, who made no move to take it. The page laid the purse on the pile of blankets and left the hall. Kitt thought of his father, so much gold paid for his blades and armour, and his habit of flinging it all into a dark room without counting, and closing the door on it. Steel was the only metal that was important to Eckehart, and he had taught his love for steel to his son, and his disdain to waste gold and silver on the minting of coins. Suddenly, Kitt felt miserably homesick for Isenkliff. But the slain of Bear Mountain kept him from going home. At first, he had not been sure that the creatures, the Hunters in the Mist, were human. Now, he knew that they were. This raised his body count to three. At least;

121

one more creature might have succumbed to the wound he had dealt him. Or her. With the Hunters in the Mist, it was hard to know apart men and women, especially when running for his life as Kitt had. That was the other problem, to know whether he had he killed one woman or two.

Kitt sat and listened to the snoring of the men in the thick air of the hall. It was out of the question to sleep here. They had shown an unfriendly disposition towards him, and if they had not been cowards, then blood would have flowed. If saving their king didn't make them his friends, then nothing would.

Kitt sat on the bench, his hand closed around the dagger hilt, while the lamps in the hall and corridors burned out. Nobody came to relight them. Soon he would sit in darkness stale with the breath of so many sleeping men. Nobody was awake now but him. Time to slip out.

He left the blankets were the page had laid them. There was a sweet smell of resin and something else that he didn't like. Making as much noise as a fragment of a dream, he stepped among the sleepers, and tried the door opposite, which opened to a stream of the clean, cold night air.

In the courtyard outside, Kitt breathed deeply, and stood still to allow his eyes to adapt to the darkness. He saw the stars as from the bottom of a chasm. Some light came from lit windows and lanterns beside a gate on the west side. It was closed and barred top and bottom, and from the two towers flanking it he heard the guards' low conversation, interrupted with many pauses.

Two inner gateways stood open. Like a shadow, Kitt stole along the castle wall towards one of them which led into another courtyard where low buildings leaned to the outer wall. Shuffling noises came from the inside, and there was a smell of fermenting shit. Stables.

The instinct to scan the outer wall for a way of escape was strong upon him, but reason told him, that the risk to scale an unknown wall in the darkness was too high. Instead, he climbed up to the roof of one of the buildings covered with reed. There he lay down with his feet touching the wall, sword hilt by his hand, and looked up at the towering black wall of the castle, and the familiar stars in the visible segment of the night sky. He heard the padding of paws on flagstones and thought of the black hounds, and why they didn't sleep.

*

Glic Tusil drew the cloth from three copper wire cages which stood on a work table. One contained two tree-cats, curled up and fast asleep, the second three falcons with their heads tucked under their wings, and the third a wolf cub, also asleep.

"Sleep, sleep, don't wake up yet. Don't wake. No, don't wake. Sleep, sleep," Glic Tusil hummed, unexpectedly tuneful, Ardri noticed.

The Master of Mirrors opened the falcon cage, and the birds did not wake up, not even when he took them out one after the other and put them into the first cage which contained the tree-cats, and the cats did not wake either. Last, the sleeping wolf cub was put in, and then Glic Tusil closed the wire door.

With fascination Ardri looked at the cage tightly filled with fur and feathers, breathing slightly in their sleep.

Next, Glic Tusil threw dry fir branches and little pieces of frankincense onto the glowing coals. When the flames began to flicker, he clapped his hand sharply. "Wake up!"

The cage erupted in an explosion of fear and fury, the hissing and screaming of the tree-cats', wings fluttering that could not break free, a round, yellow hawk's eye, and over it the howling of the wolf cub.

The alchemist lifted the cage by a handle. Blood splashed onto the work table and dripped on the floor as the alchemist carried the cage to the fire basin. Ardri looked at Glic Tusil's white hands on the handles, safely above the fury and pain that raged inside.

Although Ardri was an alchemist in his own right, he didn't move a hand to assist. That was almost as if it made a difference. If he didn't touch the cage, nor feed the fire, he was not doing this. For some reason, that was important to him. *Why?*

The Master of Mirrors set the twitching, shrieking cage onto the fire basin, and so much blood dropped into it, that the flames were nearly extinguished.

I must be honest with myself, Ardri thought, *must see my own weakness. I could stop this any moment, and that makes it possible*

123

for me to let it happen, one step after the other. I must learn to accept what must be done without such crutches for my conscience.

Glic Tusil blew into the fire and patiently fed the flames with small pieces of wood and frankincense. A sickly stench of aromatic smoke, mixed with the smell of blood, excrement, burning feathers, hair and skin, filled the room.

Look at the wolf cub, how it fights! It has already killed one tree-cat, and of the falcons, one is left alive, but in the end, it will make no difference whatsoever.

At long last, only the young wolf still whimpered. The second tree-cat's hind legs had slashed open its belly before the wolf had torn out its throat. The cub turned its breaking eyes to Ardri; it saw him, and beneath the pain and fear, he saw his own death in the wolf's eyes, a promise, bright and hard. "Such wildness. A shame that you will die anyway," Ardri said softly.

Glic Tusil heaped hands full of the sweet-smelling resin onto the fire. The flames leapt high, smoke filled the chamber, and enveloped the two alchemists.

The wolf cub cried for a long time.

It's not me doing this, Ardri thought again. *This struggle is solely between Mavors and Lute, the warrior and the mage. And again, don't fool yourself. Kitt doesn't have a chance.*

At last, the cage was still, except for the sizzling of burning flesh. The smoke hung under the ceiling in a grey, roiling veil.

When the remains of the animals were thoroughly charred, the Master of Mirrors let the flames of the fire die down and dropped ground tiger's eye and bitter salt into the hot ashes.

Then, the two alchemists bent over the cage with bated breath. Ardri forgot his detachment as he saw that something began to crystallise on the bent bars of the bloody copper cage in colours not of this earth.

"In all my long life I have never quite gotten used to the dark wonder of the transmutation," the old alchemist breathed, and the young one nodded; his eyes were shining in the same black light.

Glic Tusil poured a flask of pure spirits onto the glowing embers, and a blue flame shot up and enveloped the cage.

A cry of unforgiving fury rent the air.

124

Glic Tusil gripped the handle of the cage with the pair of fire tongs to lift it from the basin and set onto the work table. Not risking his hands, because there was life in the cage again, Ardri saw with fascination.

Blood drops ran out from under the cage onto the table -the being in the cage was cutting its own flesh on crooked, razor-sharp teeth and claws. Screaming and sobbing, it struggled against the bars. Ardri felt its hatred against everything, radiating out in waves.

With a forceps, Glic Tusil dropped a piece of wool soaked in molten frankincense into the cage. Now, the rage of the unnatural creature found an aim. Sharp teeth and claws rent the wool into tiny pieces immediately, and in its furious struggle, the bleeding thing hurt itself over and over again.

Chapter 10
The Gratitude of Kings

As he drifted between sleep and waking Kitt felt a growing tension in the air, a malicious intent. From one of the castle-windows poured a silvery sheet of light, and then it was dark again. Suddenly, a cry brought him to his feet, the howl of a wolf. It was a young animal, and it was dying in pain somewhere high up in that gigantic black mound of castle Marrak.

Clutching the sword hilt, he stood up; his hair was standing on end, and droplets of sweat beaded his forehead.

Below a dog growled and whimpered.

There was nothing he could do, and at last, it was over. In another window, a blue glow increased, high in a tower, then diminished and was gone.

*

The second scream rent the air, full of animal pain and rage.

Each step gave the twisted creature more pain, but it would not be stopped, now that it was free and had a scent, the same smell, sweet and sharp, that had been there in the eternity of hurt. Like a trail of blood, it led down the winding staircase. With a keening sound of pain and hatred, the creature flew along that spoor through the corridors.

The smell grew thick and concentrated in a body; it was the end of the trail. The creature tore into it, tore apart everything until the centre lay open like a beating heart, to erupt in a golden fire and burn the suffering, rabid thing in one last, great burst of pain.

*

The third scream was human when it began; at the end, all humanity had gone out of it, with another cry of triumph and final agony mingled in it. Big dogs began to howl with deep, melancholy voices. A noise of shouting and running came from the other courtyard, the one where the guards' hall lay, and firelight shone through the archway.

Kitt lowered himself from the roof of the building. The large dog he had heard before growled nearby, and then it whimpered. Kitt saw the eyes scintillating white, and he made a sound as if to console an ordinary dog. Keeping in the shadow of the archway, he felt the dog's big body pressing against his leg, and reached down to stroke its massive head. The soldiers who had slept in the guards' hall, stood around a blazing fire basket in the centre of the courtyard, fully armed; they turned their heads at every sound and continued to throw wood into the fire until the flames leapt high, and bathed the castle walls and their pale faces in yellow light. Kitt caught just a few words of the men's talk in the mixed language of Cryssumha and Rilante and could make only vague sense of it.

"Monster...attack...bloody mess...dead...oh yes, dead, very...who...what...gweilgi...gweilgi!"

"Nothing left worth burying," somebody said loudly, distinctly, and there seemed to be a muttered argument about that featuring the word "barbarian".

When nothing more transpired, Kitt returned to the stable roof, to sit with his back against the castle wall, his sword across his knees. His hand never leaving the hilt, he slept fitfully, and in his light sleep, he could hear the people in the other courtyard move about all night.

*

After Glic Tusil had released the creature, he and Ardri stood in the laboratory, listening.

The scream came, full of abject terror. The alchemists looked at each other.

"I think we have failed, Glic Tusil."

"Hardly. He may be big, your barbarian, but he is only flesh and blood. Somebody will come at any moment and tell us about it."

"I want to know it now," Ardri said, impatiently, and ran towards the stairs, up to the observatory, from where he crossed into the next tower. How far away everything was in Castle Marrak, and the Tower Tirdich farthest, when he was bursting with curiosity!

In the corridor which led to the guards' hall, he met Slachlan. "What was that scream? Anyone having a bad dream?"

"A monster, my king, it...it...killed..." Slachlan quavered.

"Who was killed?"

"I...can't say."

"Show me. And pull yourself together, Steward! You are a soldier, you surely have seen...oh yeuch, damn it, shit! He sure is dead." Ardri looked down at the heap of raw flesh and splintered bones mixed up with the blood-soaked shreds of fur trimmed wool blankets. All was singed and charred, and the stench of burning flesh hung in the air.

"Who is dead?" Glic Tusil's voice came from the corridor.

How the was old man here so fast behind him, that Ardri wondered.

"I can't say as yet, my Lord," Slachlan's voice was a little steadier now. "But I haven't seen the barbarian anywhere." That thought cheered him. "The big boy was sitting right here, on this very place, and those are...the blankets your servant brought for him, my Lord."

Glic Tusil approached the mangled corpse, and looked down on it with satisfaction. "As I said earlier, it is, after all, only meat, albeit a whole lot of it."

Ardri recalled the scream, so abject, to full of surprise and fear. If it had been Kitt there would be a furious roar maybe, but a sound like that, not likely. But he didn't voice his doubts again.

"Throw this offal on the dung heap!" Glic Tusil ordered.

Slachlan barked orders. Instead of obeying the soldiers retreated from the butchery. Slachlan repeated his orders, pointing his finger. With all signs of reluctance, the soldiers indicated fetched shovels and buckets.

"Bring more light!" Glic Tusil demanded.

"Oh, for mercy's sake!" somebody muttered.

Retching, the men began to shovel the bloody gobbets and strings into the buckets, as Glic Tusil looked on, vindictive satisfaction transforming his face into a demonic mask, so that the soldiers edged away from him.

Ardri thought such hostile feelings hardly warranted, as Kitt hadn't done anything to Glic Tusil -except for saving the young king of the tainted blood from a horrible death. Was his wife Neelam truly pregnant, and if so, how the Master of Mirrors could know with such certainty - a moot question; he would know.

Something metallic clattered into the bucket. The soldiers weren't curious what it was.

"What is that?" Ardri demanded.

Gingerly, a soldier picked out the purse with the gold coins.

Glic Tusil nodded and turned to go, his red robe swishing.

Ardri took charge of the purse and got his fingers bloody. Somebody offered him a large, white handkerchief and a deep bow. Wiping his hands and the brocade of the purse, the young king's attention was caught by something protruding from the bloody mess in the bucket. A closer look showed him a bronze hilt. It was that which had made the clattering noise. Ardri didn't call attention to it. It was not for Vasara to interfere in this struggle between Lute and Mavors. Glic Tusil would find out for himself, now or later. Ardri hoped to be there and see his face when he did.

*

Kitt woke from noise and motion below, water being drawn up from a well in the yard, snorting, and the peaceful sounds of the horses. The sky above the castle wall was already a pale blue, while the courtyard still lay in cold grey shadow. In the morning light, he saw a stone well with a great winch which a serf in manure stained trousers was turning, to wind up the chain. Kitt estimated that there were twenty feet of chain already on the winch.

He climbed down from the roof. Finding the stable door open, he looked in; a thick warm smell hit his nose, of horse piss and straw. The faint morning light played over glossy black skin; big questing eyes turned towards him with a thin gleam of the white showing. Kitt touched the black mane as he had wanted to do before, and felt the rough texture of the long hair, the warmth of the neck beneath it. The black stallion regarded Kitt with ears laid back, his left hoof raised slightly. To scratch the warm hide with his fingertips seemed naturally indicated to Kitt; the horse's ears slowly assumed a forward position, and the hindleg relaxed. Mindful that the horse had big teeth, Kitt moved deliberately, to pass a hand over the glossy shoulder and the slightly arched back, and feel the hard muscle gliding beneath the smooth hair.

The serf came in with a water bucket in each hand and shouldered past Kitt. He crooned to the big black stallion, as he sloshed water into a trough.

Kitt appropriated the second bucket to wash, and the man left it to him without demur. The water was cold, but of the curiously lifeless taste which he had already disliked in the hall.

The rays of the morning sun gilded the towers of castle Marrak, edging down towards the cobblestones of the courtyard. From somewhere came a smell of frying bacon.

Walking towards the archway, Kitt passed the dunghill and identified it as the source of the pungent stable smell he had perceived during the night. Two big, black dogs were sniffing at something there, irresolutely. It was a blood-soaked bundle, and a corner of it looked as if once it had been a fur-trimmed woollen blanket.

Seeing the outer gate still tightly closed, Kitt sat down on an empty barrel by the burned down fire basket, from where he could see both it and the door to the guards' hall, to watch the people who came and went on daily errands, for any indication that the gate was to be opened soon. Kitt wanted to be the first through it. Something was very wrong in castle Marrak.

The big fire basket beside him was full of overflowing ashes and agreeably warm in the morning chill.

"Breakfast, my Lord." From the guards' hall, a page boy hurried towards Kitt carrying a tray laden with a plate heaped with bread, butter, cold cutlets, and a beaker. "You left that in the hall last night, my Lord." The page set down the tray on another barrel beside Kitt and held out the purse Ardri had sent the evening before.

Kitt was about to tell the boy to keep the money but changed his mind, remembering what he had read in his books, what Eckehart's customers had told him. In cities, it was essential to have money. Maybe he could pay the smith in the main street an apprenticeship fee out of this. As he turned the purse over in his hand, Kitt noticed that the cloth of gold was stiff with dried blood. Something sharp had slit into it, and tiny blood clots and white ashes stuck to the gold thread embroidery.

"You were not in the guards' hall when it happened last night, my Lord?" the page boy ventured. "A monster came in and killed Gock."

"Who is Gock?"

"Just a soldier, my Lord. The monster tore him into so many tiny shreds, that they had to sweep him up with a broom." Besides the terror that shook in the page's voice, there was a ghoulish relish.

"Did you see the monster?"

"No, my Lord, nobody did. It crumbled into salt and ashes before anyone could get a light going. It's always like that. Ledrithud, my Lord." The page boy's voice fell to a whisper on the last words.

Kitt opened the purse and shook twelve gold coins onto the tablet. They were two fingers wide, and one side bore the image of a ship, the other a sun. Rilante coin. All were powdered in white ashes.

The page boy still hovered. "It is all there, I hope, my Lord."

"More than that." Kitt picked out a round jar which had the same diameter as the coins, and was made of dark polished wood. The screw top was not shut tightly, and the content seeped out and left a smear on Kitt's hand that smelled of resin and something sweet. Holding the jar away from him cautiously, he twisted the top. Inside was a dark paste, and with the lid open the smell was overpowering. "Do you know what this is?" he inquired of the page boy, who paled, and edged away from him. Kitt's hand shot out to grip his arm, not to hurt the other youth, but to make it very clear that escape was out of the question. "What is this?"

"It's nothing to do with me. King Ardri..." the page tugged without any effect.

"I know that. Answer me!"

"Well, sir, coming out of the woods as you do...you won't hold it against a mere page, my Lord..."

"Spit it out!"

"Your woods-smell, my Lord," the page boy whispered. "If you don't mind my saying, it's rather...rather..."

Kitt released him, and he retreated in haste, to turn resentfully at the hall door. Seeing that Kitt was still looking after him, the youth darted inside like a hare into its burrow.

Now why would he want to smell like Dodlak bait, Kitt thought, as the sweet, sharp, all-pervading aroma began to connect to the last night in the guards' hall, to fur-trimmed blankets with the same scent, which now lay on the refuse heap mixed up with the bloody, torn thing.

Looking at the food on the tablet, he realised that although he felt very hungry, he had curiously little appetite. He raised the plate to sniff carefully. The food smelled as cold roast and bread should, and so did the diluted wine. Far from being reassured, Kitt set the plate aside without eating.

Suddenly, he looked up, feeling that he was being watched, and could see nobody who paid him particular attention.

*

Finally, Ardri enjoyed the tender hours he had dreamt of, and the reality surpassed the dream, yet did little to assuage the sharp longing he had been forced to endure.

Come morning, only the thought of what had happened the night before drove him out of bed, and Neelam's white, warm arms. As he looked out of the window into the courtyard, he emitted a howl of mirth, which startled his sleepy wife. Her hair formed a black cascade on the creamy silk cushions, and Ardri just had to go back to the bed to kiss her rosy lips.

Then, there was a scratch at the door, as of a desperate dog, and when Ardri opened, Slachlan crawled into the Royal Bedchamber on all fours.

Fervently hoping that he wouldn't be too late, Ardri ran for the Tower Tirdich and descended the stair as fast as he dared. He found Glic Tusil standing among the mirrors suspended from the ceiling. Had he gone to bed at all, did the Master of Mirrors ever sleep, he wondered, and if there even was a bed in this tower.

"Good morning, Master of Mirrors! A fine day it is to teach a bright pupil on a subject dear to your heart!"

Glic Tusil stood very still; only his eyes moved slightly as he scanned the mirrors.

"Kitt is sitting in the western courtyard, eating his breakfast," Ardri said helpfully. "Strong boys need a good breakfast before their lessons begin."

Glic Tusil approached a mirror to stare into it. As he looked, the sitting figure of the wild youth appeared in the silvery round, sitting on a barrel, leather-clad, long blonde hair shining in the first sun rays, his iron sword at his side.

Suddenly Kitt raised his head, the grey eyes looking directly into the mirror. Both Glic Tusil and Ardri took back an involuntary step.

"What an instinct," Ardri murmured.

"So, who was the carrion in the guards' hall?" Glic demanded in a colourless voice.

"Slachlan has finally managed to identify a soldier the name of Gock." Ardri was thoroughly enjoying himself. "Entirely insignificant subject, certainly not worth our elaborate alchemic effort. The hangman would have been good enough for him if he annoyed you."

"Gock," Glic Tusil repeated in the same colourless voice.

This was so good, Ardri thought. Aloud he said: "Kitt must have left the hall during the night, and as it was a cold night, this Gock snagged the blankets that were meant to keep Kitt warm. The idea in the guards' hall is that Gock also stole the purse and that punishment was instant, because of the great favour Kitt enjoys for the king's salvation. The wretch probably did steal the gold. Well, he won't do it again, and it is a good lesson for Slachlan's ruffians. Don't let your pupil wait too long now, Glic Tusil. We wouldn't want him to get into a dispute with the gatekeepers, would we now! They are probably short-handed, what with Gock quitting service in this sudden manner."

There was no answer from the Master of Mirrors, except for a slight grating noise. Startled, Ardri realised that Glic Tusil was grinding his teeth, looking feral with the black eyes blazing in the very white face. Sometimes he wondered if the Master of Mirrors was a living creature at all. However, the first rule when facing monsters of any kind was never to show fear.

"Oh, Glic Tusil, where Mavors is concerned, you have again shown poor judgement! Now you have ten days to make him return to bronze, to bring him to our side."

They stared at each other, the young king and the age-old Master of Mirrors.

"I fully intend to keep my promise to teach my saviour about bronze," Ardri said in a hard voice. "That is, you will keep it for me, Glic Tusil. So, go you now to express your gratitude to Kitt again for saving the life of the King of Cryssumha in the Great Wood called Bacenis!"

"Yes, I will begin to teach your barbarian today."

"What do you think, how much can a blacksmith learn about bronze in just ten days?"

"All he ever needs to know, your Majesty."

"Be careful, Glic Tusil, very careful," Ardri said. "What you are about to try I already failed at. He is warned. You won't get him into your cage like the wolf cub."

Chapter 11
The Transmutations of the Metals

Kitt began to think in all earnest how to get out of Castle Marrak.

Mindful of the rack of bows in the guards' hall he ruled out to climb the wall. Simply request the guards to just open the gate for him? That would mean to openly declare his intention. It might just work – or totally go wrong.

As he sat there undecided, a gang of workers came through the opposite archway into the courtyard. They busied themselves with a row of spires which leaned against the outer wall. More workers appeared on the battlements above, where they installed a pulley of five castors, and threw two long ropes down the wall. The men in the courtyard attached a hook to a spire and began to haul on the other end.

Kitt watched. Anything that might afford a potential way out of castle Marrak interested him just now. He rose and wandered over, to stand beside the foreman who directed the operation, a thick-set, brown-haired, blue-eyed man, about forty years of age, and watch the tall bronze spire rise slowly up to the battlement, as the rope coiled on the pavement.

"This method needs a lot of rope," he remarked.

The foreman answered readily enough. "But we need only a tenth of the force to draw up these spires, compared to what they weigh -which are four-hundred pounds the smallest of them." Looking Kitt up and down, he took in the height, the worn leather clothing, the sword on his back, the knives, and the quiet grey eyes. "My Lord," he added as an afterthought.

The men hitched another spire to the pulley, and Kitt laid a hand on the rope. He was surprised how easy it was to move an object of that size. If it weighed ten times the pull, he estimated six-hundred pounds for this spire. "Clever."

"Eighteen are up already, eighteen more still down here. Three each on the six bastions, three each on the gate towers; the main gate has twelve. Then the castle, thirty-six there must be, six are down here. The eighty-one bronze spires of castle Marrak."

"The basic number is three?" Three princes, six-cornered houses, nine mirrors in Minit Claghini - a pattern began to emerge in Kitt's head; he didn't know yet if it meant anything.

"Three stands for tin, six for copper, nine for bronze, Dredorocht, magical numbers, but it's not my place to know about that," the foreman said. "It's all to do with the Cryssumha bronze you know."

"Do you live here in the castle?"

"Oh no, my Lord. We come from the town. Cordal is my name, and I am a rope-maker by profession."

"Nettle-fibre?"

"I see you know. We use nettle or hemp or willow-bark. Nettle is best for thin ropes, and the thinner the better for big castors like this one as you'll agree."

Kitt nodded.

Encouraged by the attention, Cordal went on. "When pulleys are needed for towers or the mine shafts, everyone comes to us. Same equipment to move heavy things up or down, you see. These spikes were taken down to be repaired, and now we put them back up. Lots of repairs in Castle Marrak just now. Didn't used to be, and everything was just tumbling down it seems. In fact, I never had been inside the castle before now, and I grew up in Dundingin." Cordal looked at Kitt sideways. "I saw you come in with the Prince Ardri yesterday, didn't I … my Lord? Slept well your first night in the castle?"

"No, I didn't," Kitt said. He looked up to count the spires on the battlements. "Must be a hundred feet, maybe a little more."

"A hundred and two, in fact. You have a good eye. Thirty more on the outside, this end. And there is the moat, another ten."

Suddenly, there was a clatter behind them, and they turned around in time to see one of the big black dogs spring away with the meat from Kitt's plate, the entire stack of three cutlets clamped in the broad jaws. Bread and wine beaker lay in the dust. The hound settled down to devour the meat within their sight, growling.

136

"Leave it be," the foreman advised Kitt, who had not moved. "The Hounds of Marrak are more dangerous than wolves."

At this moment, several women made their appearance in the courtyard, kitchen servants with red hands and cheerful faces which shone with sweat; they carried baskets with bread, trays of meat and full beer jugs.

The men interrupted their work to sit down on the barrels. Those on the battlements came down through one of the guards' towers.

"You are welcome to share our meal, my Lord, seeing as the hound got your breakfast," the foreman invited, albeit with a trace of hesitation, as he still could not quite place Kitt in the hierarchy of Castle Marrak.

Accepting gratefully, Kitt sat down beside the foreman. Although most of the workmen avoided his eye, they did not seem to be actively hostile. Little was spoken while the men ate and drank, all attention on their food. The bread was dark and rough, and the meat a little tough, but to Kitt's mind better than fine food eaten with fear of poisoning. He did not like the yeasty smell of the beer, nor its bitter taste, but it was liquid, and a light beverage, better than the lifeless water of Castle Marrak.

The black hound had finished Kitt's food with no ill effect and was now stalking the vicinity of the breakfasting workers who darted wary looks in its direction.

With a sudden snarl, the big animal jumped at an apprentice, and startled him into dropping his food. The boy's face was white with shock, and the workers muttered and gripped their tools, too afraid to do anything. The great hound seemed to sense that. Growling, it lowered its thick head over the stolen food.

Suddenly, the animal looked up again, uncertainty on the canine face. Snapping up the rest of the boy's breakfast meat it sprung away. Those who sat near Kitt had heard the low growl, which came from deep inside the young stranger's throat, and threatened a more dangerous carnivore to the hound.

"What was that?" one man asked, shaken.

Refusing to look up from his meal, his neighbour shrugged. The other workers resumed eating their food, relieved that the dangerous beast was gone.

"I can't eat anything now," the apprentice boy complained, still white about the nose, and shaking.

"Scary beasts." The foreman directed a peculiar sideways look at Kitt, who continued to eat as if nothing had happened.

Cordal shrugged, and after a little more time, he rose. That was the signal for the other workers that the break was over.

*

Consumed by cosmic wrath, Glic Tusil strode through the corridor.

A servant who saw the white face with the burning black eyes float through the dim corridor, pressed her back to the wall and prayed that their demonic look might not fall upon her.

The Master of Mirrors entered the empty guards' hall, and bared his teeth at the wet stain where the remains of the hapless Gock had lain.

As he opened the door into the courtyard, the alchemist's face was smooth again and the thin mouth curved up in a faint smile.

*

His head in the air, to see how the wheels and the rope of the pulley worked, Kitt felt his foot slip on something.

He looked down to see a human skull half-buried in the ground. Wet moss grew on it, and that was what had made him slip. Now he saw more bones among the bronze spires, of at least ten people, maybe more; a whole skeleton was half-buried at the foot of the wall. All the bones had the same greenish colour as the bronze of the spires, witness to the time they must have been lying there, without anybody caring enough, or daring, to clear them away and give them burial.

"Bronze thieves," Cordal said, following Kitt's look. "There are always those, though to dare come in here...the Castle Steward makes them sit on the spires."

The uneasiness, suspended by the normality of the workers, suddenly returned, and the courtyard recalled to Kitt the rock well, where a Dodlak had come at him out of a cave mouth. Feeling the vast pile of castle Marrak crouching in his back, he instinctively turned his head to look over his shoulder. Just then, the door of the guards' hall opened, and Kitt half expected something monstrous to come out, but it was only the old alchemist, clad in the same dark red velvet robe as the day before. As he caught sight of Kitt, he came

138

walking over purposefully. The white face creased into a smile that did not reach the black obsidian eyes.

From the corner of his eyes, Kitt observed Cordal the ropemaker move away, too casually, to stand with his back towards Glic Tusil. The workers pulled desperately so that the spire rose the last few yards quickly, and then they also went away, while those on the wall above dismantled the pulley to move to another part of the battlements.

The old alchemist seemed oblivious of the sudden shuffle. "I'm very much afraid that we have neglected you over matters of state, my young friend. Did Slachlan look after you well? He's an uncouth fellow, I know, but I assure you that he means as well as I do."

That, Kitt thought, he could believe.

Without waiting for an answer, Glic Tusil continued, "First of all, let me express my gratitude again. You have obligated all of us so very much to you. And yet I am sure you don't have the least idea of the magnitude of your feat. You just met a noble stranger in the woods and were ready to lay down your life for him."

"Never a question of that, Sir," Kitt objected.

"I see with pleasure that you are as modest as you are brave, my excellent young friend."

Kitt began to feel very uncomfortable.

Glic Tusil noticed, and his white face creased in an even more benevolent smile. "I trust that you have had your breakfast? Excellent, excellent. Are you ready now to learn about bronze?"

"Very kind, Sir. I wouldn't trespass upon your time, though." It was more the waste of his own time that Kitt was thinking about. The alchemist still did not look like a smith to him. And after last night, Kitt was not sure that he wanted to be taught magic by this old man.

"Nonsense, my dear boy, didn't I just tell you that I am forever indebted to you for King Ardri's delivery from the woods? I simply insisted on teaching you all that I know about bronze, this most royal amalgam of all metals, and his majesty was good enough to leave this important task to me."

That wasn't at all how Kitt remembered it from the night before in the throne room.

Again, Glic Tusil noticed and his thin, pale lips curved. "I must admit that at the very first I was surprised to learn that you are a blacksmith. The king told me that you have expressed a wish to learn the high arts, as such knowledge has been denied to you? You show excellent judgement to strive to better yourself. If you had come to me to learn about the stars, I would have taught you in my observatory. But my metallurgical experiments I conduct in my workshop before the west gate, my Tower Gelockefetir. Come with me then." The alchemist bustled towards the outer gate. As if scalded, the guards sprang to open up for him.

With profound relief, Kitt found himself outside the towering walls of Castle Marrak. The gate clanged shut behind him. That had been easy after all. He drew in the mild, moist spring air coming in gusts from the green meadows. Inside the walls, there had been no springtime. The vivid green of the land beyond the ancient wall surprised him all over again. One day in the castle had been enough to forget about that. He shook his head to clear the cobwebs, as he crossed the drawbridge that spanned the moat as quickly as he considered prudent.

His red robe flapping in the wind, and moving surprisingly fast, the old alchemist was hurrying along ahead of him towards the locked tower that stood in the no man's land between Castle Marrak and the town. Kitt supposed that courtesy demanded he followed the old alchemist. Maybe he really could learn something that his mother refused to teach him. Only once had he mentioned to Ardri in a half-sentence, how his mother refused to teach him any of the knowledge of Seidar and Zaubar, and for some reason, the young king had remembered it particularly. He called it Ledrithud but it seemed to be a similar art. Whether Kitt liked Ardri, or not, it was only gracious to permit a man to discharge his obligations; the Lily Knights had taught him that.

With long strides, Kitt caught up with Glic Tusil before the tower which he called Gelockefetir. About a hundred feet high, thirty feet at the base, it was topped with eight spires, one on each corner, which gave it another twenty feet of height. A clear space, on which not one blade of grass grew, surrounded the tower. From there, the hill declined sharply towards the town. The houses which stood at a distance below looked uninhabited.

Glic Tusil dug a hand-long bronze key from the deep pockets of his dark red coat and inserted it into the lock. It turned without a noise, and the thick oak portal opened upon a room which took up the whole inside of the tower. From thick wooden beams hung the things commonly associated with alchemists, stuffed bats, a big lizard head, dried snakes, bundles of herbs, flasks and bottles with coloured liquids, a crystal ball in a wire net, dozens of polished mirrors ranging in colours from silver-white to red, and bells of all sizes, from small as a thimble, to the enormous bell which took up all the space in the tower roof, and which could never have been meant to sound, as it had no room to swing in.

In the centre stood a hearth, enclosed on three sides, with a deep mould for the coal and an opening for the bellows nozzle. Beside it on a table lay clay and stone moulds, crucibles, a long-handled iron pan with a wooden grip, an open box which contained fire stone and tinder, and a hand bellows.

On a wooden beam above the hearth sat a great stuffed crow which regarded Kitt with malevolent amusement.

On the floor lay a heap of charcoal and stones, black, red, purple, green, golden speckled. Kitt bent down to look at the golden speckled rocks, it was the same kind he had seen in Minit Claghini - copper ore.

"Attend to me!" Glic Tusil snapped. "While I teach you, I am your master. That is the rule of the art, and anyone who wants to learn the art must obey the rule. You must do everything I tell you, exactly as I tell you. You speak only when I tell you. Do you understand?"

"You make yourself very clear. Master."

"A simple yes or no will suffice."

"Yes," Kitt said impatiently when he noticed that Glic Tusil was waiting for him to answer.

"You will learn the way I teach you, or not at all. Do you understand?"

"Yes." Not at all, Kitt began to think.

"All things change, become something else with time. A man is born, grows up, grows old, and dies. His dead body becomes black earth, the matter out of which new life arises. Black is the colour from which everything comes, where everything goes, black has all

141

the possibilities. You must not be fooled by rainbows of colour, as they are consequences, not the cause. Now, do you arrange the coals around and above the exact centre of the hearth, so that it may form a perfect circle."

"An open coal fire would not be hot enough for iron ore," Kitt remarked, as he heaped the coal in the hearth. "Need a special oven."

"Yes, yes. Do you call this a circle?" Glic Tusil pointed to where he wanted Kitt to adjust a piece. "Now light the fire and work this bellows."

Kitt did as he was told, using the firestone and tinder from the table.

"Spring grows into summer," the alchemist intoned. "Summer heat burns down to become autumn. The death of winter follows. From winter comes spring. Stone evolves into ore." He took up a piece of the gold-speckled ore. "See how the grains of copper ore are being born in this stone."

Kitt stared at him and wondered just how old Glic Tusil was. The curious mineral quality of the alchemist's skin, with the immobility of a porcelain mask, made it seem as if it could crack along the fine lines, and whenever he showed expression, white flakes would fall to the floor.

The alchemist spoke even more slowly and a little louder. "With time, all the stone will become ore. Given yet more time the ore will evolve into the metal. Fire shortens that time. Fire is needed to bring about the transmutation from stone to ore, and again fire is needed for the subsequent transmutation of ore into metal. Therefore, instead of the younger golden ore, we may rather look for the older black, red or green ore, because for them, less fire is needed for the smelting." Glic Tusil picked up three pieces of ore. "This black ore is the colour which copper takes in the fire. And here in the purple and red hue of this ore, we see the copper-red emerge. Now see this green ore, the colour is the same as the patina of copper."

Kitt thought that the olive tone of the ore did not much resemble the characteristic green of copper patina, but he refrained from saying so. Perhaps the old man didn't see well.

The alchemist bent down, and with each piece, he began drawing lines on the floor, stretching to reach farther in a way that Kitt began to wonder why he thought of Glic Tusil as an old man.

142

An eight-pointed star appeared the centre of which he was himself, the black line drawn with the black ore, and the green ore gave dark green lines. The line drawn with the red ore was white. When the alchemist had completed the design, he straightened up, with a movement reptilian in its fluidity.

"Does the red ore always draw a white streak?" Kitt asked.

"Can you count? How many rays does this star pattern have?" Glic snapped.

"Eight."

"He can count to eight," Glic informed the great bell above. A faint brazen note answered him.

"Is the white streak a sign for the quality of the ore?" Kitt insisted.

"Don't waste time with your silly questions, boy! Work that bellows!"

Kitt worked the hand bellows until a heap of glowing coals filled the hearth. Then, the alchemist picked up the iron pan, placed a green piece of the ore into it and held it into the fire.

"Where did you get the pan?" Kitt inquired. "Are there ironsmiths in Rilante?"

"Don't speak unless you are told!" Glic Tusil snapped.

Kitt let go of the bellows and started towards the door.

"Come back here, young fool!" Glic Tusil said in a tone almost conciliatory. "Talk breaks my concentration," he added.

Kitt stopped and turned around again, reluctantly. He rather wanted to go.

Glic Tusil sighed. "The iron pan is a spoil of war from a battle fought long, long ago, and has been in my tower since then. Are you content now? Do try not to be so touchy, this is simply the way apprentices of alchemy are taught. King Ardri himself was spoken to no different from this, during his apprenticeship, and he learned more in a year than you ever will in your whole life. It is King Ardri's express wish that I should teach you, so don't make it so difficult for me. And you mustn't stop working that bellows, or you will interrupt the process of transmutation."

Kitt shrugged and turned back to the hearth. A silence followed as he worked, accentuated by the noise the bellows made and the jingling bells. He wondered if this alchemy was really part of the

143

Seidar knowledge, the Zaubar power, which his mother kept from him? What they called Ledrithud here? All that Glic Tusil told him seemed utter nonsense -whereas his mother's methods worked infallibly. Transmutations though, that word resonated. Kitt remembered his dream in Minit Claghini, of the prisoners and the iron that had gone into the blue lakes, to be dissolved while copper formed. The iron pan had escaped that fate, but the principle was the same; iron served in the process of precipitating copper. That explained the derision of the court when they heard that he was an ironsmith, and went some way to explain Ardri's condescending attitude towards him, once he had gained his own safe ground. Kitt realised that he was useful but expendable.

"Something you don't understand?" Glic Tusil inquired.

"All to the contrary, everything begins to fall into place. Master."

"Does it?" Glic snorted. "I very much wonder."

The iron pan glowed in a bright yellow and a little puddle of molten copper formed in it, with pieces of the remains of the green ore floating on top of it.

Glic took away the pan and held it under Kitt's nose. "Stone to the ore, ore to metal," he said solemnly. "Do you understand? You may speak now."

"Yes." Kitt backed away from the fumes.

"What do you understand?"

"If I put a stone into that pan and hold it over the fire, I get the copper ore, and if I wait a little longer, I get the pure metal."

Glic Tusil looked at the big youth owlishly. "It would, of course, have to be the right kind of stone."

"Of course." Kitt grinned. "Otherwise I may get iron."

"Or worse."

Kitt decided that this point went to the old alchemist. "I understand. Go on." He reached for the pan and a handful of the ore lying on the floor.

"I didn't tell you to start smelting yet!" Glic Tusil snapped. "Pay attention to me."

Obediently Kitt laid the pan down again, thinking that maybe he would not have learned much about copper and bronze at the end of that day, but that he would have absolved a great exercise in patience. Even the Swordmaster Diorlin of Eliberre would approve of him, for once.

"With time base metals will evolve into more precious metals," Glic Tusil intoned again. "Thus, iron naturally evolves into copper. This smelting pan is of iron, symbolising the transmutation of the lower into the higher. Do you understand?"

"Yes. And if I go on heating long enough, it turns into silver and if I continue heating that I'll end up with a pan full of gold." Kitt took hold of the iron pan and held it steady as if determined to stand there and heat the copper until that happened.

"No! You don't understand!" Glic Tusil shouted. He snatched the pan from Kitt's hand and threw it at his head.

Kitt evaded the missile and it slammed at the wall with a crash and a shower of stone splinters.

"Gold is of the sun, it symbolises fire!" Glic Tusil screamed. "Silver is solid moonlight, it symbolises water! Sun and Moon are not governed by the wandering stars, as copper is!" he yelled. "Copper, silver, gold are the three aspects of incorruptible power on earth, just as the star Vasara, the moon and the sun are in the sky. Thus they cannot transmute one into the other!" He glared at Kitt with such fury that the youth wondered if he had at last annoyed the old alchemist enough to call it a day. That would leave him free to seek out the bronze smith who he had seen in the main-street of Dundingin, which he should have done from the start.

Glic Tusil's face worked as if the mask of porcelain was about to crack into white shards. Finally, he managed a brittle smile. Once more Kitt wondered why the old alchemist bothered. "To continue, metal will evolve into men. First from the base iron sprang a race of killers. The gods drove them around the whole world, and at the end of their path, the entire brood was destroyed. Then from the copper came the race of Cryssumha and from the noble bronze, its kings. Soon from silver will come the wise men. And many years from now, the perfect men will form of gold. But that lies millions of years into the future. You will not see it."

"Who were the men born from iron?"

Glic Tusil favoured Kitt with a thin malevolent smile. "They were like you. Yes, exactly like you, all muscle, small brains. And

145

so, they died because they understood nothing. You don't understand at all what I am telling you?"

"You have established that," Kitt said with an edge beneath his quiet.

"Do you look at the stars sometimes, Kitt?"

"Yes. Of course."

The alchemist raised a brow. "Of course? I'm glad to hear it. Then you know that it is the Red Star Mavors who governs iron, the Destroyer."

Kitt shook his head.

"No? What do you look at the stars for then, to howl at them? Mavors governs iron, and he is nothing but trouble. Vasara, the Queen Star, magnificently beautiful above all other stars, stands for copper. She weds Dilo, the King Star of Lightning, and when they meet, they fill the void between the stars, where Mavors once treacherously murdered his twin. Thus, bronze is born and reborn. When Dilo stands near Vasara, we make mirrors, when they stand farther apart we make bells. Then comes the Findrun and then Umharu bronze, and from them we make swords and lances. Each time that the Lightning Star moves toward the Copper Star, the bronze becomes whiter. When it moves away, the bronze becomes more golden, and when Vasara stands in the sky alone, the bronze is red. Do you understand?"

"You mean you vary the tin content of the bronze according to the position and movement of the planets in the sky."

"The stars preserve my sanity," Glic Tusil sighed wearily. "But the king bid me teach you, and teach you I will, if it kills you." His thin smile flickered on and off. "I will teach you barbarian about mirrors and bells, although I can't see the use of it. I will also teach you about the Findrun and Umharu bronze, to make swords, axes, shields, lances, arrows. You'll like that, won't you? But first, you must smelt this ore, in the way I showed you. I hope you paid attention?"

"Sure."

"You see Kitt, I am old, and can't do this kind of work anymore," Glic Tusil pursued with another abrupt change of mood. "You'd do me a favour. Not to mention, I consider it a suitable compensation for having to contend with a staggering stupidity like

146

yours. So, don't you dare come back to me before you haven't smelted all the ore, every single crumb. Then, we will continue your lessons." With a swish of the dark red robe, the alchemist turned on his heel and marched out of the door.

"Yes. Master."

Glic Tusil's back stiffened, and he wheeled round again. "And if you are too dense to even accomplish a simple task like that, don't come and ask me. Just go back to your wood and run with the other animals."

Through the open tower door, Kitt looked after the alchemist, as he hurried towards castle Marrak with the air of a raven who has wasted quite enough of his time. Then he shrugged and put more charcoal on the fire, not arranging it in a circle. He took a lump of ore and turned it in his hand that the light caught the golden speckles. "Born from the rock," he muttered, and tossed the ore back onto the heap. "Maybe you talk more sense," he addressed the great bell above.

It answered with a brazen tone, incredibly sweet and menacing. Kitt stared at it uneasily, shook his head, reached for the smelting pan and picked out lumps of red ore from the heap on the floor. From time to time he passed a chunk over the floor. Each piece drew a white line. After the red, he decided, he would try out the olive-green ore, and then the black, to see how much and what kind of copper each would yield. When the pan was full, he placed it on top of the fire and worked the bellows.

"Don't know much about the smelting of ore, do you?" a deep voice said.

Kitt turned around to see the smith from the main-street standing in the doorway. "Not copper ore," he admitted.

"I thought so, or you wouldn't be roasting the Evil Ore in an enclosed space. It can make a smith very, very sick. Has killed a good many workers until it was finally found out for the stealthy murderer it is."

"Has it?" Kitt said slowly, but the movement with which he took the pan off the fire was rapid, and so was the step that took him outside.

"Ugly death," the bronze smith elaborated. "And slow. Retch their insides out for days, pain in the tummy that makes grown men

147

cry like babies." He contemplated the eight-cornered star on the floor and nodded to himself. "That is why it is called the Evil Ore. A curse, some say. If you ask me, there are poisonous fumes released, when it's smelted."

"Glic Tusil didn't mention this little detail. Talked about the transmutation of this into that. Told me how stupid I was, and I guess he was right about that."

"Insult to injury, that's his little way. What is your name, young man?"

"Kitt. From Isenkliff."

"Isenkliff," the black-bearded man said musingly. "Minit Houarn. I heard about it."

"I'm a blacksmith." Kitt didn't mention that he already had turned in his master-piece. Here in Dundingin, this counted for nothing.

"Ah," the bronzesmith said. "Now Kitt, I won't say that the Evil Ore may not give you a good bronze. But it's unpredictable. You never know exactly what you'll get. Not worth the risk as there are other ores. Take the Double Star Bronze, which is a natural amalgam of copper and tin and almost pure, which yields much better bronze than anything you can get from the Evil Ore. Best, however, is to work with pure copper and tin. That way you can adjust the quality of your bronze precisely as you want it."

"Depending on where Dilo and Vasara stand?"

"If you like." The black eyes twinkled with amusement. "Long as you don't neglect caution. Can come to grief with bronze work in many ways, those who don't know about it."

"Could you teach me?"

"I should think I could. The Gobins have been bronze smiths in Dundingin, oh, always." The smith eyed the young giant speculatively. "So you are a blacksmith who wants to learn about bronze?"

"Yes. Do you have a use for an apprentice? I can pay a fee."

"Well, I might have a place," Gobin conceded. "Matter of fact, at the moment I don't have an apprentice, and I could do with a pair of arms like yours. That you have some experience with metal and smithcraft is a bonus, as long as you are aware that the methods are entirely different. Only, it isn't done to swipe another master's apprentice, you see."

"I have given no promise. Ardri has. To me. He promised me that I should learn about bronze."

"Promised, the king did? In those very words? That you should learn about bronze?"

Kitt nodded, a little mystified.

Gobin held out a large, black hand, and Kitt gripped it to seal the bargain.

"Come with me then. Right now. We'll explain to the Master of Mirrors later."

Kitt shook his head. "I did promise to smelt this ore. So, smelt it I will. I'll come to your house when I'm done."

Gobin opened his mouth, closed it again, and shrugged. "You keep your word, do you? See you later then."

That was the second attempt to remove the witness -or perhaps the third, if he thought about it.

When Gobin was gone Kitt gathered all dried herbs, mushrooms and bones he could find. He picked the stuffed crow from the wooden beams, its beady eyes glaring at him in outrage, and threw everything onto the ore heap. More than once he wiped his fingers from what he had touched.

As he worked, the great bell above began to speak. From the motionless dark mouth came a sound so incredibly sweet and utterly evil, that Kitt felt his skin crawl, and his hair rise on the nape of his neck. He threw the coals from the hearth onto the uncouth heap, and the flames shot high into the air and caught the wooden beams. All went up in flames, faster and hotter than it should have. Running with suspended breath, Kitt had only just time to gain the outside. From the top of the tower, a thick smoke column streamed into the sky. The great bell tolled, and from the castle, another bell began answering it.

From the town, people arrived on the scene of the fire, but not a hand stirred to salvage and rescue. They just stood around and watched the burning of the eight-cornered tower.

Louder and louder rang the great bell as if calling for help, and the burning tower swayed with the rhythm. The tolling of the bell grew so much that the spectators covered their ears and their circle widened and broke.

Suddenly, the tower leant over and collapsed in a cloud of bright yellow sparks. Burning debris flew about, and the people fled, shouting and beating at sparks in their hair and clothes.

With a deep booming crash, the great bell broke free and rolled downhill until it was swallowed in a hole that opened in the ground. It's tolling went on and on, with the echo from the castle answering. Where the bell had sunk into the earth, broken timbering protruded, and down below people were seen to mill around like surprised ants.

A thick cloud of smoke billowed above the fallen tower. Suddenly, there was a flurry in the air, of a flock of doves fleeing from a pursuing falcon. The hunt shot into the smoke cloud, and the doves fell out of it like big blue-grey raindrops and hit the ground with soft thuds; they fluttered feebly and then lay still. The falcon fell at Kitt's feet, the long sharp wings twitched and the round golden-black eye stared into the sky.

From Castle Marrak the other bell was still tolling. A trumpet signal sounded the alarm on the battlements.

*

The bells were ringing the alarm, and the soldiers of Castle Marrak formed up in the courtyard under the eyes of the Steward.

Ardri took the time to have his big black mount saddled. The idea of leaving Castle Marrak on foot just didn't appeal to him. There was no hurry, he felt, even if the whole of Dundingin was burning. Still, he was the residing representative of the royal family of Iwerdonn and had to make a show of leading things as if he cared.

The Master of Mirrors fidgeted beside him; there was no other word for it. Was Glic Tusil afraid? Ardri wondered with amazement.

The west gate opened, and the horizon lay clear before him. It took him a moment to realise what had happened. The tower Gelockefetir had gone. Completely gone. Beside him, Glic Tusil's face was a complete blank.

"What happened to your tower, Master of Mirrors?"

"It must have succumbed to barbarian stupidity."

Ardri attempted to suppress a bubble of laughter; it had a tinge of hysterics. He rode across the drawbridge, with Slachlan and the soldiers on foot trying to keep up with him.

His face the usual immobile white mask, the Master of Mirrors moved beside the horse without straining himself, stepping on his own road. His dark red coat caught the wind that it stood behind him like a serpent's hood.

When the young king drove his horse through the crowd, redhaired Rilantemen cursed him, and dark-haired Cryssumha people cringing out of his way. From the vantage height in the saddle, he surveyed the ruins of the tower, the hole the bell had torn into the mountain side, and Kitt, who was raking energetically among the charred embers with a fire hook.

The mask cracked, and the alchemist began to shout. "You clumsy barbarian, what did you do now, what did you do?"

Kitt straightened up from the thing he had dragged from the debris. Ardri saw a smoking shapeless lump of a sickly white colour lie among dead birds, a whole flock of doves and a falcon, and he knew at once what Glic Tusil had attempted. How much of the poison had Kitt swallowed, if any, and what had he realised, those were the questions.

The giant youth dropped the firehook and carefully wiped his hand on a rag. "Here's the copper. Master." Kitt pointed to the mass at his feet. "Smelted it all, as you bid me. What do we do now? Will we let Dilo shine on it until it turns into bronze? Or will we put it on the highest tower, for lightning to strike, thereby shortening the process?"

Ardri sniggered. For an apprentice, this was advanced alchemical joking. Again, he heard that grating noise as the Master of Mirrors gnashed his teeth.

"May lightning strike you, you savage!" Glic Tusil turned on his heel and stalked away in the direction of the castle.

Kitt picked up the smoking lump of hot metal, and quickly, before it could burn his hands, threw it after the alchemist. The heavy mass thumped the earth hard at Glic Tusil's heel, and those standing near felt the vibration of the impact through the soles of their feet. Glic Tusil stopped dead, but after a moment he continued to walk. Ardri had to admire the old man that he didn't run. On the other hand, the king wasn't sure that the Master of Mirrors could be killed by dropping a massive lump of anything on him. *Here we have the irresistible forces of nature*, he thought, *Lute and Mavors clashing*.

151

Slachlan looked upon the burning ruin with a curious expression on his face, what was visible of it under the dark beard. It almost seemed as if he smiled. "You'll have to come along and explain this, big boy."

Kitt didn't answer. Just looking at his face Ardri knew that the young barbarian could not be trapped behind the walls of Castle Marrak again.

Slachlan seemed to read his mind too. "We'll make you come, never fear."

"You didn't bring enough men."

"No, we didn't," Ardri muttered very lowly, hoping that Slachlan heard. "What happened here?" he asked aloud. "Please do enlighten us, Kitt, because we are consumed with curiosity. There must be a sensible explanation, though what that could be..."

Kitt shrugged. "Master Glic Tusil told me to smelt the copper ore."

"And..." Ardri waved a hand in the direction of the devastation.

"And I did." Kitt grinned broadly. "Lightning must have struck. Dilo you know."

"Funny," Ardri said. "As you and Glic Tusil don't seem to agree, I shall have to find you another teacher."

"You have already done enough for me."

Ardri's eyes narrowed. So, the barbarian boy was offering him sarcasm, but he wasn't going to acknowledge that he had noticed. Twenty armoured soldiers were not nearly enough.

Sudden shouting broke out and grew to a pitch; two young men were fighting. Others joined in on both sides.

"On the king!" Slachlan brought his men up to surround Ardri's mount.

From farther down the hill came the sound of commotion.

"That will be the city guards," Slachlan said. "Taking their sweet time, they are."

"All the better, that leaves you enough time to arrest anyone who resists and bring them into Marrak. Some of these Rilante curs dared to curse me. I want an example made. But don't on any account get into a scruff with the city guards."

Ardri wheeled his mount and galloped back up the hill. On the drawbridge, he caught up with the Master of Mirrors.

"Yes, my king." Slachlan bowed to the crupper of Ardri's horse. "Arrest anyone who resists." He turned back to arrest the barbarian first, but Kitt was gone.

The city guard came up the hill, with Captain Warmond in the lead, his distinctive white and black mount setting a leisurely pace. His helmet was hanging from his saddle-bow, and his red hair stirred in the wind.

"Get a step on!" Slachlan snapped. "The arsonist has just escaped."

"One criminal? What have you lot been doing then; you've been first on the scene?" Warmond's face was unreadable due to the thick scar that split his features.

The Steward of Castle Marrak knew that the Captain was grinning.

Chapter 12
In the Streets of Ulud

Six dark alleyways opened among the conical six-cornered houses – Kitt had to choose one to enter in a hurry.

The buildings of the quarter near the place where Glic Tusil's tower had stood, looked old to Kitt, ancient as Castle Marrak itself. The reek of sulphur stung in his nose. Nothing green grew anywhere as if the breath of a dragon had gone over the earth, and from time to time, slight tremors shook the ground. Out of pale faces, dark eyes watched the stranger. This was a different kind of wood, one where Kitt didn't know the rules, which made it another death trap after his escape from castle Marrak.

Underground the great fallen bell still boomed remotely, and the earth trembled. The way he had come through thronged with soldiers and he heard Slachlan's command. Kitt dived into an alley on the east side which he hoped to lead into the main street. Walls ran left and right uninterrupted by windows or doors, and there were no people.

A basket suddenly appeared beside Kitt, filled with gold-speckled greenish lumps, and then the head which supported it appeared and rolled black eyes at Kitt. The man came up from a hole in the ground. He was small as a ten-year-old boy, but his face was lined and twitched. As he went on along that street, Kitt had to balance between a wall and a chain of holes. Smoke issued from one and steam hissed from another. Somewhere under his feet was a constant sound of picking and mechanical squeaks.

He turned corners, always at obtuse angles, never right or acute. A six-cornered outlay took shape in his head, like a honeycomb. The alley Kitt was in petered out before a wall, and thus interrupted the honeycomb pattern, and forced him to retrace his steps until an arch opened into another lane which ran its crooked path among the high backs of the six-cornered stone houses. The ground became more uneven, and the quarter he passed through appeared even more ancient and was blackened with soot.

Kitt crossed stairs and doorways and courtyards.

The people he saw in that quarter were all stunted; few were over five feet tall. There was a peculiar restlessness about them, heads shook, lids twitched, slack mouths drooled, and restless limbs threw frantic shadows on rough stonewalls. Through an open door, he observed a shadow dancing around a fire like a troll from a fairytale. In a courtyard, a brilliant stream of molten metal was poured into a mould by artisan whose hands and heads shook, but the hot flow of liquid metal poured steady and true.

Another bell began to ring from Castle Marrak, now high above. Other bells answered it from all over Dundingin.

Suddenly, three gangling youths blocked Kitt's way. They were comparatively tall, the corners of their mouths hung down slack, and their fingers shook. The footlong bronze knives they held were rock steady, and so was the malicious look under the nervously twitching lids. Kitt sensed more movement in his back, but he did not turn, and he did not stop.

The middle youth said something in the language Kitt did not understand, and the other two laughed, a gurgling sound.

"Are you talking to me?" Kitt inquired in the language of Rilante.

"Animal! Arsonist!" the middle youth accused in the same language, with an accent even thicker than Kitt's.

He felt a rush in his back, and stepped aside, caught hold of an outstretched arm with a knife, and hurled the figure attached to it at the three assailants who confronted him. It was another youth just like them, and they all went down in a tangle.

As Kitt walked past them, the youth who had spoken got up and tried to rush him. Kitt arrested the knife arm with his left and caught hold of the stringy throat with his right; he lifted and smashed the youth into the wall to the left. The air expelled from the lungs by the impact could not pass the compressed throat, the youth's eyes opened wide and snapped shut, and for the moment the twitching of his various body parts stopped.

155

"It was a work accident," Kitt said and threw the dangling body into the other assailants who had just begun to rise. They all went down in a heap again.

Another bronze knife flickered. Kitt felled the wielder with one swing of his right fist that flung the assailant against a man who carried a basket with flat, black, cakes of a glassy material, which fell to the ground and shattered. Kitt knocked the third youth down again. Heedless of the fight, the man with the basket crawled about the floor to reach for the spilt contents.

As Kitt passed the first assailant, he stepped on the wrist which stuck from a grey sleeve and the youth yelped; his numbed hand opened and released the knife.

And still the big bell from the castle boomed, and the small bells were jingling and yapping at Kitt's heels. Many more dark eyes turned towards him with recognition and intent.

Yet another bell began to ring from Castle Marrak in a strident tone; before his inner eye, Kitt saw this bell, that hung motionless in a spire where there was no room for it to swing, shouting from a brazen mouth. More and more bells gave tongue, falling in behind it, one by one, and like dogs followed the white-faced hunter.

The crooked alleyways began to fill up with people, from each doorway came purposeful movement and hands reached for Kitt's legs from burrows in the ground. As yet he was able to free himself with determined brutality.

As he turned a corner, Kitt found himself free of the crowd, only for a moment, he knew. He jumped high and drew himself up to the ten-foot mural. It was three feet wide of roughly cut stone. Below, the alley filled up with dark heads and shaking limbs, milling about and searching; none of them looked up.

On the other side of the wall, a strange ritual seemed to be in progress, heedless of the commotion outside. Kitt observed men shovel coal dust into a cauldron which contained molten copper. A young oak tree was pushed in, and the metal bubbled. The workers sprinkled more coal dust over the surface of the molten metal. Absorbed in what they were doing, they still paid no attention to the mob surging through the lane outside.

One of the smelters took a ladle of the liquid, let it solidify and threw it into a water trough where the hot metal burst. The man fished out the pieces and they all looked at the dark red breakage. Crouching right above, Kitt looked as intently as they. Blisters could not be good, he thought. The smelters shook their heads -at least this was what it looked like to Kitt; they shook so much.

The men repeated their ritual with the coal and another tree and the water. The second time, the colour of the breaks was brick red with a satiny shimmer, and the smelters seemed to nod, but again it was hard to tell because of their twitching.

Filing away this observation, Kitt made his way along the wall, then across roofs, and skirted more six-cornered yards.

Once, the copper sheet roof which covered an inner yard felt hot under his feet.

Once, he came to a tower crusted all over with yellow sulphur flowers.

He saw a pale girl sitting in a window frame, swaying and watching him silently; long dark hair poured down her back like a wave of mystery.

In a courtyard, men were pouring metal; they also did not look up from their work. In another place, women were engaged in breaking the glittering ore to lumps the size of hens' eggs with round stones for hammers, such as are found on the seashore, hundreds of miles away.

The next courtyard was square, and the house had a rectangular roof. There was a right angle formed by a long low house and Kitt looked down into a wider thoroughfare - the main street. There, many Rilante people stood still as they listened with all signs of unease to the jangling of the bells all over the town, and the booming of the bell up in Castle Marrak and the fallen bell underground.

Kitt climbed down from the house; he remembered the wooden gallery from when he had entered Dundingin the day before, what seemed an eternity ago. At his sudden appearance from seemingly nowhere, the woodsrunners and hunters interrupted their eating, drinking and quarrelling. An excited mutter rose, and hostile stares were directed at him, which Kitt gave back directly. His fighting mood still held, and he did not mind if he knocked over some more challengers, as many as liked to come at him. The men sensed that clearly, and after a quick survey of the broad shoulders, ready hands, simple weapons, and cold, grey eyes, they looked away one after the

157

other, except for the big black-haired man. It was a sober, experienced look out of those ice-blue eyes which Kitt returned in kind.

He was not far from the city gate and the guards there had donned their helmets and were scanning the main street towards Castle Marrak. What did the hunting of the bells mean to them, would they feel obliged to intervene, Kitt asked himself and stayed in cover behind the corner.

A trumpet sounded before the city wall. The guards went to throw open both wings of the gate for a rider to come through on a black horse; he was clad in black armour with the visor of his helmet down, which made him look inhuman. Behind the black rider, more armed horsemen thronged through the gate. Kitt saw the Amhas customers of the tavern melt to the background, and heard the mutter of "Lord Morrik!"

Lord Morrik turned his helmeted head left and right like a lizard and Kitt saw black, unwinking eyes glitter behind the eye slit, and rest upon him for a moment.

As the black lord and his warriors passed and rode on towards Castle Marrak, they bore down deliberately upon the red-haired people in the street who made room with ill grace.

"Lord Morrik!" they murmured, and it sounded like a curse. The black-haired, dark-eyed, pale people came out of the alleys for the sole purpose to bow. Some knelt. How many of these had been searching for him, thought Kitt, and that now they seemed to have forgotten about him.

Chapter 13
The Last Laugh

On his way to Gobin's smithy, Kitt followed in the wake of the riders at a judicious distance. He towered over the crowd with head and shoulders, and there was always space around him as if people saw something big coming and gave it room.

The shops were taking in their stock for the night. Empty farmer's wagons drawn by sturdy horses went in the opposite direction on their way to the gate. He passed another tavern on the right-hand side a notch above the first where farmers and tradesmen looked up from their drink and fell silent to watch Kitt stride past. The mainstreet turned west rising slightly, and he felt like going in the wrong direction, into the town, towards Castle Marrak.

The next tavern to the right Kitt remembered as the one with the two red-haired women. The girl had served beer to Ardri on his return from the Bacenis -which he hadn't drunk, Kitt had noticed. As he passed, the door flew open, and a man reeled out. He ran into the street and grabbed Kitt's arm. "There he is!"

Kitt freed himself with a light push, enough to knock the man backwards. He sat down in the dirt of the road, and beamed up at the youth. "Good boy, burned that old buzzard's tower. Dunno why we didn't think of that ourselves." The man's speech was slurred, and his eyes glittered. "Have a drink! We all have a drink."

Another man appeared in the doorway, who wore the breastplate of the city guards. A scar divided his face from the right cheekbone down to the left side of his neck. Kitt had seen the guards' captain before - Warmond was the name.

"Come in, young man! We're off duty. All friends here."

The captain's invitation was seconded enthusiastically from the four windows; the establishment seemed full to the rafters of red-haired men in different stages of shedding their regulation city guard armour for comfort who were calling out to Kitt in a friendly manner.

There was nothing left but to surrender to what seemed the exact opposite of being arrested for public wrongdoing. To enter the tavern, Kitt had to bend head and shoulders and go a little sideways to get through the doorway.

After straightening up, his head was just below the ceiling, and a set of six bells swung directly before his face, jingling in a sweet high tone. Kitt brushed them away, feeling that he had had enough of bells for that day.

The air of a room full of people smote his senses, the noise setting upon him like a swarm of buzz flies. Hands reached out and shouted greetings.

Beset by second thoughts, Kitt retreated slowly backwards.

Feeling the door frame touch his back, he bent head and shoulders to back out of the door. So it was that he suddenly came face to face with the girl Blaitisin, who had giggled, Kitt remembered well. The halo of her bright red hair gleamed in the candlelight, and cornflower eyes widened into his. "I saw you throw the copper after the old alchemist," she said breathlessly. "Two men could not lift that bar."

She drew him back inside, and Kitt followed captive, and she pressed him down on a seat with her small white hands. "Shame you didn't hit," she giggled, and the wind chime's six bells rang with her words like laughter. "Why did you miss?"

"You are a fool, my girl," the older woman admonished. Kitt remembered her name also, Beibini. She had the same bright red hair as the girl, lines of habitual laughter crinkled the corners of the same cornflower eyes and her hips had a comfortable width. "They are all fools here, which includes my husband, the mighty, righteous captain of the city guards." She gave the scarred man an affectionate nudge and put an earthenware mug before Kitt. "As for you, young hero, you better look out double careful from now on. You are a marked man."

Kitt looked at the mug full of a dark liquid with speckles of white foam on it, and then at the woman. "Drink!" She laid her hand on his biceps and squeezed it. "Beibini invites you. It was a splendid joke, but we won't laugh for long."

There were not a hundred people in that room, as Kitt had at first thought. About two dozen men with hair varying from strawberry yellow to flaming red crowded around five tables pushed together, city guards by the look and talk of them.

At the sixth table, where Blaitisin had put Kitt, sat four traders in their shirtsleeves, having doffed their fur-trimmed caps and cloaks. They were sturdy men of indeterminate age who resumed their animated talk about fur prices, quality and the iniquities of the Woodstalkers. Their light eyes glittered moist in the lamplight.

In the corner place sat another man, young, of tall and rangy built, who more resembled the woodsrunners Kitt had seen in the first tavern; he was steadily drinking a brown liquid from a glass and said nothing. His freckled face had been burned by the sun often, and deep lines crossed the cheeks and surrounded the intensely blue eyes.

The sixth man at the table was an Amhas, sitting beside the woodsrunner and clad alike, except for the necklaces of claws and teeth, including human teeth; he stared into his glass and the dark animal eyes were glazed. A tall, green glass bottle stood between the two woods-runners. The freckled man refilled for himself and the Amhas. Silently, he raised his glass to Kitt who took a doubtful sip from his mug. He hadn't much liked his first taste of beer in the courtyard of Castle Marrak. Taste and smell of Beibini's dark brew were much stronger, more bitter, and he was not yet sure what to think of it. Others obviously were. Mugs were raised all around with relish.

"Good, isn't it?" the captain of the city guard grinned. "The best in Dundingin." He took a deep draft, which Kitt imitated out of courtesy. A moment later, his head felt curiously light and almost absent-minded he drank for the third time.

"There seems to have been some trouble at the Alchemist's Tower," the guard's captain remarked conversationally. "We arrived after the fact, and nothing people said made sense. You were mentioned. We are taking no notice whatsoever. The least said the better." He winked and took another draught.

Kitt followed suit, and that emptied his mug. The red-haired girl brought him a plate heaped with bread and meat and another mug of beer. Kitt ate hungrily and washed the food down with more of the beer. It tasted good now. Suddenly he felt like laughing, and he threw back his head and laughed, and the other guests smiled and raised their mugs to him. Everything was so easy now that he was out of

Castle Marrak, and everybody in Dundingin was kind and hospitable.

The girl came back with another mug. The third beer tasted much better still. She leaned against Kitt's shoulder, and he looked into her cornflower eyes, and her smiling face was swimming before his eyes. She kissed him, and it tasted like a rosebud dunked in beer.

"Tell me your name!" Kitt demanded because he wanted to hear it from her.

She said that her name was Blaitisin, and the chimes above his head rang.

"There are iron bells too," Kitt remarked. "But their tone is not the same." His tongue felt a little unwieldy.

"Bells of Cryssumha bronze. The Green Man sells them," somebody said. "He gets them from Gobin."

"Not Gobin. Gobin makes arrows, armour, blades, sensible stuff not playthings. He is alright for a Cryssumha man."

"...he said he has them from Iwerdonn."

"Nonsense, all bronze is made in Western Cryssumha."

"I have a wonderful mirror, shows my face ever so clear." Blaitisin wrinkled her little nose.

"Come the time when you won't care for mirrors no more. And what you got then?" Beibini scolded. "Come old age, the only friend left to a woman is money. Now serve the guests another round, can't you see that they are waiting!"

Blaitisin pouted and winked at Kitt, who rose and reached for her.

"And you sit down and be good now!" Beibini ordered.

Kitt, who had forgotten that there were other people in the room beside the girl, sat down again, feeling a little silly.

"How that Green Man talks, he can't stop no more than one of his wind chimes in a gale. They say Glic Tusil put a curse on him, for talking back. He doesn't like backtalk, the alchemist doesn't," somebody was saying.

Kitt thought of the bells in Glic Tusil's tower, the great bell trapped up in the top, and the hundreds of small ones, but Blaitisin returned with another full mug and kissed him again, so he forgot about it.

162

"Blaitisin!" Beibini called. "Damn the girl! Up to bed with you, it's late."

Kitt watched the girl's white dress disappear in the gloom of the corridor. He wanted to go after her, but as he half rose, another frothing jug appeared before him, and a small but firm hand pressed him down on his seat. "This is all you'll get today, young hero," Beibini said.

Kitt idly wondered if he should continue on his way to the bronze smithy, but he didn't move except to take a sip from the fresh mug of beer.

"I say he's found a treasure. Piles of ingots," another man, just beyond the edge of Kitt's curiously narrowed vision, said in a conspirator's tone. "But where, that he won't tell, however much he talks."

"Many people used to search for old bronze in the ruined places in the woods. Many got killed by the Woodstalkers. The Amhas sometimes guided them, but they are too afraid now."

The tall, broad Amhas raised liquid, dark eyes towards the speaker. "Hawkwing not scared. Hawkwing hunt beaver, marten, tree cat, fox, hunt..."

"My friend Hawkwing hasn't brought me a single pelt in months," one of the traders remarked. "Afraid of the Murder Bear like everyone else?"

Canaras Muntrer, Singing Bear, everywhere, all the time, slay warriors, eat hearts. Canaras Muntrer great Mirril magic. Spalouer Askel, Hawkwing, find great Mirril magic. You see Dshooka-man, you see."

"Magic indeed," a trader said lightly. "Some bored ladies in Iwerdonn set great store by the Amhas witchmen's mumbo jumbo, the drugged smoke, the senseless drumming and chanting. Nobody can tell me that these dirty savages know something about you or me that we don't. Or that anything they know is worth knowing. If it were, they wouldn't be the defeated drunken lot they are." He laughed. "Except skulking through the woods, they do that as well as the wild Woodstalkers."

"Take away Hawkwing's honour," the Amhas was saying, his tongue stumbling over the words.

"When he starts talking about his honour, it means he's stinking drunk."

"The price of skins has doubled," another fur trader said acidly. "When it has trebled, Hawkwing will find his courage again. Much Uskeva dream water for skin, hey?"

"More Uskeva for bronze, especially if it is Findrun."

"It is time somebody skinned that Murder Bear."

"Hawkwing not scared." The Amhas emptied his beaker. "Hawkwing go Bacenis now take honour Canaras Muntrer." He rose and made for the door; there he paused and swayed. Holding on to the door frame, he slid down, and by the time he reached the floor, he was snoring.

"Won't he be surprised when he wakes up and hears that he's pledged to go after the Murder Bear?" Laughing the fur traders returned to their drink.

"Who is that Murder Bear?" Kitt asked.

"Don't you know?" The young freckled man in the corner, who had been silent so far, suddenly spoke. He shrugged. "Sorry." He turned his gaze back into his glass.

"Who is the Murder Bear, you ask?" One of the traders snorted with anger. "A Woodstalker devil. Nobody has ever seen him because nobody lives to tell."

"Why on earth does Hawkwing call him Singing Bear?" the trader's companion asked. "First I hear."

"I don't know if he sings. Don't care. He kills anyone who searches for the bronze of the lost cities, and has decided to ruin the fur trade too."

"Hawkwing will go back to hunt when he has drunk up all his money and so will the others. Trust me, not even the Murder Bear can stand between an Amhas and a bottle. In the meantime, the skin prices rise, and with the money, they can get drunk longer, so the prices rise more. The woodsrunners, now that they can't go into the Bacenis at all any more, they're getting into a truly vile mood, afraid, and ashamed of their fear. Landlady doesn't like to see their kind in here, and I don't blame her. Some may be Rilante men, but they're worthless all the same. Most are bastards from Amhas women. Often drink too much and then quarrel."

"Live too close to death to respect anything and anyone," the young freckled man said.

"Well, you should know all about that, Faibur," the trader said. "Faibur here is the exception to the rule about woodsrunners that I just mentioned, naturally," he explained to Kitt. "I didn't mean offense."

"None taken," the freckled man said peaceably.

"He said the Singing Bear had taken away his honour?" Kitt asked, speaking lowly so as not to wake the drunk Amhas.

The woods-runner called Faibur also lowered his voice. "Hawkwing told me about it once, another time when he was stinking drunk. Don't think he remembers it, and frankly, I wouldn't want him to. When sober, Hawkwing is quite another matter."

"Except he's never sober if he can help it," the trader beside him interjected.

"Hawkwing told me that Canaras Muntrer, that is the Murder Bear, once attacked this Amhas village. He was way ahead of his warriors, as is his custom and charged right in among the Amhas warriors. He was alone, but the Amhas couldn't take him down, and the Murder Bear felled them right and left. When Hawkwing saw that he was the last warrior alive of the whole village, I told you he is a brave man, he is that, as I should know, but this time he hid among the women. The Murder Bear found him there and struck him in the face, and that way took the Hawkwing's honour because he didn't even bother to kill him. He's been drinking ever since."

Kitt looked at the snoring bundle by the door with a queer muddled feeling of compassion and contempt.

"I had a friend once, Amhas, a true friend," Faibur was saying. "Stone with Horns. When you hear me talking about him, you know I'm drunk. You won't find friendship very often between Rilante and Amhas, but we understood each other and did good business together. We used to go into the Bacenis, to hunt, and trade with the Feen. Skins, fur, ivory, the occasional bronze bar. Never know where you are with them. Then the fear had a new name, Murder Bear, and I became tired of being afraid. Stayed in my father's shop here in Dundingin, and Stone with Horns brought me skins until he didn't come to my shop no more. Later I heard that the Murder Bear had

165

caught him. They said that he lasted the whole night at the stake and that he died as well as he had fought."

Somebody sat down on the bench beside Kitt. "See you've met Faibur. He and his father have the fur shop beside my smithy."

"Gobin!" Kitt beamed at the bronze smith.

"Master Gobin, my friend!" Faibur said thickly. "Long time since you came here? Well, now you are here, you must drink. I am already drunk."

"Not yet, Faibur, I think you must drink more. You'll have to keep us company, Kitt, that's your first duty as my apprentice. Caught together, hung together, as the saying goes."

The other traders had drawn away, leaving Kitt, Gobin and Faibur at one end of the table. Beibini set a full tankard before Gobin.

"I didn't know this place served Cryssumha degenerates," one of the traders grumbled.

Beibini whipped round. "Nobody will be denied a drink here unless he makes trouble. And you take care that you won't be reminded of your words in the Hot Pit when you beg the Punishers for a drink."

"There isn't much love lost between Rilante and Cryssumha either," Faibur said heavily. "There isn't much love anywhere."

"Smelted the ore, I heard." Gobin took a deep draft and wiped the foam out of his black beard with the back of his hand. "Didn't use that little pan, after all, I heard," he pursued, and his dark eyes twinkled.

"Job would have taken too long to finish."

"So it would, so it would. An eternity of pain."

"And a hot smelting fire that was!" Captain Warmond called out. "We drink to that!" He rose to help his wife to serve the beer as fast as the guests were drinking.

The laughter branded up again so loud that it shook the bells of the wind chimes into a mad giggle.

*

Her eyes dreamy, Blaitisin sang to herself in her little room.

How big and strong he was, this Kitt, and how handsome, although he was a smith. He need not take second place to anyone, no, not even to Prince Ardri. Maybe this Kitt was not a simple smith

166

at all, but a warrior prince who wandered the world in disguise to find a woman who would love him just for himself. He had kissed her, and she hugged herself at the memory and did a little dance across the floor.

The bronze bells tinkled. She had three windchimes of nine bells each to ring out so beautifully when she whirled about on her toes, with her skirt flying out. Blaitisin's head was full of romance, and she knew she was beautiful.

She picked up her mirror that was always so clear. Her rose mouth curved in anticipatory pleasure as she raised the mirror and looked into the perfect round, expecting to see her red-golden hair, her milk-white skin, her cornflower blue eyes. What she saw in the mirror was a monster head, gritty eyes, grey skin, coarse hair stubble, a grinning mouth, that now opened into a scream.

"If you scream, they will come. Then he will see you like this," the bells told her.

"No, no, no, no, no!" She flung out her arm, but her fingers would not release the mirror. She could not even turn away her head, couldn't close her eyes to shut out the sight. She had to look at the monster head. Her other hand flew up to her face, and she felt the clammy skin, the bristly hair. Her hand in the mirror was a grey claw with long, dirty nails.

"Be quiet, or your mother will come," the bells said. "If she sees what is here in the room of her beautiful daughter, she will shout until men come and break your bones with sticks."

"Mercy, mercy!" she whimpered, on her knees, still looking into the mirror.

"Go, monster, go!" the bells said. "Hide, monster, hide! You have no more place here."

Blaitisin looked round in despair, her eyes lighting on the familiar things, a necklace, a camisole as if they were straws to hold on.

"Would you like to put a ribbon in your hair, monster?" The mocking bells would not let her be. "Don't bother! Just go, monster, go!"

Blaitisin opened her door and stole downstairs, along the dark corridor, clutching the mirror in her hand. She could see inside the candle-lit guest room, her mother smiling, and the long hair of the young smith fell over broad shoulders and shimmered like barley in the sun.

"Hide, monster, hide, don't let anybody see you. You don't want him to see you, do you! When he sees you, he will draw his sword and strike that ugly head from your shoulders."

Nobody saw Blaitisin as she stole along the back alleys, the mirror in her hand. All over the town, the bells told her where to go.

*

"Time to go home." It was as if Gobin spoke from a long, long way off.

Kitt rose and had to sit down again, heavily. His body did not seem to be quite his own any more.

"You'll look after him, Master Gobin?" he heard Beibini say from somewhere. "That's good. He could sleep here of course, but maybe it is better that he goes with you. I don't trust my Blaitisin at all. Not that I blame her." She emitted a rich chuckle. "She's developing a good taste in men. All the women in our family have it." She nudged her husband, who grinned drunkenly.

"I take him home. He is my new apprentice."

"I'm sure he'll do well for you."

"His references aren't too good," one of the soldiers remarked. "I hear the Alchemist of Castle Marrak couldn't do anything with him."

This was considered another excellent joke. A storm of laughter accompanied them out of the door. The bronze windchimes jingled merrily in tune.

*

When Kitt awoke the next morning, he felt that crows had decided to roost in his mouth. His head was swollen to the size of a mountain, and behind his brow, Jarnmantsjes had taken up a significant mining operation. No precious ore there -nothing but dead stone.

He stared at an unfamiliar clay ceiling. In some places, he could see the willow wands poke through. Looking at them tired him. The idea of turning his head to find out where he was did not bear thinking. A black fog had swallowed a large part of the night before, and left only dim shadows of more things that did not bear to think about either. It was gloomy and he heard the quiet rush of rain. How long he had slept he had no idea either, except that it was not enough.

168

The smell of sizzling bacon and eggs smote his nostrils. Another thing he did not want to contemplate just now.

"Yesterday he was so glad. Today the world is sad, sad, sad," a deep, rumbling voice sang.

Kitt remembered the voice; it belonged to Gobin the bronzesmith. This brought a remote recollection of wandering through a street which weaved in the moonlight, the black-bearded smith pulling him out of the way of walls that moved with inconsiderate suddenness.

"Not feeling quite the thing, young man?" Gobin asked in an unnecessarily cheerful voice.

"Something I ate?" Kitt croaked.

"Something you drank."

"The beer was bad?"

"Only the seventh or so tankard."

A plate with steaming bacon hovered above Kitt. "No, thanks."

The plate disappeared, but Gobin still would not leave him in peace. "Sit up, young man!"

Manfully, Kitt sat up and willed the room to stop spinning around him.

"Easy does it." Gobin pushed a clay cup at Kitt.

Just to look at the milky white liquid made his stomach rise again.

"Don't look at it, drink it down. It'll settle your insides."

Since he had no strength to object, Kitt drank it down as ordered, and felt the liquid slip down his throat, lining his stomach. The relief was immediate and immense.

"Never again," he said.

Gobin gave him another cup which contained a green liquid. Kitt recognised the bitter taste of willow bark. He drank it down, and a little later, the headache receded and left only a numbness behind the eyes. He suddenly felt more than ready for breakfast. When he had put himself outside an enormous amount of fried bacon and eggs, he was prepared to face the world. "What is that white stuff?"

"Ashes of Waterman's Fire, collected when the full moon looks into Struenfoly's mirror."

"Does everybody in this place talk gibberish?"

"It's a valuable secret. How much is it worth to you, each moment that the pain eases?"

"You must be rich."

"Benefactor to humanity. No business sense, alas." Gobin held a white piece of rock under Kitt's nose. "I grind this and dissolve in water. Not that you'll need it again, as you've just forsworn drink forever."

Kitt scrutinised the rock, tasted, and recognised it. "Simple enough."

"Most things that are good are simple. Not all though. That would be too simple." Gobin turned the white rock in his large blackened hands with black tufts of hair on the back. "And many things are both simple and complicated. People, for instance, you think you know all about them, and then find you that don't. Or the other way around."

"I've never seen so many people in one place. I don't know what is going on here. I'm blundering," Kitt confessed. "Something is going on in this place. Isn't it?"

"Oh yes, you might say something is going on. If you were to put it tamely. And somehow, I have a feeling that you are in the middle of the whole damned mess. And that is a very bad place to be."

A noise arose, of people calling in the street, and it came steadily nearer.

"Something has happened already. It had to." All the good humour left Gobin's face. He stepped under the door of his smithy, where Kitt joined him.

It was still raining, and water was running in the wheel runnels of the wet pavement. Four men came past from the direction of Castle Marrak, and between them on a plank they carried a white dripping thing. The men slowly passed with their burden, and Kitt saw Blaitisin's white still face. Dark red coils lay over her eyes and mouth, and her right arm lay limply on her bosom, but her hand clutched a bronze mirror.

"She went into the moat," one of the men said to nobody in particular. "The water was only knee-deep where we found her, but she drowned in it all the same." He raised pale blue eyes towards the grey bulk of the castle. "It was the Monster of Marrak."

Staring down at Blaitisin's face, Kitt remembered the taste of rosebud and beer, her lips on his, and her laughter about Glic Tusil's tower. As if in a bad dream, he stepped forward and took the dead girl into his arms, accepting the burden of guilt and the men who were carrying her gave her up to him without question. They were now surrounded by what seemed to be the whole Rilante population of Dundingin. All looked up at Castle Marrak with eyes that were afraid. They made way for Kitt and the dead girl.

Beibini stood in the middle of the street. "We did not laugh long," she said. The lines of laughter in her face were like inscriptions on a gravestone now.

Kitt carried the dead girl into the tavern. The windchimes jingled. Beibini threw open the door to the left and Kitt laid Blaitisin down on a table there.

Her mother tried to prise the mirror from her cold hand and could not, the dead girl clutched it so hard. Kitt attempted to help her, but Blaitisin's death grip was like iron.

"Take it away from her, please! Take it away, anyhow!" Beibini sobbed with terror and revulsion.

The cold fingers broke with a snap one by one. Kitt felt sweat break out on his forehead. Sick to his heart, he had the mirror at last and looked into it. For a moment, he saw black obsidian eyes mock into his. They were gone in a blink, and he saw only his own grey troubled eyes looking back at him.

"It wasn't your fault, Kitt, don't you blame yourself, boy," Beibini said as an echo to his unspoken thought.

Women bustled in, and Kitt left Blaitisin there on the table.

Captain Warmond came in, his face so pale that the scar seemed red, and the windchimes jingled again. "I am sick of bells." The father reached up, ripped them off and threw them down. With hellish laughter that would not stop the bells rolled around on the floor. White-lipped Warmond stomped them into crushed metal. "Nobody blames you, Kitt. Not for a moment," he echoed his wife. "We know who did this, but we can't do a thing about it."

Kitt did blame himself. He felt that Blaitisin was dead because he was alive, because he hadn't died poisoned in the alchemist's tower like the falcon and the doves. When he returned to Gobin's smithy, something slipped from his hand and he stopped and saw

171

bronze blink in the mud. It was the mirror; he had not noticed that he still held it. He picked it up, and again looked into the bronze oval. Had he really seen the black, mocking eyes in it?

The bronze smith stepped out. "Give me that mirror, give it to me!" He attempted to take it from Kitt's hand. "Don't look into it. The mirror is a trap for any who looks into it, and that trap can be sprung again."

"She wouldn't let go of it." Kitt didn't let go of it now. Gobin led him into the smithy where he sat down heavily. "She was like a flower."

"It wasn't your fault, Kitt."

"Beibini also said that it wasn't my fault, Warmond said it."

"And they meant it."

"What do you know?"

"Dundingin is a town full of mirrors and bells; that is what is happening here, and always has. It is said that when Lute stands in the west, nobody must look into mirrors. But here in Ulud, in Dundingin, nobody must look into mirrors at all. Now, give me that thing!"

Kitt held out the mirror, the last thing Blaitisin had touched, and Gobin took it with a sigh of relief. He slipped it into the forge, face down, heaped coal onto it and worked the hand bellows. "Better that way. A connection has been established."

"With her murderer?" Why did Gobin destroy the evidence? How could Kitt bring home the crime to him now? Blaitisin had spoken of the Green Man who sold mirrors. Did that man have something to do with Glic Tusil?

"You are confused and suspicious," Gobin said. "When young men are confused and suspicious, they get angry, and then they do something stupid. I don't want you angry. I'll explain all that happened, beginning with what Glic Tusil tried to do to you."

Chapter 14
The Secret of Bronze

13th day Ceitein. Quicksilvery Srad leaves the Star Pattern. The Courtier, who was he?

Ardri, King of Cryssumha, Star Observation Journal

Gobin took up a piece of chalk, and began to draw on the grey stone slab covering the table.

Kitt watched suspiciously as a star emerged. "Six," he said. "Your star has six rays; Glic Tusil's star had eight."

"I saw it," Gobin said.

"Ardri talked much about a Star Pattern."

"And now you wish you had listened. Never mind, I'll show you. Vasara is the star of copper, my star, six is her number, and she is the Queen Star. Glic Tusil's star is Lute, the star of the Ledrithud magic and Dark Lute's number is eight. The white line was all wrong, and the green was not right either. Black is uncertain, with that colour you never know. Many things can hide behind it, good or bad, but I would stake this smithy on a bet that Glic Tusil's black line was not healthy. I'll show you what is. Wait!" He went out of the back of his smithy.

Kitt just sat there, not really waiting -trying not to think.

Something hard hit the door to the street.

Kitt went to open.

Outside stood five young Rilante men with blond and red hair and thin beards. They looked surprised at being confronted by Kitt. "What are you doing with the Cryssumha scum? Haven't you seen what they are like?"

"I'm Master Gobin's apprentice."

Just then, two guardsmen came along the main street; Kitt remembered them from the Mocking Bird tavern the night before.

"Off with you!" they addressed the five angry young men. "Master Gobin is an honourable man. He's got nothing to do with..." their eyes went to Castle Marrak.

"That's what you think." The emphasis was on "you".

"What Captain Warmond thinks. Good enough? Listen, boys, we understand. We are as cut up about poor, dear Blaitisin as you are. But Gobin is a good smith, an honest one. He works for the guards' force."

"What is going on?" Faibur inquired, as he arrived from the neighbouring house looking hung over and accompanied by an elderly man, tall, stooping, with an amiable freckled face.

"Don't mess with Gobin, lads," the guard said reasonably. "His neighbours defend him, we do, Kitt here does."

"You shouldn't!" the first angry young man said bitterly. The five moved away, unappeased.

"We have a lot more of that now," the guardsman said. "We're glad that you are here with Master Gobin. You can count yourself lucky he took you on. He is the best in the land, you know. Fashioned our armour and weapons." The soldier touched his bronze helmet and the hilt of his short stabbing sword. "And this too."

At Kitt's request, the guard handed over the lance, for him to appraise the flaring edge and rounded flanks of the lancehead and run his hand over the rows of lines and circles that decorated the whole blade except for the edges. "Nice."

"Call us, if you need a hand," the second guard said. "Not that you look like you ever do."

They were all gone from the door when Gobin returned inside the house, and Kitt didn't mention the incident.

On the broad calloused palm of his hand, the bronze-smith held lumps of black and red ore with a metallic shimmer. "This black ore is good, but I cannot prove it to you, as it looks just like the bad, same colour, same lustre. And this red ore, it is almost black, but it draws a red line, not a white one." He demonstrated on the table. "White is most unhealthy. Stay away from the white line, Kitt. I don't work this Evil Ore, and you won't find it here in my smithy. If there is no other ore available, do not breathe in the fumes, while you smelt it. Not so much as a whiff."

174

"He gave me fair warning. Even drew a picture for me," Kitt said with disgust as much about his own ignorance, as about the alchemist's treachery.

Gobin laughed. "That's Glic Tusil. The Master of Mirrors he is also called. Smoke and mirrors are his metier. Though you did show him a thing about smoke." Chuckling, the smith opened a copper-bound chest and from it took a green, bubbly, shining mass speckled with deep blue. "And here is the best ore you could wish to find. Claghin, the queen's ore. It does almost give pity to smelt it if it were not for the beauty of copper itself." He drew it along the stone slab. "See, this pale green line is not like the other green. It does almost look like copper patina. Now you know the copper ores."

There was another knock on the door. Gobin rose, but Kitt was faster to open the door. Outside stood the same two city guards with a heavy basket between them. It was full of mirrors and bells. "We brought away every single thing the Green Man sold in the Mocking Bird. The poor, dear girl had three windchimes in her little room. Once we started, all the neighbours took down theirs. We want you to smelt all, make them into lance heads."

*

Kitt weighed the windchimes and the mirrors as Gobin told him to. "Eighteen pounds of bells, twelve of mirrors."

"Keep that in mind! Now hack up everything in as small parts as you can manage."

Kitt didn't ask why. He set about to destroy the bells and mirrors with a will, starting with the lump of bronze that had been Blaitisin's mirror, and crushing the bells with his fingers. The fragments he carried into the back yard, and placed them all together in a tall clay crucible, as Gobin told him.

When this was done, Gobin talked. "With three parts of tin out of seventy-two the bronze is copper red. That is Umharu, which is used a lot since the tin has become scarce.

With more tin, the alloy changes into golden yellow, and with six parts of tin, we have Findrun. Both are used for weapons but for the king's arms only Findrun. The lighter the colour of the bronze, the harder it is, and the less malleable.

At twelve parts tin, the hammer rests. Because the bronze would crack, were you to attempt to cold-forge it.

175

At twenty-four parts tin, the bell is cast, dull in colour, clear in tone and at thirty-six parts the mirror bronze, radiant and white and brittle. This is what we have here, a mixture of Bell Bronze and Mirror bronze. Can you tell how many parts of tin we have?"

This was talk that Kitt understood and the thought that now, at last, he would learn the art of making bronze, and the calculation almost took his mind off Blaitisin. He calculated eighteen times twenty-four plus twelve times thirty-six, this sum divided by thirty. "Twenty-eight parts in seventy-two plus eight-tenths of one part. What will we do with this bronze?"

Gobin showed him the mould for six lance heads; it had two halves that fitted together.

"You really want to make lances out of that metal?"

"Once smelted, the bronze doesn't belong to the owner of the old form. Don't you let yourself get rattled! We smiths will always have the last word with the metal, and nobody else. Don't let anyone tell you different! Now, casting is a work that has to be done very fast. Reheat bronze too often, and the tin will boil out of it. You can neglect the eight-tenths of a part that you so conscientiously calculated because it will boil away."

Kitt nodded. "There are some iron alloys that you can heat only once."

"Then, I reckon you have already learned to work fast. Now tell me what you do to put an edge on your iron?"

"I heat the blade to a red glow, and hammer until it fades, and then I heat again. Need to time everything. Then comes the hardening and sharpening."

"Well, if you treat bronze like that, it will break, for hot bronze is brittle. Therefore, bronze is hammered when it is cold. Now, how much copper do we have to add to our smelt so that you may hammer the bronze?"

Kitt calculated again; this was a little harder.

"Forty pounds, for twelve parts of tin. For six, seventy pounds more. Gives one hundred and forty pounds of Findrun bronze."

"Not afraid of numbers, you aren't."

"Give about one hundred and forty of these lance heads. Do we have so many moulds?"

"You'll see," Gobin said mysteriously.

176

After dinner in castle Marrak Lord Morrik's mailed glove crashed on the table, and set wine bottles and beakers dancing. "This barbarian should never have got to Dundingin! Or at least, he shouldn't be walking the streets now!"

"What I said, my Lord," Slachlan muttered in the corner, and emptied his wine beaker.

Lord Morrik was from a younger branch of the ancient royal family of Cryssumha and having been the de facto ruler of West Cryssumha for so long, he did not seem to feel that anything had changed with the arrival of the young king. The young Queen being lord Morrik's daughter guaranteed him a senior position.

Ardri sized up his father in law, the carefully groomed black beard, the carriage of the tall, massive figure and the haughty black eyes. Where he sat was the head of the table. That would have to change. He set down his goblet with a sharp crack. "Your king would have been in the belly of a Bethrek before he could have been crowned with Fenifindrune. Your king would have bled at a Woodstalker stake if it had not been for this young barbarian. But for him, Fenifindrune might be lost in the woods altogether, and all hope of restoring Cryssumha terminated." He fixed lord Morrik with a hard stare. "Would I begin my rule of Cryssumha with the destruction of the man who I have everything to thank for, my life, and my crown?"

"That is exactly what a king must begin his rule with. A necessary and correct deed. Your Majesty." The mailed glove did not come into play again.

"A stupidly dangerous deed. I watched this boy eat the heart of a Bethrek. Raw."

There was a momentary pause. Ardri grinned, as he watched them picturing it. Slachlan drained his wine in one gulp and reached for the bottle.

Lord Morrik raised an expressive eyebrow. "Indeed. Well, I don't know any man who killed a Bethrek."

"With a knife."

Lord Morrik's eyebrow went up even further. "Indeed," he repeated.

"Not his first, either."

Lord Morrik's saturnine assurance was wavering, a priceless sight. "I begin to understand your point," he said pensively.

Slachlan scowled. "Attack him from behind, or in his sleep."

Ardri shook his head. "I wish you had seen him fight the Maldryg guards of Minit Claghini and Kione Lonnir. Foul wood's sorcery which Glic Tusil is powerless against." Ardri looked around the table. "The sooner you all get it into your head that this barbarian is like nothing you have ever seen, the better, so that we won't lose more time with unprofitable chatter about what I should have done."

"The outcome would have been uncertain, I see."

"Not merely uncertain, Lord Morrik. There was too much certainty for my liking."

"I think I saw your barbarian when I came into Dundingin. Hard to overlook him in fact. Very impressively built. Young, an adolescent."

"In case you draw the common inference from his being very big and very young, that he is needs stupid, I should better warn you, that he has the cunning of a Woodstalker, paired with quite an unexpected sophistication. He's given me many a nasty surprise."

Lord Morrik nodded. "I took your meaning when you mentioned that he killed a Bethrek with a knife. But then it should interest us all the more, what exactly motivated him to help you, your Majesty."

"You won't believe it, I didn't either at first. He took it into his head that having saved me from the Bethrek made him responsible for me, so he had to continue saving me." Ardri smiled. "With all his strength and skill, he is good-natured and honest. Which is just what makes him dangerous. He is sixteen years old. The day when he learns that good deeds are rarely repaid in kind I don't want to be anywhere near."

"I see. Full of ideals." Lord Morrik also smiled. "Unwilling to face the facts of life. And they feel invulnerable, then."

"He is a creature of Mavors, Lord Morrik." Glic Tusil's tone was thick with meaning. "Where such a one treads, there foundations shake, schemes crumble, patterns break."

"Or towers burn down." Slachlan's dark face twisted into a grin it wasn't accustomed to, and that didn't improve it.

Glic Tusil did not deign to answer that. "The first time I attempted to remove him from the Star Pattern, the spoor we laid so carefully directed the magic creature's rage to another man. That could have been chance. The second time my tower Gelockefetir before the West Gate burned down, by accident while smelting ore the city guards say. I don't require a third thing to happen, to be certain of what he is. He is destined to be the antithesis of chance, he is, as your Majesty says, a certainty. It will be almost impossible to stop him."

"A foot-length of bronze through his belly will stop him, alright. You are old Glic Tusil, and even when you were young, you found a sword too heavy for you to carry," Slachlan jibed. "Stick to your potions and stinks!"

Glic Tusil turned to the steward and smiled; it was a thin, poisonous smile. "You get on my nerves, numbskull."

Slachlan choked on his wine, coughed so hard that it hurt and looked uncertain.

"You know that I'm not at all sure about the nature of Mavors," Ardri said. "So far in Kitt's person, the Red Star has been a friendly influence, even necessary, more than necessary, vital. What exactly is the nine-fold nature of Mavors, what aspects are essential, how do they change, when, under what circumstances? There are so many possible errors, and only one right course."

"The slightest doubt calls for decisive action," Glic Tusil said, contemplating his nails.

Ardri frowned. "Apart from that, I like him."

"Irrelevant."

"I beg your pardon, Lord Morrik?"

"Gasda will be here soon, your Majesty," Morrik reminded. "He may be the Dog of Rilante, but he is no fool, and he will ask a lot of questions."

"I have an answer to all of Lord Gasda's questions."

"So has this Kitt. Gasda mustn't get a chance to talk to him."

"He gave me his word that he will not talk, and I trust his promise."

Lord Morrik shrugged and exchanged an eloquent look with the Steward.

Glic Tusil had spotted a dust speckle on the red velvet of his sleeve and snipped it away.

***

179

"Clay, sand and straw," Gobin explained. "I mix as much sand into the clay as I can, without the thing to crumble, and some straw so that the clay won't shrink when the mould dries."

He began kneading the leather-coloured, sticky mask, and Kitt joined him with enthusiasm; he had always loved messing around with clay.

An injured voice said, "I think you could have trusted me, or at least my father, with mixing the clay for your mould, master Gobin." A young man had come into the yard through the side gate bent under a heavy basket. His long white face framed with locks of sleek black hair peered up at the smith.

"I trust your father like myself, dear boy," Gobin said. "And you, for that matter, Young Crochen. But I want to show Kitt here how to make a mould. He is my new apprentice and needs to learn everything. Just put it all here my boy, thank you."

The potter set down his basket and peered up at Kitt's great height, and then turned his eyes even higher, to heaven. "All the stars, Gobin, you don't think you can turn a barbarian into a smith. What are you laughing about, barbarian?" the young man inquired with a loftiness that was quite an achievement, seeing that he stood a head and a half less than Kitt.

"What you think makes no difference to what I am." Kitt shrugged. "Or vice versa." He had borrowed this line from the Aurel Liber by Vero Annio, the famous Daguilarian philosopher.

Standing with his mouth slightly open, the young potter visibly tried to work out whether he had been offended.

"My compliments to your father," Gobin said, and the young man retreated with a venomous glance at Kitt.

***

Gobin was the only one of the black-haired, dark-eyed Cryssumha people on main-street among the Rilante traders, and his house did not follow the six-cornered pattern. His neighbours down the street were the fur traders, seven shops, and then came Beibini's tavern. Left and right Gobin's smithy bordered on the yards of his street neighbours. But his yard was more extended than theirs and seven-cornered.

Kitt was presented to Gobin's neighbour on the other side of the backyard, the potter, a cheerful rotund man, who made crucibles from a mixture of clay and ground quartz stone. "How often does the crucible melt, or the bottom fall out of it, but mine are fired so hard that you can use them for twelve castings, at least, is that not so, Master Gobin?"

And Gobin agreed that was so.

The potter's son was there, and Kitt nodded to him. The young potter smiled. "What I think of you, or what you think of me, isn't it?" He chuckled, as about an excellent joke.

The other backyard neighbour was the beekeeper who supplied the wax for Gobin's models. The high clay walls that enclosed the beekeeper's yard hummed with the thousands of bees that lived in caverns with small slits for an entrance, and on a sunny day, the furry insects formed a cloud above the yard. The beekeeper was a tall, thin man who smiled with vague amiability, and spoke little. He presented Kitt with a six-cornered pottery jar containing last year's honey. The beekeeper's wife was even taller and thinner than her husband; she had long black hair and a long white gentle face and said nothing at all.

The third backyard neighbour was also a neighbour of Faibur's, who worked in leather and skins for the lining of armour and making of weapon belts with his wife and eight dark-eyed daughters aged six to twenty years old.

*

Gobin lit the fire under the crucible on the hearth. "You'll work the bellows."

"And how." They were smelting the bronze from the bells and mirrors, which Kitt had already reduced to the smallest particles he could.

Gobin placed the two halves of the mould into the other half of the double oven. "When pouring the bronze, the mould must be dry and hot and clean, or Dilo, the Lord of Lightning, will throw the molten metal back at you."

It was Kitt's task to take the hot mould out of the oven, and stand it upright in a wooden block, while Gobin took out the crucible and poured the liquid metal into the top.

Later, when the mould was cracked open like a walnut, inside was the bronze tree, the raw shape of six lance heads that gleamed with a pale gold shimmer.

"Now try to work the raw shape into something a soldier will consider useful."

Kitt nodded and set to work.

Gobin watched him as he swung the hammer, first slowly, experimentally, scrutinising the effect of each blow, then beating harder and faster.

"That's the way to go about it," he said.

***

Kitt handed the mended copper pan to the customer, a slim girl with a mass of blonde curls and rosy cheeks. She looked neat in a cream-coloured linen blouse and linen skirt and sturdy wooden shoes and a blue kerchief that brought out the colour of her eyes. She reminded him that her name was Deridere and seemed inclined to chat.

Standing on the porch of Gobin's smithy, Kitt looked up to Castle Marrak, and wondered how he always forgot about it once it was out of sight. Had Castle Marrak forgotten about him? He could not chance it. So he muttered that he had to get back to the smelting oven and turned his back on her and her pot, hoping she'd be safe.

In the backyard, the double oven was glowing every day to deal with the bells and mirrors the Rilante people of the main street kept bringing. The bronze was smelted in a crucible on one side and several small moulds heated in the other. Kitt shovelled coal, which was being mined practically under their very feet by the underground people of the city. This was his work, as the apprentice.

"You must be getting tired of mending all those copper pots and pans and buckets the girls keep bringing," Gobin said jocularly.

"My father says to repair mundane things brings good luck."

Gobin grinned. "The darlings must be running out of broken items. I suspect some of them even stave in their cooking utensils deliberately. They can hardly pretend an interest in lance-heads, can they, eh Kitt? Haven't you noticed?"

"Noticed what?"

"The girls! They're not coming to see me. Could have done that any time for the last twenty years I've been a widower, but they never did. Both Rilante and Cryssumha girls too. Which do you like better? Or is there just one?"

"If there were, I'd be careful not to point her out. But there isn't."

182

When he was done shovelling the coal, Kitt worked the bellows. Each knew what to do, and the precision of the mechanical work took his mind off all else.

"We will add a bit of lead to the bronze, one part in a hundred to make it flow better, get a finer cast," Gobin remarked. "Not to mention lead fits in just now with the rising star constellation, which is called the mirror, because Vasara, Lute and Mavors stand in a triangle."

"My main consideration."

"Such a tone is not fitting in one so young. We will also add some Galmei to add to the bronze. This is also the way to make fine jewellery."

They poured the bronze, and then Gobin fell into one of his silences; he seemed to have something on his mind. Kitt did not ask. If Gobin was anything like his father Eckehart, then his secrets were many and deep, and he wasn't going to share them all. Since Kitt had realised that his father Eckehart also kept secrets from him, he was perfecting a habit of looking and listening for as many clues as he could. So he pretended not to notice when Gobin unwrapped a wax model he didn't want his apprentice to see, yet in turn, pretended not doing anything special. The glimpse was enough to recognise the minute masks and swelling shapes as something Kitt had seen in his dream of Minit Claghini. Gobin was making preparations to form a mould for a sword sheath.

"What is it, Kitt? What do you see?" Gobin's voice said in his ear.

"You tell me what I see."

"I see an honest young man who keeps to his word. And I don't know what to advise you, Kitt. This insistence of yours to keep your word seems a weakness that can get you killed. But at the same time, it is a strength that raises you above all others. If you are strong enough. Only the truly strong can afford this kind of folly...or think they can."

"As you say, a folly."

"Maybe the trick is, to be honest always, while never expecting the same from others. Makes no sense that, what, son?"

"All to the contrary Gobin, it makes good sense."

"And for some nice surprises, now and again. Now, we have worked hard all day and yesterday and the day before. Go you to the Mocking Bird. You haven't been since you started working here and it won't do. In a city a man must be neighbourly."

"But I don't know if Beibini..."

"She isn't well these days, doesn't often rouse herself enough to serve drink, and when she does, she forgets to take payment. Warmond can't always be around. His men can't stand that look in her eyes and don't come to the Mocking Bird so much, but there are others, and she gets taken advantage of if there isn't one of the neighbours to look out for her. So we'll look in now and again, least we can do. I will join you later. Your beer today is on your master."

It was evident, that the bronze smith really didn't want his apprentice present. That was alright with Kitt. He didn't really want anything to do with that Sword of Cryssumha.

*

Faibur and his father were in the Mocking Bird with a bottle before them, and Kitt sat down at their table.

Beibini brought a mug of beer. The bright, empty stare of her blue eyes was not easy for Kitt to face. But she smiled at him, patted his biceps, and briefly looked like her old self. He gave her one of his twelve gold coins, carefully wiped clean from all traces of ash.

"That should take care of a couple of massive hangovers and open you a snug credit," Faibur said.

"Don't you go for the bottles though, you are too young for Uskeva," Fidcal advised.

The tavern door opened, and two big city guards came in, a girl between them. She was thin, about twelve years old, her bare feet scratched deeply, the strawberry blonde hair was full of burdock. Her blue eyes were frightened and painfully aware.

"This one came to the gate," the guard told Beibini. "Didn't say a word, it seems that she can't. Her folks had a farmstead near the Struenfoly. Captain has gone out to the Fota farm with the off-duty men. But you see how she is, so captain said to bring her here."

"He did well, of course. What's your name, child?"

The girl looked at Beibini mutely. It didn't seem so much that she couldn't speak, but more that she couldn't understand a word said to her.

"Do you know her name?"

"We know her by sight; her folks came to the market often. But not to speak to."

"In a year or two perhaps I'll ask," the guardsman said with a grin that exposed a perfect row of white teeth under the thick red moustache.

"And I'm sure she'll give you the reply you deserve, handsome. You are lucky that she's lost her speech."

The guard stroked his moustache. "I'm pleased to notice that you've regained yours, Beibini."

"Are you now?" His comrade chuckled. "Told you just where you get off, she did, right away."

"Back to the gate, that's where," the soldier with the red moustache said. "One quick beer, thank you." His face darkened. "It does look bad."

"I dread the news the Captain will bring," his companion said. "Woodstalkers, I'm afraid. Those bloody Amhas at a guess, and they'll shift all blame on the Murder Bear. I don't believe he even exists."

"Or that he'd bother with farmers. How we listen to the lies of those savages and not knock off their heads..."

Beibini took the girl by the hand. "Come, child, sit here by me behind the counter and let me get something warm into you and see to your poor feet."

After sunset, more city guards crowded into the tavern, headed by Captain Warmond. "Nobody there at the farm," he said. No dead bodies, not a trace. Just an empty house. They had lots of bells and mirrors. They had ploughed their fields, but what they wanted to sow I don't know. There was no seed, not one grain. It makes no sense."

Of the girl, the top of her red-blonde head was visible behind the counter. They all looked over to her.

"So, Woodstalkers?" the soldier with the red moustache asked in a low voice.

"Where are the bodies, then? There should be a horrible mess if it were Woodstalkers, torture, mutilation. And the house wasn't plundered, the kegs untouched. Wasn't Woodstalkers."

"Warmond, sit your men down to eat!" Beibini led the girl from behind the counter by the hand. "Come then child, there's an empty

185

room upstairs just ready for you. We'll be an odd pair, two maimed ones. I have just lost my daughter." Over her shoulder, she called "Time gentlemen!"

Chapter 15
A Cloak for a King

Before the open city-gate stood three tall, dark figures, Woodstalkers; with black facepaint and their dark eyes without the whites showing, they looked utterly alien. These Woodstalkers were wild ones, not the tame Amhas.

They were clad in leather leggings and loincloth, tied to a girdle with leather thongs, in which copper knives stuck. On their feet, they wore wrappings of soft leather.

Two of them wore strings of teeth and claws round neck and upper arms and in their long, blue-black hair. One bore a brace of brick red fox pelts, and the other had both arms around a voluminous skin with the inside out, so that nobody could see what kind of animal it had belonged to.

The third was the leader; he was taller than his two companions, steel cord muscles which suggested unusual strength and reflexes played under the sleek bronze skin decorated rather than marred by white scars, scratches and dots, particularly on the legs and arms. Across his eyes ran a broad stripe of black paint, and two lines at the corners of his mouth accentuated the animalist fascination of the finely cut face made wild by a long white scar across his forehead. His only adornment was a curved fang the length of a man's hand which gleamed white on the bare chest.

The warriors stood there as if it didn't matter to them how long, and the guardsmen's curious and hostile glances bounced off them like water from a rock.

Captain Warmond interrogated them in person, using a mixture of Rilante and Amhas language, and declared himself satisfied. He knew that if he turned away these hunters, the fur traders would lynch him. So little pelts had come in of late, these were only three men, and he didn't believe they had anything to do with the incident on the Fota farmstead. He didn't even bother to ask them to leave their knives and short lances.

A hush fell over the lower end of the main street and spread as the warriors walked along with the arrogant poise of great cats followed by suspicious looks and whispers, until the first fur trader caught sight of them, and tried to engage them in a deal.

The stir was such that Fidcal stepped out of his shop. When he saw the three warriors approaching, he called for his son. "These are more savage than we are used to seeing."

"Be quiet father, for the Wild Hunt's sake!" Faibur muttered from the threshold. "Mangan Sorkera himself, walking slap bang into Dundingin."

The three warriors stopped before Fidcal's premises; behind them crowded the rivalling fur traders. War leader and woodsrunner measured each other, black animal eyes mocked into the blue.

"Long time Faibur not hunt in Sreedok, that he calls Bacenis," Mangan Sorkera said in the language of Rilante.

It was Fidcal who answered. "The Bacenis is full of bears. Fidcal now waits for the pelts to come to him on Woodstalker legs. So cut the cackle and show what you brought."

Just by lowering his lids, the war leader contrived to express utter contempt.

"Allow me, father," Faibur interjected.

"Mangan Sorkera heard there is a king come to Cryssumha."

"Who told, the wind, the trees?"

"A guard told, the guard of Gliyet-Sotal."

"The war leader must be careful of the names he speaks in Dundingin, or he may never leave it again," Faibur muttered.

"Mangan Sorkera will leave Dundingin when and how Mangan Sorkera chooses. But Faibur will not leave, is afraid of bears."

Faibur flushed an angry red.

Mangan Sorkera motioned behind him, and the warrior who bore the large skin in his arms stepped forward and began to unfold it. The two warriors took the extended pelt at one fore and hind paw each and held it up with outstretched arms. They were tall men just over six feet, and even so, the other two paws touched the ground. All around caught their breath at the sight of the fur, coal-black with silver spots, that fell in folds like heavy silk.

188

"Sheh Ri," Fidcal murmured. "A Mooncat."

His commercial instincts asserted themselves, and he began to look for holes and cuts. "Through the eye, as befits a good hunter. I give the great warrior a great price."

"Twelve Findrun lances," Mangan Sorkera demanded.

"Twelve Umharu lances, very good."

"Twelve Findrun lances."

"Six."

"Twelve Findrun lances."

Thoughtfully, Fidcal caressed the Sheh Ri skin "I could maybe manage..."

"Twelve Findrun lances."

The trader stopped smiling. The prices for Findrun bronze were sky high in these times, and therefore, the profit would not be as substantial as he had hoped. He could save the transport fees to Iwerdonn if he sold the pelt on Castle Marrak - thereby drawing attention to himself - and if he discounted the uncertain favour of royals - being of a sceptic turn of mind, Fidcal was inclined to discount it. Most of all, that Woodstalker gave him gooseflesh, those calmly mad animal eyes, the predator's poise. Who was he really? Faibur seemed to know more than he told, and his father was not sure that he liked that. As keen as he was to make any fur deal at all, let alone the splendid chance to buy the skin of such a strange animal, Fidcal was about to give it a miss.

*

"Is there something outside that you're afraid of?" Gobin chuckled. "that's what you look like, I swear, peeking out of the window like a scaredy-cat."

It was instinct with Kitt to hide whenever he saw Mangan Sorkera, the Feen war leader. He realised the nonsense of that in the middle of Dundingin. "I've only ever seen the pelt of such an animal," he said without thinking. It was a ceremonial cloak in the vision of old Cryssumha where Kitt had seen this same fur pattern, this liquid shimmer. "Not really seen it," he amended, "It was only a dream and now it's come true."

The master smith seemed galvanised by what he saw through the window. Kitt followed Gobin out into the main street to Faibur's shop.

"Faibur, my friend!"

Upon seeing Gobin step out of the crowd, trailed by his big, warlike apprentice, Fidcal breathed again. The boy had a reputation.

Kitt approached to touch the Sheh Ri skin; it felt soft and slick and cool under his hand. He noticed that Mangan Sorkera marked his position, just as he marked the war leader's. The other two young warriors Kitt knew from the night of the Mik Shini; they had done their best to make it hot for him at the Feen torture stake. Now, he could detect no resentment; they looked at him openly, curiously, with almost friendly recognition.

Gobin drew Faibur into a corner and began to whisper urgently, while Mangan Sorkera watched with another sarcastic lowering of eyelids.

"...king's cloak," Kitt overheard Gobin whisper.

"Your damn dreams of Cryssumha," Faibur muttered. There was more argument from Gobin until Faibur threw up his hands. "All right, all right. We'll put this through for you."

Fidcal attempted to continue the haggling with Mangan Sorkera, but the war leader ignored him, and looked at Kitt. "Gawthrin Lye can fight like strong warrior. Fight Agetool A Shushei. Why Gawthrin Lye hide like fox, run like stag?"

Kitt shrugged. "Feen are slow like sloths, blind like moles. One day I may wait for them in plain sunlight."

Mangan Sorkera turned to his companions, and apparently translated what Kitt had said all too well because the young warriors glowered at him.

Faibur returned to the shop, followed by Gobin who carried a bundle. "Here, as you ask." With a clank, he dropped the heavy load onto the arms of one of the young Woodstalkers. The second warrior pushed aside the cloth to reveal the pale-golden gleam of the Findrun lance blades.

"Oh, don't wave this about!" Faibur hissed.

Fidcal made a movement with his hands as if he was washing them. "I leave you to this, you don't seem to want me, and I don't want any of this business."

"Don't worry, there will be a commission both ways. See you in the Mocking Bird."

"For the next couple of days," his father said over his shoulder, already on his way to Beibini's establishment.

At a brief command from the war leader, the other Woodstalker threw the fox pelts at Faibur's feet, and both young warriors strode down the main street of Dundingin with the distance-eating trot of the woodsmen.

The war leader turned to follow his men when Faibur spoke to him. "Mangan Sorkera cannot win his war against Rilante. Not even with Findrun lances."

The war leader turned around again. "Why then is Faibur afraid?"

The forest runner felt Mangan Sorkera's dark eyes on him, and the future seemed to open before him red and black. He shivered.

"You found my Bethrek skin?" Kitt demanded.

Mangan Sorkera smiled, and the deer eyes looked deceptively gentle. "Fox cub hunted, bear took the game."

"Hunt your own, Mangan Sorkera. There are enough Bethrek in the Sreedok Bacenis for both of us."

"Mangan Sorkera's women cure Graykhol Rere Bethrek skin. Gawthrin Lye come Bacenis Sreedok and fetch." The finely cut lips twitched in a curiously friendly smile. "Gawthrin Lye come soon. Mangan Sorkera waits." With that, he followed his warriors.

"So you have a name with the Feen," Faibur said. "A good name too. Gawthrin Lye, fox cub, clever child. A rare compliment. Usually, they just call everybody not a Feen a Dshooka, that means bad, stupid people, and to them, all Dshooka are the same. You must have impressed the Singing Bear."

"I just keep running away." Kitt did not mention that on two occasions he and Mangan Sorkera had faced the same adversary, though far from being allies.

"Then you're the first who escaped." Faibur laughed without mirth. "If he ever catches you, you will die the Red Death, hard and long drawn out. And that will be a compliment too, as the Feen understand it. By the way, that was a fine bit of woods diplomacy, compliment for the war leader, and challenge from an equal."

"That's how I meant it."

"Well, well, let's contemplate just what you've bitten off there. You know this Woodstalker by the name of Mangan Sorkera,

191

Singing Bear, in the Feen language. The Amhas call him Canaras Muntrer, crazy, savage, raving mad bear. But this side of the Struenfoly they call him the Murder Bear as if he was a rabid animal, and he truly is the most dangerous predator the Bacenis has seen. Till today maybe." Faibur appraised the youth standing there with the unconscious arrogance of strength, the grey eyes narrowing like a cat's, deceptively lazy, yet hearing and seeing everything around him.

"So that's who he is. I wondered if it was the same man. Why did he come here, Faibur?"

"Why did he come to Dundingin at all or why did he do me the honour of his exclusive business, carrying that Sheh Ri pelt past six shops and the Stag and Bottle Inn where all the itinerant traders lurk?"

"Both."

"I don't tell all I know, and that may be the reason why some skins still come my way, as did the Sheh Ri pelt just now, while other traders are long out of business. I might be afraid of Mangan Sorkera, or I might have totally different reasons."

"Tell me?"

"Insistent, are you. I could, but for that, I'll need to be drinking, and you pay the Uskeva."

"I have money. Gobin wants no apprenticeship fee, though I offered to pay."

"You'll pay him yet, somehow or other. Nothing in Cryssumha comes as a gift. Now let's go to the Mocking Bird."

"Go, Kitt," Gobin said. "This is a big day. You have no idea. Or maybe you have. If so, I know you will be careful what you say, even after a beer or two or three. I will join you later."

*

"Is it permitted to enter?" Prince Ardri stood in the door of the smithy. He was clad in black velvet and soft leather, and he wore the polite expression of somebody who owns everything but is not going to make a particular point of that.

Gobin bowed deeply. "My king!"

"I hear that you are having a cloak made, master smith? That you paid a high price for a pelt, and I have come to assure you of the royal sanction for the transaction. Don't worry at all, dear Gobin."

"Never, my king!" the bronze smith said and bowed again.

"I further heard that you have taken in Kitt as your apprentice. I'm very grateful for that, Master Gobin. I owe much gratitude to Kitt. I had asked the Master of Mirrors to teach him about bronze, but the two didn't see eye to eye."

"I know." For the first time, Gobin dropped the deferential, non-committal mask to smile into his bushy beard, and the black eyes twinkled with amusement.

Ardri grinned back with malicious enjoyment. "You should have seen Glic Tusil's face when the tower Gelockefetir was gone, wiped off the horizon, just like that." He sobered. "Something will happen soon."

"It already did." Gobin's face became stern and forbidding. "A harmless girl was driven into the moat. She'd just had a little joke with Kitt. This was a nasty deed, done to cause him grief and make him feel powerless and guilty."

"I have to hand it to Glic Tusil, to go for the vulnerable spot with such fiendish accuracy. This over-sensitive feeling of responsibility for all his actions, it's Kitt's chink. How did he come by that, I wonder? Who did it to him? It seems such an unnecessary waste. Glic Tusil does have his reasons, though. He is convinced that Mavors is the danger that threatens to disrupt the Star Pattern."

Gobin shook his head. "The Master of Mirrors errs. He errs badly."

Ardri nodded. "Unfortunately, he persists in that error."

"Glic Tusil thinks he can discount Dewar Farwar's walk across the sky. He is wrong. The Hero passes the dance of the wandering stars; he follows his own unchanging path as they weave their pattern. Occasionally, they make new patterns with the bright stars of his shoulders, his knees, his girdle, patterns that mean something to those who watch the wandering stars, but to the Hero they are quite meaningless."

"So that is the way your thoughts run, Master Gobin? Not Mavors but Dewar Farwar, the Eternal Hero? I suppose you know that Kitt saved my life over and over in the Bacenis wood?"

193

"I heard rumours about that, but nothing from Kitt. He just clams up whenever the talk swings in that direction."

"Then you wouldn't be worried that he might let slip a word by accident, not meaning any harm?"

"Not he. You can be sure of that my king." Their eyes met. "You must not fall into Glic Tusil's error."

"Telling your king what he must and must not do?"

"Warning you, my king. It is as much as your life is worth."

"Threatening your king?"

"Warning my king not to spoil a good thing. I won't allow it."

"I can't let you talk like that, my dear master smith. I face enough disrespect as it is."

"They won't stop you, my king. Nobody can stop you now. Unless it were yourself."

"I know what you want to tell me. Enough! A change of subject is indicated. How is Kitt succeeding in his studies of bronze? You know he is a lowly ironsmith. Does he have even the smallest aptitude to attain a higher understanding of bronze?"

"He is the best apprentice I ever had. Need to tell or show him everything only once. He is one of those who talks to metal, and the metal answers, holding nothing back. Talent like that must not be wasted. I won't allow it; I won't allow the old monster to destroy his soul."

"How you insist, Master Gobin. I hear you. I heard you the first time."

"I didn't let him see the moulds but not for that reason."

"Better that way. How fortunate that you still happen to have those ancient moulds."

"Fortune had nothing to do with it, my king."

"Of course not. Manner of speech. You have held the smithy of Ulud long, dear Master Gobin?"

"My family has always held it, your majesty, from father to son. This is ending now."

"You don't have a son yourself?"

"I had sons. All stillborn. My wife died at the birth of the sixth. Ulud is not a good place for the young."

"That will change. The stars are coming right again, and the long down-swing is at an end. The star of Cryssumha is rising, as Vasara

194

and Dilo in the heavens, so copper and tin on earth. On the day of the mirror, the sword Slatynrigan will be forged in Ulud. The copper from Minit Claghini and the tin of Gwinminit Meingloud, the White Mountain Mine, will be brought to you. Do you know that I saw White Mountain with my own eyes, and it is nothing but a hole in the ground in the Bacenis."

*

When Kitt and Faibur arrived at the Mocking Bird, the tavern held only two guests.

Fidcal sat in his regular place at the window table, before him a half full glass of shining amber in the light of the sun sinking below the roofs of Dundingin.

A leather-clad man sat in the corner by the door leaning his back on the wall. Kitt knew him by sight; it was the big, dark-haired hunter from the Stag and Bottle Inn with the ice-blue eyes, Cynan Concen. He didn't seem to take notice of the newcomers, but Kitt sensed that to be as much camouflage as his own studied disinterest.

Beibini brought a glass and an Uskeva bottle for Faibur and a mug of beer for Kitt, and patted his biceps. "Your gold coin is still good."

"Would master Fidcal also accept a drink?" Kitt said.

"Supercilious pup. Where did they teach you that glib tongue?"

The Red Lily Knights had taught Kitt how to turn polite phrases, though he did not mention that. They too had secrets.

"What my father is saying is that he will allow you with pleasure."

Beibini topped Fidcal's glass from the bottle.

"Leave the bottle here, dear Beibini," Faibur requested.

She did, and her blue eyes filled with tears. "Everybody is so kind, but it makes me cry."

The smell and taste of beer brought back Blaitisin's face and her kiss. Kitt emptied half the tankard in one. It had no effect.

"Now, what do you want to know?" Faibur asked.

Kitt roused himself from his horrible reverie. "Many things. What did the war leader call the Bethrek?"

"Graykhol Rere. The Feen consider that beast the same as a warrior, a strong, cruel one. I once saw a Graykhol Rere, a Bethrek, from enough distance, so you see me sitting here. The way it looked at me...that's another thing I don't care to remember when sober. Like he knew me. So you killed a Bethrek?"

"Yes."

"Where's the skin?" Fidcal asked with his commercial interest aroused.

"The Murder Bear seems to have it," Faibur said. "Come on, Kitt, you got to tell me something sometime."

"Why does he," Fidcal said. "He's paying your drink."

"The other day you said Mangan Sorkera killed your friend? If you will speak about it? I try to find out as much as I can about the Feen."

Faibur waved his hand. "The Feen want to be spoken about after they are dead, for their deeds to be remembered. So I do. The least I can do. He was my Feen father, rather. As a boy, I was lost in the Bacenis once, and Stone with Horns found me."

"Rub it in!" Fidcal was scowling.

"I wanted to go with the hunters, father. But I was too young and clumsy. They left me behind, and I don't blame them. They were on the run. They're dead now. Stone with Horns saved me, taught me. Yes, it was Mangan Sorkera who killed him. He only took his heart and skull, not his honour, because my friend was a brave man, as the Singing Bear is a brave man. I wouldn't have wanted to see him like Hawkwing; it is better that he is dead, and so my friend thought too. They are not that different, the Amhas and the Feen, they don't recognise any way of life but their own. If you want to be their friend, you have to do everything their way. Exactly. They tolerate nothing else."

"Needless to say they don't have very many friends," the big forest runner remarked. His voice was deep and sober, and his broad sombre face with the bright blue eyes was impassive. "I knew Stone with Horns. Tried to kill each other a couple of times. So that's how he died. It is true that he grew grey like a badger and he must have slowed. Not even the Murder Bear would have caught him otherwise."

Faibur drank fast. "When the Feen kill a brave enemy in battle or under torture, they bury the right leg and left hand on the north side of the village, and left leg and right hand on the south side, the trunk west, and the skull in the east. But only those they respect.

196

They do the same with a Bethrek, a bear, or an Archantel lion. I guess they did with the Sheh Ri carcass too. They must have done it with Stone. They would do it to you. When he came...Mangan Sorkera..."

"The Murder Bear," Cynan Concen said. "Yes, I knew who he was when he came past the Stag and Bottle Inn."

"And you didn't say anything either?" Fidcal said outraged. "I would have called the city guards. What's wrong with you and my son? Been in the woods too long, that's what's the matter with you, have it on your brain. I believe you're fond of those murderous Woodstalkers."

"I'm fond of you too, for no good reason either, father. I thought Mangan Sorkera was daring me to come and avenge Stone. But for him to bring the Sheh Ri pelt might show that it is Kitt here foremost in his mind, because of the Bethrek skin. That doesn't mean he didn't challenge me also. I think he did."

"You don't have to go into the Bacenis any more, that's for the likes of him." Fidcal motioned to the big forest runner. "And he's afraid too, aren't you, Cynan Concen?"

"I don't bring mine to you. You're a miser."

"You don't have any to bring, daren't set foot into the Bacenis."

"I wait for the prices to go up, when you fat traders finally realise that your supply dried up for good. I won't risk my neck for little coin paid over with a grudge."

"Afraid, for all that you're as big a lug as this boy here. He dares what you don't."

"You're drunk, old man. And why not, but don't quarrel with me. Have another, this round on me."

"You came sniffing after the Sheh Ri pelt, that's what you're after," Fidcal accused.

"Of course. Any hunter would," Cynan Concen admitted. "And now there's talk about Bethreks. Hoped to overhear where they lair." He looked at Kitt.

"Latunsrigo."

"So." The big man didn't seem surprised.

More guests came in, and now all the tables were occupied.

Ryoni helped Baibini serving beer and food, but the waif still didn't speak. Beibini intercepted her when she headed for the table

197

where Kitt was sitting with the fur traders and went to serve them herself. "Here you go, gentlemen! The same again."

"She looks better, must be for seeing you, Kitt," Faibur remarked.

"But..."

"Nobody blames you. Blaitisin liked you, the last thing she fancied. Grief takes strange forms. I should know all about that."

An Amhas approached, attired in stained leather breeches and a dirty linen shirt that flopped around his emaciated frame; his hair was chopped untidily at shoulder-length.

He addressed Faibur. "I saw you sell bronze teeth to Canaras Muntrer." His voice was high and excited, and heads turned towards them.

"You've been having a nightmare, Lost Dog. How would he be in Dundingin?" Faibur muttered. "I just traded for skins today."

"Lord Morrik not like hear," Lost Dog said with a cunning sneer.

"He might feed your loose tongue to the Hounds of Marrak."

"Some say Prince Ardri nice new cloak. King's cloak. Lord Gasda not like hear. Lost Dog hear Lord Gasda come Dundingin."

"Rumours, my friend, rumours. Very unhealthy. Might get Lost Dog killed. Better drown them in the Stag and Bottle Inn?"

Coins clinked.

"Thankee Sir, Lost Dog didn't say nothing, didn't see nothing Sir, don't mind poor drunk Amhas. Lost Dog not always this man's name, Seven Steers this man's name, when Amhas great but now Amhas finished, and this man called Lost Dog."

When the Amhas slunk to the door, Cynan Concen stood up from his place in the far corner and came forward.

Lost Dog shrank before the icy blue eyes. "Gruk Radam let Lost Dog be. Lost Dog say nothing."

"See that you don't, or I'll give you yet another name. How does Lost his Balls sound to you?" Cynan Concen shouldered Lost Dog aside that he fell out of the door and sat down at Kitt's table. "So, Faibur," he muttered. "With Mangan Sorkera walking out of the gate there went the only chance you ever had to avenge Stone with Horns. You must know that if you're realistic."

Faibur glared. "I wouldn't have Mangan Sorkera torn to pieces by the mob of Dundingin. That's the last thing Stone would want. Not that I think they could get him. He didn't think so."

"Or he knows and trusts you."

"If he knows me, he must also know that one day I will go into the Bacenis after him."

"Then, Faibur, you will die." Cynan Concen merely stated a fact.

"As you say, then I'll die. And all I'll ask of any god is that I may die as well as Stone with Horns did."

"You're drunk. Talking rot. Both of you!" Fidcal took a hefty swig himself. "Turning the boy's head with your irresponsible nonsense."

"He called you Gruk Radam," Kitt blurted out. "Is that Amhas language and what does it mean?"

Cynan Concen regarded Kitt for a moment before he replied. "Kills on Sight," he said. "The Woodstalkers know that when they come within bow reach of me, I shoot, and I hit. The only way in the Bacenis."

"He knows already," Faibur said. "His name with the Feen is Gawthrin Lye."

"So," Cynan Concen said. "Now Latunsrigo, that is Kra-Tini Feen land, and right across the whole Bacenis. Did you come to Dundingin through the wood? From Isenkliff?" When Kitt looked bewildered: "You mentioned it in here the other night." He grinned.

"I came in on the river Zinnfluss this time. Farther south."

"Still across all the Bacenis."

Kitt really did not want to talk about the dead Woodstalker and the Hunters in the Mist.

Cynan Concen seemed to notice. "Another time," he said.

"Is the Amhas language like the Feen language?" Kitt asked. "Their word for bear seems different? Or do they mean different kinds of bear?"

"What do you want with their language?" Fidcal objected.

"Anything you could say to a wild Woodstalker is best said with something hard, sharp and heavy," Cynan Concen agreed.

"Where the man's right he's right, ruffian as he may be. Better it would be if you never went into the Bacenis again."

"But master Fidcal, I have to go. The Murder Bear has my Graykhol Rere, I mean Bethrek skin. That is the second one I lose to him."

"To lose one Bethrek skin is bad luck. To lose two is careless." Faibur snorted into his beer.

Even Cynan Concen allowed himself the tiniest twitch of his mouth.

Fidcal frowned. "Anybody can be a mangy forest runner and hunter; I have been one myself and had nothing from it but grief. But there are few smiths with a feeling for metal like you seem to have, from what master Gobin tells me. One mustn't praise apprentices to their face, it's bad for their character, and master Gobin won't like me to tell you. But I will say it. You are the best apprentice he ever had and one day you will be a great craftsman, one of the very great in fact. Gobin says so in these very words, and he knows. If you don't waste your talent on foolishness and get yourself killed before your time."

"Not everybody can kill Bethreks and outrun the Murder Bear either," Faibur said. "No to mention to babysit our precious prince in the Bacenis, for very little thanks, graceless bastard that he is."

This seemed to be common knowledge, not from him, Kitt hoped, horribly aware that he might have said more and not remember it. He put down his mug without drinking.

"Point is, being a good hunter is a scarce talent too," Faibur concluded.

"I drink to that," Cynan Concen said. He waved to Beibini.

"Brawny fool," Fidcal muttered.

Chapter 16
Bells and Mirrors

On the 4th day of Mezheven, Vasara, Mavors and Lute will stand in a triangle. That constellation is called The Mirror.

Ardri, King of Cryssumha, Star Observation Journal

The chimes jingled, and the bronze disk hummed, and Ardri looked into the shiny surface of the large mirror on the wall.

What he saw there was not his own face, but a room in the royal palace in Iwerdonn. He saw King Tirnmas sit with his large-knuckled hands folded in his lap, staring ahead with empty blue eyes. Beside him stood the Crown Prince Nolan Ri, called Flannan because of his thick, dark, red curls and sunny temper. Ardri's half-brother wore a simple leather tunic, breeches, and knee-high boots; on the leather were green marks and shiny places from the wearing of bronze armour.

"Lord Gasda? To Dundingin?" Flannan's voice came from the bells of the windchime above in a deep vibrating tone.

"He'll unite forces with Lord Morrik. They'll find Ardri."

"Something is not right there." The Crown Prince frowned, his pleasant hell-raiser face serious for once, as searched for words to express his unease. "It is just a feeling I've been having for some time. Father?"

Reluctantly, King Tirnmas met his son's and heir's eyes.

"It's that bad, is it?"

"Yes, brother, it's that bad," Ardri whispered.

Prince Flannan gave a start as if he had heard something, and Ardri stepped back from the bronze mirror. "I don't want to kill you, Flannan. If only you don't oppose me. You can board a new land like you board a trader. You can still be a king somewhere, brother, I would be glad for it, and if ever you should steer your ships towards

Cryssumha again, I shall be waiting on the shore with ten thousand soldiers to receive you in state."

Flannan made a full turn on his heel, his red curls flaring out behind him. "I'm going mad. Hearing voices."

"I hear voices all the time," King Tirnmas sighed. "Tell the servants to call my Queen Serenaiba, that she may come to me."

"I'll go get her myself."

"She'll get you," Ardri said.

The mirror fell dark, and the bells were silent.

***

Prince Flannan stormed through the palace corridors, and stopped before a high narrow wooden door inlaid with mother of pearl. A servant woman sat beside it. The prince did not wait to be announced, did not even take time to knock, but gripped the ivory handle and threw it open. The protest of the serving woman bounced off his back.

By the high window stood queen Serenaiba. She half-turned at Flannan's stormy entrance.

"That must all be your doing, Serenaiba!"

The Queen of Rilante looked at the irate Crown Prince out of her dark eyes, shining like the black star sapphires around her neck, and giving away as much. Just looked at him; she did not bother to explain or justify herself, as nine out of ten women, or more, would have done. Not for the first time, Prince Flannan thought what a remarkable queen this was, how dangerous in her quiet way, and how beautiful in her black and white fragility. No one would have thought she had three adult sons, with two of them probably dead. As always, she instantly contrived to make him feel like a brute, within the first minute that he had stomped into her room, bewildered and inarticulate. But this time he did not lower his voice. "What did you do with my last little brother? He always was a weird fish, but I happen to like him, and now I hear that he's lost too, like Ridevin and Kuranori?"

"Your father sends lord Gasda and a thousand men to Cryssumha to find him."

"He told me just now, and I wondered at once what devilry you are up to!" Behind his ferocity, the Crown Prince was very uneasy. If Queen Serenaiba thought that her Cryssumha faction was strong

202

enough to take on Gasda, then either she or Flannan was about to make a bad mistake.

"I think you meant to tell me that my husband wants me, Prince Nolan Ri?" Queen Serenaiba was the only one who didn't call him Flannan. She came towards him, and he gave way, as always. She laid a long slim hand on his chest, for a brief moment drowning him in the blackness of her eyes and the musk and lilies of her perfume. "The Royal Court is no place for you, Nolan Ri. You want planks under your feet, the sea wind, the chase."

Then she was gone. "Now where did I hear this today," Flannan muttered, several minutes late.

*

All that happened in Iwerdonn played out before the watching eyes of Castle Marrak, the mirrors of the Tower Tirdich.

Had it always been like that, Ardri wondered, and thought of his childhood, and his youth. It was difficult to comprehend that he had always been under the eye of the Master of Mirrors. "What will happen when my son is born, my first dark-eyed son, Glic Tusil? When I...disappear...who will reign, until he comes of age?"

"If anything untoward should happen to your majesty, for which I currently don't see any indication in the Star Pattern, your wife, Queen Neelam, would naturally reign for her son. She would be advised by a Throne Council consisting of the Prince Angkou and Queen Serenaiba -and my unworthiness."

"My mother." She was the focus, the catalyst, that never changes itself, Rivin Claghini, the Queen of the Mountain, Serenaiba, Neelam. Sometimes Ardri thought that it was the same woman always, different mirror images of the Eternal Queen of Cryssumha. "What I'd like to know is this: who has the upper hand, the Queen or you, Glic Tusil? Frankly, with the utmost respect to your abilities, my coin is on Serenaiba."

Glic Tusil bowed. "Your bet would win."

With one finger, Ardri traced the lines of the Star Patterns engraved on the smooth top of the bronze table. "Why didn't my mother marry lord Morrik, who is of the blood, even though a younger branch? Wouldn't that be the more direct way, than me marrying Morrik's daughter? Not that I'm complaining. She is a girl like a magnolia blossom. But she can hardly like being married to a,"

203

Ardri paused. "A mongrel. Her manners are, of course, too good to mention it."

"Because of the sun and the moon both involved in the Star Pattern."

"You mean because it was necessary to take Rilante first. Serenaiba would already have done that, like a beautiful mantis takes her hapless husband, as easily, if it wasn't for Flannan. Why haven't you been able to do something about him, Glic Tusil? You might not believe it, but I do like my big brother. You weren't considerate of my feelings, I take it?"

"Naturally not, and yes, it has been tried. The difficulty with the Crown Prince is that when he looks into a mirror, he sees only himself. Mirrors, I may remind you, are divides between worlds, where you are on one side, and your monster on the other. All the dark instincts rejected and left behind are there, waiting for you. If a man breaks his mirror while looking into it, then he and his monster come together and devour each other. Often, the better a person is the more powerful...and depraved...is the monster in the mirror. But Nolan Ri has never lain in conflict with himself, he has never wanted what he couldn't get, has never harboured feelings of hatred and rancour in his heart. He is a veritable Sun Child, and there is no monster waiting for him on the other side of the mirror. There are few men like that."

Ardri stepped close to Glic Tusil. "You are not to attempt my brother's life ever again, Master of Mirrors. I forbid you! Flannan is to sail away unharmed!"

"But will he, King Ardri?" Glic Tusil muttered at the closing door.

"How long?" A clear, sweet voice asked, and Queen Neelam stepped into the room from behind the tapestry, where she had been sitting in a recess and listening. She wore a long coppery brocade dress and held herself straight, her back arching slightly. Her dark, lustrous eyes looked intently at the Master of Mirrors who bowed very deep.

He knew immediately what the young Queen was asking him. "Only the one intermediate step is required. Queen Serenaiba bore three sons of mixed blood. But your son will be of the pure Blood of Cryssumha alone. Entirely. Perfect. It can be done."

"Do this!" she said. "I cannot stand more." She turned to go and turned back again, the train of her dress swishing over the floor. "Is it in your power to remove the taint from my husband, Master of Mirrors?"

"If he will take my lead."

"He won't," she said. "Can you do it, Glic Tusil?"

"It can be done. If you will trust me, and help me, Queen Neelam."

"I will," she said.

Once there had been nine Masters of Mirrors; of them, only Glic Tusil of Ulud survived, protected by the weapons of Rilante.

Ever since Rilante troops, loggers and farmers had extracted Ulud from the thick forest, Glic Tusil had striven to call back Cryssumha, again and again, and every attempt had failed. None of the royal blood of Cryssumha had succeeded in winning the crown Fenifindrune. Never had Glic Tusil come so near to his goal as now. The king of tainted blood wore the bronze crown; tainted blood would rule Cryssumha for a long time, but time did not matter to Glic Tusil, the last Master of Mirrors.

His eyes on the highly polished surfaces of his mirrors, he watched as the mirror constellation sank in the west, with Vasara, Mavors, and Lute forming a perfect rhombus with another small star, that was of no consequence at all, except on this day.

Chapter 17
The Forging of Slatynrigan

Today is a perilous day, the tenth day of the month Mezheven. Today, Vasara and Mavors will almost join. Dilo is still standing aloof, but soon he and Vasara will meet, and for that day Slatynrigan must be ready.

Ardri, King of Cryssumha, Star Observation Journal

The air was delirious with late spring. Kitt returned from an errand of Gobin's.

On the veranda of Fidcal's shop sat a pale young woman, a daughter of the left-hand yard neighbour. She was busy lining the Sheh Ri pelt with red and silver brocade. The shimmering black folds of the thick fur flowed around her like glistening tar. Biting off a thread with sharp pearly teeth, she smiled at Kitt from big black eyes, and he smiled back at her - and remembered that he should not do that. He often noticed a tendency to forget the existence of Castle Marrak, which took up half his horizon. This time also, again, he hadn't thought about it. He began to suspect that he was not the only one afflicted by this sporadic blindness towards the grey stone structure that squatted above Dundingin.

As he traversed the short distance to Gobin's smithy, he did not smile any more. In the courtyard, his eyes fell upon a heap of copper cubes, gleaming red, their regular shape betraying it to be the copper Ardri had brought from Mountain Minit Claghini. There was also the tightly woven packet, which Kitt knew contained grey sand, the tin ore from the Towers of Lightning. He still marvelled how Ardri had never dropped all this on his anxious way through the woods, pursued by the Woodstalkers.

"You know what this is, and you are wondering how it came here," Gobin remarked, and Kitt realised that an expression of the face could betray secrets as inevitably as a loose tongue. "Glic Tusil brought it in person. He came on business for the king. I thought it better that you and he wouldn't meet. You had differences."

In the excitement of learning so much about bronze, Kitt had almost forgotten about the alchemist too. Only when he woke in the dead of night from nightmares of black eyes in a mirror mocking him across the drowned Blaitisin, did he remember Glic Tusil. With the rise of the sun and the beginning of the noise of daily business around Gobin's smithy, the alchemist retreated into a realm of black fog.

"I had to lug two hundred pounds of scrap copper through the whole of Dundingin because you worried about that wizard's safety?"

"I'm sure a mere two hundred pounds didn't get you into a sweat. But it slowed you down."

"What are we to make of that ore?"

"The Sword Slatynrigan, the Findrun blade which the Kings of Cryssumha used to sacrifice to the mountain. You see Kitt, in the old times, if the mountain were given no blood it would take it, ten-fold, a hundred-fold. Mines would fall in and crush the workers, and stones would roll down the slopes and find flesh and bone. Therefore sacrifice was one of the main duties of the king and Slatynrigan is one of the royal regalia. The sword was lost when Cryssumha fell. Tonight is the night Glic Tusil has calculated for the new casting. It is the night when the constellation of the Mirror is perfect, when Vasara, Mavors and Lute will be standing at the exact same distance from each other."

"Is this the mould?" Kitt scrutinised the four feet long stone and turned it around; but he didn't find what he looked for, the crack that held the two halves together. It was a solid piece, with a small opening at the upper end. "How did you get the shape inside?"

"I didn't. This mould has been hidden, waiting for this day."

Kitt wondered, why was Gobin telling him all this, as this had to be one of the Cryssumha secrets and he wasn't sure, that he wanted to know more about it.

"Why am I telling you all this? The forging of Slatynrigan is another work I have to do alone. But you can help me with one thing if you do exactly as I say. Will you do that one thing for me?"

"Anything," Kitt said mystified. "What?"

"Go now and stay inside the smithy, do not come out tonight. Whatever happens, on no account cross the threshold. When you see me come running, close the door behind me as fast as you can. I know you can be very fast, and that's what I'm counting on."

"Can I watch from inside?"

"I hope you will, and not miss the moment when I start running. As long as you don't cross." Gobin pointed to the threshold which consisted of a long stone slab sunk into the earth.

From inside the smithy Kitt watched as Gobin placed the crucible filled with the copper and the tin ore in one oven and the stone mould into the other. The smith seemed a black giant before the firelight, his face lifted up to the sky. He closed the doors of the oven, locking in the firelight. Then they waited, each in his place, for the metal to smelt.

Kitt looked up into the darkening eastern sky where the wandering stars were already visible. The constellation known to Kitt as the Southern King hove up over the roofs of Dundingin to rule the sky with the splendour of many bright stars outlining the figure of a broad-shouldered man - from the belt on his slim waist hung a sword, and two more bright stars, which were the knees, became visible. The Rilante saw their Torin Daraval in this constellation, and Gobin called it the Eternal Hero. Kitt looked out for the changing patterns both Gobin, and Ardri, had pointed out to him. All he saw were six and eight-cornered patterns combining into a spider's web above his head, waiting to close around him. Idly he wondered what Mavors was doing in the Star Pattern of the sword Slatynrigan. It stood for iron, Ardri had explained.

The light of the stars was so bright that Kitt could see everything in the yard. His attention returned to where Gobin took the heated stone mould from the first oven and stood it upright. Then, with whirling hands, he took out from the other oven the crucible with the molten bronze and poured it into the mould in a fiery stream.

The moment when the thin, glowing metal stream broke off, the bronze smith dropped the empty crucible and came running towards the house on the road of firelight that was pouring from the open shutters of the ovens.

Suddenly Gobin stumbled as over an obstacle, although there was nothing visible. The big man crashed to his knees with an anguished cry.

Kitt darted out of the door, grabbed him by the scruff and dragged him across the threshold with one hand, pulling the door closed with the other. Something sharp thudded into the wood like the claw of a thwarted bird of prey; the thick planks bulged and creaked. The door held.

From outside came a shattering crash and a high-pitched scream. Panting, the smith rose from the floor, terror still filling his eyes. "Didn't I tell you to stay put? On no account come out? Thank you, Kitt! That was close. One day you must tell me, when you do as you are told, and when not. I'm sure I'm not the only one who'd dearly like to know."

After a while, Gobin opened the door a crack, and they looked outside, cautiously.

In the light from the two ovens mixing with the starlight, they saw the stone mould. The upper part of it had disappeared, and only the base still stood. In it stuck a sword shape, glittering with the silvery yellow of Findrun bronze.

"It is over," Gobin said. "We can come out." But he didn't move yet.

Suddenly, from the other side of the wall, rose a keening of women's voices. Kitt ran out to look over the wall into the pottery yard. In the bright light that poured from all the windows of the house, he saw that not one plate, jar or crucible was left whole. The potter lay on top of his pulverised earthenware, blood and brains splattered over the shards. There could be no doubt that he was dead. The wailing inside the house continued, but the door remained closed. As Gobin came across the yard to look over the wall, the lights in the potter's house went out abruptly.

Kitt threw a handful of straw onto the glowing coals of the smelting oven, and flames went up; their orange light washed into every corner of the yard and over the new sword. He looked around for the pieces of the upper part of the mould, and didn't see any trace of it - no splinters anywhere. He took hammer and chisel to crack open the rest of the mould so that Gobin could liberate the sword.

"A perfect cast," the bronze smith said, looking over the shining blade with satisfaction. He carried the new sword into the smithy, while Kitt remained outside. What had just happened, he wondered, as the straw fires burned out and it went dark. He looked up to the sky and watched as the gleaming pair of Vasara and Dilo sank west. From inside the workshop came the sound of hammering.

Kitt crossed the yard and opened the door. Gobin was working on the blade, hammering the edge. "This is the sword Slatynrigan," he said into Kitt's silence, interpunctuating every word with a hammer blow. "The mountain gives nothing without sacrifice. You get something, you must give something. This knowledge is in the blood of every man and woman in Cryssumha; every child is born with it. All the neighbours who chose to live beside a forge, they know. Potter Crochen, he knew. The Rilante can't understand this, but you can. You are a smith."

"The prices are high in Dundingin – Ulud."

"That they are."

"You didn't want to pay the price yourself. And I helped you get away with it."

"So, potter Crochen's death is your doing."

"No, it's not," Kitt said with sudden illumination. "It's yours."

"Yes. And so, it's on my conscience, not yours. What's more, you aren't responsible for all my actions hence just because you saved my neck now." Gobin paused his hammering to cock his head and grin at Kitt. "You aren't responsible for what Slatynrigan will do, either. For you, that is a valuable lesson. Take it to heart!" He resumed his hammering along the edge of the bronze sword. He didn't ask his apprentice to take a turn, and Kitt didn't offer.

The night was pitch-dark outside, past midnight, when Gobin laid down the hammer. For the first time, Kitt really looked at a bronze sword as a weapon. Before that day, bronze blades for him had only been pieces of old metal discarded for the superior steel. This sword lay on the anvil new and gleaming, and there was a red light wavering about it that was more than the mere reflection of firelight on metal.

Kitt's hand neared the blade, and hovered without touching. His fingertips tingled, and he felt the hair rise on his head. This sword had power, a smouldering, impersonal, aggressive magic. He had thought that the alchemist was just an old fool. He had disregarded Gobin's talk about star magic, dismissed Ledrithud as something less consequential than his mother's Seidar and Zaubar. He pulled back his hand without having touched the bronze. "I should have paid more attention to what Glic Tusil said."

"That's as may be. If he told you something worthwhile, it was likely to be a tiny grain of truth hidden in a cloud of mysterious hints. Only another adept would know what he meant."

A knock came on the door.

"Talk about a devil," Gobin remarked. He didn't seem surprised despite the hour.

Kitt opened the door. Outside was the hunch-backed boy in the black-and-copper page livery of Castle Marrak with both arms around a big bronze jug with a lid.

"Ah," Gobin said, "A jug of wine to refresh ourselves from the hot work. Tolosan?"

The hunchback nodded, sidled in crablike and stood the jug on the work table by the window. Relieved of his heavy burden, he sidled out again without having spoken a word.

"The good Glic Tusil, how thoughtful. That was Graup, his page boy. Never speaks. I don't know if he's been forbidden or prevented. I know that you have forsworn drink...at least you said so once." Gobin's black eyes twinkled almost in the old manner. "I advise you to firmly keep up that resolution where this wine is concerned."

Kitt eyed the bronze jar with the joint lid. "You think he did something to it?"

"Of course he did."

"Poison?"

"Worse." Out of a silver casket, Gobin took a polished golden disk. "My brother Eurich, the goldsmith, sent me this from Iwerdonn." He placed the disk upon the lid of the jar. From inside came a gurgling and hissing; it sounded as if the wine was boiling.

Gobin chuckled. "Just as I thought. The thing can't come out now, because of the gold. These creatures can't stand gold, or silver. Listen to its raging!"

"You don't seem to mind?"

"Not at all." Gobin chuckled again. "I don't think Glic Tusil seriously expected this to work. We know each other so long, the

211

Master of Mirrors and I. It's just customary to try, good form, you see. Indeed, if he didn't attempt my life tonight, it would almost be like accusing me that my work was not good." He yawned. "We can sleep now. I am dog tired. It must have been the running. I'm not a young man, and I feel these things in my bones. I never ran so fast in my life. And it nearly wasn't fast enough."

Gobin threw himself down on the long wooden chest that was his bed and dragged a woollen blanket over himself.

*

Lying on a stack of cowhides which served as his bed behind the anvil, Kitt felt the stars moving in their courses above. He didn't need to see Dilo, the Lord of Lightning, to know that he stood deep over the western horizon. He thought that he felt the other Wandering Stars weaving their pattern beneath the horizon: Vasara, Lute, Mavors. The lid of the wine jar rattled faintly. At last, Kitt slept, waking fitfully from time to time to see if the gold disk was in place.

And then in the darkest hour of the night, the hour of thieves, and nightmares, the rattling grew louder. The gold disk fell off, and a hard black head with long jaws spiked with sharp teeth lifted the lid and rose out of the jar. Spider limbs ending in obsidian claws propelled the thing to where Kitt lay, unable to move hand or foot. Only when the nightmare was above him, Kitt regained the use of his limbs. His hands found a hilt; and it was not the hilt of his iron sword, but that didn't matter right now. He gripped the strange hilt, and his hand slipped just a little, so that he hit out with the flat of the blade. The monster was flung against the wall screeching.

Then Kitt woke up, to find himself standing in the middle of the room with the new bronze sword in his hand, the sword named Slatynrigan. He heard Gobin curse and saw sparks glimmer and a small flame flicker up.

Gobin lighted a wax candle, another, and a third. In their light, they saw Slachlan, who was lying crumpled up by the wall, a long knife beside him. The gold disk on the jar rattled faintly.

"I dreamt it had fallen off."

Gobin sprang towards Slachlan and yanked the slumping body into a standing position against the wall. "Thank Rivin Claghini, Queen in the Mountain, no blood," he breathed.

Kitt laid the bronze sword back on the anvil and stepped away from it, opening and closing his hand to get rid of a feeling as if thin hot wires were pulling at his nerves.

Slachlan laughed, it was a happy sound. All the lines in his face had smoothed out as if a dark cloud had lifted, and sunlight streamed over a desolate and barren land. His eyes were not black now but brown, of such a light hazel colour that the change was visible in the candle light.

Gobin released the smiling Steward of Castle Marrak, and he just sat there and hummed a little tune with a rusty voice more suited to command the burning of a village, the torture and death of bound victims.

"Slatynrigan has drunk his mind," Gobin said.

"How?"

At the sound of his voice Slachlan turned his idiot's smile onto Kitt.

"I have forged the Queen's Ore at the conjunction of three wandering stars and the sword Slatynrigan has returned. It is not merely like the ancient sword - it is the ancient sword itself. Each time Slatynrigan is swung, it takes something, a life, a soul, a mind, and what it takes it keeps. Hundreds of generations of sacrifices, and they are all in this blade that I made."

"Why did you make a thing like that?"

"That is what I do. I am Gobin. There always is a Gobin in Ulud, and when there is a king in Cryssumha, the Gobin alive in that time forges the sword Slatynrigan."

"This thing needs the sheath," Kitt said. "No, we need the sheath. You made it, I know. Where is it?"

Gobin brought the sheath, a long object of shining bronze, which seemed to bud and swell into strange fruit. He slipped the blade into it. "I should have done that first thing. Why didn't I?"

Kitt recognised the globular design, the smooth ornaments on the lip and wondered if the sheath was an improvement of the situation. He looked at the sword, laying there on the anvil, so like the one he had seen raised in sacrifice in his dream of Ancient Cryssumha. He thought that he still was in that dream, that they were all dreaming it, Ardri, Glic Tusil, Gobin, Slachlan, and he. The dream was becoming more real every day, and the Bacenis wood and

213

the kingdom of Rilante were becoming more unreal. More and more, he became aware of a strange element marring that dream, an asymmetry that had to go before the vision of Cryssumha could finally become real. He, Kitt, had to go.

He woke with a start. Incredibly he had slept again, dreamed with that sword on the anvil near him, Slachlan giggling in the corner, and Gobin looking at him with his black Cryssumha eyes.

Kitt sat bolt upright.

Gobin wasn't looking at him, he was asleep.

"Glic Tusil didn't bring the mould," Kitt said aloud.

"Eh, what?" The bronze smith sat up, rubbing his eyes.

Gobin had been so very secretive about those moulds and Kitt had thought himself very mature for not asking about them. Now he felt only naive. "You said it had been hidden. That is even true, you had it here all the time. You said you didn't make it, but you must know how the shape got into the stone?"

"Can't I get any sleep in my own house tonight?"

"I don't want to sleep. Let's work! There are more than a hundred lance heads to finish and forty pounds of bells and mirrors to smelt."

"Pain in the butt, that's what you are," Gobin muttered. "I don't blame the Master of Mirrors for losing patience with you. Fire the oven then. Just don't burn down the house, is all I ask." He scrambled down from his bed.

Moving the clattering metal, the smiths shattered the grey silence of morning.

"Where are the tongs?" Kitt looked around for the tool he used to move the hot clay moulds.

Slachlan crouched in the yard giggling like a spiteful child. "You'll never find them now."

"Blast the imbecile!" Gobin was annoyed. "Better find them fast, or the tin and lead will boil out, and the metal won't pour properly."

Kitt found his tongs in the water trough.

They worked until the sun rose.

***

214

This night of the great conjunction, the Master of Mirrors did not sleep, nor did Ardri, King of Cryssumha.

It was the night when the sword Slatynrigan would return, the last and most powerful of the Royal Insignia. The crown Fenifindrune bestowed the legitimation. The Mooncat cloak signified the vanquishing of the savage woods, a symbol without power that Ardri promised himself to one day fill with meaning. Slatynrigan gave the power.

The young King of Cryssumha and his alchemist faced each other across the patterns engraved on the round bronze table in the conservatory of Castle Marrak. In the tall bronze mirror on the wall, their images stood eye to eye. Above reeled the Wandering Stars. Already, the Mirror constellation was less perfect.

"Your Majesty, even the slightest doubt at this time that the sword Slatynrigan has returned..."

"I am certain now. You have been blind, unforgivably blind. It is the Eternal Hero! Not Mavors!"

"It makes no change. Both are a terrible danger. If you think you can dominate him, you are in error. You cannot even predict him. Your barbarian pet is a monster, your Majesty. I have found out that he has bad blood, the worst that ever tainted the earth, descended from a long line of iron-willed slayers."

"Why Glic Tusil, that is too interesting. Please tell me more."

"Did you ever, your Majesty, in the course of your studies, come across records speaking of the Kri?"

Ardri whistled. "The perfect warriors who destroyed the souls of men as well as their bodies, and you say one such is here? Yes, I too consider that a portent. I was right about him, again I was right."

"They went armed with iron and their god was Iron Mavors."

"So what if it was? Can't you see that they were mere weapons themselves, that anyone could grip the hilt? And all you can think about is to destroy a precious and powerful weapon like that, possibly the last one left? You are getting old, too old; I am right about that too. You are afraid of risks, and that is why your star pattern is old and crusted and as fragile as a spider net, a pattern that was broken once by savage stone axes, and never mended properly. It can be broken again."

215

"Not this time. I won't allow anything that can break the pattern. Nothing." The alchemist and the king faced each other like duellists. "Prince Angkou taught you well, King of Cryssumha, but from the beginning, I have seen the flaw in your calculations."

Ardri spoke low, evenly. "Glic Tusil, you serve Cryssumha without needing to sleep, you lurk in mirrors, and you speak in the voice of the bells, but your star is Lute, and the number of Lute is eight. Beyond eight no Master of Mirrors can see. The number of Mavors is nine, so what can you know about Mavors? The King of Cryssumha can see beyond eight because the sum of six, Vasara, and three, Dilo, is nine, and so can Gobin see, because copper is six, and tin is three, and the sum of copper and tin is bronze. Realise that you have overstepped your boundaries. You won't keep me from gripping the hilt of the perfect weapon, to cut the strings of your royal dancing puppet."

Glic Tusil bowed, deep enough so that his long black hair curtained the white mask of his face. Once again, Ardri heard the low, ugly grating noise of the Master of Mirrors grinding his teeth.

***

"Is it permitted to enter?" Prince Ardri stood in the door of the smithy. On his shoulders lay the cloak made of the Sheh Ri pelt, and the crown Fenifindrune sat on his black hair.

Slachlan crawled towards him on his knees and buried his big hands into the thick fur, burbling with delight. With a quick, brutal movement, Ardri pressed Slachlan's wrists. The knotty fingers opened, and the big man cowered whimpering and nursing his numbed hands that hung down limply. Ardri's eyes lit on the blade lying on the anvil, then looked at Slachlan.

"I had finished the sword Slatynrigan and we slept, when he came. "Gobin said. "We did not recognise him. The sword …"

"What happened here, Gobin? You know, that nobody must blood Slatynrigan but a born King of Cryssumha in sacrifice. Tell me about it, leave nothing out!"

"There was no blood. Kitt hit him with the broad side, and Slachlan became like you see him. But there was no blood, not one drop, not even a red scratch."

216

Kitt thought he saw a moment of fear in Gobin's eyes, and that surprised him. He had thought that the bronzesmith was afraid of no-one.

Ardri stepped inside the smithy to the anvil; he touched the sword hilt. "A pity about Slachlan," he said. "His family has served mine since the days of Ancient Cryssumha."

"Until last night," Kitt said, warily watching Ardri's hands.

Ardri tore his eyes away from the sword and looked at him with eyes that were black, not blue. "He was jealous of you, Kitt, because it was you who protected me in the Bacenis. But I did not think he would attack a friend of mine."

"You must forgive me...friend...that I suspect you sent him because I know your precious secret. You couldn't take me out by yourself. Not by creeping up from behind and in the darkness."

"Have a care, Kitt! You are speaking to the king!" Gobin said in a shocked voice.

None of the young men paid attention to him, and he turned his back and leaned at the doorpost to look out into the main street.

"You know, I may have done so," Ardri admitted. "Entirely unintentionally, of course. I told him that you had pledged silence about what you saw in the Bacenis and that I trusted you. But it seems he was not prepared to take any chance."

"Your tame alchemist wasn't taking chances either."

"Glic Tusil?" Ardri looked puzzled. "I asked him to teach you about bronze as a special favour to me, and he agreed. And you burned down his tower."

"It was the only way to smelt the Evil Ore, as he demanded that I do. He talked about stars and transmutations. Not a word about the poisonous fumes."

"I didn't know anything about the Evil Ore."

"Looks as if a king doesn't need to know everything. He doesn't even have to want anything. It's all done for him." The lid on the wine jar rattled, and Ardri looked at it. "I didn't send this wine," he said quickly.

"What about the flask you kept offering me in the Bacenis?"

"I drank that wine myself, you saw me!"

His mother's, the healer Aslaug's, attentive pupil, Kitt could think of more than one trick to accomplish something like that, and

217

he smiled cynically. It was the first time that such an expression marred his face.

Ardri shook his head. "Dead men keep their mouths shut, that's an old and tested truth to which I subscribe, and I don't deny it. But you have too quick an eye, and even if I had managed to slip you a dose, you might still have lived long enough to lock those big hands of yours around my neck. It was too dangerous, and only a fool would attempt it. I am not stupid. Therefore, the wine was all right. Surely you can give me credit for intelligence, if for nothing else."

Kitt shrugged without even bothering to answer that.

"A king must not be ruled by emotions," Ardri went on; he sounded as if it was important to him, that Kitt should see his point. "The King of Cryssumha follows his star pattern. Glic Tusil reads the same stars, and he acts on it. Incidentally, we cannot agree on the nature of the Red Star Mavors."

The way Kitt watched his hand that touched the sword recalled to Ardri the memory of the iron blade at his throat in Minit Claghini. He shook his head, smiling ruefully. "Poor Slachlan. This was my slim chance, and he spoiled it. Look at him, playing with his knives and not cutting himself even now. His head has forgotten, but his hands have not. A useful tool, but far from perfect. You would have been perfect. I would have taken that weight of responsibility, of doubt and regrets, from your shoulders, and you wouldn't have minded killing anymore."

Ardri lifted the sheathed sword, very slowly; he kept his hands away from the hilt. Kitt's light-grey eyes reminded him of the wolf cub, promising death if he made a wrong move now. Even so close to success, Kitt's iron sword, never far from him, could hew through the web of the Star Pattern with one slash.

A noise of drumming and hoofbeats coming up the main street broke the tension.

"We have company," Gobin said from the door.

A column of mounted soldiers came in sight. The first rider was a tall, red-bearded man on a huge brown stallion, who held himself erect in the saddle, his mail a dazzle of gilded Findrun bronze. Out of cold blue eyes, he looked down on Dundingin.

"Lord Gasda, in person," Ardri said and retreated a step inside the smithy.

218

The Dog of Rilante went past without noticing the crowned King of Cryssumha in his full regalia. Behind Gasda came horse soldiers four abreast, compact red-haired men, in silvered mail.

"A hundred," Gobin said when the last had passed.

"Nine hundred are camping outside the gate," Ardri added. "They make absolutely no difference, not now, because everything is coming together on earth as in the skies." With the pelt coat swinging, he turned around in a flash and with the same movement drew the bronze blade and struck the bench by the window. It fell into two pieces.

When he completed his turn, Kitt had his sword in hand.

"You are nervous, my friend." Ardri laughed.

"With friends like you, I need no enemies."

"With enemies like you, I feel safer than with my friends." Now by the door, Ardri's eyes were blue again. "I trust you, Kitt."

"I don't trust you, Ardri." The bitterness had disappeared from Kitt's face; he even smiled. It was a hard smile, and there was finality in his face, a judgement.

Ardri saw it, and he flushed. That surprised him. "So you have lost that childish naiveté of yours, touching, but stupid. You know what, Kitt, you do owe me thanks for that lesson."

"Let's call it quits then."

"I don't think that I can. My life is worth a lot to many, and I feel that I still owe you."

Ardri's upright figure was silhouetted briefly in the square of the door, and with another swing of the Sheh Ri pelt cloak, he was gone. Slachlan shambled after his master.

Kitt considered the ruins of the stone bench. He didn't know how to fashion a steel blade that could have wrought this sort of destruction.

Chapter 18
Chaining the Dog of Rilante

Ardri overtook Lord Gasda and his men on an underground lane of ancient Ulud, delirious with the knowledge that Slatynrigan could cut his way through them if he so chose. He did not choose because he had plans with Lord Gasda. There was a worse fate possible for the Dog of Rilante, and Ardri meant for him to have it and taste it to the full.

One of Ardri's earliest memories was Lord Gasda leaving the Sun Temple of Iwerdonn at the winter solstice, his blue eyes shining in a fanatical light. Striding past the Stone Ship where the Royal Family stood in their place before the golden column, he saluted King Tirnmas and the Crown Prince, and his cold blue eyes passed over the three younger princes, the mixed blood. Then and later, he never bothered to salute this royal child, Serenaiba's son, who was taught in arcane knowledge since he could speak and understand words.

Gasda had worshipped the first queen, Murine, Flannan's mother. As all soldiers of Rilante did, he adored Flannan, the Crown Prince. Flannan, strong and bold and always laughing, appeared to be the one standing in the sun always, while Ardri stood in the shadows, waiting.

Arrived in Castle Marrak, he had just time to get to the Royal Tower Tirbrennin to divest himself of the crown Fenifindrune and lay down the sword Slatynrigan.

Through all of this, he was watched. The Master of Mirrors had no access to Tirbrennin; Ardri had revived that ancient spell. But there in the mirror was the pale face, the image so clear that it was the same as an actual presence. Ardri wondered if Glic Tusil intended to leave him alone sometimes.

"By the way," he addressed the mirror image, "Kitt doesn't seem to drink wine. At least, he wouldn't accept any from me, when I offered. I didn't mention this little detail, not knowing what you planned."

The Master of Mirrors shrugged thin shoulders. "There will be something eventually."

"Whatever you're up to where Kitt is concerned, it won't work. You're wrong about Mavors, but you are so persistent in your error that you may yet infuse it with reality and turn Kitt into my implacable enemy, and then you'll say you were right all along. That, Glic Tusil, is the only danger coming from Mavors."

Noise surged up from the usually silent courtyard, calls and the stamping of horses. Ardri ran to the window facing the town and looked out, swiping aside a crow which was balancing there. It cawed angrily and flapped its wings.

The young king saw the body of a hundred riders amassed at the gate. Farther down, he could see another troop of soldiers in the main road. They moved purposefully, stationing men at every corner.

"The city of Dundingin is taken. They feel in control, and they are." Ardri laughed. "Lord Gasda has arrived at the gate. I must hurry and greet my father's most faithful general without delay. Excuse me, venerable Master of Mirrors."

Glic Tusil's image bowed, smiling a thin smile that seemed in danger to crack the white mask of frozen fury.

Ardri kept on the Mooncat cloak. This animal hadn't been seen in Cryssumha for centuries, and there was a chance that no Rilanteman knew what it represented. But even if they did, it needn't worry him. Besides, this animal skin had been the talk of the town for days; the Sheh Ri could not be kept a secret. And not last, Ardri felt splendid in that cloak, and that was how he wanted to meet Lord Gasda. The delicious innuendo was another bonus.

Before descending from the King's Tower directly into the throne room, Ardri picked up two golden discs four inches wide with a ship on one side and the sun on the other, with the name of each lost prince engraved on both sides, once in reverse and once right. Ardri owned such a disc with his name, and so did Flannan. These were the seals of the Princes of the Royal House of Rilante, destined to be found on their bodies if they died. Ridevin and Kuranori had divested themselves of these vestiges of Rilante before they went into the Bacenis as Kings in Waiting, just as as their youngest brother had. Their reign of Cryssumha had been short; to this day, Ardri did not know when Kuranori's death had made him the King in Waiting.

"Lord Gasda!" the new Steward of Castle Marrak announced and threw open the high bronze doors.

Ardri received his father's general in the middle of the great hall. The tall windows were obscured by long swathes of thick dark red velvet, and hundreds of candles burned, but only in the first part of the long room, while the back with the dais and the throne remained in the shadows.

The young King of Cryssumha watched Lord Gasda walk towards him, tall and golden in the bright, gilded Findrun bronze mail. He had taken off his yellow-crested helmet to reveal short curls of strawberry-blond hair which proclaimed his race like a banner.

Behind him came Captain Warmond and a soldier in black leather with bronze rings sewn to it. His short hair and beard were of the brightest red Ardri had ever seen, his features unremarkable, sunburnt and freckled.

Lord Gasda still looked at the youngest Prince of Rilante with the same disregard as he had then, but this time he did of course salute. "The king will be overjoyed to hear that the Prince Ardri is alive and well." Gasda himself did not appear overjoyed. "When the prince is ready to journey, we will return to Iwerdonn."

"Delighted to see you, my dear Lord Gasda. We won't go back just now. I am needed here."

The Dog of Rilante stiffened even further. "The orders of the king were explicit. To ride to Dundingin and if need be into the great woods called the Bacenis, to rescue the Prince Ardri from whatever danger threatened him and bring him back to Iwerdonn. Now that I see that you are safe..."

"Yes Lord Gasda, I am back from the Bacenis. And I have found Kione Lonnir."

For a long moment Gasda stood as if struck, staring at Ardri in mute surprise. Slowly, another expression began to form on his face, that of a man desperately yearning to believe. A shadow of distrust passed and went, like an unwelcome guest.

Ardri was ready for him with a face radiating enthusiasm. "Only three days from the Struenfoly."

Cold formality dissolved into speechless joy, a change Ardri thought was almost comic in this correct soldier. "My lord prince, I thought...they said..."

"I know what they said, Lord Gasda. My brothers went into the Bacenis before me, to search for this lost place most revered in Rilante, also marking the easternmost border of the realm. To prove that we are Princes of Rilante to those who call us the Cryssumha brood." The bitterness in his words was genuine. He had the satisfaction to see a flush creep up in Gasda's cheek. "My brothers are still there. I could not bring their bones through the Bacenis, only this." From under the She-Ri cloak he brought out the two royal seals.

The three Rilante officers stared at the two golden disks.

Ardri drove home his advantage. "The Princes Ridevin and Kuranori never returned, but I did. The legends are true, Lord Gasda. It is all true. Golden Torin Daraval stands still there, in the prow of his ship Murdris, behind him his twelve shipmates, held by bands of foul Donadroch woods magic. We will mobilise all troops and take Kione Lonnir back into Rilante."

Ardri approached the general, laid a hand on Gasda's arm, and looked into the blue eyes, fascinated with the spectacular results a simple gamble on a childhood memory had paid. A minute ago, that man had been his implacable enemy, and now he was his own just as completely.

Ardri smote a bronze gong and a page came running. "Tell lord Morrik to come here, at once." The page darted away.

"Morrik doesn't...share my feelings about Kione Lonnir, naturally," he said confidentially. "But he is willing to do the favour to me, and naturally he aches to avenge my brothers. He just wasn't sure that we were strong enough. Now that you are here, our force will win through and what is more, hold the place."

Lord Gasda cleared his throat. "By your leave, my prince, my men will be sufficient."

"But the Woodstalkers! You see, there is an agreement with the Amhas that the troops of Rilante would not cross the Struenfoly as long as it runs to the sea. That agreement is null, naturally, considering that we had no knowledge of Kione Lonnir being in the treaty area. There will be trouble, though."

"The Amhas." Gasda snorted. "Those sorry, drunken savages."

"True, they are just downtrodden curs but consider how they kept the secret of Kione Lonnir from us, all this time. And we are not sure how many of them there are now. They must have been breeding like rabbits under Rilante protection. Also, there are other wilder Woodstalker tribes, deeper in the woods. There's the Murder Bear, and he might force the Amhas to join him and attack us." Ardri saw Warmond nod to his every word.

"Time we sort him out too, as we're at it. This border area has been a mess for too long. We'll ride at once."

"Surely not today, nor tomorrow, lord Gasda. Your men have just arrived after the long ride from Iwerdonn. You will want to take in stores, plan carefully."

Again, Lord Gasda snorted impatiently.

The saturnine figure of Lord Morrik appeared in the doorway, and Ardri turned towards him with a show of eagerness.

"Morrik, at last! When can your men get ready to cross the Struenfoly?"

"We can start requisitioning the barges tomorrow at dawn, if you will it, my...prince, and move the day after tomorrow."

Gasda barely acknowledged Morrik. "It's not necessary Prince Ardri, and frankly, my men would not like it."

Ardri seemed blithely unaware of the tangible antagonism between the two army leaders, one a lord of Rilante, the other of Cryssumha. "Do you think we should send an embassy to the Amhas before taking any action? We might give them a chance to comply of their own accord? They should leap to it, considering. And if they don't, we know exactly where we are with them."

Lord Morrik looked at Ardri carefully. "I've always said wipe out the whole dirty, devious, useless gaggle of paupers down to their pups. All I need is the order, and I'll do it, at once, and I'll not ask anyone's help."

"I and my men will ride to Kione Lonnir today. Alone!" Lord Gasda said with finality. "Just provide the barges for the river-crossing."

224

"Banquets await you in castle Marrak. I simply insist. And as you will need me to describe you the way, you will have to humour me."

Gasda looked at Ardri as if he would have liked to put him to the question. "Tomorrow then."

"If you're sure, lord Gasda." Ardri studiously avoided meeting Lord Morrik's eyes. That easy, he couldn't believe how easy this pious ass made it to get rid of him. To be fair, it was a good story, apparently backed by hard proof, and he couldn't blame Gasda for falling for it.

He waited until the bronze doors closed behind the Dog of Rilante pacing away impatiently, before he allowed himself to give in to the laughter that shook him. "Many more heads for Kione Lonnir! I shall fill that valley with enough skulls to put a final stop to Torin Daraval's ship!"

Lord Morrik witnessed the outbreak impassively. "What if this fanatic wins through against all the odds?"

"If anyone can, it would probably be Gasda. I'm the first to acknowledge that, even though I can't stand the dog." Ardri laughed, it was normal laughter this time. "Why, then I'd be rid of the Woodstalkers, and it would be extraordinary bad luck indeed if that victory doesn't cost Gasda most of his men. I cannot lose." Ardri fixed his father in law with a hard stare. "No, I cannot lose. Better get used to it."

"Yes, your Majesty." Lord Morrik bowed, deeply.

*

The barracks of the Dundingin city guards were abuzz with preparations to cross the Struenfoly.

On the porch of the commando barrack, beside the impatient Lord Gasda, stood the soldier with the bright red hair and beard, who had accompanied the Dog of Rilante into Castle Marrak. He was known by the name of Gilroy and his official rank was that of a captain of the queen's bodyguard, the late Queen Murine's, naturally. They were still called the Queen's Service, but they did not serve the present Queen of Rilante. There had always been a lot of circumspection about the Queen's Service. Now Gilroy wondered if it fell to him to prevent the Rilante host from rushing across the

Struenfoly into the Wood called the Bacenis populated by savages, how many, nobody knew.

Torin Daraval, his ship Murdris, and Kione Lonnir, the place where it stood still, had been the shimmering mirage on the Eastern horizon for as long as he could remember listening to fairy-tales and heroic ballads. How did he feel about his hero becoming real? One part of him felt the same excitement as he saw glowing in Lord Gasda's face. As the ranking officer of the Queen's Service in Dundingin, he felt profound distrust for all things Cryssumha, and that included Prince Ardri.

"Have you perchance had a good look at Prince Ardri's cloak, my Lord Gasda?" he finally ventured.

"Cloak? What do I care what the Prince wears?" Gasda said absently. "There's Warmond, at last."

"It's a Mooncat pelt."

"Is it?"

"Surely you know what that means, my lord?"

The blue eyes became cold and hard; for a moment, the old Gasda was back. "I didn't know that you cared so much about fashion, Gilroy."

"Fashion? Oh, yes, fashion. The fashion of Cryssumha. Must I really remind you, my Lord, that the Mooncat cloak is one of the insignia of the Kings of Cryssumha? Since the fall of the citadel of Minit Claghini that animal was never seen again, it disappeared into myth. So where does that cloak come from?"

"An heirloom, I should say. His mother is of the ancient royal family … which, in all fairness, can't be helped. Are the provisions coming?" This was directed at Warmond.

"As fast as they can," the Guards' Captain said. "Not the best time of year, just before sowing."

"That is what I'm talking about, Sir," Gilroy persisted. "The Mooncat cloak was worn by all kings of Cryssumha. What do you think will happen when it is being paraded in this part of Rilante again? By one of the Cryssumha Brood, no less? There will be unrest at the very least."

"A cloak doesn't make a king," Captain Warmond said. "The crown Fenifindrune, the sword Slatynrigan, those are the main insignia of Cryssumha. They were lost when the Woodstalkers tore them from the bloody body of their last king so many generations ago. I have nothing to say against Prince Ardri, he appears wholly loyal to Flannan...I mean to say the Crown Prince. I was there the day when some Woodstalkers brought in the Mooncat pelt to sell, this is a coincidence."

"They say Prince Ardri has journeyed to Minit Claghini, the old Cryssumha citadel, in the quest for Fenifindrune," Gilroy persisted.

"His quest was Kione Lonnir," Gasda said firmly. "Naturally, he and his brothers wanted to redeem themselves. In my eyes, they did. That Ardri found Torin Daraval's ship is proof enough."

"It is said that Prince Ardri only returned alive, because he had the help of some barbarian woodsrunner who kept him safe from the Woodstalkers. That barbarian is still in Dundingin, and he could tell us where Prince Ardri really went."

Warmond rubbed across the scar that split his face. "You mean Kitt, from Isenkliff. I know the boy, he's an apprenticed smith. He doesn't talk about what went on in the Bacenis. Not at all. But somebody on Marrak wants to make sure. There have been...attempts to shut his mouth for good. They didn't succeed."

"That means we can pull him in for questioning," Gilroy said. "Tell me where I can find him!"

"Don't waste time with side issues," Gasda snapped. "When we have Kione Lonnir, the insignia of Cryssumha don't matter anymore. We have to get ready to cross the Struenfoly the day after tomorrow. What about the river barges?"

"On the way, my lord," Warmond said.

"Why does everything take so long?" Gasda burst out. A wagon column hove in sight, and he jumped down from the porch and strode away to meet it.

Guards' captain and serviceman did not look at each other.

"Kione Lonnir, three days from here," Warmond said pensively. "I never thought. None of the woodsrunners ever mentioned it."

"There is no...error possible, do you think?"

"You mean do I think Prince Ardri told a barefaced lie?"

"Well, do you?"

"I don't know you so very well Gilroy, and I never quite knew what your position was."

"Queen's Service. We serve Flannan, you and me both. And I wonder if Prince Ardri told this lie about Kione Lonnir to divert attention from his real purpose? That he may as well have found those Royal seals in Minit Claghini, because the other two Cryssumha Brood princes had the selfsame traitorous intention?"

Warmond nodded. "He didn't mention Kione Lonnir when he returned, not a word. He may have had his reasons to keep that up his sleeve, but it seems strange. Now that Gasda arrives and would ask questions, he springs it on him. And I will say that three days into the Great Wood called Bacenis may be a longer way than anyone thinks. Prince Ardri spoke the truth about that at least, and it worries me."

"Feen, Amhas, all the same."

No, it is not! The Amhas are beaten, the Feen are not. That is the difference! The outcome of such an expedition is by no means certain; you can take that from me."

"What can we do?" Gilroy asked. "There is no doubt that we will cross the Struenfoly tomorrow? The provisions and boats will be there?"

"They will," Warmond said grimly. "There may be a delay. A day, at most. That's all I can manage, seeing Gasda's present mood, and he'll bite off my head for it."

"No time to be lost, then." Gilroy squared his shoulders.

Chapter 19
Monster in a Jar

A crow flew into the Mirror Chamber, cawing with a loud abandoned noise that reverberated from the walls, drowning the voices of the windchimes. It was the same crow Ardri had seen before, and it settled on the window sill, tilted its head and peered at him sideways.

In mock imitation, birdlike, Ardri also inclined his head. "What are you up to again, Glic Tusil?"

*

With the authority of two mailed soldiers behind him, Gilroy planted himself in front of the fur trader's porch.

"Master Fidcal?"

"Faibur. The son."

"So, Faibur, what do you know about a cloak, a king's cloak? Made from the skin of an animal of legend, a Mooncat?"

The trader answered readily enough. "The Mooncat skin, yes. Woodsrunners call it a Sheh Ri, and as you say, it is a beast of legend; some say it is extinct, some say it never lived. I never saw one in my time as a woods-runner. But I bought a fur a few days ago, and it was accurately as the old tales describe, black as night with white spots, just like moonlight, and a silvery shimmer like silk, only more precious. The most beautiful thing I've handled."

"You bought it from the Woodstalkers?"

"Who else would I buy it from?"

"Sold it?"

"The same day."

"Who to?"

"It was offered it to Prince Ardri first. Naturally."

"Indeed. Just out of curiosity, what did you pay for it to those Woodstalkers?"

"I can't see what business..."

"Twelve Findrun lances price for Sheh Ri," the Amhas called Lost Dog said; he suddenly stood at Gilroy's elbow.

"Twelve Findrun lances for the Woodstalkers?"

"Why not?"

"Where did you get so much Findrun from, when Gasda can't find enough good bronze to arm the royal troops?"

"This was Cryssumha once, soldier, and is now the bronze heart of Rilante."

"And you, trader, are you still a Rilante man?"

"And you look like a simple soldier, so why do you talk like an officer?"

"Faibur had no Findrun, but Gobin the smith had twelve Findrun lances," Lost Dog interjected again.

"Gobin, not a Rilante name. So you, a Rilante man, conspire with these degenerates? Where does this Gobin live?"

Lost Dog pointed to the smithy next door. Giving Faibur a hard stare, the soldiers turned towards it. The Amhas intercepted Gilroy by tugging his mailed arm, and he threw down some small silver coins. They rolled in all directions, and Lost Dog scrambled after them.

Before he could gather them all, Faibur had set his foot on two coins. "Thanks a lot, you cur. I won't forget that."

"Faibur take foot off coins. Lost Dog no tell Canaras Muntrer Dundingin." The dark eyes looked up at Faibur craftily.

"See that you don't, because the Murder Bear may hear his name spoken, and then he'll come and take your worthless hide for shoes, and that is all you are good for, to be trampled on."

Under his tan, Lost Dog blenched and his face looked pinched.

Faibur took his foot from the coins.

Lost Dog scraped the silver out of the dirt and slunk away to the tavern by the gate, the Stag and Bottle, that served drink to all who could pay, even a ragged Amhas.

*

Kitt was hammering out the edge of a Findrun lance; a basket with the raw shapes and another with the finished blades stood by the anvil.

230

Gobin was in the yard, busy smelting another batch of the bells, wind chimes and mirrors that the Rilante people of Dundingin kept bringing in.

A shadow darkened the door of the smithy. Straightening up from his work Kitt saw a man in the bronze and leather mail of Rilante; he was stocky, with bright red hair and beard cropped short, with indifferent freckled features, and shrewd light blue eyes. He was followed by a mailed soldier whose helmet with nose protection gave his face mask-like expression.

Gobin stumbled in from the backdoor that led to the yard, pushed by a third soldier. The bronze smith looked outraged, which meant that he was alright for now.

Holding the hammer in the right, the unfinished lance in the left, Kitt moved back a little to keep all men in his sight, and be near to his sword, which leaned on the wall.

The freckled man noted his movement and grinned hardily. "You are the one who came out of the Bacenis with Prince Ardri?"

Kitt looked from one soldier to the other without answering.

"Seems a deaf-mute," the soldier said. "He looks stupid."

Kitt remained silent. He was a stupid barbarian who didn't speak the language; that was the way to play this one.

"Oh, no." The freckled soldier shook his head slowly, the pale blue eyes narrowing. "Not stupid at all. We know about you, boy, so you can stop dissimulating."

"What do you want?" Gobin demanded.

"We will presently take your statement about Findrun lances given to Woodstalkers in exchange for a Mooncat pelt, master smith," the freckled man said almost civilly. "But first, your apprentice shall answer me. This doesn't need to get painful, but that's entirely up to you both."

Kitt continued standing as still as the anvil and saying as much. The soldiers prepared to corner Kitt, and he gripped hammer and axe harder, still without a word.

There was a raucous cry. The freckled man ducked, and half raised his hands, as a crow came flying into the door above his head. "What the..."

The crow wheeled under the roof, cawing, and landed on the gold disc that covered the wine jar on the table. There the bird

231

stepped from one foot to the other like dancing on a hot stove while a rasping tune emerged from its strong, black beak. The golden disc lifted and clattered from one side to the other. The soldier holding Gobin started laughing.

The golden disc slipped, and the crow took to the air with a screech. The disk clattered onto the table and down onto the floor. Standing on edge, it rolled towards the middle of the room, wobbled and fell over.

Out of the wine jar came long, black legs ending in sharp claws, and waved in the air. A monster emerged, far too big to have fitted into that jar. It had a round head with eight red eyes, two large and six small, which shone like glowing coals, and long rattling serrated razor jaws.

Kitt threw hammer and spearhead at it, which glanced off the black, keratinous head without effect. The beast flew at him. Kitt lifted the stone anvil, muscles and tendons standing out in ridges on arms and shoulders and legs; he raised it above his head and heaved it at the oncoming monster. It went down under the weight.

Immediately, the anvil began rising, and the long black legs snaked around blindly, feeling into every corner.

That gave Kitt the moment he needed to jump across the room and pick up the golden disk.

The anvil fell to the floor with a thud.

Kitt threw the golden disc and the edge cut across the red eyes. The monster exploded into salt and smoking ashes.

Kitt wiped away the grains stinging his face to look out for his lesser adversaries. The soldiers had run.

*

"What are you gibbering about?" Captain Warmond demanded of the shaken and pale Gilroy. He had found him and two soldiers in the Mocking Bird.

Beibini set down a bottle of the strongest Uskeva. When Gilroy had downed half a water glass of the burning liquid, he was able to speak. "A monster in Gobin's smithy. Just when we wanted to pull in the suspect. I saw it, like a black, red-eyed spider bigger than a hellhound and that was only its beastly swollen body...the legs, oh the damn black legs!"

"We aren't safe," Beibini said, her blue eyes tragic. "With Lord Gasda and a thousand Rilante soldiers here, we aren't safe."

"My dear," Warmond said.

With a sob, she clutched his arm and briefly laid her head on his shoulder. Then she went out, and the men heard her crying in the kitchen.

"The thing went straight for him. The big boy," one of the soldiers said. Joso, Warmond recalled the name. "Which gave us the chance to bolt. It makes no sense, but I saw it."

"Oh, the monster makes sense," Warmond spoke gruffly, hoping to quell the panic he heard squeaking in the voices. "What makes no sense is you bothering Kitt and Master Gobin. I know that boy, I told you he's straight. And so is the bronze smith. He works for us, makes all our arms and weapons. Findrun bronze too and only charges for Umharu, with your Iwerdonn brass unwilling to pay the increased prices."

"They're dead," Joso croaked.

The other soldier nodded. Lase, his name was.

"Don't think so," Warmond said. "Kitt is the one who burned the Alchemist's Tower. Unfortunately, Glic Tusil was not in it."

"The white-faced phantom nobody ever saw?"

"The same. All of Dundingin is afraid of it, him, and yet nobody could swear that he even exists. He appears unreal, a spectre. I think he killed my daughter with his Donadroch sorcery." The Captain swallowed, his face contorted with grief. "He also sent your spider monster."

Gilroy considered Warmond with astonishment. "I have heard of Glic Tusil, the old fiend that has risen from the graves of Cryssumha, but I thought he was just something mothers scared their children with. You think this phantom wizard killed your daughter, maybe those folks too, yet you're not sure he exists?"

"Glic Tusil is real enough." The Captain looked very tired all of a sudden. He looked around to make sure Beibini was out of earshot. "When you meet him in the street, he seems just like a strange old cove, an alchemist. I've even talked to him and at that moment, never thought...of monsters. I forget most of the time, and it is only now that Blaitisin is gone that I remember. But nobody else seems to be aware. You've come to a bad place, Gilroy. Everything is

233

contaminated by Evil thousands of years old. Rilante is like a newly born infant before it."

"About this apprentice boy, Kitt. He burned the tower of the phantom wizard? Then where does he stand?"

The Captain shrugged. "Nowhere I'd say. Kitt is interested in the working of metal, the mining of ores, and the wild things in the Bacenis, and he's beginning to discover the girls. My Blaitisin took a right shine to him and him to her." His face twitched again. "He's a good boy, no harm in him at all."

"You aren't going to have a look if they are alright in that smithy." That was not a question. "I'm not going back either," Gilroy pursued. "Joso, Lase, drink up and go get me Brodi and Neilo. We'll cut right through the centre-knot."

When the soldiers were gone, Gilroy poured just a sip and then pushed away the bottle. Beibini came to the table again bringing pork crackling. Her eyes were still red. "Is Lord Gasda really going into the Bacenis?"

"Yes, and do you know who told him about Kione Lonnir?" Warmond looked at Beibini with angry eyes. "Prince Ardri told him." Beibini lifted her hands to her mouth. "Mother of Thirteen, protect us! We should never have come here, into this land, where the ground is hollowed out like a maggot-eaten carcass, where houses disappear into holes and where things come out of the tunnels."

"You know that I was under orders. Her orders, Serenaiba's, even if the words came out of the mouth of the king. She wants to deprive the crown prince of his friends. She has her work cut out, as he makes new friends daily." He even smiled a little.

"What shall we do?"

"Exceed my orders," Gilroy said. "The official part of it."

"At least you'll get your delay," Warmond said. "We have to range far inland for the provisions. There isn't a grain to be had near Dundingin, as if it is all running out at once. This is the time of sowing, the fields are ploughed, and there is no seed. Where has it all gone? When you ask the farmers, they can't give you an answer that makes sense. I wonder if the disappearance of the Fota farmers fits into all this?" He looked over to the redblond girl who was serving a

234

table with grain traders. "That is Ryoni. Her family disappeared from their farmstead. Without trace. She hasn't said a word yet."

*

Attired in cloak, boots and light armour for setting out across the Struenfoly, the Dog of Rilante towered above Ardri and glowered. Some of his distrust had visibly returned as he was baulked from setting out for Kione Lonnir at all speed.

"I could not say my dear Lord Gasda," Ardri said with all signs of puzzlement. "Where has all the grain gone?" Into Ulud below in the mountain. Grain wagons had come into Dundingin daily, but nobody seemed to make the connection. Glic Tusil's finest work, Ardri was the first to recognise that. "It is bad, you say? I don't know about agriculture." That last was even true, Ardri didn't have the slightest notion how anything was grown. All he knew was that it involved getting dirty. And boorish. "Provisions? Of course, let us see what we have here in Marrak."

Together they went to the kitchen courtyard where the stores were kept in deep underground vaults. "Calves liver, river crabs, asparagus. Sugarbread, raisins, almond cake. Not campaign-rations maybe but they are food. May I present Glic Tusil, our astrologer?"

Lord Gasda was startled by the sudden appearance of the old, white-faced man with the dusty-looking long dark hair, clad in a dark-red velvet robe. Glic Tusil had donned spectacles, which he didn't need, and bore a register with columns of numbers and letters. Ardri just barely kept his face straight; this was almost too much attention to detail – a mockery, really. "The venerable Glic Tusil is responsible for the storage spells," he explained. That, at least, was true. "These larch tongues have been laid in before I was born."

"I even have something more rare and delicate." Glic Tusil pottered among the crates and amphorae, looking like a genuine cellar-master. He brought forth a basket with nine fist-sized, golden balls, unlike any fruit grown in Rilante. "Paradise apples. As fresh and ripe as on the day they were plucked. My finest result."

For a moment, Gasda seemed diverted from his single-minded purpose. "I saw such fruit just once on the table of the Queen Murine."

"Those were a gift from Castle Marrak on the occasion of her Majesty's birthday. They came from this very basket, which held a dozen."

The last birthday Queen Murine ever celebrated. Glic Tusil couldn't resist, Ardri thought with dismay. What if the Dog of Rilante made the connection? He took one of the fruits, began peeling it. "I understand that these fruits won't spoil as long as the skin is intact. That is essential." The peels dropped on the floor, and a fragrant aroma filled the vault.

Ardri broke the fruit in two and handed one half to Gasda. At once, he separated a slice from his half and put it in his mouth. No fruit tasted like this, very sweet and slightly sour, sun-ripe, fresh. It was no wonder that Queen Murine had consumed all three paradise apples without sharing with anybody. Waiting, whether Gasda would eat, Ardri ate a second slice.

Lord Gasda frowned. "There were rumours of sorcery..."

"I know," Ardri said. "People call Glic Tusil an alchemist, but you'll agree that storage spells are most important. Everything is at your disposition, my dear Lord Gasda, take all you want, take it all. I care nothing if there is no dinner table on Marrak tonight. You must not be held up any longer."

Lord Gasda followed Ardri's example of separating a slice and putting it in his mouth. For a moment, his face lost its rigidity, as he tasted paradise, like Queen Murine had.

Chapter 20
Journeyman

Everything in the smithy was down on the floor; the soldiers in their panic had run into tables, banks and walls.

Kitt and Gobin were picking up the shambles when Ardri appeared in the door. He wore the Sheh Ri cloak. "Trouble with the might of Rilante?"

"They weren't any trouble," Kitt said.

Ardri considered the golden disk stuck in the smoking heap on the floor and exchanged a look with Gobin. "Another attempt?"

"The crow."

"I see. I need Kitt to come with me."

"I'll never go inside Castle Marrak again."

"Ironic, that it was Glic Tusil himself who led you out. He underestimated you. Well, he hasn't seen you in the woods."

He'd been dense and had more luck than he deserved, Kitt thought bitterly. Ardri praising his wit made him very uncomfortable; it had to mean that he was overlooking something vital.

Gobin seemed to read his mind. "Do listen to the king, Kitt," he said quietly.

Ardri frowned. "The Star Pattern is not yet resolved. As long as Lute still stands above the horizon, the attempts on Kitt's life and sanity will continue. One day I will control the Master of Mirrors. Entirely. I have been King of Cryssumha a short time, and my power is waxing as his wanes. Already, he cannot go where I forbid him, cannot touch anyone I name and mark as mine. I want to offer you the position as my High Steward and right hand, Kitt. Poor Slachlan, alas, will not be able to serve me as he did before, though he is very happy now."

"I should not be as good at...misunderstanding you."

"Your answer is no? That's a pity, but I expected that. Then I will fulfil my first promise to you. You asked me for a boat. You remember?"

Kitt had not really forgotten, but there were those strange days of oblivion when all he thought about was bronze. Suddenly he was very eager to leave Dundingin.

"I hate to lose you," Gobin said. "But I release you from your apprenticeship and give you your freedom as a journeyman." He grinned at Kitt's surprised look. "That is the form. I have the power as your master. For what that is worth. I couldn't protect you from Lute. Here are your wages." Gobin picked gold disc out of the ashes and the chucked it towards Kitt, who caught it neatly. "Seek out any smith and mention my name. They'll see you're alright, and in time will accept your master piece. I hope that one day, I'll hear what it will be."

Kitt nodded and began to pick up his belongings. He didn't have much, lance, bow, sword, his weapons belt holding three knives, a leather bag, a long leather coat consisting mainly of straps, pockets and belts, which the girls in Faibur's shop had fashioned according to his ideas, the purse with what was left of Ardri's coin. Kitt slipped it into his bag along with the golden disk. He was a long way from home and when among people you needed money.

He was about to ask Gobin to tell good bye to Beibini and the waif Ryoni and Faibur and Fidcal, but he didn't speak their names, not with Ardri present.

"Thank you for everything, Master Gobin," Ardri said with earnest gratitude. "Come now, Kitt! I hid the ship in the old harbour. Nobody knows...except for the river-men who brought it there."

So, nobody knew, Kitt thought, appreciating the pause.

Ardri didn't want them to be seen in the mainstreet. They stepped into the courtyard, and from there into the leather worker's yard and out into the alley.

"Won't you change your mind and join your fate to mine?" Ardri pursued. "Now that the best smith in Cryssumha taught you about bronze, don't all other metals pale to you, by comparison, even silver or gold? You can't possibly still prefer iron? Iron is corrupt, Kitt. Bronze cannot be corrupted."

"Iron can be made incorruptible."

238

"What?"

"On Isenkliff we forge incorruptible iron. Never rusts, never corrodes, never weakens."

"I didn't know that," Ardri said. "If only I'd had that piece of knowledge before. But it fits, and how it fits. Proof that I was right about Mavors in my pattern."

"Yes, the Star Pattern. The use of iron to precipitate copper." Kitt smiled. It was one of the new smiles that he had learned in Cryssumha, and that didn't reach the eyes. "The iron dissolves in the process."

"It is an old way and not necessary for me. There are other methods. You don't believe me. Maybe you can believe that I prefer you alive because Glic Tusil wants you dead? He's been so persistent that he even went against my direct order. I can't accept that and dearly want to put him in his place. You surely can appreciate that?"

Kitt nodded, because he could, and shook his head, because he wouldn't change his mind.

When they emerged from the crooked lanes between the six-cornered artisan's yards, and came into a broader thoroughfare, the attack happened fast and relentless. Two men with long knives moved in, competently, business-like.

Kitt moved faster. His right hand lashed out, crashed between the eyes of the first assassin who attacked Ardri, and rocked back his head. Without watching him go down like an ox struck by an axe Kitt turned on the second assassin whose knife was inches away. His left fist caught him square on the breastbone and threw him back against a clay wall, and the impact expelled the air from his breast in a whoosh. Seconds after the assault had begun it was over.

The first assassin lay motionless where he had fallen. Uncharacteristic for a Rilante man he had dark hair standing stark against a deathly pale skin. The second assassin arched his back, fighting for breath, whistling noises coming from his throat. He was a slim, wiry man, with a head full of yellow curls, and a short yellow beard and moustache. The memory of laughter nested in the corners of the blue eyes that now were clouded with pain. Both were clad in military looking leather hose and tunic without insignia.

239

Kitt crouched down beside the dark-haired man and felt for his neck, checked the pulse and breathed a sigh of relief.

"They are alive," Ardri said amazed. "I'd forgotten how fast you are and how hard you hit. Still don't like killing?"

"Why would I? I have nothing against them." Kitt grinned, and his grey eyes were hard and cold.

The blond assassin rolled over. Coughing he stemmed both arms against the ground, trying to heave himself into an upright position. Kitt sat him with his back against the clay wall.

"That hurt! You pack a serious punch, kiddo!" His hand sneaked towards one of the knives that lay near him.

"Don't try!"

"Always worth a try." The assassin smiled a quick, rueful smile.

"I brought Ardri out of the Bacenis," Kitt explained. "Can't let you kill him." He shrugged. "That's how it is."

"That's just plain pig-headed, kiddo. You haven't had much thanks for keeping him alive, have you?"

"How do you know that?"

"I just know." The man grinned. "His kind gives you nothing but grief. Sometimes it's best to cut your losses. What say, you scratch him yourself, as you're so particular? You got the right. His life is yours, and he's forfeited it when he betrayed you. Then we'll all have a drink together? I badly need one. I'll buy."

"Cut your losses yourself. Soldiers coming. Heavy footed." Kitt heard the marching steps coming their way, faintly.

"It's the officers, they like to demonstrate strength. Considerate, always know where they are, no need for argument. We should be on our way, is that what you said just now, kiddo?"

"Can you stand?" Kitt held out a hand.

The assassin gripped it and drew himself to his feet. He laid back his head to look at Kitt squarely. "You know kiddo, I had a funny feeling the moment I saw you, but no idea how funny this was going to be." He bent down to his companion whose eyes were closed, the lids twitching and shook him by the shoulder. "Wake up man, Dundingin's finest will be here in a moment, and I don't know what to tell them."

240

"Oh my head!" the dark-haired assassin groaned. His hand was sneaking towards a dagger in his girdle steadily, as if independent of the limp body.

His companion intercepted his hand. "Nothing doing brother."

The first assassin looked up at Kitt. His eyes were steel blue and implacable. "Some other time then." Supported by his companion on one side and Kitt on the other the first assassin staggered to his feet. Struggling to stand, his eyes fell on Ardri, who had not moved during the episode. "That really is a Sheh Ri pelt," he said. "There is no room for another king in Rilante."

"I couldn't agree with you more," Ardri retorted.

"Come along, lean on me." The blond assassin looked over his shoulder at Kitt. "Er, thanks for the break, kiddo."

"My pleasure."

"I wouldn't call it a pleasure, but it was an education."

"Anytime." Kitt chuckled.

Ardri noted that there was no grudge on either side. The blond assassin looked upon Kitt with respect and genuine liking, and even the silent dark-haired one managed a crooked grin. Kitt's eyes were alive with mischief. The guarded, careful expression seemed to be reserved for Ardri. He felt a pang of loneliness that he would forever be excluded from that brotherhood of fighters. He burst out laughing, and sounding a little hollow. "You do exactly as you see fit, eh Kitt? No matter that I'm the king of the land, all I can do is watch you impose your rule wherever you happen to be standing. Seems my opinion doesn't matter."

"It doesn't."

"Explain to me, why did you first strike down the assassin attacking me, and only then took care of the knife intended for your own back?"

Kitt shrugged. "No difference in the outcome."

"Well, I suppose you're perfectly entitled to deliver lines like this. You know Kitt, since I met you I have wondered how it would feel to have a conscience. It must be as comfortable as carrying around an anvil. That weight must be heavy even for you." He frowned. "A conscience is an affliction only the very strong can afford."

"Without conscience, the strong stand alone," Kitt repeated what his parents told him often.

"Kings always stand alone. We don't have friends, only allies."

"Maybe because kings make rotten friends."

"Harsh. Kings don't have friends because friendship is a muddled principle, unreliable and bound to be unstable. It's far better to have power. Then you know where you are, and so does everyone else, and everything becomes beautifully clear. It's time you cast it off, this heavy anvil Kitt. The relief will be instant, believe me."

Kitt didn't need to answer that, as the city guards came swinging around the corner and bore down upon them in a way that made it very clear that the law had arrived, and order was restored to this part of town. "My prince, we received the report of a fight?" the guards captain inquired, concern furrowing his brow.

"I wouldn't call it a fight exactly. No, no fight as such, not a chance."

"Your royal highness is unharmed?"

"Oh, yes, I'm perfectly alright."

"The perpetrators escaped?"

"They had fair warning. Fine marching, my dear Captain Warmond. We could hear you from a long way off. Safe feeling, to know the law's arriving. I'll sponsor drums and cymbals for you, make a good show."

"Your royal highness is generous." The guards' captain bowed.

"You deserve it," Ardri said graciously.

Captain Warmond seemed to remember his duty. "Do you wish for our protection for your further way, Prince Ardri?"

"No, my dear fellow, that's not necessary. I have all the protection I need."

With a face devoid of recognition Warmond mustered Kitt, who said nothing. The captain saluted smartly, snapped a command that made the guards swing around, moving as one body. They tramped up the alley again.

Ardri stared after them. "Now I wonder if the good Warmond is really all that stupid. The way he went royal this and highness that, was he taking the piss, as the soldiers so elegantly express it?"

Kitt had nothing to say about that. As they continued their way, they met a sedan chair, born by four stocky, black-haired men with blank faces. The silver brocade curtain was jerked aside by a slim, white hand, and huge black eyes looked out. Ardri bent over the white fingers with the long transparent nails. It was the girl Kitt had seen in the throne room on his first day in Dundingin, who had been kneeling down so gracefully. "I heard there has been an attempt on your life, my king!" her voice murmured like water tinkling into a bronze bowl.

"Now how did you already hear Neelam my Evening Star? It happened only a few moments ago."

"The bells, of course," she whispered.

"Of course. Dundingin is full of bells. And mirrors. My dear, Kitt has just saved me again for the, how many times was it, Kitt?"

"I didn't count," Kitt said absently, taking in the sight of skin like curdled milk, the indescribable wine-red bow of the mouth, the black hair weighing down a neck like a flower stalk, and hematite eyes. These luminous, dark eyes looked at him curiously as if he was a clever performing animal. "Protect my king well!" she said, smiled and jerked the curtains closed.

They both looked after the sedan chair as it swayed up the street.

"It's good not to be a heap of cracked bones in the Bacenis," Ardri remarked. "I'll not cease to be grateful to you, Kitt. I know that you're not my friend, and you don't trust me. That may be all for the better, because we can work together on a sound, clear-cut base of mutual benefit. Whatever else, I owe you a reward and I don't stint. Won't you reconsider? No?"

"No."

There was it again, that hard judgement, against which no appeal was possible. He was alone, Ardri realised, and it was time to accept that and stop trying not to be alone. "Then Slatynrigan is my only protection. I didn't dare to carry it openly, with Gasda still in town. If I had brought Slatynrigan now, I would not have to be saved by you again. An army couldn't withstand me. I don't really need men to serve me."

What was he doing, Kitt wondered? Going away while Ardri had that sword? Should he go after Captain Warmond and warn him?

He turned around to see the street filling with crowds of small dark-haired men, twitching, blinking, shaking in that way they had, and at the same time, implacable. They came out of the alleyways and seemed to be emerging from the ground.

"You would have to fight your way through them all the way," Ardri said, apparently reading his mind. "I know you don't want to do that. Cryssumha will rise, and there is nothing anyone could do. The Wandering Stars will it so. Don't worry about the Rilante people. They are warned. Why do you think did that attack happen? They know what is up, and they'll realise that they must give in or go. You have to go too, Kitt. I was wrong to ask you to stay. I couldn't be the king with you present, I realise that now."

*

Incoherent with fury, Captain Warmond stormed into the command barrack.

"You said you'd take care of the mongrel, Gilroy. But when I come upon the scene of the prince's violent demise, I find him standing there grinning and giving me shit about cymbals. What the hell happened?"

"Your Kitt survived the monster, that's what happened. Or rather, who."

Warmond waved aside the nicety of speech. "Yeah, so you had a grammar tutor, Gilroy. Doesn't it hurt you in a moment like this? At least your bunglers knew enough to get clear. I couldn't have done anything but to arrest them."

"Neilo and Brodi are the best."

"Not for that job, they obviously weren't. And I don't talk about their brawn, but their judgement."

"Why don't you reserve your judgement until you've listened to their account?"

When Brodi and Neilo appeared, Captain Warmond noticed that they walked uncertainly, like men who weren't quite sure how badly they were hurt. "The kid just flattened us." Brodi shrugged. "One hit each, and down we went, never saw it coming."

"Aren't you ashamed to show your faces after being bested by a sixteen-year-old apprentice boy?"

"Not a bit." Brodi stared back squarely at the irritated guard's captain. "I could as well be ashamed of having been bested by the Bethrek of the fable."

244

"Which animal does exist in the Bacenis," Warmond said slightly calmer. "I know the boy. He wears a Bethrek tooth around his neck. I warned you about him. But you had to go for him like a pair of tavern drunks. Be glad that you got away on your two legs."

"They didn't get away, he let them go," Gilroy said.

"Prince Ardri let you go?"

"Not Ardri." Brodi chuckled. "The prince stood aside looking pretty while the kid sent us on our way. Without asking us any questions. And without so much as a by your leave to high and mighty."

"What did Ardri say to that?"

"Nothing. Like I said, the kid didn't consult him."

"The kid won't talk either," Brodi said. "He's not the kind."

"I trust Brodi's judgement," Gilroy said. "If he says the kid won't talk, Lord Morrik will have nothing to go upon, should he make inquiries. Now just get a hold on yourself, captain. We've both served under Flannan, who called us his friends. Now he's surrounded by Cryssumha people, King Tirnmas grows weaker every day, Ardri is scheming here in Dundingin and Gasda insists on going into the Bacenis with his whole force to take Kione Lonnir from the Amhas. Leaving Morrik in charge of Dundingin. While you have nothing better to do..."

"I beg your pardon, Gilroy." Warmond looked a little ashamed of himself. "Fact is, I do believe every word your ruffians say. I hadn't foreseen that Kitt would still protect Ardri, seeing the sort of thanks he gets for his troubles, but I should have, and I'm angry at myself."

"Why should you have foreseen that?"

"Because I know him. Somehow, he got a funny idea of returning good for bad. I call it the perversity of youth. Besides its Glic Tusil who's the master of monsters. Ardri is careful to keep his damn kid gloves spotless, makes a big show of breaking free from his influence. He fooled me for a time. So Kitt can't be sure. It's all perfectly done."

"There really are bethreks?" Neilo asked.

All looked at him because the taciturn assassin was known to speak less than once in a year.

"And the Mooncat too," Gilroy said. "That's what we are here about."

*

Kitt and Ardri arrived at a part of the old city wall that had been incorporated into the defensive structures around the town of Dundingin. There was a small, but very sturdy bronze gate, looking unbelievably ancient without being corroded in the slightest.

"Eastern Gate," Ardri said. "It was locked years and years, that's why there is no guard." He produced a bronze key which he inserted into the lock; it turned smoothly, and the door opened without noise. They stepped through and looked down upon a marshy area. There was a disused quay and beside it lay a small one-mast ship. From the height they were standing, it looked like a forgotten toy.

"There it is. The channel is silted up, but I ascertained that it is still sufficiently deep for this vessel, which has a flat bottom, I am told."

"You kept your word fully, Ardri."

Ardri cocked an eyebrow. "Besides the art of bronze smithing, you have learned sarcasm, Kitt. It doesn't really suit you, and moreover, you're wrong. I am not your enemy, for the simple reason that I fear you. I suppose you can accept that? I understand that you can't believe that I mean you well because I like and admire you, though that is the case also. Thirdly, I am truly grateful to you for saving my royal ass, as you put it so inelegantly with your blacksmith's charm. If this sounds like a farewell speech to you, then you hear right. You must go. Now. You heard my queen, the bells tell everything, and this ship won't be a secret much longer. Don't bother to bid me an affectionate farewell."

Taking Ardri at his word, Kitt walked away, down Ulud's steep and crumbled Harbour Stairs. The young king watched him setting his feet surely, never slipping, never stumbling. Not looking back.

An overgrown road ran past buildings which had sunk halfway into the swamp, and empty windows stared above stagnant green water like the scared eyes of drowning men, and across an arched stone bridge to a basin fringed with reeds, the water in it intensely blue. An open water lock led into a channel beyond.

When Kitt reached the quay beside the ship, he turned and looked up the mountain, up and up. Ardri couldn't see the expression on his face, that far below, and wondered, if he now saw Gitirafon, Ulud's River Gate, the entrance into the world below Dundingin. But perhaps he only saw what the Rilante-people had seen for hundreds of years, a rock-face with a chance resemblance to a gigantic façade.

For a ridiculous moment, Ardri hoped that Kitt would wave. Of course, he could wave himself. But he wasn't sure that Kitt would respond.

Chapter 21
The Boat

Vasara and Dilo completed their conjunction. Lute has gone on his way and disappeared into the sunset glow. Mavors is there to stay.

Ardri, King of Cryssumha, Star Observation Journal

Kitt made his way across pastureland and fields, using the paths of the cattle and the wild animals.

It had rained with the fine drizzle that was not cold. Now the sun shone, and above the emerald green river valley, the misty air was like a warm opal. He breathed with animal pleasure, and was asking himself, how he had stood it so long inside city walls.

Since Ardri had explicitly wanted him to go in the boat, walked him to it, too, Kitt hadn't taken it. As an extra precaution, he kept away from the channel. He could see it from above, running at the foot of a chain of hills; the water flowed slowly, shining in the sun. Maybe he was paranoid, but he had to wonder, where Ardri's queen had come from in her litter. She looked like one born with magic power in her body, this girl of magnolia, ebony and haematite. Furthermore, when he waited to see Ardri gone, he had looked up the rock-face above the disused harbour basin, and it reminded him of Minit Claghini, with its eroded gates. Underground Ulud had seemed very near there, and it was the same extended hill that had Castle Marrak on top of its western and northwestern part. As he wandered along, he still felt it brooding in his back.

Ahead lay a hillock crowned by ruins, four-cornered structures, so Kitt wandered towards it. It seemed to have been a watchtower once. A stump was left, of three storeys, built of square, rough stones, and the ceilings had fallen in. Kitt climbed up from the outside, without taking off his boots; the craggy stones afforded him ample hold.

From the top, Kitt could see far across the Struenfoly valley. He studied the course of the broad stream, watched closely how it meandered across the vast plain from a point beyond Dundingin towards the northern horizon, where it would turn West. Kitt knew that from asking casual questions in the Mocking Bird. From up here, the extended loop was not yet visible. On the eastern shore, trees grew down to the water, the green fingers of the Dark Wood Murkowydir, also called the Great Wood Bacenis.

West, south and north stretched the meadowlands of Rilante. Kitt's eyes rested on the place where he had come ashore with Ardri, and wandered to a bend downriver. That had to be the place he was looking for.

After climbing back down again, he found that his hands black with soot and looked inside the tower. Human bones mingled among the fallen stones. Nothing seemed to die naturally in this land.

*

"Everything is lost," Captain Warmond told his wife.

Beibini's blue eyes widened. "So quickly?"

"Gasda has crossed the river on this wild goose chase and he took more than half of the city guards into the Bacenis with him. We haven't had word from him since, no news whatsoever. I only have a skeleton crew left, and he grudged even that. Ardri is in possession of Dundingin. We have nothing to stop him; I make no mistake about that. If Gasda returns, he will have lost many men, and if he is beaten...that is a possibility, I'm afraid. You must leave, at once. You'll lose everything, but you'll live."

Beibini's eyes wandered through the tavern, lighting on the bottles, tables, earthenware and glass. "If Kitt was here. He wouldn't let harm come to us. Monsters can't touch him. But he's gone, Gobin told me."

"He saved Prince Ardri's skin yet again."

"The poor boy can't distinguish right from wrong in this serpents' pit, and that's not his fault. If Blaitisin hadn't gone into the moat, he would have stayed. Maybe that is why she had to go."

"You may be right," Warmond said with sudden grievous illumination. "But it's too late now. Listen Beibini, in the old harbour lays a ship, a sturdy vessel, with all the tackle in order. I cannot find out who put it there. Could be anyone; we all expect catastrophe.

249

Well, he'll have to get away in something else. I put a guard on it, two men laying low; they'll go with you and Ryoni. Pack very little, so that the Cryssumha people don't realise what you're up to, and then go straight to the eastern gate, it's unlocked. As fast as you can, promise you won't wait for me!"

"No!" she protested.

"Yes! Please, my wife! I can act much better if I don't have to worry about you too. Make your way through the channel into the Struenfoly; the men will need to sweat a bit with the poles. From then it will be easy all the way downriver with the current. Somebody will see you at Bilawini, and help you land before you get swept out into the sea."

*

The canoe lay where Kitt had expected, in the shallow, caught in the branches of a fallen willow tree.

He had not expected to also find the bodies of the three Amhas rowers, but they were there, slumped over, their long hair stirring in the air. They were less decomposed than could have been expected from so many days exposed to the open air. Their lips were drawn back in a rictus of pain; all had vomited. The bottom of the canoe was covered with something dark and viscous. Kitt hadn't seen people killed by poison before; his knowledge was purely academic. This had to have been something fast-acting. His mind ran over all the dangerous substances connected with copper and bronze, slow-acting poisons all. His mind ran over all the dangerous substances connected with copper and bronze, slow-acting poisons all - unless laced with some kind of Zaubar magic -Ledrithud, Donadroch, whatever it was called.

He tipped the canoe over so that the corpses fell onto the shore. To clean out the dark liquid, he pushed the rim under to scoop river water inside. He sloshed the water by dipping the canoe back and forth and sideways, while carefully avoiding any drop to fall on him. That took some time to accomplish, but he knew he must not be hasty.

He then filled the canoe bottom with rushes, fresh green mixed with dry stalks from the year before, and picked up the Amhas' weapons, the bows with arrows, the lances, the small round shields made of wood and leather and bronze knives. Before he stowed them in the canoe, he inspected them for traces of the dark liquid and washed off every speck he saw.

As he made the canoe shoot into Struenfoly, Kitt hoped that this was where he left Ardri's Star Pattern. He kept in the middle of the stream, where the main current ran just out of bowshot from the wooded shore.

*

"An Amhas? What does the dirty cur want?" Ardri demanded from his new Steward. Slachlan would never have allowed a savage from the woods to smirch the threshold of Castle Marrak with his noisome presence.

"He says he has news from Gasda."

Ardri descended to the Southern courtyard where the castle guards held a dishevelled Amhas whose stink of stale spirits and worse came at him in waves.

"This man Lost Dog," he said and continued to gabble in a barbarous accent of which Ardri understood little except for the mention of Gasda and Kione Lonnir.

"He says the Murder Bear has ambushed Gasda's soldiers in the Bacenis," one of the Rilante men working by the castle wall said. He looked horribly upset. "I am used to their strange way of speaking the Rilante language, my prince, as my mother cooks in the Stag and Bottle Inn. This can't be true, my prince?" The man's eyes were begging him for reassurance.

"He's a drunken wreckage. How can he know anything about it?" Ardri demanded. "Ask him!"

The man asked something, almost shouting, and the savage gabbled some more. With barely concealed impatience, Ardri waited for the man to stop asking unintelligible questions and translate.

"He says he saw the tracks and found the bodies. He said Lord Gasda demanded guides and the Amhas Woodstalkers refused. He destroyed one of their camps, and they fell upon him. Gasda killed them all. Then the wild Woodstalkers attacked him in Kione Lonnir. Maybe it isn't all that bad."

"Ask him who he told about it."

"You dirty rat!" the workman said passionately. "My lord prince, this piece of shit has known for a couple of days but didn't

251

tell anyone because he wants a reward from you, my prince. I hope you'll reward him as he deserves!"

"I'll reward you both," Ardri said. Obeying his signal, the guards took hold of the workman and marched him away together with the Amhas.

The shocked yells of the workman faded underground where the prison cells were.

*

Kitt's canoe drifted in the main current of the Struenfoly river when he saw a man ahead, gesticulating frantically by the river's edge, on the wrong side. He heard him shouting, too.

Fragments of bronze mail and bright red hair showed him to be a Rilante man, who apparently knew no better, to call attention to himself like that for everything with teeth and claws, knives and arrows.

The canoe drifted nearer in the current, and Kitt recognised the soldier who had come to the smithy to ask about the Sheh Ri pelt and Findrun lances. Their eyes locked across the expanse of the Struenfoly. In a few moments, Kitt would pass, and then it would be difficult to reach the man.

"Hey, big boy, get me out of here!" the man cried and waved both arms.

"Jump in and swim!" Kitt called back. He wouldn't go near that shore, not after the racket the soldier had made, but he took the canoe out of the current nearer the Bacenis side and let the paddles trail, scanning the trees carefully, in his left one of the small Amhas round shields.

The soldier waded into the river until the water stood to his belly, then his chest. He began to swim, and the current took hold of him. Kitt let the canoe drift downriver, to overtake the man struggling in the water, but he wouldn't make it to the middle of the river; he was not swimming strongly enough.

Kitt let the canoe shoot towards the shore, conscious that some Feen might lie in wait for just that manoeuvre, and hoping to see the arrow in time to drop to the bottom of the canoe.

He reached the soldier as he was sinking, stretched out an arm to collar him and pulled him into the canoe, at the same time using his

252

weight to prevent the light vessel from tipping over, making it veer around.

Still no arrows.

The canoe shot into the main current again with the soldier lying lying on the rushes in the bottom, gasping. "Lord Gasda was taken captive by the Woodstalkers."

"He's dead then. Or wishes he was."

"Where are you going in that canoe?"

"Home."

"Take me to Dundingin!"

"No can do."

"You must!"

"Have you more questions to ask me, soldier?"

"I don't need to ask you anything. All is clear to me." He lounged with a knife.

Kitt caught his hand easily. "You can't row upriver. You are too weak."

The man fell against him panting. "Been on the run in the woods without food or sleep for days. You can throw me overboard now. I can't do anything anyway. I just had to try."

Kitt released the man, who sank down in the boat. He veered out of the current with a couple of powerful moves of the oar. They landed on the opposite shore, less than five miles from where Kitt had started. The soldier attempted to scramble to his feet. He was pale and shaky and the water running out of his clothes was pink.

"Are you wounded?"

"Just some scratches."

Kitt uncorked his water bottle and held it to the soldier's lips. Then he cut little pieces of bread and fed four of them to him, and gave him a sip of water after each.

"Why don't you stick to nursing, boy, you got a talent for it," the man said when his face had gained a little colour. "Name is Gilroy, I'm lord Gasda's...attendant. I'll walk from here. I must get to Dundingin before the news gets there about the army's defeat. Once Ardri knows, the Cryssumha degenerates will massacre all the Rilante people; that was the plan all along. They've bred and multiplied, nobody knows how many there are. Most of them were

253

living underground, hidden by sorcery. And you had to go and save Prince," Gilroy spat out "Adri again. It was you who defeated us."

"What difference which brother is on the throne?" Kitt objected.

"It's not that simple. Ardri wants to turn back the time, before there was Rilante, for Cryssumha to rise again. For that, all our people just must be wiped out. Like washing a plate."

And that was why Ardri had wanted him gone; it made horrible sense now. Beginning the ardent upstream row, Kitt thought of Beibini, the waif Ryoni, Fidcal, Faibur, Warmond. All in mortal danger, by saving just one life in the woods, and then saving it again. While he rowed along the western river shore towards Dundingin, he saw before him Blaitisin's face.

Chapter 22
Cryssumha Rising

Ardri, King of Cryssumha, walked in his full regalia through the main street of stricken Dundingin.

Tunnel entrances had opened in the pavements, and whole sections had fallen in, to reveal the vaults underneath milling with pale, dark-haired, dark-eyed people. With the same colouring, the similarity to the Cryssumha-inhabitants of the surface ended; these subterranean denizens had small, deformed, twitching bodies which were full of purpose like ants, and they boiled out of the ground like tar. No red-haired Rilante person was visible anywhere.

Wherever the Cryssumha people caught sight of the Mooncat cloak and the crown Fenifindrune, they dropped to their knees and lowered their heads. *Just as well*, Ardri thought, *what if they see, really see, that my eyes are blue*. He laid his hand on the hilt of the Sword Slatynrigan.

He took a turn to retrace the way he had walked with Kitt. The east gate swung open. Ardri tried to recall if he had locked it again. Below the ship was gone from the basin.

Somehow Ardri had not dared to believe that Kitt would simply leave on the spot, because of that chink he had, the anvil of responsibility he carried around. The only explanation was that he had not realised the immediate danger for his Rilante friends. That also surprised Ardri. He suspected that he had been intimidated by the young giant, because of the way he had anticipated every event in the woods and evaded every one of Glic Tusil's attacks. Perhaps he had given too much credit to those clear, light-grey eyes that seemed to look beyond the horizons and deep into everything. But the dangers of the woods were nothing compared to the wiles of Ulud. If Kitt had been in the city when the massacre began, things might still have been dangerous for the King of Cryssumha.

Even from this far above Ardri saw that the blue of the water of the little harbour basin was tinged with red, and a nasty smell stung his nose, the stench of finality. Something was dead down there. He strained to see what it was, and took a step forward, then another, down the Harbour Stairs. He had to know.

The water stank of rotting blood and mud, and in it swam the planks of the little ship, that had not sailed, after all. A movement among the reeds caught Ardri's eye. He stopped, fascinated and afraid. *Is it Kitt, and is he hurt? Enough to make it safe to approach? Careful now, make no mistake, because it would be my last.*

Setting down his foot from the last step of the Harbour Stairs, he looked up. Eastern Gate was high above, far away. *Too far?* But he just had to see. He had Slatynrigan, need not be afraid anymore, not even of Kitt.

Still unable to make out what was stirring there, he approached the basin across the bridge, where the reeds were now stirring violently. He bent aside the tall green stalks and saw a woman with long red hair, who was trying to drag herself out of the water. As Ardri watched, her arms gave, and she sank down, one side of her face buried in the mud. Once she had been a beautiful, voluptuous, ripe specimen of womanhood. Clothes and skin had been torn with something long and sharp, and the lower half of her body which lay in the water was a mass of lacerated skin and flesh; the white of the thigh bones gleamed among the red spongy mass of her legs. She must have been trying for a long time, succeeding only for the infinite distances of a few inches.

Ardri knelt down and lifted her head. She tried to look at him. He turned her around, and she cried out like an animal. One half of her face was deathly white, the other black with the mud of the swamp. Her eyes were very blue and looked into his with an odd intensity. "Blue eyes. Not black," she whispered. It seemed to give her consolation. "Boat full of people...go to Bilawini. Bell...rang and rang...under our feet...bones turned to water...ship fell apart...we fell...where the monsters are."

"The bell was in the ship?"

"Yes, ship."

"Was Kitt with you? Gobin's apprentice? Young barbarian very tall, very strong, long blond hair, grey eyes?" Ardri spoke slowly and clearly so that the dying woman might understand.

"If Kitt had been here, we would live." Her face softened. "Invincible."

"Yes," Ardri said. So Kitt had not trusted him enough to embark in the ship after all. That realisation stung more sharply than he would ever have expected, and this emotion mingled strangely with his relief that Kitt must be alive - and far away.

There was more which bothered Ardri. He had taken all precautions so that nobody but he and Kitt knew about this boat. But somebody else had also known. "Nothing I want or do seems to matter," he murmured, and rose to his feet. "So am I part of a cosmic pattern, or am I a mere puppet on the string of a puppet-master? The puppet-master, the Master of Mirrors, Glic Tusil? Have all the kings of Cryssumha always been no more than that?"

Suddenly the woman's eyes focussed on Ardri's face. "You! You!" she whispered. "Wizard prince! Curse you, devil, that your blue eyes deceived me! You did this!"

Ardri drew his knife from his belt, an old blade made entirely of silver -intended for monsters, not for people. Not the sharpest edge. He braced himself for what he would do, and cowered down again, buried his hand in the long, red hair and with a quick, brutal movement stabbed the woman through the neck.

"I didn't," he said when the blood stopped spurting from the severed carotids, and she did not move any more, told the blue eyes, that would not fade.

Cowering there in the black mud he wiped the woman's blood from the silver blade with his fingers and looked at the bright red drops that coursed over his hands. "And that is the last blood of Rilante left in Dundingin." A crazy, mirthless chuckle bubbled up in his throat. "But for that which runs in my own veins."

*

At the sound of a blade leaving its scabbard, Glic Tusil looked up from the star chart to see Ardri standing in the door of the Mirror Chamber, on his head the crown Fenifindrune, the Mooncat cloak over his shoulder, in his hand the naked sword Slatynrigan.

Glic Tusil bowed.

257

"The player bowing to his puppet? You have played well, Glic Tusil. The back of Rilante was broken in Dundingin."

"I have always served the Kings of Cryssumha."

"Yes, it was always you. Only the kings changed, father, son, grandson, the whole line of the blood. All your puppets Glic Tusil! Should it not be you, who wears the crown Fenifindrune? Do you think the Mooncat cloak would suit you, as the true ruler of Cryssumha? Do you covet the sword Slatynrigan?" Ardri lifted the blade slightly and stepped into the room.

Glic Tusil looked shocked. "Only the blood of Cryssumha can wear these insignia."

"Yes," Ardri said pleasantly. "The blood. But my blood is tainted. And my eyes are blue." He stepped closer. "I am your tool, to produce the true King of Cryssumha. How many generations, do you think?"

"Your son will be of pure blood."

"Now, you are honest, Glic Tusil, you do not lie at a direct question. How do you plan to get rid of me, Master of Mirrors? And isn't water also a mirror, and its surface easily broken - is that how you killed the Rilante fugitives?"

"The fugitives?" Glic Tusil looked truly surprised. "Why should I waste my considerable abilities to wipe out the sorry remnants of Rilante? If they flee Dundingin, then they will die in Iwerdonn, Carrameille or Bilawini, or any other place where Cryssumha rises."

"Are you saying that it is not Rilante blood that is rotting in the old harbour? Whose is it then, Glic Tusil? Who do you hate and fear so much that you go to such length to destroy him? Did you use my Queen Neelam to accomplish it? We met her at the eastern gate. What inducement did you hold out to her? I do not blame her, never her, but I judge you!"

"The barbarian blacksmith was the one who could break the Star Pattern. He could have done it even now. The Queen was aware of the danger." Glic Tusil stabbed with a long white finger onto a point on the table with the star map, then to another. "My star is sinking; dark Lute is sinking, but Mavors still stands bright and high even as Dilo and Vasara rule the sky. Now is your time, King Ardri, it is you who must prevail."

258

"I know that. But tell me, what monster rose for Kitt from the mirror of the water in the old harbour? You must have put it there because there was no harm in the boy, none, no more than there is in Flannan. He should have waded to the shore and shook himself, then come straight here to cut our throats for what he must regard as base ingratitude."

"His monster lies in his blood, the blood of a long line of killers. I told you."

"Nonsense. Kitt was a smith, like his father, and I ascertained that Eckehart of Minit Houarn does not stand in the Kri bloodline. It was all a chimaera of yours. In fact, there are no more Kri. They were all killed."

"Yes. A mere sixteen years ago." Glic Tusil laid a world of meaning in his words.

"I said nonsense. Kitt a Kri? Then why didn't he like to kill? The length he went to avoid bloodshed was quite ludicrous. You wasted an extraordinary amount of power to slay a strong, but essentially harmless, apprentice smith. Might I prevail upon you to dedicate what remains of your waning power to the rise of Cryssumha?"

Glic Tusil regarded Ardri levelly. "Mavors still blazes red, and that disquiets me. The stars are in this barbarian's favour also, and it has proved very difficult to destroy him. I wonder has he escaped again? Is it possible that you know that he is alive, King Ardri?" The white mask that was Glic Tusil's face remained immobile, but the black eyes blazed hellishly. "Oh, yes, that is it. For a moment I thought that I had succeeded, that at last we were rid of him, but you want to mislead me into thinking that, don't you, as you did in the guards' hall when you knew perfectly well that the bloody carcass was merely the worthless soldier Gock?"

Ardri stood his ground before the enraged Master of Mirrors. "Your star is sinking Glic Tusil. Lute is sinking at last, but not before you have succeeded to turn Kitt into my enemy while failing to neutralise him!"

"Your Majesty, if that barbarian is still alive, you must leave Ulud and hurry to Iwerdonn, before Mavors can break the pattern." Glic Tusil's voice had a sound that was almost pleading, and stood in a marked contrast to the stiff white face and the black eyes glowing in their unholy rage.

259

"You mean before he returns to take off my head for the tricks you played on him, you old bungler? Or because he must believe that it was I who killed his Rilante friends in this utterly senseless and filthy manner?" With cold fury Ardri began to stalk around the star table towards Glic Tusil. "I'll take your advice, ride to Iwerdonn today, with Neelam, for our union to receive the blessing of my father and my mother, my king and my queen. And I think it is time Cryssumha is also ruled by a dynasty of kings. Not by an undead Master of Mirrors."

The sword Slatynrigan neared Glic Tusil's chest.

The Master of Mirrors took one backwards step, and another until his back was to the tall mirror. There he took another step back, and rings began to run across the mirror surface like ripples on water. Glic Tusil disappeared sinking into the mirror, a moment before Ardri could reach him.

While the young king still stared, the sword Slatynrigan hanging forgotten in his hand, the surface of the mirror became opaque, like a lake freezing over, until only a circular black centre was left, and he thought that he saw things writhing in the darkness of that hole. Then the mirror surface closed with a little cracking sound and was smooth again. Ardri saw his own reflection, which caused him to close his mouth.

Something clattered onto the floor, and he saw a dark red jewel, such as the copper miners sometimes found and called the Heart of Ore. He sheathed Slatynrigan and picked up the jewel. "So, the monster was on this side of the mirror."

Now to find a golden casket.

The gem danced on the smooth gold like a drop of water on a hot hearth and Ardri grinned as he closed the lid.

One faraway day a pure-blooded King of Cryssumha would lay the red jewel, the Heart of Ore on a surface of polished bronze and conjure the last Master of Mirrors. By then Ardri would long be dead. It was good to know that he would never see Glic Tusil again.

*

Trusting that nobody expected him back, Kitt ran the canoe into the channel; it was the quickest way. In the harbour basin, the water had turned a brown colour and stank of death.

"I'm too late. It has already happened." Gilroy slumped.

Kitt looked at some pieces of wood that drifted in the glutinous water, and smiled grimly. "That boat was my reward."

"Can I guess what for? And who? You saved his life more than once. Why did you keep faith with him for so long?"

"Nothing to do with him."

Unexpectedly, Gilroy nodded. "You just kept faith."

They crossed the bridge, passed the ruined buildings and ascended the crumbled flight of stairs.

"Old Dundingin," Girlroy said. "It had another name once. Ulud, the charnel house, the stone tomb. Here's the east gate. Now how do we get in?"

The gate turned out to be unlocked, and Kitt pushed it open a crack. The thoroughfare onto which the six-cornered houses backed was deserted. Warily they stepped into Dundingin. On their way to the main street they had to circumvent deep holes in the street - structures like honeycombs were visible inside.

"Torin Daraval, turn your ship around!" Gilroy whispered. "Mother of Thirteen protect us! How didn't we know about this?"

Kitt turned into a narrow alley, ducked through an arch and came into the courtyard of the potter, where the shards had been swept away and new pots and bowls dried on racks. The young potter Crochen had obviously taken over from his father, but he wasn't in his yard. Quickly, they went through into another courtyard, that of the beekeeper. From there a small gate led into the backyard of Gobin's smithy.

There was no fire in the smelting ovens. Kitt opened the backdoor into the house, and found Gobin sitting at the table, his big black hands before him idly. He didn't move or speak. Kitt went past him to the front door and looked out. A torrent seemed to have gone through the main street, and left broken flotsam of furniture, wares and glass shards.

"Dundingin is gutted like a fish," Gilroy said beside him. "I see no dead bodies, though."

"They've been eaten! Even the bones!" Gobin shuddered violently. "The news of Gasda's defeat came last night. All the bells started ringing, it was an infernal noise. The mob of Cryssumha surged through the streets. Those of Ulud who have lived and bred underground came up. I didn't know there were so many of

261

those...such creatures! The city guards made a stand, but they had no chance. The enemy was inside the gates."

"What happened to Beibini? And Ryoni?"

"They went away in time. The Captain got them out before this started. He was warned."

"Yes, he was," Gilroy agreed. "He knew what was going on. There was no way for him to stop Cryssumha from rising, but they could prepare themselves."

"Fidcal and Faibur?"

"Faibur wanted to go with lord Gasda to serve as a scout, he and Cynan Concen and some other woodsrunners. But Master Fidcal prevailed on Faibur to stay." Gobin looked strained. "They left the city with Beibini, and took nothing but their lives. All their wares are lying in the street now, you saw."

"What did Prince Ardri do?" Gilroy interjected.

"King Ardri of Cryssumha had only his own body bodyguard because Lord Morrik's troops had gone to the rescue of Lord Gasda. When the mob began to crawl out of the tunnels, Ardri sent out messengers. They intercepted Lord Morrik as half his troupes had already crossed the Struenfoly. So he turned back, but was too late to save the Rilante people."

"Neat!" Gilroy spat.

Kitt and Gobin looked at each other.

"Was that not what you wished for, bronzen Cryssumha restored?"

"And now look what it is to have your dearest wish granted," Gobin said. "Learn from that, Kitt. Don't worry about me, though. A smith is always on the fringe and yet always needed, be it war or peace. We don't have enemies. I'm sure your father told you just the same thing, and you'll find it to be true."

"Yes, he did."

"So, no need to drive this responsibility thing too far, you know. You'll find this kind of thinking tends to get out of hand if you don't draw lines."

Kitt nodded slowly.

Gobin looked before him on the table. "King Ardri and Lord Morrik left with the troops only a little while ago. They go to Iwerdonn."

"I have to get there before them!" Gilroy said urgently. "Prince Flannan must have a chance to defend the capital city of Iwerdonn." With two steps, the soldier was beside Gobin and gripped his arm. "If you betray me, you're dead, Cryssumha-smith."

The smith did not move. "You won't change anything, Rilante-man. Cryssumha is rising. You can't fight the Wandering Stars."

"I have to warn them in Iwerdonn." Gilroy released Gobin and looked at Kitt, whose grey eyes had been upon him during the interchange. "Come with me! What you have to tell will shake King Tirnmas out of his apathy if anything can."

"No. I go home," Kitt said with a finality that cut off any further argument.

Gobin and Gilroy watched as Kitt crossed the backyard in three steps, went over the low wall like a cat, then he was gone.

"You can't leave by day, Rilante-man. If you try, you'll be caught and ripped apart. Leave by night," Gobin advised. "Rest up, nobody will look for you here. We'll use the soot in the oven to hide your hair colour, and you can go after dark when they can't see your eyes."

"Why would you help me get out of here alive?"

"Because Kitt saved you."

"Nobody got out, did they, Cryssumha-smith? Why did you tell lies to the boy? Do you know the old harbour is foul with blood?"

Gobin suddenly looked tired to death. "It is all Glic Tusil's doing; he is going out of his way to destroy Kitt's soul. But I won't allow it. There were so many people plotting, Ardri, Glic Tusil, Gasda, Morrik, not least you and Warmond. Kitt was in the middle of it all, and whatever he did, whichever way he turned, somebody would come to harm. That's why I lied to him."

"Saving one life, the life of Prince Ardri, your Kitt spelt death for countless others. You don't want that he realises that either?"

"What for? To demonstrate to him how bad things arise from good deeds? What use is that to anyone? You leave the boy in peace! He saved your life too!"

"Fair enough. He pulled me out of the river, despite the run-in we had here earlier."

"Because you were in danger. Just like Prince Ardri. It is that simple."

263

"Yes, I see." Gilroy really did see. "But life isn't that simple, and if you think you can shield the big boy from that knowledge..."

A great bell tolled from Castle Marrak, and all the smaller bells of Ulud pealed and jingled. Gilroy sprang up pale-faced, his hair standing on end.

"The bells!" Gobin groaned. "Silence the bells!"

Chapter 23
Prince on the Run

The bronze disc in the Mirror Chamber in Castle Marrak emitted a bright tone, but nobody heard it in the empty rooms in the tower Tirdich. In the silvery bronze mirror on the wall appeared the bewildered face of King Tirnmas, talking to himself. "Weak, I am weak, and old. I was a man once, I was a king. But what is kingship, when she looks at me with her black, beautiful, merciless eyes."

Crown Prince Flannan burst into the room. "So my little brother Ardri is found. But now Lord Gasda has gone into the Bacenis. Kione Lonnir, again! And Ardri has married Lord Morrik's daughter!"

"You suspect your brother Ardri of duplicity?" King Tirnmas demanded heavily.

"Naturally," Flannan said cheerfully. "I like my little brother. But that has never blinded me to the fact that he's crooked like a cloak needle. What I should have done, long ago, is take the treasury and buy steel blades and hire men to wield them. I should have gone to Isenkliff where the Eternal Smith has his forge, to replace the bronze with cold, clean steel."

"Steel," Tirnmas said. "It would strain our precarious hold on the Cryssumha province because many would not like that."

"Of course not. Steel will end their world. From the beginning, Rilante was tied to Cryssumha by chains of bronze. I will cut through our dependence with iron blades. I will go to Isenkliff. So many warriors have passed our coast on their way there. Nobody even knows where exactly that island lays, not even those who've been there. May take months to find it, months to get what I need from the Eternal Smith. I have lost too much time."

"You are the crown prince, Flannan, you have the right to shape the future of Rilante, beginning even now. However, your brother Ardri..."

"You know father, I would not have minded to cede my right of primogeniture to Ardri. He always wanted to rule so much more than I did. And I was almost prepared to take my ship, my crew and strike out for new land, cut into it like Torin Daraval and carve out a kingdom as far as my arm reaches, then leave my descendants to the weary task of holding it together and governing it. But this I can't allow, this filthiness and sorcery that was Cryssumha to arise again."

"I don't understand," Tirnmas said. "What is it you are talking about Flannan?"

"Cryssumha rising. They want to bring back Cryssumha, Ardri, Lord Morrik, a sorcerer name of Glic Tusil and...and..."

"Queen Serenaiba?"

She stood in the door, slim and upright in her purple pleated gown, her long black hair slick and straight around her perfect face. Tirnmas stretched out his hand to her in an odd supplicating gesture, and she came and took it in her own paper-white fingers.

Flannan's face hardened, suddenly he looked much older.

"Don't listen to him, my husband!" Serenaiba said in her low husky voice. "Ardri comes to present his bride. Is it not the most wonderful news? Neelam is a dear girl and so beautiful! And I believe she is expecting." The last, she whispered. "We will be doting grandparents, Tirnmas."

Nobody had ever looked less like a doting grandmother to Flannan. "So, Ardri is coming? You should know, Serenaiba. Then he will be here in a few days. Lord Morrik means at least a thousand lances, and better than ours. I bet he has as much Findrun bronze as he wishes. We should hire Nordmänner. They sign on by entire ships and are the best warriors within reach, able to face down Morrik. We will have to get rid of them later, or at the worst cede them some ports for the time being. I will prepare Iwerdonn for a siege."

"Prince Nolan Ri has gone mad!" Serenaiba cried. "He is talking of steel and closing Iwerdonn against his brother Ardri!"

King Tirnmas drew himself up. "You can't hold the city against our ally Lord Morrik, and I don't want you in Iwerdonn when your brother arrives. Will you go, Flannan! At once! I order you to! I am still the King of Rilante, not a swaddled baby for which you seem to mistake me."

266

Flannan looked at his father keenly because for a moment Tirnmas seemed the king he had been twenty years ago, the adored hero of Flannan's childhood, standing tall with a whimsical smile on his lips.

"I'll be as fast as I can, father."

The Crown Prince strode from the hall, the war banner of his long red hair blazed for a short moment in the sunlight streaming through a window, and then the door closed behind him.

When Flannan had gone, King Tirnmas' figure crumpled. He was an old defeated man again, but the shadow of that whimsical smile still hovered in the corner of his mouth.

The mirror image faded in the empty tower Tirdich of castle Marrak.

*

There were no mirrors or bells in the wing of the castle which the Crown Prince occupied. Nobody saw him go into the part where he hosted special prisoners. Flannan believed in courtesy towards your enemy.

"Lynch!" he addressed the pirate captain with the wild red hair who inhabited a comfortable suite with a sea view. "I have to find Lodemar again and you are going to help me!"

***

Aware that his canoe was visible as a black bug on a silver plate, Kitt kept his eyes on the right river shore. The Struenfoly was too wide for arrow volleys unless the attackers took to boats. But single shots by an exceptional shooter with an exceptionally powerful bow could hit.

If there was such a shooter, his chances were growing slimmer. The river widened along its run with small tributaries adding their water. The starry sky above turned slowly and the river changed direction in a long loop, beginning to run west-south-west, away from the Murkowydir. Now, the green pasture land, dotted with solitary trees, extended on both sides of the river.

The sun came up in Kitt's back, and the bed of the Struenfoly had widened still more. Strips of mud appeared on both sides with the tide beginning to go out. Now, he met shipping craft on the river, shallow-bottomed single-masted boats with triangular sails crewed by Rilante-men who looked out curiously as the canoe shot past them downriver.

Then, the breath of the bay was in Kitt's face, strong and mild. The town of Bilawini lay on the left shore, her harbour a forest of masts and serpent keels.

In the middle of the bay was an island with another small harbour where two three-masters were moored side by side. One was about one hundred and fifty feet long, including the beam and two and a half decks, and had elegant racing lines. It showed signs of extensive repair and a new foremast was being rigged.

This ship was dwarfed by the other, double as long, two hundred and eighty feet precisely with another thirty-six feet for her beam and a one-hundred-and-fifty-foot mainmast. Kitt knew the larger ship very well; it was the Birlinn Yehan, which had visited Isenkliff several times. She was the most wonderful vessel that he had ever seen, with a steel skeleton beneath her wooden hull, steel plate enforced bottom and three and a half decks.

Kitt rowed in under her curving stern and then alongside until he spotted a sailor. "Permission to come aboard Potrek!"

The sailor peered down to him. "Well, I never! Kitt! You here!" he disappeared.

Kitt held his position; he didn't have to wait long until a rope ladder came down. "Skipper says, come up directly!"

Kitt fastened his canoe to the hooks of the ladder and climbed up. On deck, he came face to face with Captain Lodemar, a lithe man above middle height in his thirties with blond hair he wore in a clubbed braid and the beardless face of a scholar. He was clad in cloth breeches, a blue shirt with a brown brocade waistcoat and over-knee boots.

Beside him stood a younger man; he was tall, wide-shouldered, wiry, with natural grace, his freckled pirate face framed by a fiery bush of thick, dark-red curls. His strong chin was clean-shaven and showed a deep cleft; he had a hook nose, a long mouth and vividly blue eyes. He wore a bronze ringmail tunic, with a blue silk cloak hanging from his shoulder.

"Well, well. Seems it comes all together now," Captain Lodemar remarked. "Couldn't make head or tail of the things your man told.

268

Just didn't make the connection. Kitt, this is Prince Flannan of Rilante, and he is telling me..."

"Excuse me just a moment, Lodemar," the man in the blue cloak requested. "Brodi!" he shouted; his voice carrying easily above the noises of the ship and sea.

A soldier in worn leather and bronze stepped briskly across the deck followed by a tall, slim dark-haired man in a black leather kilt and vest. At the sight of Kitt, he grinned, showing a row of even white teeth in a short blond beard. The other man raised a dark eyebrow. Kitt knew these men.

"Kiddo! You here! My prince, this is the kid who..."

"I know who he is." A peculiar expression of mixed emotions crossed the young royal's face as he looked Kitt up and down. "Yes, I have heard your name, and felt, even more, the consequences of your actions."

Sailors and soldiers drew nearer across the deck, and Kitt noted where each man stood, how each was armed while keeping his attention on the prince; he was the most dangerous, and he was irate.

"What I want to know," Lodemar spoke up, "How come and what you're doing here, Kitt?"

"Yes, that's what we want to know and what the hell you mean by it," the prince said. "Where ought he to be then, Lodemar?"

"Why, on Isenkliff! He is master Eckehart's son and a deuced good blacksmith in his own right. A master, don't be fooled by his young age."

"I was cut off in the Murkowydir, the Bacenis. Have to go home the long way around. Hoped you could spare me a boat."

"Isenkliff." Again, the prince measured Kitt up and down, his face unreadable, and then he smiled a tight little smile. "You went there, Lodemar."

"Guilty as charged," the captain said. "A good sword Master Eckehart forged for me. Feels like an extension not only of my arm but my will."

"You showed it to me the last time, when we met in the middle of the sea." Prince Flannan smiled. "That's when I conceived a wish to go to Isenkliff myself to have an Aurora blade made. And maybe a cannon."

269

"We blew his Golden Hind out of the water," Lodemar indicated the two iron cylinders mounted on the bow and the repairs on the neighbouring ship. "It was Kitt here who thought that they could be made of iron instead of bronze."

"Indeed," Flannan frowned.

"Had to cast the metal," Kitt provided blithely. "We don't often do such work on Isenkliff."

"They functioned as you thought, too, which didn't stop Flannan from boarding me but he sure was impressed with the Aurora Blade. Wanted to hear all about it."

"That is why I went after you particularly," Flannan said. "Now I'm wondering about the cannon. Did you think that you were arming my enemy? As Lodemar was then."

Kitt hadn't thought about Prince Flannan at all at the time and just stopped himself from saying so. "Lodemar is my friend."

"That is so," Lodemar said.

"They say, anyone who wants an indestructible Aurora Blade, must fight a giant first," Flannan said with a hard look at Kitt. "Are you that giant? Must I fight you?" The prince's sword hand hovered near the hilt, his eyes sparkling in a mad blue fire.

The men stirred, pushing Brodi in the back, who stood rooted to the spot.

"If we are to make a sword for you, we will cross blades. To find out your weaknesses and strengths. To adapt the sword to the fighter.

"My strength and weakness?" Flannan raised his brows. "You can test me right here, right now, Kitt of Isenkliff."

"Not before breakfast," Lodemar said with authority. "Come to the cabin! You look hungry, Kitt."

"Three days on the Struenfoly." Kitt was already halfway along the deck, leaving behind a suddenly bemused crown prince. He spotted Pots, the cook, waving to him from the ship's galley and grinning. "I'm frying some extra lamb cutlets!" he called.

Kitt made to go down the companionway to the sailors' mess. Lodemar laid his hand on his elbow. "Main cabin!"

The Birlinn Yehan had a big cabin with a long table, which was now laden with dishes under metal covers, scrambled eggs, sausages, black and white pudding, and fried bacon, by the appetising smell.

Slabs of yellow butter reposed on glass dishes, and there was dark and white bread. Kitt smelt the incredibly rarefied aroma of coffee. Pots the cook came in carrying two roasted geese on a huge silver platter.

Kitt went to the table end where the youngest ships officers usually sat.

Lodemar intercepted him again. "Sit here by the crown prince and me," he invited, leading the way to the head of the table. "Flannan has questions, and I am bursting to hear your tale."

"So am I," the prince said grimly, apparently not mollified by the generous spread.

The cabin filled with men. Kitt was on Lodemar's left, on the right was the prince. A boy took up station behind Flannan's chair. Lodemar's First, his younger brother Karnatz, took the chair beside Kitt. He was a sailor as capable as the captain, the mirror image of him, and the cause for the legend that Lodemar never slept. Sailmaster, quartermaster and steersman sat down at table, all professional men who knew Kitt well and were as pleased as they were mystified to see him. Three men well-dressed in blue linen were unknown to Kitt, the prince's, he guessed. As everybody was sitting, there was no immediate threat. Behind Kitt was the window of the main cabin, panels of thick round glass that let in the light, mounted in wooden frames. A fragile structure. Kitt thought that he was not as hemmed in, as it might appear.

"So Kitt, going back for the end of the sailing season?" Lodemar remarked, carving a roasted goose. "You'll be on time, though no ship from the south has passed Cape Akla these days."

"You should know, my dear Lodemar, with your habit of lurking in the Koim waters," Flannan said easily.

"I feel at home in the islands." Lodemar grinned unrepentantly.

"Which of them you call home, I never found out. That is rather the point, I do understand, though I hope that one day you will invite me. I beg your pardon, I interrupted."

Lodemar proceeded to deposit an entire goose leg on Kitt's plate. It dripped with yellow fat, and the skin was crisp brown. Kitt started eating. Noticing that he was the first to dig in did not make him stop. All the men began plying their cutlery without further ceremony. For a time, nobody spoke.

271

We know Kitt well from Isenkliff," Karnatz was resuming the conversation. "He is Master Eckehart's assistant, who is relying on him for many things." he explained to the Rilante-men.

As always when he thought of his father working alone, Kitt felt a pang of bad conscience. For a moment, it spoiled his appetite. A young smith was expected to journey to learn from other masters, as Kitt had learned from Master Gobin. It was an excuse that failed to convince him.

"He presented his master-piece already two years ago, didn't you, Kitt?" Karnatz pursued.

"And overdue even then, by Gavido Lord of Smiths!" the sailmaster exclaimed. "Your braces are holding up wonderfully, Kitt my boy. Never had trouble with them since."

"What was your masterpiece?" Flannan inquired.

"A sword for an old fighter."

"Diorlin of Eliberre," Lodemar elaborated.

"Indeed," Flannan raised his red brows. "Of course, I heard of the Swordmaster of the Red Lily Knights, but I had no idea that you knew him."

"Last autumn I ran into him and his knights on Isenkliff, fresh from being taught some humility. They were so embarrassed by being whipped by a fifteen-year-old smith, as Kitt was then, that they hung one of their fancy cloaks over him and made him a knight. Right, Kitt, you're a Knight of the Red Lily!"

"Not for real," Kitt said doubtfully.

Pots appeared behind him and plunked a stack of three lamb cutlets right onto his plate and poured hot mint sauce over the whole. Kitt applied himself gratefully, the goose leg having taken but the edge off his appetite.

"You are wrong not to take such an investiture seriously," Flannan remarked. "If you are a Lily Knight, you owe them aid, and they you."

"A Red Lily Knight? That makes for an interesting diplomatic complication," one of Flannan's men said. He was older, and the net of lines around his bright blue eyes deepened as he smiled.

"Lord Bonyd of the Queen's Service," Lodemar informed in an aside to Kitt; by his tone this seemed to be important, and the older man heard and sketched a slight bow.

"So, as you are a blacksmith." Flannan poised his butter knife in the air. "Will you make a sword for me?"

"Yes!" Kitt's flush of excitement spoke more than that one word. He itched to get his hands on steel again. Not only did the Crown Prince of Rilante seem a capable fighter from what Kitt could see. Forging a sword for him after fashioning a blade for Diorlin would make his reputation as a blacksmith. And incidentally, solve any issues the prince might have with him, Kitt hoped. Flannan certainly looked pleased for the first time.

"I better warn you right now Kitt," Lodemar said. "You won't have it all your own way with the crown prince like you did with those hapless young Lily Knights. And me, truth be told. But you won't be able to beat him either, Flannan. Right impudent jackanapes with a blade. Nobody got the better of him yet, not even Swordmaster Diorlin of Eliberre."

"But I didn't get the better of him either," Kitt said. He had no idea what caused both Lodemar and Flannan to laugh out loud.

"Right," Lodemar wiped his eyes. I'll get us out of the harbour on the tail of this tide. The Golden Hind must follow when she can, poor buggers. Be feeling safer at sea. I really want to be far away from Clencarde."

They all looked to backboard as if they could see the island, barren and unprepossessing with bare rock and stunted shrubs.

"There's a sunken garden in the middle, flowers of all colours as never grow on the mainland, and marble columns and golden fountains, every rock is a gemstone and it's full of butterflies and dragonflies. All so beautiful to make an old salt sailor weep," Lord Bonyd said, intended for Kitt. "The Sunken Garden of Clencarde belongs to a beautiful Cryssumha lady, or so the tale goes for no one has ever seen her."

"It was that sort of thing that drove me out to sea," Flannan said. Everywhere in Rilante, you find something ancient of theirs, a six-cornered house, eight cornered tower, sunken garden, hidden wells, a disused mine that seems bottomless. Even in Iwerdonn, and I suspect something like that stuck in the heart of the royal palace. As a kid, I measured every room, and the floor plan just never added up."

"That's what I mean," Lord Bonyd said. "My people are from Gollien. There is a stone tower all grown over with roses, and in it a

273

princess has been sleeping for centuries, white as snow, red as blood and black as ebony. The neighbours' son went to wake her with his kiss and never came back. He was not the first nor the last. In winter, when there's no leaves nor roses, if you look closely, you see white bones deep within the thicket. Never went back home, not that I could have, because all roads lead away from Gollien, and that's another sorcery."

The breakfast round disbanded. When the men came on deck, the broad mudflats to both sides of the river were narrowing with the incoming tide.

"And now you'll see something," Lodemar said to Flannan. "We'll just steam out, and no sailing craft will be able to tail us with this west wind." He went away shouting commands that sent sailors running; down in the ships belly wheels were turning, and the two propellers at the stern churned the water. Out at sea, the sails of the bowsprit went up and caught the breeze. A gust of wind hit their faces as the Birlinn Yehan cleared the island of Glencarde and ploughed into the western sea. Flannan breathed in deep that his broad chest widened, and so did Kitt.

For the first time, the Prince laughed. "What if we sail on westward and never turn back? There are rich lands under the sunset. Mind, we would have to do a lot of crossing against the wind, but with this ship, we can do it."

"The Nordmänner say there is a passage directly to the Islands Beneath the Sunrise. Far enough even for dragons to live there."

"Why, you look like you want to go at once?"

"Every time I see a ship, I wonder where it's going, and I'd like to go with it."

"I believe you," Flannan said. This went a long way to explain how Kitt had wound up in Rilante, he thought.

Chapter 24
A Sword for a King

Vasara eschews war, doffs armour and blade and contemplates herself in mirrors. Battles will be fought with iron, and an ironsmith will be the last to know the mystery of the bronze blade in the stone.

Ardri, King of Cryssumha, Star Observation Journal

The feeding and watering of the sheep and cattle were over. This was a big part of the day. The Birlinn Yehan was used to carrying animals, but this time the whole lower deck had been converted into a stable and store for the hay and grain and the separate water supply. Prince Flannan had worked with the men. Now he stood on the freshly washed upper deck in a blue hose and tunic. He wore no mail. His dark red hair was tied back in a knot.

He drew his sword, it was a golden, gleaming Findrun bronze blade. "Ready when you are."

Kitt drew his steel blade and placed the simple sheath by the middle mast beside the goldstudded one of Flannan's sword. When they saw their Prince square off with the newcomer, the Rilante men drew a ring around them. Flannan noticed that most of them kept their hands near their hilts.

"...I've heard that name, isn't that the bastard..." he heard one of them mutter.

"Don't talk nonsense, Coil!" Brodi snapped.

"Will you look at that brute! The prince shouldn't step in front of that one?" Flannan could see what caused that remark. The boy was three inches taller than the crown prince and built to scale, with the impressive shoulders and arms of a blacksmith. At sixteen years old he was probably stronger than Flannan at twenty-five. Strength was not all, least workman's strength.

"He'll step, and he'll hit," another soldier said.

"Give us more room!" Flannan demanded, a sharp tone of command in his voice that was enough to drive the men back, and the circle widened. "I want you to keep the men in order, Brodi!"

"Yes, my Prince!" Brodi glared at the men. "Neilo, give me a hand here!"

Neilo stepped forward, tall and rangy, his dark leather clothing flapping in the wind like crow wings. His steel-blue eyes passed from one face to the next. Everyone took back two steps. Neilo had a reputation that still fell far short of what he could do, Flannan knew.

Iron and bronze met with a clash. Flannan's eyes widened a little, and he strove to hide his surprise. It was a hard hit. The next blow was even harder, but this time Flannan met it without giving way. Kitt increased the force, and yet again with each passage, and then suddenly desisted. Their eyes met for a moment while the fighters retook their positions.

"Had enough, barbarian whelp?" Coil shouted, and the others laughed.

Not too bright, they weren't, Coil and his friends. Kitt had just found the limit of Flannan's resistance, but the merry comments from the Rilante men assured the crown prince that only he and Kitt were aware of that. *How long? What does the boy intend?* It was a nasty situation, which Flannan had not foreseen. Lodemar had tried to warn him.

During the following fast passage of arms, the blades flickered like pale gold and white lightning in the summer sun. Kitt worked out three advantages, none of which he pressed. The Rilante men all celebrated each action of their prince unconditionally. Fine beads of sweat stood on Flannan's face. As they continued fencing, Flannan noticed a slowing of his movements, beginning to tire. With a sharp, vicious slash, the iron blade bit deeply into the bronze. Everybody who heard it flinched.

Kitt stepped back and lowered his sword. "I know all I need about you, Prince Flannan, and what sword to make for you," he said formally.

Flannan expelled the deep breath he had drawn in. The men still hadn't realised how their prince had been played. Except for Neilo, who had both his hands in his leather sleeves, around two knife hilts, the prince knew.

276

"Iron to cut the bronze of Cryssumha!" he called out loud. "That is how we shall win back our land. We go to Isenkliff, and every man will carry an Aurora blade back to Rilante! All my men armed in iron, an iron blade for each, spears, axes, armour."

The men cheered again without reserve. Flannan was relieved at this reception of his radical plan. "So we'll go to Isenkliff together. What do you think of my plan?" he asked so that only the nearest men heard. "You don't look happy? Well, I tell you, you're coming. Rilante can't carry you."

"That's true," Brodi said, "Boy like that, beat us at every turn. What you'll be when you grow up, kiddo? Just hope I'll not be anywhere near then."

Flannan's eyes challenged Kitt. "Do you intend to stand in my way when I take back Rilante?"

"Not at all. I'll go home. Never to come back. Ever."

"I'll make sure you get home. But now, you get to work! Thanks to you I'm not only a crown prince without a crown to look forward to but one without a sword. That is an intolerable position, don't you think?"

Kitt nodded. "Iron is the only chance for you."

"You agree? You know, you interest me strangely."

"The forge is in the forecastle," Lodemar said. "Kitt knows all about it, as he set it up for me. There's a lot of iron on this ship. Gero will have the coal brought up, and then he can be your handyman like last time."

"Aye Captain," Gero said, a shade resigned it seemed to Flannan. Gero was the Birlinn Yehan's smith, but apparently only when Kitt wasn't aboard. Lodemar really did make much of the boy. So did the rest of the crew. The prince wondered if that was justified. After all, the lad was barely sixteen years old. And fought like an entire Nordmänner ship's crew, he reminded himself. Without making an exhibition of it. His men hadn't realised.

Kitt found the forge on the forecastle as he had left it a year ago, battened down with a tarpaulin.

He fired the charcoal and then waited for it to glow through, watching the slow passage of the cliffs, white beaches and meadows of the luminous green that he had first seen in Rilante. He had

277

smelled the animals when coming aboard. He had heard some talk that Flannan was going to Asringholm to forge an alliance with the Nordmänner who used the Rilante ports, and noticed the northward course of the ship. Kitt had meant to ask Lodemar for a boat at the height of Kallasness to make his way east on the route the warriors took who came to Isenkliff by ship. He had looked forward to doing that so much that it had become a sort of certainty with him. Now it had turned out, however, that the talk of Asringholm had been to mislead casual listeners in Bilawini port. In truth, all the cattle were intended for Isenkliff. Lodemar knew what he had to bring, having made the run more often than any other sea captain. It was the part of the transaction Kitt liked least but without the Jarnmantsje, the Lütte Jotun, there would be no forge on Isenkliff. They supplied most of the iron ingots and the coal; they had to be compensated with meat. Since he knew how many of the Lütte Jotun lived under Isenkliff, he knew that he could never feed them singlehanded, however much he hunted. The Birlinn Yehan took enormous amounts of iron to maintain and repair. And on this occasion, an army needed to be outfitted with steel. It wouldn't be the first time that such a thing had been accomplished by Brynnir's Forge. Flannan in Isenkliff, blaming Kitt for the happenings in Rilante, meeting his mother – it did not bode well.

The forge held an even bed of glowing coal, and Kitt rummaged about the pieces of steel, selecting several and placing them to heat. Gero went down the hatchway to bring up more coal from the ship's belly.

Flannan did not intend to leave Kitt to work in peace. He sat down on the tool-chest as if he had found his abiding place for the day. "Brodi tells me that you came out of the Bacenis," the prince said far too casually.

"Never meant to come this far," Kitt said. "I was cut off by the Hunters in the Mist."

"What, they really exist?"

"I was caught in a battle between the Feen Woodstalkers and … them. Ended up in their mountain. Full of bears."

Gero returned and began to work the bellows. The way he moved told Kitt to let him get on with it by himself. Gero was grouchy sometimes.

278

"Brodi said that Woodstalker chief, the Murder Bear also was in the area. That he was seen in Dundingin. Somebody sold him Findrun lances. What do you know about him, Kitt?"

"He wears a Bethrek tooth."

"Human oyster, aren't you Kitt? Do I have to drag out every word? Tell me about the Woodstalkers and the Hunters in the Mist, as you must know more about them, than most."

Kitt didn't intend to tell how he had slain three of the mist creatures, one a female, a woman. Nor about his frequent run-ins with the Feen and Mangan Sorkera. Nor what had happened in Minit Claghini and Kione Lonnir. "They eat human flesh."

"The bears or the Woodstalkers or Hunters in the Mist?"

"All of them. But the Hunters in the Mist knock their meat on the head first. And they don't torture. So I guess they're human for that."

"Or not. An interesting philosophical question."

Kitt continued sorting through the pieces of steel.

"Iron is not as beautiful as bronze," the Prince said, turning a piece of iron in his hands. "A bronze sword is a jewel as well as a weapon. Iron is just a tool."

For all his love of iron Kitt understood the beauty of bronze, had felt the enchantment in the warm, rosy gleam, the heavy, slick smoothness. But he wasn't going to admit that.

"Don't touch anything!" He took the iron from Flannan's hand. "Got the fresh coal going, Gero? Then work that bellows!"

The older workman worked the bellows vigorously, muttering: "Slave driver, that's what you are, at your young age too. What you'll be when you grow up..."

"Everybody seems to wonder that." The prince's mouth twitched. "A dangerous nuisance comes to mind. Why couldn't you stick to smithing? You seem to know that well enough?"

"Damn it!" Kitt pushed the steel bar into the forge with unnecessary violence. "I found your brother in the woods! How was I supposed to know?"

"A just remark," Flannan said with feeling. "Very just indeed. But you must understand that your impact on the affairs of Rilante has been impossible to neglect. In fact, when I heard your name shouted on this deck, I wondered whether my little brother had foreseen my move and that you were coming for me. Seems you didn't, because you could have killed me at will. I handed you the opportunity on a silver platter."

Gero turned around to gape at them both.

"Not easily. You are good."

"But you are better. Much better."

"Yes."

"Yes," Flannan mimicked. "Well, why bother with phrases of polite denial, if that's how it is. I'm glad that you're not fighting on the other side."

"Why should I fight on any side?"

Flannan cocked his head. "There could be so many reasons."

"No." Kitt shook his head. "There are very few reasons. The best fight is the one avoided."

"Come now, Kitt!" Flannan protested. "Nobody learns to fight like you do, just to avoid it."

"Wrong. You see, if I am good, nobody can force me to kill them if I don't want to."

"Force you to kill them if you don't want to," Flannan repeated, staring at the youth. "You have truly extraordinary ideas. Must have surprised Ardri. Didn't he offer you a place with him? I can't believe he willingly let go of a weapon of your calibre."

"He offered. But I'm not going to take mercenary service. Or any service. And I didn't trust him. He didn't trust me either. Attempted twice to shut my mouth for good. That's only counting the times I realised." There had been at least two or three more occasions when Kitt hadn't been sure. "Others also tried. I don't know how much Ardri knew about that." Kitt lifted the smoking iron block out of the forge and threw it on the anvil, hot ashes and sparks scattering about. He took the hammer from Flannan's hand and beat the iron relentlessly, tirelessly, slag splinters flying to all sides; some hit Flannan's face and hands like small hailstones.

Flannan grinned crookedly. "Then excuse me, Kitt, but why..."

"Why did I keep your brother alive again and again?" There was a rawness in Kitt's voice and the following sentences he interpunctuated with hard hammer blows. "When I saw - Prince Ardri – he didn't know he was doomed - deep in the Bacenis - hadn't the least chance - couldn't think how he even got that far."

"Don't mistake my brother for an anaemic scholar nor a royal wimp. He's a skilled warrior, brave and astute, and a cunning hunter."

Kitt waved away Ardri's accomplishments with the hand that held the twenty-pound-hammer. "It's entirely the wrong kind of skill and cunning to survive in the Murkowydir that you call Bacenis. That day it was my decision if Ardri lived or died. Didn't like that decision, had to make it all the same, in the time it took a Bethrek to jump – and they are fast." Kitt pushed the iron back into the forge. "Work that bellows!"

"Yes, your high and mightiness," Gero muttered.

"You would always decide in favour of life, is that right, Kitt?" Flannan seemed to understand unexpectedly quick.

"Life is the right decision. From then on, I felt responsible for Ardri. So I continued to save him. I blamed all on his royal birth. That star pattern. The old kingdom of Cryssumha. I think now that I was afraid to admit that I had made a mistake that cost – lives." Kitt passed his hand over his face, thinking of Blaitisin. "I should have stood aside, let those assassins do their job."

"Assassins?" Flannan roared. "Brodi! Neilo!"

"They tried to stop what was going on in Dundingin," Kitt said. "It was the last chance. If you turn against your men you don't deserve Isenkliff steel. How do I even know you're the righteous one?"

"Now don't you take that tone with the crown prince!" Gero admonished.

"Work the bellows!" Kitt and Flannan said in unison.

Flannan grinned. "Well I am the good guy, but you won't know that by my telling you so. However, being the crown prince at least goes to show my birthright. You may not be impressed by it, but it can't be set aside by anything less than a unanimous decision of the full throne council, and then only if I became incapable or insane. Also, you won't hear many complaints about my conduct from citizens, only from pirates and the like lawbreakers. I am really a useful member of society and can bring quite a number of testimonials to my character."

"Truth under the sun, that is," Gero said. "We were on the wrong side of the law, Lodemar and Lynch and all of us, but we made the full turn, we did, and there are no hard feelings now."

"Come around at a time when I'm heir only to the clothes I'm standing up in," Flannan said. "I won't forget that, Gero my friend, whichever way this mess pans out. Truth is I wouldn't have been averse to let Ardri king it in Rilante. But Cryssumha rising, that is another matter."

"Don't you even think it Prince Flannan," Gero protested, "or what are we all here for?"

Brodi approached across the deck at a run. "My prince?"

"Nothing Brodi, my friend. Just a minor point concerning the events in Dundingin, which Kitt here has been able to elucidate to my entire satisfaction. He speaks well of you and Neilo."

"Why, thanks, kiddo!"

"Stop calling me kiddo!"

"Whatever you say, big boy." Brodi grinned like a maniac.

"Don't misunderstand me," Flannan said, "Ardri is after all my brother, and I've always been fond of him. Still am, strange as that may seem. So, I am grateful you saved his neck. But I must stop him."

"And how!" Brodi agreed.

Flannan sighed, fidgeting with the iron. "Ardri is a thoroughly rotten brother to me, but I feel it is not his fault so much, but that of his mother, Queen Serenaiba. She isn't my mother, thank goodness. My mother, the Queen Murine, was beloved by all."

"The Mother of Thirteen bless and rest the sweet lady," Gero and Brodi muttered reverently.

Flannan's face softened for a moment, then hardened again. "But Serenaiba, my father's second wife, she comes from an indecently old Cryssumha family. Seemed a sound political idea at the time to link up the royal house of Rilante with the old Cryssumha nobility. Unfortunately, they are Donadroch sorcerers. Not that you'd notice it looking at Serenaiba. She's so very beautiful." For a moment, Flannan seemed to pursue a disagreeable thought. "Ardri is caught up in a net, hers and that sorcerer's, Glic Tusil. The Spectre in the Mirrors. For years he's been coming and going in the castle of Iwerdonn and...things happened. But there are still people who think

282

he's a ghost. I know how that must sound to you. I express myself badly." Flannan frowned with the effort.

"It was the same in Dundingin," Brodi said. "The Monster of Castle Marrak. But Glic Tusil the Alchemist seemed just an old guy, and somehow you didn't even think of snuffing him. I'm still not sure..."

"I know Glic Tusil." Kitt kicked at a piece of coal that it clattered against the side.

"Well, Serenaiba is much the same. Picture that old rook of a Donadroch sorcerer as a beautiful woman, white as snow, red as blood and black as ebony."

Kitt stopped working to stare at Flannan. "I refuse to try."

Flannan chuckled. "Did you see Ardri's bride Neelam? What's she like?"

"Just beautiful. Like you say, white as snow, red as blood and black as ebony."

"She would be. Never mind. All three of Serenaiba's sons were fine boys."

"By your leave, my Prince." Brodi turned his back and walked away.

"Nobody liked them much." Flannan sighed. "But they were my little brothers. I taught them the bow and lance and sword, took them to hunt, and to sail on my ships, and they looked up to me. Then, suddenly, Ridevin and Kuranori started to avoid me and looked at me as if I was the lowest beetle. And then they both disappeared, one after the other. Only Ardri was left, Ardri who I liked best." Flannan's face worked. "When I first saw the same change in him, I could not bear it! But I think he still preserved me some fondness, like for an old dog, maybe. And now I can't help feeling that it is not really him who does some of the things he does."

"The Star Pattern of Cryssumha," Kitt murmured, and gripped the glowing iron with the tongs.

"Of course, you know what I'm talking about!"

"I do." Kitt laid down a crashing hammer blow. "Ardri...does nothing...against his will...at first...I thought like you...that he was caught...star pattern...he kept talking about...that it wasn't his fault...how daft I have been."

The hammer banged down with the same measured force as before, the rhythm hadn't changed. Flannan observed the young smith curiously, the set mouth, tense body, the way the big hands gripped the hammer.

It was at himself Kitt was angry, because of having been seduced by Ardri's natural charm, a grace of manner he felt he did not possess. Because of having let himself be flattered by open admiration of his strength and woods skill. Let himself be disarmed by his frank gratitude and trust, even when the prince's ruthless cunning had become apparent.

"Once...back in Dundingin...Ardri called all the shots...I was like a child in the woods...blindfolded. All those people...living so close together inside a wall...afraid of the woods beyond the Struenfoly...all these people selling something to the next...miner sells ore to the smelter...smelter sells copper ingots to the smith...smith sells a bronze knife or a bracelet...for coin which buys him food...from the farmer. I'm used to doing everything myself."

Kitt stopped hammering and put the iron on the hearth to reheat.

"And even out of your depth like that you succeeded in tipping all the scales in Dundingin. Or maybe because of that." Flannan picked up the hammer, weighed it in his hand, and estimating it at twenty pounds.

Kitt shrugged. "Ardri promised me the secrets of bronze. Then he wanted me away because I wouldn't serve him and knew too much. So he gave me a ship, as he had promised. Only he and I knew about that. But I didn't sail in it, because I didn't trust him." Kitt thought of the day when he had seen the broken planks swimming in the harbour water, fouled with rotting blood. The question whose blood it had been, had tormented him ever since. "Somebody else must have found that ship and tried to flee Dundingin in it, and that was their death. When we came into the town again, Gilroy and I, we saw the remains."

"You know Gilroy?"

"I fished him out of the Struenfoly. After Lord Gasda's thousand were defeated in the Bacenis."

"What is that you're saying, Kitt?"

Gero stopped working the bellows. "Yes, what are you talking about? The Dog of Rilante cannot be defeated! Only run away from.

284

When we got wise that he was anywhere over the horizon, we packed on sails and piled the coal, whichever got us away faster."

"Have you seen nobody come from Dundingin? Gobin had told me that Beibini and the waif, Ryoni, left together with Faibur and Fidcal, before the city guards were attacked by the mob. I hoped that Captain Warmond had got away too?"

"Our Lady Mother to Thirteen Shining Sons, give me patience!" Flannan exclaimed. "For the love of the Sun Kitt, will you speak already! Why was there a mob? Didn't Ardri and Lord Morrik take control of Dundingin and West Cryssumha?"

"Lord Gasda went into the Bacenis with his thousand to take Kione Lonnir."

"Brodi told me that. I couldn't believe that Gasda went after that fever dream and left the field to Morrik, but nobody said anything about a defeat." He shouted, "Brodi, come back here and bring Neilo! And ask Lodemar to step here for a moment!" To himself, he added, "He may want to revise his decision to join me."

"Never," Gero said stoutly.

Flannan considered the captain of the Birlinn Yehan and his officers. They looked shocked, which was surprising when he considered Gasda's relentless persecution of pirates and smugglers. Maybe they were thinking of the thousand soldiers lost in the Bacenis.

"The stone ship and the stone men, twelve silver and one golden," Kitt was saying in answer to Lord Bonyd's questions. "Ardri and I saw it. The Fihen, the Waldpirschers, didn't enter that valley. Because of the undead guards. No, not any more. Good place for us to sleep."

"So, Kione Lonnir exists." Flannan groaned. He had always loved the legend, but never expected it to take substance at the worst of times.

"I didn't see any survivors besides Gilroy," Kitt answered another of Bonyd's questions. "He said that Mangan Sorkera, I mean the Murder Bear and his Fihen, his Waldpirschers, killed or captured them all."

"Where is Gilroy now?"

"Left him in Dundingin with Gobin the master smith. I didn't want him with me as he'd attacked me once already."

285

"I see," Flannan said. People weren't safe where the business of kings was concerned, that was what Kitt thought, he knew as if he could read the boy's mind.

"Gilroy thought you were in Iwerdonn. Ardri left Dundingin with his queen and Lord Morrik and a thousand lances. Gilroy wanted to overtake them and warn you."

"But I already knew that Ardri was coming." Flannan laughed mirthlessly. "The pretence was that he'd come to present his bride."

Kitt looked to ask a question, changed his mind, but Flannan answered anyway. "Yes, I knew Ardri would come to Iwerdonn with Morrik. In fact, that very day I set out for Isenkliff. And I am still going after steel. The slaughter of Dundingin is past helping. That you saw no more fugitives, and that we didn't see any in Bilawini, may be a sign that Gasda has managed to gather the survivors and is making his way back. Gilroy should have lain low to warn them from entering Dundingin again, but Gasda will know anyway that he's been tricked." He desperately wanted to believe that.

Kitt shook his head. "Gasda is dead or captive. Dead is better."

Chapter 25
To Land and Sea

The day of the Black Sun falls on Atenu of the month Gorseren, seventh month after Winter Solstice. Then the Star of Cryssumha will be brightest. After the Sun returns, Vasara, Dilo and Lute go their separate ways. All that is set in motion then will reach completion.

Ardri, King of Cryssumha, Star Observation Journal

Unsuspectingly, the Rilante people had built their settlements on top of the old Cryssumha places.

Now, the old mine shafts opened, and ancient cellars and tunnels gaped, disgorging dark haired pale skinned people, curiously bent and twitching, to worship their king.

The crown Fenifindrune on his head, his shoulders wrapped in the Mooncat cloak, his hand never far from Slatynrigan's hilt, Ardri advanced west. The subjects of Cryssumha worshipped him, and the Rilante people just disappeared under them.

It was as if a black wave rolled on to Iwerdonn that engulfed all Rilante settlements in its way, with Ardri riding on top. No survivors escaped to carry a warning to the next Rilante towns which lay in his way.

*

The Birlinn Yehan made her way up the rough Rilante coast crossing into the steady north-west wind. Her crew was saving coal, using the steam prudently - they used the steam wheel sometimes to round one of the many capes. Their progress was helped by the northern current.

Being in a hurry, they still took the time to put into one of the many bays to warn the few settlements that Cryssumha had risen. The people did not panic. They listened to the crown prince of Rilante as he explained his quest for steel. Flannan wondered if he would be in time to justify their trust, and how long could they hold out. As long as they must, their grim faces told him.

As the ship proceeded almost straight northward, it began to rain every day, a steady drizzle of fine droplets. On the horizon rose brown hills to towering height and there was something eerie about them. The moors, Flannan explained to Kitt, wondering what might be sleeping inside those symmetric elevations. The big boy was extraordinarily easy to talk to, attentive to any information that came his way - to tell too much at times, Flannan found, but he could not stop.

The crown prince was on the forecastle often. The crown prince was on the forecastle often. He took over the duties of firing the forge and working the bellows from Gero who was pleased to escape Kitt's exacting demands. He was an older man who had been the ship's armourer until Kitt climbed onto the deck and re-organised the smithy to the acclaim of the crew, relegating Gero to an assistant role. He watched amazed as Flannan took over menial duties, carrying coal and ashes. The crown prince felt fine with being sent here and there with brief commands. Kitt meant no slight; he just made use of another pair of hands. Flannan found that the simple tasks took his mind off his worries. Even so, the crown prince watched with mixed emotions how his sword took shape. To him, it seemed an uncouth dark thing, and the blacksmith work an arcane rite involving fire and water and indescribably noxious substances such as boiled goose feathers and unwashed entrails.

Finally, Kitt declared the blade finished. It had the light colour of steel now and still didn't look more attractive than the first time Flannan had remarked on that. He refrained from saying so, not caring for another look from those grey eyes. Not scornful, not questioning, not arrogant. He struggled to find a word for that utter indifference.

Kitt laid the blade onto the anvil. He dipped a rag into a can of what he called Oil of Iron. Some ingredients had come from the cook, who had given them readily. Nobody on board the Birlinn Yehan was inclined to argue about anything with the young smith. He just expected everyone to comply. Just like he did himself as a Royal, Flannan admitted to himself, and perhaps with better reason. After all, the crew depended on the stability of iron, for being afloat and staying above water, trusted their lives to it and therefore to the smith. A king might well aspire to something like that, he thought.

As the rag passed across the blade, Flannan caught his breath at the pattern that sprang to life, dark and light circles and parallel lines along the edge. The broad hardening line gleamed like thin ice.

"This iron is beautiful," he acknowledged. "More beautiful than bronze even."

"The pattern has no value as such. Steel is either good or not. This steel is good. But you said blacksmiths can't do beautiful. So, I used every showy trick."

"You don't have to explain; I see the beauty." Flannan pointed to the seven dots. "Is this your signature? The northern chariot?"

"We call it the Hay Wagon. You want your old tang and grip? If you do, you will have to give even more attention to keeping the metal dry, especially at the junction, as corrosion may set in there."

After brief consideration, Flannan decided that he would, tang and grip being bronze that had come from Cladith Culuris with the first wave of settlers. He weighed the pommel in his hand, a golden lion's head. "This was part of the sword Torin Daraval gave to his younger brother, Conner. With this, he crushed the head of Star Cloud. He was the supreme Woodstalker chief and Donadroch magical warrior who held the lands now cultivated and called Nenaghen." Flannan handed over the pommel. "I wonder how Sidrum Castle has been faring. They lie on Ardri's way to Rilante."

"Old place?"

"Yes. On a mountain. There are caves." Flannan met Kitt's stricken eyes. "My brother is a big boy," he said. "His actions are not your fault."

"Say you," Kitt muttered, as he fitted the grip to the tang. So many men had told him that, his father, Grimwolf the Heerking, Gobin, and he wondered if he could he ever believe it.

"You can believe me," Flannan said.

*

When Ardri rode through the scoured town of Carrameille below Sidrum Castle, a Rilanteman stepped out of a doorway swinging a long double-bladed axe, which got stuck in the spine of the Cryssumha youth who threw himself in front of his king.

This gave Ardri time to draw the sword Slatynrigan. The assailant cried out as the bronze blade leapt forward and touched his head. Just a soft touch, not a blow or cut. A ripple seemed to run over his face from top to bottom, smoothing out the mask of hatred. The man ceased the struggle to free his axe and stood with his arms hanging down. The crowd of Cryssumha people tore him apart.

Before sheathing Slatynrigan, Ardri held the rose gold gleaming blade before his eyes. The reflection it gave back showed him that his eyes were not blue any longer, but black.

He looked at Neelam, his wife, his queen, and for the first time, she met his gaze fully and she smiled. For this smile alone, Ardri would destroy father and brother, and the whole of Rilante.

*

Kitt presented the hilt of the finished sword across his left forearm. "You want to try it out?

Flannan didn't really look forward to another bout with Kitt, but he could hardly say so. They faced off, and the ship's crew drew around. Their blades flickered in the rhythm of the precise figures Kitt had learned from Swordmaster Diorlin of the Red Lily Knights, the prince parrying in kind, and finally disengaged to the thunderous applause of crew and soldiers.

"Well, this was more like ballroom dance," Flannan hissed through his teeth. "Another showy trick Kitt?"

"Maybe a bit."

"Have you been called an arrogant pup before? I would like to call you something original, but you probably heard it all already."

"I'm not more skilled than you are. A little faster and a lot stronger. I'm stronger and faster than most men. Something I'm born with, nothing to be proud about."

"Now, who told you that nonsense? You're incomparable. I never met a swordsman like you. How does it feel to be invincible?"

"Nobody is invincible. At any one time there will be at least one man somewhere, but maybe two or three, who are better than I am. And then there is luck, too, if luck turns against me..." he shrugged. "Neither skill nor strength will save me then."

"Very proper reply. And another example of arrogance thinly disguised as humility. Like your Hay Wagon. You should watch that Kitt, it's not a trait to endear you to anyone."

"How can it be arrogance if it's the truth?"

"Sometimes I forget that you are a sixteen-year-old dolt because you're so big and silent. Then you open your mouth and remind me."

Kitt flushed. "Sometimes I forget you're a royal and Ardri's brother."

"Trying to forget it myself," Flannan said, soberly. "I keep imagining what damage is he inflicting while my back is turned? On Rilante, my father?"

*

On the third day of Mehefin, the sixth month after Winter Solstice, Ardri prepared to enter Iwerdonn, the capital of Rilante. On the eastern horizon, Vasara and Dilo stood as one star, the Star of Cryssumha.

The sun rose and for a moment the morning light drowned the Star of Cryssumha in the morning sky, but not quite, it was visible as a bright dot even by day.

And then the portent happened. The disk of the moon passed in front of the sun and slowly obscured the red disc until a fiery ring was left. All the world was dark while the Star of Cryssumha blazed in the east, reaching westward with fiery tendrils.

Ardri felt more than heard the shout arise from many throats mingled with a wail of terror.

"Only one more year," he said to Neelam, his wife, and wondered, how conscious she was of the Star Pattern that enveloped her life. "Seven years ago, I watched from the tower Brontigern as Vasara passed before the sun. It was the day after, that Ridevin left to find Fenifindrune. Stood you on one of the towers of Marrak to watch, Neelam? You were but a girl then. What did you make of this first groom and then Kuranori, the second betrothed who also left you in Ulud, never to return?"

"Ridevin, Kuranori, those were hardly names of kings of Cryssumha," she said in that bell-like voice of hers. "I was always waiting for the third to come."

Ardri shivered. "We'll watch together as Vasara conquers the sun for the second time and then the rise of Cryssumha will be irrevocable."

*

"It is always winter on this island," Lodemar said. He wore a sturdy sheep-skin jacket, and beside him, the crown prince wrapped his blue velvet cloak tightly around his shoulders and shuddered.

The Birlinn Yehan was being swept past Eissee by the current turning from straight north to north-east. Black and white trees stood in the fog, bare, without leaves; perhaps they were not alive any more. Through the gnarled trunks, they saw a small lake, and in it, naked men submerged to the hips. The mermen were hairless, jetblack, of exquisite proportions and moved very slowly in the dark water, in ever-narrowing circles as the lake froze. Some stood immobile in a ring of ice like the tree-trunks. As the Birlinn Yehan passed, they all turned their dark, symmetric faces to mournfully watch the ship through the trees which surrounded the lake like the bars of a cage.

"They have been like this every time I passed here," Lodemar said. "Never get used to the sight."

"Is there nothing in a book?" Kitt wanted to know. He was standing there with bare arms, apparently impervious to the cold. "A story, legend? Something about a curse and how to break it?"

"Not that I know," Lodemar said.

Flannan shook his head. "Not in the library of Iwerdonn. I have read everything that pertained to the seas. But you are thinking of rescue, aren't you Kitt? Find it hard to sail past and do nothing? I understand you for that is how I feel myself. Lodemar?"

"No!" the captain said decisively. "We don't know if they are even men."

"Exactly," Flannan said. "We don't know. What if they are?"

"I could take a boat," Kitt said. "You go on."

"Absolutely not!" Lodemar said. "What would I tell your parents?"

"What you saw here."

"You'll not have one of my boats. And you'll not go in that canoe you paddled about on the river. This is the ocean."

Kitt said nothing. His grey eyes challenged the older man. There was no way the captain of the Birlinn Yehan could keep the big youth from doing anything he wanted, Flannan thought. And Kitt knew it. Lodemar was aware, and every man aboard. Nobody would step in his way; it was as simple as that. Flannan thought that all the boy's courtesy and good manners and deference to his elders were no more than a thin veneer, an affectation even, and he wondered how to head him off. "Is this the main shipping route to Isenkliff?" he inquired of Lodemar. "You say that you saw these...mermen...here on Eissee every time you passed?"

"It is the main route, and I've been taking my bucket along here three years now. Always the same sight."

"There's a good chance then that they'll keep. But for now, Kitt, I will honestly tell you that I prefer you not meddle in yet another thing in Rilante. You tend to make a marked impact, and we cannot know if there isn't a connection between the Donadroch magic of Eissee and Cryssumha." A low blow, he acknowledged to himself.

The grey eyes were on him now. Not exactly a pleasant sensation, Flannan thought. Suddenly he sensed a wavering, a doubt. "When the troubles with Cryssumha are over, I'll send an expedition. No, I'll come myself. I promise you, Kitt."

"And you keep your promises," Kitt said, his voice colourless. "I know because Ardri did, too."

As far as low blows went, this was a well-aimed comeback, Flannan thought, and if he was giving enough credit to the boy -and how dangerous he was, what would happen if that wilfulness became more pronounced, who could rein him in then and if one day there would be no other remedy left than simply killing him.

There was a shout, and several sailors pointed upwards. An indescribable pall fell upon the world as the black disk of the moon was moving in front of the sun. The sunlight continued to fade. There were shouts of consternation on the ship.

"It's a celestial phenomenon of the sun and the moon!" Flannan shouted in his battlefield voice. "No danger!"

The dimming light lit the different expressions, fear, wariness, Lodemar's stolidity, Lord Bonyd's studied blankness, Kitt's eager face. Sailors were running and climbing to take in the sails.

"We're firing the kettle, in case," Lodemar said in a low voice.

"That's what I call being on your toes," Flannan said lightly. "No wonder you eluded me so long."

Kitt looked excited. "It was due. But somehow, I didn't believe it would really happen. I never saw an eclipse before. Only read about it in books."

"The moon?" Gero asked.

"Moving before the sun. Because it's nearer to us," Kitt explained.

"Sun and moon are the same sizes," Brodi objected. "You can see that. So they must be the same distance. How you talk, Kitt!"

"He's right though," the prince said. "You may take it from me Brodi. My little brother forecasted this eclipse; he was always calculating the course of the stars. He knew where the sun and moon ran their courses, every moment of the day. So that's why Kitt and Ardri got on so well. Both calculating the stars." Flannan couldn't see Kitt's face now. He heard Brodi's expelled breath.

"I don't believe in Star Patterns," Kitt said, "I need to know the tides. And times of light and darkness."

High waves were breaking around Eissee, the white foam shining in the growing gloom.

"The island is sinking!" somebody shouted.

"Springtide," Flannan said loudly.

The darkness grew deeper. The crew were muttering unhappily.

A final bright sunray winked out. In the black sky flamed a ring of fire, a feathery crown of light. The men on the ship fell silent. The sea rose and lifted the ship. Night winds were blowing. Brilliant beside the ring of fire a star glowed, bigger and brighter than all the other stars in the dark sky. The Star of Cryssumha, Kitt thought. Aloud he said, "Conjunction of the Wandering Stars, Blodstarna and Meginstarna, the Nordmänner call them." He didn't want to say the Cryssumha names "Conjunction, how you talk, Kiddo," Brodi sneered.

"You won't see this again in your lifetime," Flannan added.

"I hope not," Brodi said, almost inaudibly.

After what seemed a long time, but were only minutes, a bright ray of light appeared on the edge of the black disk. It grew into a half-moon shape that widened. The men sighed and then laughed with relief. When half of the sun was released from the black disk, they cheered. All suddenly felt that they could win.

Kitt kept his eye on the bright dot shining in the Eastern sky, drowned out by the light of the freed sun, but still there.

Eissee was slipping beneath the western horizon. Some of the crew were convinced that the island had sunk. Flannan told them that

294

was not so, and they didn't contradict. It was touching to see how these rebels had come to acknowledge him as the crown prince and to trust their lives to him. But that was far from believing what he said about the sun and the moon.

Flannan thought that perhaps he shouldn't have mentioned Ardri's name during the darkness of the swallowed sun. He wondered if he was underestimating the depth of the animosity and distrust the Rilante-people felt towards their Cryssumha-born Queen and her surviving son. It worked in his favour now, but Flannan was thinking of the future, and did he still have a brother, or was he the only Prince of Rilante - was he alone?

Chapter 26
Sacrifice

A lance of light appeared as the moon released the sun. The cycle that had begun seven years ago with the passage of Vasara was now almost completed.

Ardri faced Iwerdonn, the doomed place on top of ancient Mechanon, of which only the tower Brontigern remained above ground. The underground was another matter.

Only three months had passed since the seventeenth day of Merzeh, when Ardri had stepped from the portal of the tower Brontigern to mount a horse and ride out of the East Gate of Iwerdonn. To him, it seemed a year.

As the King of Cryssumha approached at the head of his host, the double wings of the gate began to close. One gesture of lord Morrik's mail glove sent forward a hundred of his Cryssumha knights. Between them, they were swinging a beam tipped with copper on leather loops. They had been carrying it all the way from Ulud for this moment - to crash into the closing wings.

The gate swung wide open, and showed the Rilante people standing in the main street, red-handed. The light of the new sun exposed their crime of murder. From the gate to the centre, the bodies of Cryssumha people covered the granite flagstones which had caved in places and below the inside of a tunnel was visible.

Lord Morrik's thousand thundered through the streets with their glittering bronze lances lowered, spitting the exhausted Rilante defenders. It was over quickly.

Ardri followed with Neelam, and together they rode up the hill of Kaisil towards the palace, without sparing a single glance for the Rilante dead nor those of Cryssumha. The thousand Cryssumha warriors drew up in front of the royal palace, to form a lane for Ardri and Neelam to ride through, with Morrik waiting at the foot of the stairs.

"Where is Flannan?" Ardri wondered. "Why isn't he defending the capital city?"

"All the better your Majesty?" Lord Morrik ventured.

Ardri shook his head. "No Morrik, all the worse."

The gate of the palace of Iwerdonn opened and at the top of the stairs stood Serenaiba. Twitching figures shambled around her. Ardri ascended the stairs, Neelam's hand on his right, his left on Slatynrigan's hilt. He saw that something lay at Serenaiba's feet. It was King Tirnmas, weighed down with bronze chains heavy enough to crush such an old man, and yet the King of Rilante seemed more alive than he had the last time when Ardri had seen him sitting on the throne.

"Where is Flannan, father? Why isn't he here to protect you?" It was a genuine question as a part of Ardri felt shocked to see his father like this.

"You are no son of mine you degenerate Cryssumha brood, by whatever Donadroch sorcery you were spawned. You have no right to the crown of Rilante." King Tirnmas' voice was surprisingly loud.

It didn't matter. There were no Rilante alive to hear him.

"There is no such thing as the crown of Rilante," Ardri said gently. "There never was. I am King of Cryssumha, crowned with Fenifindrune. I wear the Mooncat cloak around my shoulders. And most importantly, I carry the sword Slatynrigan. You can be proud of your youngest son."

King Tirnmas spat. "How did you betray Lord Gasda you bastard?"

"Betrayal, father? Not at all! You see, I really did find Torin Daraval's ship Murdris. I told Gasda. He went into the Bacenis to take Kione Lonnir from the Woodstalkers. It was the last thing he saw in life, so he must have died happy."

King Tirnmas closed his eyes and sagged in his chains. He raised his head once again. "Flannan...the crown prince...my heir … he will return with an iron army."

"But you won't need to see him defeated. I can do that for you, father. No pain. And there will be no pain for Flannan either. This, I promise."

Ardri drew the sword Slatynrigan. With the tip, he touched Tirnmas' forehead, very lightly, and watched fascinated as the old king's eyes emptied of expression and his face smoothed out.

"Behold the First Sacrifice!" the Prince Angkou said in his beautiful, sonorous voice. He was sitting in his wheeled bronze chair farther back in the portico.

"What are you thinking uncle?" Ardri laughed. "His Rilante blood is no good for sacrifice, and you know it. For the First Sacrifice, I need Cryssumha blood." He pointed Slatynrigan first at this man and then at another.

They all knelt to it.

"Stronger still in sacrifice is royal blood." Ardri pointed the shining blade at lord Morrik, and after the slightest hesitation, the supreme warlord of Cryssumha also knelt.

Ardri sidestepped into the portico. He seized Angkou's long black hair, drew him out of his chair like a stuffed doll and dragged him to the foot of the stairs.

"I grant you the boon that you shall look upon completion with your own eyes. Behold the blood of the First Sacrifice!"

The sword Slatynrigan cut into the High Prince Angkou's neck, first the left artery, then the right. Adri kept hold of Angkou's head, forcing him to see his own blood washing down the palace stairs. He felt his mother's eyes upon him and Neelam's. When he released the High Prince, he fell forward, the blood still pumping from his body. Ardri waited until the red flood stopped, before he gave his order.

"Lord Morrik, complete the sweep of the city and the countryside."

Morrik rose out of his kneeling position and descended the palace stairs. At the foot, he turned to kneel again and bow his forehead to the ground.

Thus rid of Glic Tusil, the Master of Mirrors, and his mentor, the High Prince Angkou, with Lord Morrik put in his place, and King Tirnmas robbed of his mind – Ardri felt that he was King of Cryssumha at last. There was just one loose end left, Flannan. And Kitt, wherever he was – perhaps back at Minit Houarn, his native Isenkliff.

Queen Serenaiba spoke. "Nolan Ri left three days ago even though he had received warning that there was a king in Cryssumha.

298

He intends to seek the temple of Mavors on Minit Houarn to arm with steel. He has planned to turn to iron for a long time."

For a moment, Ardri felt as if he had been bitten by an old loved dog. "Glic Tusil warned me, but I did not believe," he said, more to himself. "I saw Flannan in the mirror, heard him speak about Minit Houarn, but I didn't believe he'd really do it. I never expected that he would abandon father to your mercy. If he could do that...what else? Flannan and Kitt on Minit Houarn...there it is, the final aspect of Mavors. It could not be worse." On this also, the Master of Mirrors had been right.

"But my love, this Kitt, he is only a murderous brute." Neelam shuddered delicately. "I saw him standing over his kill, and I spoke kindly to him because he served you. That's all he is suitable for, to serve his betters. Otherwise, you will simply destroy him."

"Yes my dear, that's how it must have appeared to you," Ardri said, not deeming it necessary to enlighten her on every single one of her points.

"One year until Vasara's final victory," Queen Serenaiba said. "A long time for Mavors to wreak damage. Unfortunately, at sea, Prince Nolan Ri is out of our reach."

Could his mother read his thoughts? Or was the conclusion just so obvious? "Flannan was never within reach, even here in the palace, or why didn't you do something about him?" Never before had Ardri spoken to her in this manner.

Only much later Ardri realised that he had omitted to seize that moment on the palace stairs to neutralise his mother, Queen Serenaiba, along with his uncle, the High Prince Angkou. By then, it was too late. He knew that now he could never muster the courage.

***

Kitt saw the white cliffs on the horizon, Latunsrigo, the King's Seat.

He went below decks where a sleeping place had been allotted to him, which he only used to stow his few possessions, preferring to sleep on the upper deck beside his anvil. He took his weapons, bow, short stabbing spear and one of his belts with bags and pouches. Hoping to look casual, he went to the place where the canoe lay on the foredeck. He would throw it overboard, jump in after it and save himself discussions with Lodemar and Flannan.

Just as he put spear and bow into the Amhas canoe, the prince's fiery head poked from the companionway. "Aha! The white cliffs of Latunsrigo, is it? Are you thinking of jumping ship?" His pleasant ugly head turned up to Kitt with a whimsical smile twitching the long mouth. He did not seem to consider his vulnerable position.

"I have to go there," Kitt said gruffly. "Can't I do something without you catching me at it?"

"Be reasonable, this is a ship full of men! Everybody will know everything within moments."

As if to illustrate his words, Brodi and Neilo came wandering over. Kitt sighed.

"What is there for you at Latunsrigo?" Flannan insisted.

"There is a Feen village about ten miles from here. Mangan Sorkera, the Murder Bear, as you call him, he lives there. He has something that is mine. Challenged me to get it."

"The Murder Bear? You surprise me," Flannan came up from the companionway. "This far east?"

"He is everywhere he wants to be," Kitt said ruefully.

"So. Would you perchance see something indicating Gasda's fate? And his thousand? There must have been a lot of loot. You know the regulation equipment."

"Maybe I'll see something and maybe I won't," Kitt said cautiously. He might see more grisly trophies, he thought.

"Just so. Kione Lonnir is a long way off. Well then, I'll square Lodemar for your boat, yes I insist. The royal house of Rilante seems to be owing you one, and I'm good for my brother's debts. Forget this canoe; it is suitable for rivers, not the sea, no better than swimming."

Lodemar was on his bridge when Kitt and Flannan came in search of him. "Here we go again," the captain said, looking harassed. "You well know your father doesn't like you going off into the Bacenis. And as for your mother..." he made a significant pause. "What will I tell them?"

"What, the big boy is afraid of his mother?" Brodi laughed.

"Just you wait," Lodemar said. "You'll be afraid of the lady Aslaug too.

"Tell my parents that you told me not to go." Kitt shrugged. He wanted to be off. The longer the Birlinn Yehan was before Latunsrigo, the higher the chance that the vessel would be spotted and watched.

"Kitt tells me that the lair of the Murder Bear is near." Flannan looked haggard. "Perhaps he will see something of Gasda's Thousand. Their fate. Naturally, we'll wait for you. How can I meet the smith of Minit Houarn and tell him we sailed out on his son?"

*

The Feen village seemed to be empty; there were no warriors, women or children among the reed-thatched clay houses standing around the paved stone square, nor were there any Jays in the surrounding trees.

It was the hour before sunrise. A drum muttered nearby from the grove of the great red Tini trees. Before one of the houses, a tawny skin hung on a pole like bait on a hook. Bethrek, Dodlak, Graykhol Rere, Death Smile Cat, those were the names the sabre-toothed beast was called in the different languages of the North.

A dog was crouching beside the house; it was a human dog, with matted red-blonde hair and beard, bones like sticks in a sack, the pale skin crisscrossed with a net of long scarlet knife scars. His blue eyes were empty. The naked man was tied by the neck with two leashes, and another trapping the left foot, in a way that he could not untie any of them without choking.

Kitt neared the tied captive apprehensively as if it really was a dog. "Are you still a man?" he asked in a barely audible voice.

"I was the Dog of Rilante. Now I'm only a dog," the man whispered. "The dog must bark, there is a stranger in the village. If he doesn't bark, they will torture me again, and I couldn't stand that. They despise me for screaming under the fire and the knives. How they shout, Dshooka, Dshooka. I don't know what that means." Kitt examined the leashes which tied the captive. He didn't cut them but took time to unfasten the knots so that it would seem that the prisoner had somehow managed to free himself.

"Impossible to flee," the man murmured when the loose ends of his bonds dropped to the ground. "Tried it, they brought me back. Played with me, pretended not to see me crawling, hiding in the dirt.

Then when I thought I'd made it, they caught me again. Hope, the worst torture is hope. Can't you just kill me?"

"Kill yourself." Kitt pressed his knife into the man's hand. The dirty fingers closed around the hilt with a soldier's instinct. "Or go south-east until you hit the coast. Then follow the waterline south to Ferysland. Don't attempt to go back to Rilante, it's too far. Cryssumha has risen."

He didn't know whether the dog who had once been Lord Gasda had heard him, so he repeated his instructions. He extracted the dried meat from his satchel, unhooked his water flask and put it all in Gasda's lap. The freed captive would use the chance, or he wouldn't, it depended on how much of his soul was still left. There must still be a spark, for he had not barked.

"South-east," Kitt repeated for the third time. He turned towards where the drums muttered. He knew that area well.

The red Tini trees surrounded a circular paved place with the stone laid in concentric rings around a stone pillar twice the height of a man. The firelight played over the warriors forming the inner circle; there were hundreds, many more of them than lived in the village. Women and children stood in the outer circle on the edge, among the trees. The stone pillar in the centre of the place was flanked by two fires, their light shining on a man tied to it. The man was bright red from the blood that was streaming out of his many wounds, a dark circle spreading around his feet, widening with every beat of his heart.

Slightly ahead of the circle of warriors, facing the pole, stood a tall figure with snakeskins draped over the gaunt limbs, an enormous serpenthead shadowing the face, the skin falling down to the ground and trailing behind the masked man for ten feet.

The fires died down, the drumbeat ceased. The sun rose big and red, among a mass of fiery clouds brewing on the horizon, boding a day of wind and rain. The rosy light streamed through a gap in the trees, lighting the red trunks and the red man at the stone pillar, who raised his head slowly, his blue eyes blazing.

The masked serpent figure stepped forward, and with a slash of a stone knife in his right opened the chest and tore out the heart with his left. He showed it to the red man at the pillar, who saw his own beating heart in the hand of the masked man before he broke to his knees in the pool of his blood.

Out of the circle of the warriors, one stepped beside the masked serpent man, who offered the red heart to him. Mangan Sorkera. The war leader bit into the heart and blood spurted over his face. Slowly his head turned around, blood running down the chin and forearms; as he scanned the deep shadows among the red trunks of the giant trees, the deceptively gentle deer eyes met Kitt's.

The war leader had seen him, this time there was no doubt. Mangan Sorkera raised a red hand and drew it across his eyes, smearing his face with blood, and turned back to the fire, where the warriors cut pieces of flesh from the slumped body and ate them raw, dipped hands into the blood and drew them over their faces, shoulders, arms, chest. Two women also stepped forward to eat from the warm, bloody flesh and smear the blood over their breasts and bellies.

At last only bloody bones were hanging from the stone pillar. Warriors came to cut off the limbs and the head. The right leg and left arm were buried on the north side of the stone-paved place and the left leg and right arm on the south side, and west, what was left of the trunk. The upper part of the skull was set aside, and also the teeth, and the remainder of the skull was buried in the east of the place. As the holes were dug, bones from earlier burials came to light.

Mangan Sorkera had not called pursuit. Kitt retreated slowly and returned to the deserted village. On the border of the stone pavement, he stopped dead. Pressed into the soil in front of him was one canine paw print. The Feen had never had dogs before, not real dogs. He was glad that out of habit, he had approached the village upwind, even though he thought it empty.

The human dog who had been Lord Gasda was gone.

Kitt took down the Dodlak skin; it was heavy and felt soft and pliant. He rolled it up into a bundle, knotting the paws. Then, he ran straight towards the coast, making no attempt to disguise his tracks, nor his direction, thus giving Lord Gasda of Rilante a desperately tiny chance as Mangan Sorkera pursued Gawthrin Lye.

*

303

Mangan Sorkera considered the trail blazed towards the coast.

Once again, Gawthrin Lye was trying to bring a Dshooka through the Sreedok. This time he would die for it. The young Stag warriors fell in behind him, led by Shaluwa.

The rain that had threatened all morning finally broke, dissolving the track before Mangan's eyes. That mattered not. He knew where the youth was heading, Kadyokanap Askai. Did Gawthrin Lye really think he could use the same trick twice on Mangan Sorkera? Two capital mistakes were too much - unless Mangan Sorkera had made a mistake of his own in his estimate, and he did not think so. But maybe the youth was reckoning on Mangan's thinking just this way. Gawthrin Lye was very cunning.

The rain ceased, and the Feen picked up the track again, it was fresh. Mangan Sorkera continued with mounting doubts. The pursuit should long have come up with the broken dog that had been the Dshooka war leader from Rilante. Not even Gawthrin Lye could carry both the man and the Graykhol Rere skin at a run. That he had even attempted to take both was the height of audacity. That he still had not dropped one or the other was remarkable.

When the track vanished where the rocks began, the war leader knew. It was only Gawthrin Lye's track they were following. Mangan Sorkera's error had bought the Dshooka dog time for his flight, but he did not care about that. The Dshooka couldn't survive in the Sreedok wood, and he hadn't earned a Red Death. With signals of a bone whistle and a few gestures, the war leader divided his men, one party to the top of Mark-Nidyas–Rerenejish, the other to the little beach of Kadyokanap-Askai nearby.

They followed his command at top speed, but Mangan himself hesitated. Gawthrin Lye had no way of knowing how much of a head start he had, but the fact that at this point he had taken to concealing his track indicated that he reckoned that it was little. He was in the habit of coming by boat and must have hidden it somewhere. There was little choice on the Kadyokanap-Askai coast of steep cliffs and high tide. Gawthrin Lye had hidden inside of Mark-Nidyas–Rerenejish before, right within the cave inhabited by the Graykhol Rere pride.

Mangan Sorkera looked down into Death Hole, the Good Spirit Dalyon's place, at the bottom of which was a cave entrance. White bones lay in the grass at the bottom of the rock-well, with the long fangs broken out of the skull. Gawthrin Lye had killed that Graykhol Rere three great suns ago, but there were always Graykhol Reres in Mark-Nidyas–Rerenejish.

A pebble was dislodged from the steep rock wall, and beside the skull, a footstep in the grass had been hidden skilfully, but not well enough for the eyes of Mangan Sorkera. Knowing that the tide was still in and filled the cave mouth on the other side of of the cliff, he exulted in the knowledge that he and Gawthrin Lye would meet at last, alone.

Mangan Sorkera hesitated, contemplating the Graykhol Rere skull. Those faint traces he saw below – were those deliberate? A cunning invitation by Gawthrin Lye, a calculated insult –kill a second Graykhol Rere first, like I did, then face me! Such a fight would demand the last of Mangan Sorkera, and he'd have little left to put up against Gawthrin Lye. Mangan Sorkera was sure now that the cub had grown up and turned at bay.

A roar reverberated down in the cave. About to descend into Death Hole, something held him back, a word at the back of his head: *Bear not fight Graykhol Rere, Mooankayit one sun circle.*

Mangan Sorkera now possessed the knowledge that Gawthrin Lye's shape in Nyedasya-Dyarve, the real world, was a grey lion Mooankayit. His given name of a fox cub in Nyedasya-Aurayskahan-Ashyalish, this World of Illusion, made no difference to this, and thus Shangar Shaark Ayen's words were not open to interpretation. When he had still lived in the simple world of the warrior, nothing would have held him back from a struggle like this, where life and death would meet so narrowly, where the reward in the real world was immeasurable. But Shangar Shaark Ayen had spoken, and a war leader of the Feen did not disregard the advice of the Ludoshini.

Mangan Sorkera retreated to take up station on top of Mark-Nidyas–Rerenejish. His warriors assembled around him, stringing their bows. It would only be another waste of arrows, the war leader was sure.

*

Kitt heard a vengeful roar behind him as he waded into the subterranean tidal lake. In the uncertain light, he saw the tawny shape pace up and down by the water's edge, the green eyes scintillating, snarling as if he smelt the Dodlak skin.

Would it come in - Kitt didn't know if Dodlaks could swim and how well. He waded into deeper water where he would have a better chance if the beast did spring into the water. It did not, as if it knew as well as Kitt that the tide would soon go out in an irresistible stream.

Where was Mangan Sorkera, he wondered, while striving to keep in position against the water pressure as he watched the pacing, snarling Dodlak. He had planned to let the war leader and the beasts fight it out between them who would get to tear his heart out. But the war leader did not show.

The water pressure ceased, and for a moment, there was no current. Then, the flow changed direction. Kitt went with it to where the tidal lake narrowed into a tunnel. There he had secured the boat. He threw in the Dodlak skin. Now he had his hands free.

The last ray of evening light shone into the cave and converted the tawny pelt of the Dodlak into gold as he followed the receding waterline. Kitt strung his bow.

The Dodlak crouched with his belly on the ground, and for a moment, Kitt thought that he would jump. He drew the bowstring and the Death Smile Cat turned tail and bounded back into the darkness of the cave, weaving and bouncing, as if it knew exactly what a bow was.

For a brief moment the light streaming into the cave turned brighter as the opening widened and then dimmer as the light went out of the sky. It was dark outside when Kitt cut loose the mooring rope. The boat shot out with the last tide stream and passed under the overhanging rock. There was a moment of danger when somebody hanging on to the cliff could have sent an arrow into the boat or sounded the alarm, to bring down the concerted volley he dreaded. But it didn't happen. The King's Seat soared above, a pale, silent shadow in the darkness. He thought that he saw a dark figure standing on top, but that might be the memory of another day, another flight.

No arrows came down out of the night. The retreating tide carried the boat out of range. Kitt was pleased. This time the Dodlak skin would remain whole, not ripped to ribbons by arrows like the one three years ago had been.

*

Once again, the Feen war leader stood high up on Mark-Nidyas–Rerenejish, watching Gawthrin Lye out of sight, imagining more than really seeing the boat in the darkness. The fox cub must be wondering why Mangan Sorkera had refused his challenge, and this thought irked him beyond endurance.

Chapter 27
The King of Rilante

Brodi and Neilo looked down at Kitt asleep by the anvil, wrapped head to foot in a tawny skin.

Then they looked at each other; Neilo grinned and Brodi tiptoed to the hardening trough to fill a pitcher with the rusty water.

"You dare, you'll drink it," Kitt said.

"Well, well, the fox doesn't sleep, he merely reposes," Brodi recited the old proverb. "We didn't notice you come aboard last night kiddo. The watch will have some explaining to do."

"He wasn't asleep."

"Just didn't notice more than six feet of blacksmith clamber aboard with a great fur. Why that's alright then."

Kitt unwrapped himself from the fur and the Rilante soldiers lifted it high one forepaw each. Finding themselves far too short, they laid the skin out on the deck. The sailors gathered around to marvel, and Gweronell, one of Kitt's old friends, a Woodstalker turned sailor, stood white-faced and stared first at the skin and then at Kitt. "Graykhol Rere," he said.

They made room for Prince Flannan and Captain Lodemar.

"Is that a Bethrek?" Lodemar exclaimed. "I never saw one, but it couldn't be any other animal."

"I didn't believe such a beast really existed." Flannan touched the tawny white speckled pelt, and lifted it to look at the inside. "Nicely cured. And you stole this from the Murder Bear? What did he have to say about it?"

"Didn't steal it, it's mine. The one that attacked Ardri."

"How did you kill it?" Flannan had grown pale.

Kitt touched the long knife.

"You went against that beast with a blade little more than two handspans long?" Flannan looked at Kitt as if he saw him for the first time. "What a hunt, I salute you. No wonder you wanted to retrieve such a trophy."

"And you had to slay this fine fellow just to save the Cryssumha brood," Brodi muttered.

"That's quite enough! You speak of a Prince of Rilante!" Flannan snapped.

Brodi looked unrepentant. "You got the teeth, haven't you? Show!"

Kitt detached the bag tied to his belt and produced the long, white, curved dagger-like canines.

Neilo whistled.

Brodi measured one of the teeth with thumb and forefinger, and probed the points. "Longer than your knife. Surely would have put an end to Cryssumha rising before it began. Well spilt milk and bolted horses."

"I said enough! Did you see any indication of Gasda's force, spoils, trophies, prisoners?"

"I saw Gasda himself." Kitt told about the encounter in the Feen village, but not about the man who suffered the Red Death.

"Might Gasda be trying to follow you?"

"I told him to go South-east."

"Why? Did you tell him we were near?"

"I didn't."

"Care to explain why not?" Flannan asked between clenched teeth, and his face was tense.

"So I could draw the pursuit. He might have tried to reach you and would have been caught. There is only one low access to this coast, which is always guarded." Kitt pointed to a low beach west of the King's Seat.

"We go in," Flannan said.

Kitt shook his head. "There are too many Feen...Woodstalkers...in the area and they are led by Mangan Sorkera...the Murder Bear. Gasda had a thousand men at arms, you have a hundred."

"You know the Bacenis as nobody else does. Could you chance a guess where Gasda is likely to end up if he follows your advice?"

309

"You ask me how far a man exhausted in body and mind would crawl? Who can hardly stand up to make sure of his direction, needs to hide and lay low, and won't find food?"

Flannan winced. "You put it brutally. I suppose you think it rather a stretch of the imagination, but if you'd oblige me?"

"I can try."

They went to the main cabin in search of maps. Flannan cleared the table with a sweep of his arm that sent glasses and jugs crashing to the floor, and Lodemar extended a parchment with part of the coast roughly sketched, and pointed. "Latunsrigo."

Kitt picked up a piece of graphite and drew a dot and some lines. "The Feen village. There is a creek, in a valley, so he will end up there. The creek runs due west. I told him to go south-east towards Ferysland. It would mean to cross and go uphill. He may not have the strength or will. If he does, somewhere he'll hit the coast and go south, passing Bear Mountain in the distance. Here. There is a chance that the Mother Boys find him first and recognise my knife. If the pure-bloods find him, he'll end on a spit."

"You talk like imperial signal code," Flannan complained. "Please elaborate! I understand that with Feen you mean the Woodstalkers, but who are these Mother Boys and pure-bloods and is it true then that the Woodstalkers eat human flesh?"

"Only in sacrifice. And it's an honour not everybody merits. The Hunters in the Mist...for the pure-blooded of them we are just so much meat. They killed and eat the warriors of the village near Bear Mountain. There are no Woodstalkers in their area."

"One thing is clear, people that eat Woodstalkers for breakfast must be truly frightful," Brodi commented.

"They are. The most dangerous thing in the woods. They can't run fast, so they hunt together. They pass their prey from one group to the next until it becomes exhausted and makes a mistake. They have an extra sense, can find anybody by something they call Sheen. That is the greatest danger for Gasda."

Flannan looked at Kitt curiously but said nothing.

"Then he has to cross the river Zinnfluss, which is a mile wide in this area. There are lots of reeds, lots of fallen trees. If he does cross, he may be washed out to sea, and if he doesn't drown, some Ferys fishermen might pick him up."

"That's a lot of ifs but each surmountable by itself. I say we'll just sail south along the coast and keep a lookout."

"If he takes my advice. But if he's too exhausted to think clearly and heads back south-west, he'll have to cross six times the distance through Feen territory. The creek south of the village is joined by another creek running south-west, that's the only crossing he'd have to make, it's not too deep, but the state he's in he may drown." Kitt drew more lines into the map. "There are two more creeks further down running north-west, and the whole river veers west-south-west and runs into the Struenfoly. But it's too far." Kitt shrugged.

"And if he does reach the Struenfoly, on the other shore now is Cryssumha. You told him?"

"I did. Don't know if he understood me."

"What we'll do is we sail along this coast. And if we don't find him, we return to Rilante and go up the Struenfoly. I allowed my father to send out Gasda to save my little brother because I totally misjudged the situation. Knowing that Gasda is near, I can't just sail on to Isenkliff and have myself a nice suit of armour made. Even if I do lose the crown. Lodemar, I know this is a change of course in every respect but can I prevail upon you...I will make it up to you."

"Along the coast." Lodemar nodded.

"We might have a better chance to retrieve Gasda if Kitt acted as our guide to the Bacenis?"

"I go home."

"Meaning you don't believe Gasda's got a dog's chance? Damn what a rotten crack. What on earth is that you have there?" The last was directed at Neilo who had opened Kitt's satchel and was laying out hand-long pale yellow wicked looking claws on top of the map in neat rows of five and four.

"Are those the Bethrek's? Some hooks, don't think anything ever escaped them. Now, wait a moment..."

"Particularly as there appear to be twenty-one," Brodi said. "Unless a Bethrek has more claws than all other cats- come now Kitt, give!"

311

Neilo turned the satchel upside-down. Ten gold coins fell out, a gold disk and a bronze pendant cast in the shape of a flower with a girl's face.

"Where is the rest of that second Bethrek?" Brodi demanded.

"I remember...Warmond told us...let's see what you have tucked away in your shirt Kitt?"

"Hands off me!" Kitt protested.

"Hold still! Upper canine number three. A necklace like a Woodstalker, be ashamed of yourself, except Woodstalkers decorate much less ostentatiously, wolves, bears and bits of other Woodstalkers but Bethreks hardly ever. My prince, this boy here..."

"Bagged two Bethreks. Be assured, dear Brodi, that I can count and draw conclusions as well as you. How did you kill that one, with a knife too?"

"It was three years ago."

"Oh, that's alright then," Brodi sniggered. "You were what age, thirteen? Then it doesn't count anyway."

"Did you kill it with a knife?" the Prince repeated his question.

Kitt shrugged, took his satchel away from Neilo, swiped the rows of claws into it, collected the pendant, and tied the string.

Neilo shoved the gold at him.

"Don't need it. It was for the boat."

"No use my offering you a heap of gold for your help then, is there Kitt?" Flannan's face was grim and pale. "Seems I'm lucky Ardri couldn't buy you either."

"He almost did, with bronze. The knowledge of working it. That was the bait, and the sword Slatynrigan was the trap. One touch with that blade would have made me his mindless tool."

"Did he...?"

"He didn't dare attempt it because I was warned."

"It is true then."

"All of it. So you couldn't have won a direct confrontation." Kitt concluded, looking squarely at Flannan. "If that's what's bothering you."

"A whole lot is bothering me, you whelp. Now let me get this clear. You told me that nobody can escape the Murder Bear, but you do it at will. You said not even the Murder Bear could stand against the cannibals of Bear Mountain, but you did. I never heard of anyone who killed a Bethrek, let alone two. With a knife. If anyone can extract Lord Gasda from the Bacenis, it's you."

"So you must go, Kitt," Lodemar said.

Kitt looked at him uncertainly. "You both wouldn't let me see if those men on Eissee needed help. Now you want me to help Gasda?"

"That's different, you must realise that?" Flannan said gently.

"Not different to me." There would be a pursuit and Kitt didn't want to have to kill more Feen warriors. He hadn't wanted to do it for Ardri, and he wasn't willing to do it for Gasda, a man he didn't even know. He knew that the Rilante would never understand; for them, the Woodstalkers were inhumane enemies.

Flannan looked at him sharply. "I can't fault your argument," he conceded. "Listen, if you help me get my friend out, I'll be in your debt as long as I live, and whatever you did to aid and abet the rise of Cryssumha, I'll call it forgiven. And forgotten. Never to be spoken about again."

Kitt heaved a deep sigh. "I can go south with you towards Zinnfluss and scout the woods for signs of Gasda. That is all. Back to Rilante or Cryssumha, I won't go. I learned enough not to expect gratitude from kings or princes. All I ask is that you promise that you won't mention that...anything...to...to anyone at all?"

"Fair enough. I promise."

"They too." Kitt looked from Lodemar to Brodi and Neilo.

"Sure thing kiddo. Not keen to tell the world and his uncle how we've been walloped by a blacksmith of sixteen. Those that don't know what you're like don't have a hope to understand," Brodi said, and Neilo nodded.

"None of my men to say a word," the prince said. "No records in the library of Rilante. You have my promise."

"We won't rat you out to your mother," Lodemar added.

Kitt glared at him, and Brodi guffawed but stopped at a sharp look from Flannan.

Pots judged the moment prudent and tiptoed in with a plate heaped high with fried eggs and bacon and a pot of coffee, which he placed before a grateful, very hungry Kitt.

***

The dogs barked at a boat which lay dry on the beach just above the low-water line among some boulders, hard to see because they were

313

of the same colour. There was nothing about the Dshooka-made vessel to indicate that it was Gawthrin Lye's. But Korikuta was sure all the same that here was the chance to force respect for the Zoyamizoyi.

The catastrophe at Glatogami, Bear Mountain, should have led to a seamless joining of the two Feen families, the Kra-Tini having lost all their old warriors against the Lychyen-Amangan man-eaters, and the Zoyamizoyi had lost all their strong warriors. But no Kra-Tini warrior was prepared to cede position to the Zoyamizoyi elders exiled to their bitter charity. They would, once Korikuta trapped the fair-haired Dshooka cub, who mocked and challenged Mangan Sorkera himself.

The Kra-Tini had many stories about Gawthrin Lye. How as a young boy he had killed in a fight man to man Agetool A Shushei, blood-brother to Mangan Sorkera and their second strongest warrior.

How he had brazenly run into Mukine-Kad-Nidyas and when they came to the part where he had transformed into an eagle and flown away from the roof of Karabfrak's house, all closed their eyes to tease old Shak Lagat, Hawkeye, the famous hunter who had overlooked the infinitesimal signs of Gawthrin Lye's escape. Shak Lagat had died in Glatogami, but the Kra-Tini still closed their eyes at the end of that story. They then went on how he had turned into a Graykhol Rere and crossed the caves of Mark-Nidyas–Rerenejish, then changed into a seal and dived to evade the Kra-Tini arrows. They didn't close their eyes throughout that story, but Korikuta felt that they ought to.

Being old Korikuta knew that there was a grain of truth in the Kra-Tini's fantastic tales: that Gawthrin Lye was a very dangerous enemy. Those of the Kra-Tini warriors who had been at the end of Gawthrin Lye's massive fists called him Djanadir Thomiat, Hammerer.

And now, there was a new story just a few days old, how he stole the Graykhol Rere skin from Mangan Sorkera's house. Gawthrin Lye, Djanadir Thomiat, was the weak spot of the Kra-Tini Feen, their war leader's own failure. He would stand among the Tini trees from sunset to sunrise, and it would be Korikuta to devour his heart instead of Mangan Sorkera.

314

Korikuta blew his whistle. The warriors who would follow his call were all of them either too old or too young for this kind of hunt. They would win or perish. That also would be a victory over the Kra-Tini because besides Agetool A Shushei, Djanadir Thomiat had never done any of them the honour of taking their lives.

*

With infinite caution, Kitt moved through the no-man's-land between Bear Mountain and the Feen territory, nearing the Kra-Tini Feen village from the south-east.

He checked out all the obvious hideouts a city-bred man like Gasda was likely to make for. He thought of the paw print he had seen and that the Kra-Tini now had dogs, and how much harder that would make everything. For the unlikely case that he found Gasda alive, he had laid his plan and prepared their retreat. It would work, or it wouldn't. He was acutely aware that with every step further inland, the odds for success were growing slimmer.

Suddenly he stopped and did not move at all. He had a glimpse of black and white, and then he spotted a Woodstalker who was lying on top of the ridge just ahead and watched something in the valley below. So intent was he that Kitt caught a very good sight of him. It was a young warrior, a Stag or even just a Jay. His blue-black hair was very long with feathers braided into it.

On the other side of the valley was another movement. Kitt caught sight of a second Woodstalker heading down. There was the sound of running feet, and the first Woodstalker slipped over the ridge.

Kitt took up the vacated position. Below, he saw the man he had freed, Lord Gasda, Dog of Rilante, lurch along at the bottom of the valley, flanked by the two Feen who drove him into headlong flight, by disappearing, then showing themselves again, playing the same cruel game as they had with Ardri. The hunt headed east and uphill. Kitt followed, unseen by all three men.

They had gone on for about three miles when Kitt heard a whistle tone from the south-east, the direction where he had left the boat on the line of low tide, barely hidden from sight among some boulders. It sounded different from the war leader's whistle, which he knew so well.

*

The young, cold voice had told Gasda to go south-east. It wasn't the voice of an enemy, but indifferent and yet commanding, overriding his instinct to just crawl west where Rilante lay, so far away it could as well be on another star. Cryssumha had risen the voice had said. Gasda staggered up the slope and stumbled, sank down to one knee. He saw the two Woodstalkers again, attempted to rise and couldn't at first. It was over, he knew, but still he reeled onwards.

The Woodstalkers closed in like wolves on a wounded wisent. One stabbed at his chest with a lance, and drew a deep, long cut; blood welled up and ran down his chest, but it didn't hurt. He slapped aside the lance shaft and couldn't prevent the second Woodstalker to slice his lance across the first cut. The double pain hit with delay and Gasda cried out, rose and stumbled down the slope, the two Woodstalkers close behind, stabbing at his back. He fell and rolled down until he hit a boulder, and the air expelled from his lungs in another cry. He drew himself up until he sat with his back to the stone and raised the knife. They wouldn't take him, bind and drag him back; he wouldn't ever again bark like a dog.

His tormentors dawdled on the slope in full sight. They were still boys, soft faces like girls with very long raven hair, and deceptively gentle animal eyes.

Suddenly, a third man was there. Gasda hadn't seen him until he was already halfway down the slope. The Woodstalkers didn't notice him either, as he came up behind them like a big, tawny cat.

He clouted one over the head with the right fist that held a dagger, which threw him flat on his back, and as the other turned around, he hit him in the stomach so that he doubled over and then lay retching. The first Woodstalker attempted to rise, and the fair-haired newcomer was above him with a long stride and hit him on the chin that his head snapped back. He bent down to the stricken Woodstalkers, gripped them by their hair, dragged their heads together and tied the long strands. That really was an excellent idea, Gasda thought.

Then he bound their feet together with a leather cord, and once he had secured his victims, he took the rest of their hair, stuffed it into their mouths and tied their loincloths round.

Gasda laughed.

316

The youth tied the Woodstalkers' arms together at the wrists with strips of their leggings, bound more strips around their feet and retrieved his leather cord. Every movement was economical and fluent. Big as the stranger was, he was not much more than a boy either, fair-haired, light-eyed; there couldn't be two like this one.

He straightened and moved down towards Gasda. "Prince Flannan sends me." It was the cold young voice that had told him to go south-west.

Gasda closed his eyes briefly, tears running out from under the lids. He felt the youth bend over him and lunged with the knife. He missed. He opened his eyes again and saw the youth, standing just out of arms reach, frowning down on him.

"I saw you at Dundingin. You are Ardri's pet wolf. Your master trapped me using Kione Lonnir, and now you plan to trap Prince Nolan Ri by using me. I'll rather cut my throat with this knife you gave me."

"I have no master. Flannan is on the Birlinn Yehan just off the coast."

"Lodemar's in this?"

"Yes. I'll bring you to Flannan, in exchange for...something he promised me."

"Shame, you'll miss out. I came as far as I could."

"No, you didn't. There's still about...five miles to go."

"I can't stand up. If...if you're honest...tell Prince Nolan Ri..."

"Can't or won't? You want me to tell your prince which?"

"That he is not to endanger himself on my account." Gasda grinned. "I can't take the chance that you're Ardri's."

"I'm no one's," the youth muttered. "Just want to go home. For that, I need your prince's promise. You'll have to promise too."

"Promise what?"

"That you never saw or heard of me before. You don't promise now. When I got you safe." The youth bent down, took the knife from Gasda as from a child, hoisted him up and slung him across his shoulders. It didn't seem to cause him any effort.

Hanging over the broad shoulder like a butchered deer Gasda met the animal eyes of one the young Woodstalkers, full of terror and hatred. Alien race as they were, he knew how they felt. They hadn't made a noise. He wondered if they would rather spend any amount of time trying to free themselves, than call attention to their embarrassing plight. Young men were foolish, and some grown-ups too.

It was hellishly uncomfortable being carried upside down with his face rubbing against the leather of the boy's tunic, which smelled of forest and animals, feeling the muscles move underneath. The ground shifted past with speed, making Gasda dizzy. He fell into a stupor of misery, from which he was roused when the youth shifted him in mid-run.

There were, in fact, almost ten miles south-east to where the boat lay. If it was still there. If the Feen did what he thought most likely they would.

Kitt started to run east directly towards the coast. This detour would prolong the way he had to go, but it took him away from the straight line between the Feen village and the boat. It might have been found by now. Sometimes it seemed to him that Mangan Sorkera, also called the Murder Bear, was all-seeing and omniscient.

Gasda was a tall man of over six feet but weighed less than a hundred and fifty imperial pounds, starved as he was. Kitt didn't stop once until he reached the high shore about two miles north from where he had left the boat. The sea lay before him, grey, foggy and empty, and of the Birlinn Yehan, nothing showed, not so much as a mast top.

Kitt set down his burden and leant Gasda against a rock. His eyes were closed and lay deep in their sockets, his lips pressed together, his forehead wrinkled with pain.

From his satchel, Kitt took sugar lumps which he had asked from the cook, dropped them into his water flask one by one, added a pinch of salt from the package he always carried, shook it and held it to Gasda's lips. He took a sip, and then another and opened his eyes, very blue against the grime and stubble of his face.

"The sea," he murmured. "Out of the damn trees."

Kitt tied the leather cord around Gasda's legs and back. The Dog of Rilante tried to shove him away. "Damn it, boy, enough of this! I can go by myself now."

"But I can't wait for you and the tide won't." Kitt hoisted him onto his back like a rucksack, careful to draw one of his arms over his shoulder and the other around his chest and secure them with a cord so that Gasda wouldn't attempt to throttle him. "Hold fast. We mustn't lose the tide."

"I'll have to kill you!" Gasda whispered.

With the Rilante warlord on his back, Kitt turned south, in the direction where the boat lay. Overhead the clouds raced from west to east, and it began to rain. Now and again, Gasda shivered violently.

As they approached the place where he had left the boat, Kitt moved more slowly, taking time to skirt possible hideouts, scrupulously keeping upwind, remembering the sound of the whistle, the paw print in the Feen village and a dog yip he thought he'd heard in the woods.

The boat lay as Kitt had left it, and nothing indicated that it had been discovered, but he had a suspicion bordering on certainty that the Feen were hiding nearby, waiting for him to come out into the open on the shore. It was what he had counted on, the one reason for them not to remove the boat. He could also be quite sure that they had not damaged it because this boat was original to the Birlinn Yehan and had been fashioned from thin steel sheets. With the tide reaching its apex, the boat was already in the water but not yet floating because of its metal weight. There couldn't be many Feen in hiding though, or the hollow they sheltered in now would have been manned.

Kitt left Gasda to sit with the flask containing the sugar water and began to scrape away the soil. Something golden appeared close to the surface. He carefully removed all the adhering earth from the sun pattern embossed in gold and silver on the broad, curved bronze sheet, wondering whether there would be some sun rays to make their run across the shore more spectacular, but the weather didn't look like it.

"The crown prince's shield! What...?"

Kitt's hand shot out and covered Gasda's mouth. "Quiet!" he mouthed, putting his face near. "You'll run to the boat, with the shield on your back. It's about a hundred yards. Can you do that?"

Gasda looked at him dumbly.

"Can you?" Kitt hoped the Dog of Rilante wasn't still imagining that he'd lugged him all the way just to play him a dirty trick.

Gasda nodded.

"Good. Keep under the shield, don't lose direction. Don't fall! Don't worry about the Woodstalkers; I'll take them off you. Just concentrate on running."

Gasda nodded again.

Lying flat on his belly, Gasda looked over the ridge, feeling his saviour's hand upon his neck whenever he raised his head to see better.

He saw the boat lying in the water of high tide, such as the larger seagoing Rilante ships carried. In a little time, it should float in the rising water. For some reason, it didn't yet, seemed extraordinarily heavy. But soon it would.

Incredibly, salvation was a possibility. First, Gasda fixed the position in his mind, then the way down and across rock and pebble, which did not present any obstacles; the last bit would be through the surf. He saw no sign of Woodstalkers; there was some hoary joke about that.

He appreciated the youth's plan which involved the tide and the shield. It was tall, wide and curved enough to protect most of the body from arrows, and it was such a splendid item that the Woodstalkers must be confused for vital moments, when they saw it move towards the water, apparently on two legs. When they recovered, they would maybe shoot and then give chase. Once they closed in on him, their arrows would not come into play anymore. Then the big youth would move in. There was a good chance that he'd be upon them before they noticed. A picture came up in Gasda's head of another bunch of Woodstalkers with their hair tied together and he stifled a hysterical giggle.

Such a simple plan revealed disquieting premeditation and cunning in a boy of at most sixteen years of age. Gasda couldn't think of any reason he mightn't do just as he said, or why Prince Ardri might want him alive. But then, he hadn't seen the trap behind the news of Kione Lonnir either. He winced at the memory. No time for that now. He was a seaman, and the consciousness of the tide was in his blood. All would depend on whether he could keep running towards the boat. He felt stronger due to the salty sugar water, but he knew what an interminable distance a hundred yards could be in a fight. In his mind, he broke them down into stages to master one after the other.

He stretched his legs and arms, tensing his muscles, relaxing, tensing again until he felt something like warmth. He took some more of the salty sugar water. It would have to do.

The youth looked relieved and nodded slightly.

Gasda didn't even know his name; Gilroy had mentioned something, but he hadn't listened. He resolved to ask the boy his name if he lived and to kill him, if necessary. Perhaps it wouldn't be required. As he retreated back down into the hole on his belly, there was a slight noise, and the boy frowned. He moved in the grass like a serpent.

They rested until the tide was at its apex, and that was the moment the boy had waited for. He fastened the shield to Gasda's back, and never had a shield felt this heavy. If he fell, he would resemble a tortoise, possibly unable to get up again. If he fell in the surf, he would drown. He resolved that he wouldn't fall.

"If you do fall, just get up, go on! Think only of the boat." The boy's voice was no more than a murmur of air.

Gasda crawled upwards again and felt the boy's hand press on the shield. He understood that he had to start his run from below the ridge, or the shield would be spotted too early. In his mind, he concentrated on the location of the boat.

The pressure lifted from the shield. Gasda sprang up and over the ridge. He was in the open. First, the run down the steep coast; he made it without falling and came onto the stretch of rock and pebble. Something slammed hard into the shield, and then he heard the hated sound of their yelling. His eyes fixed on the boat he could hear them come rushing behind, overtaking him. Then the yelling stopped and was replaced by sounds of a scuffle. A Woodstalker came flying across his field of view. There was the sound of a hard crash to his left.

Gasda plodded on.

Something heavy weighed down the shield, and he fell with his face in the sand. The weight came off, and he scrambled up again. And again.

A Woodstalker was in front of him and lunged with a knife; the boy landed a terrific punch on his temple, and there was a crack of bone.

The pebbles before him were wet, and a wave came running up to him. There was the boy again, and he gripped the leather thongs which secured the shield and loaded Gasda on his back as he waded into the surf.

Something slammed into the shield hard, it sounded like a gust of hail and then another. Gasda felt two impacts on his right leg; it did not hurt, but he knew that he had been hit by arrows.

Then he was kneeling in the boat, held up by the shield, and there was another clatter on metal, and two arrows fell in front of him, spent.

He hadn't seen how Kitt managed to get into the boat, but there he was, tying a rope to the tiller and then came towards him and took off the leather cord so that Gasda could lay down, with the shield settling above and blotting out the sky.

*

Mangan Sorkera strained his eyes for the Dshooka sail on the horizon, not listening to Korikuta who explained how they had almost caught Gawthrin Lye, if he hadn't escaped their ambush, dragging with him the Rilante dog, cracking the heads of the young warriors and breaking their bones for the old. The fools had been dazzled and surprised, gaped at a gilded bronze shield and closed in stupidly, leaving their shooting far too late. If they'd disabled the Dshooka dog fast enough, Gawthrin Lye wouldn't have stood a chance to get them both into that boat.

Too many questions ran through his head: why the youth had run this enormous risk for a Dshooka so much inferior in strength or courage – whether it could be the same reason why he had protected Liba Ri Cryssumha, and whether it was possible that he made no more difference between the different Dshooka factions than the Feen did themselves. Except the Feen killed any Dshooka who they found in their territory while Gawthrin Lye seemed bent on saving them from the consequences of their weakness and blundering. The war leader just did not understand that boy.

The old fool finally stopped jabbering. The Zoyamizoyi men stood around him with hanging arms, their eyes full of resentful resignation. At least two men would not survive the knocks Gawthrin Lye had dealt them, and two more would be either crippled or dead. The war leader knew what the Zoyamizoyi had been trying to accomplish, as he knew that the Kra-Tini wouldn't forgive their deviousness in the face of their failure.

"Go untie those other long-haired weak-heads," he said in a voice that held no expression at all.

So far his warriors had stood behind him in impassive silence, but at the mention of the two Zoyamizoyi Stags tied together with hair, hands and heels, there was a noise like a sneezing tree cat. Fitcher had made it; he was the youngest of the band of young warriors who followed the war leader.

Mangan Sorkera felt his own mouth twitch. He dropped his weapons, spear, knives and club, and walked away from the coast, back into the Sreedok, empty-handed and unarmed. He needed to enter the real world Nyedasya-Dyarve to look for Gawthrin Lye's traces there, so that he could finally understand why he acted as he did and find a way to make use of his weakness.

Shaluwa picked up the war leader's weapons and followed. He had claimed and won the right to watch over Mangan Sorkera, the Singing Bear, in this world of shadows Nyedasya-Aurayskahan-Ashyalish, as once had his blood brother, Agetool A Shushei, killed by Gawthrin Lye four sun squares ago, and old Brule, who had died in Glatogami.

***

The Birlinn Yehan stood below the horizon a day's sailing south of the King's Seat.

The Crown Prince leant on the rail and fretted. He couldn't see the sunrise for thick clouds, and it was raining, not hard, but persistent. Flannan was not used to wait while somebody else was acting. Kitt had been right, he minded terribly to have left Iwerdonn behind without defence and abandoning his father because he judged that he could not win there. Now from a distance, he doubted that judgement. Realising that he had always blamed his father for falling prey to the beautiful mantis Serenaiba made it all worse. King Tirnmas must have paid the price by now. That was why Flannan couldn't bear to abandon Lord Gasda, called the Dog of Rilante,

323

because he was so unswervingly loyal always, so true to the memory of Queen Murine, Flannan's mother.

"Kitt said to expect him with the end of the tide, but he didn't say which tide. This is the fourth. If we could at least see something!"

"Can't take her farther in," Lodemar said for the tenth time. "Kitt said not to show so much as the tip of the mast."

"Who is giving the commands here, Kitt?"

"Well, you did agree to everything he asked. So did I. He doesn't want the Woodstalkers to home in on his line of escape. Makes sense."

"I practically blackmailed him into going," Flannan said unhappily. "All he wanted was to go home and never hear of Rilante again. I don't have the right to blame him, not for saving my little brother or anything else. I have no claim on him, at all. How far is Isenkliff?"

"Some people have been at sea for months without finding it, confounded by mists, driven off course by erratic currents and unseasonal winds. But my estimate is a good three hundred miles east-north-east as the bird flies."

"And he proposed to sail there in an open boat by himself?"

"I understand he's done it many times. His parents aren't happy with his going about like that, but Kitt can't resist the adventure and who can blame a boy that age. The stories he told of the animals in the Bacenis Wood and the Graumeer, and his run-ins with the Woodstalkers...but only when his parents didn't hear."

If Kitt knew these waters like his own bathtub, what would keep him from simply giving them the slip - nothing but the promise of discretion. He'd seemed very anxious about that, though. "Think he'll come back then?"

"If he can he will, and if there's anything left of Gasda, he'll pull it out. Because he said so. And...because you promised him."

"That's why he agreed in the first place, I'm aware of that. Is his mother so much worse than the Murder Bear?"

Brodi laughed a little. "Funny."

"Not really," Lodemar said. "Always down on the boy, she is, and he tries so hard to please her. Something's always wrong, and then she tells him off in such a manner, and he can't understand it, and truth to tell, neither could I when I was there. What can be wrong with a boy to grow up into the best warrior he's capable of becoming, and not a nursemaid? Because that's what she wants him to be. She has a little girl now, so she could lay off the boy, but will she? She is a woman of lofty thoughts, the lady Aslaug, and makes no sense to a simple man. But Kitt doesn't protest, not a word. It's like whipping a puppy for licking her hand. If she gets hold of this Cryssumha mess-up, he won't ever hear the last of it. Give the kid a break, will you!"

"You're a soft-hearted bastard Lodemar, I'm surprised at you." Brodi shook his head.

"What does the father say?" Flannan asked.

"Speaks up for the boy when it gets too bad. Taught him his trade, works him hard, turned him into a damn good smith as you've seen yourself, my Prince."

"Turned him into damn good fighter too," Brodi said slowly. "What with that business of testing the warriors who come for Aurora blades the boy must have learned weapons and modes of fighting from all known countries, and then some, learned it with the experts too. Travel to Isenkliff is no walk in the garden, it's a veritable feat, and those who make it are the best. Seems to me that smith wiped his lady's eye thoroughly. Whom did you see when you were there?"

"It's no good you pretending to be the tough guy for the rough, Brodi. One of Gilroy's bunch of spies you are alright. Questions, questions."

"Well, I can see the lady's point, the boy is a terror. One day he'll grow out of the apron strings and then everyone will run for their lives. I'd rather anticipate him. To see him clamber aboard just when we thought we'd escaped Ardri's Donadroch sorcery, how did that make me feel, what do you think?"

"Why don't you ask a direct question? Was Kitt sent by the Cryssumha brood to get the crown prince, is what you want to know? What a twisted imagination you have, insinuating things!"

"Just what I need for outguessing that twisted shoot Ardri."

"I suppose I can't prevail upon you to use civil terms when speaking of the youngest Prince of Rilante?" Flannan inquired resignedly.

"Not Kitt," Lodemar said stoutly. "Completely unthinkable. The boy is straight. When he gets back, I'll tell him you need another clout on the head before you go on from mistrusting him to suspecting yourself. You may have been doing this double thinking too long, you know."

"The kid did behave rather well towards Neilo and me," Brodi admitted. "If he'd offed us, nobody would have brought warning that there was a king in Cryssumha. On the other hand, this was just what could give Ardri a bearing on Flannan."

"Really my prince, the mere idea is preposterous!"

"You put a lot of trust in Kitt my dear Lodemar, and you know him longer than I or Brodi do. I've learned to consider your judgement, and I'm prepared to wait here; however long it takes. Hopefully not too long, now, though."

A shout drifted down from the lookout. "Boat! Boat! Boat!"

The drift anchor was hauled up before Lodemar could even give the command; the sailors had been waiting on deck in the rain. Steam came out of the side as the vents were thrown open and the central wheel turned within moments of the signal. The two propellers began to churn. The Birlinn Yehan steamed against the north-west wind, towards the shore, to meet the dot which came running towards them across the chopping waves, and grew into a sail filled to bursting with the wind.

Flannan laid both hands to his mouth, and called up the mast. "Do you see one man or two?"

"One."

Flannan's shoulders sagged. "Well, it was a long shot. I should be grateful that we didn't sacrifice Kitt as well. It would not stand us well with his father, and frankly, it would be a damn shame."

Lodemar gave the command for the steam to be shut down. The ship slowed down as the boat came up, dropped her sail and was driven against the backboard side by the wind.

Kitt gripped the rope a sailor threw down to him and fastened it to the bow. He was soaked head to toe, the hair plastered to his head.

"Boy looks a sight," Lodemar commented. "Heat water, jump to it, Pots! And get me every spare blanket!"

"Water is hot, and blankets are warm these last days," the cook yelled up from below.

326

"How you coddle the terrible kid, you sod!" Brodi jeered.

The whole crew was hanging over the rail to see.

"Back to your stations!" Lodemar yelled.

"My shield looks like a hedgehog," Flannan remarked. "They must have shot at very short range. There's something under it!"

Kitt drew the shield aside and there in the bottom of the boat lay a naked, dirty, skin and bone relic of a man. He lifted him in his arms and into the quickly lowered rope net. Then the man, who nobody recognised as Lord Gasda, Dog of Rilante, lay on the Birlinn Yehan's deck with his eyes closed, a blue tinge around his mouth and eyes. Temporary wound dressings were soaked with blood. The crown prince knelt to wrap him into his own coat.

Kitt vaulted over the rail and Flannan sprang up to embrace him, getting water all over himself.

"I want to redress his wounds. Where..."

"My cot, naturally," Flannan said.

Kitt picked up the unconscious man and carried him to the main cabin.

Flannan watched Kitt clean and dress the wounds and frowned. "He isn't coming to?"

"Exhausted and hurt. He's a brave man. Hot bathwater!" he threw over his shoulder.

"Just waiting for you to ask," Pots the cook said as he provided white linen and cans with steaming water.

Admirable man, the cook, Flannan thought gratefully. The boy seemed to know exactly what he was doing, and he did it with surprising gentleness. He had a satchel full of different drugs and implements, the prince noticed. What else, he wondered.

Gasda awoke and took a swing at Kitt. The boy evaded it easily without damaging him further and without any sign of irritation.

"Get some hot soup or tea!"

"It is here," Pots the cook said. "Duck soup, extra salt, as you asked. And that tea you gave me, nice and hot."

"Allow me!" Flannan raised Lord Gasda with his arm around the bony shoulders. He was shocked at how little the once burly man weighed.

"My prince, be careful!" Gasda said urgently. "This young man here..."

327

"Kitt is on our side now," Flannan said and raised a spoon of duck soup to the gaunt face. The wounded man took the nourishment.

Kitt packed up his medicines. "Once we get to Isenkliff, my mother will do the real healing."

"You'll see and won't believe," Lodemar said. "Just let's get him there alive. A spark of life is all we need to keep glowing."

Flannan looked at Kitt with a shining face. "You did save him!"

"No. You did. If you hadn't made me, I wouldn't have gone. I was wrong."

A cheer rose on the deck outside, "Long live King Flannan!"

The men could put two and two together, Flannan thought; they had to realise that King Tirnmas was dead.

"Where's the Bethrek skin?" Kitt asked.

"Bring the kid his Bethrek skin," Lodemar said, looking as mystified as Flannan felt.

Neilo brought the tawny pelt and Kitt held it out to Flannan. "For a king's cloak."

"You risk the Red Death of the Woodstalkers to retrieve this, and then you offer it to me? Why?"

"Because you insisted to go for Gasda."

"I told you I could do nothing less."

"Yes."

"I never felt so useless in my life, standing here on the deck and waiting for you to pull the chestnuts from the fire."

"Kitt is right; none of us would have given a broken grappling hook for Gasda's chances. But you wouldn't give up my king, and that's why you deserve a Bethrek cloak, to remind the people that when the odds are endless, their king will come for them, as surely as he took back Rilante."

"Great speech, Lodemar. And I mean it!" Brodi took the Bethrek skin and threw it over Flannan's shoulder.

Flannan stroked the tawny pelt. "With a cloak like that, I can only be king or be buried in it, so let's better win this war. Gasda saved is a victory after a string of losses. Maybe you have turned the tide for us, Kitt."

"He turned it for Cryssumha, why not for us. It might work." Brodi said. "Normally I don't believe in highfalutin nonsense, but sometimes patterns do exist."

"Bethrek fights against Mooncat! Let the fur fly until there's nothing left!" Neilo laughed.

They all stared at him.

"He's already spoken once this year," Brodi said. "And then he didn't laugh."

***

The three Nordmänner came across the stone pavement of Iwerdonn castle like rolling sea mountains, with their long yellow hair running into wild beards, huge hide boots and intricately wrought bronze armour.

"Glad to see you looking good, King Tirnmas," the foremost said. "We heard that Rilante had fallen and you were in trouble."

"And you came at once, how good of you!" Ardri drawled. He stood beside the golden throne, his hand on his father's shoulder. Serenaiba sat on the smaller throne beside her husband, upright in purple, her beautiful rose petal lips curving upwards.

"Well!" the Nordmann spread his long arms in an expansive gesture. "There is the question of harbour rights. We heard Captain Flannan, I mean the Crown Prince Nolan Ri, has left Rilante?"

"He is trying out his new ship. It is a big armoured one."

"Lodemar's Birlinn Yehan, we heard. So he'll be back?"

"Expecting him to dock any day. There was a minor uprising in Eastern Rilante, but that was controlled by myself. The Crown Prince didn't need to intervene."

"He sent Lord Gasda east."

"To deal with the Woodstalkers. High time too. Those blood-soaked savages are squatting on some of our richest tin and copper mines and practically halted the fur trade, as they killed hunters and farmers. Lord Gasda is sorting them out for good as we speak. The news we receive from the campaign is excellent."

"I am glad to hear that nothing has changed in Rilante."

"Only for the better. Therefore you will oblige us all, my father King Tirnmas, my brother Prince Nolan Ri, and me, by relating what you saw and heard here to any others who might be misled by rumours they may have heard because," Ardri smiled deprecatingly, "you know how it is, sometimes false alarms are just as apt to cause problems as real unrest. And we don't want anything to disturb the bronze trade, just when the crown is regaining full control of the Cryssumha mines beyond the Struenfoly."

"Well, well, well, that is very clear." The Nordmann emitted another of his big, dishonest laughs. "Good of you to grant us this audience, King Tirnmas. And your queen."

They turned their broad backs and ambled out of the throne room.

"Just one truth you spoke to these sea wolves," Serenaiba murmured. "Nolan Ri will return."

"And none too soon. We will need Flannan here to deal with threats from seaward. This was only the beginning. There will be more scavengers coming to divide the carcass of Rilante, thinking that her defender is gone. I'll fetch him back myself, with Slatynrigan, all the way from Minit Houarn if necessary. Flannan can sail ships in his sleep, won't need his mind to fight battles. You thought of him only as something to be got out of the way, mother, because you don't understand hard facts and fighting men. Leave the work of ruling to me, the King of Cryssumha, and attend to your woman's sphere. Go look after your daughter in law, my beloved wife, Neelam. She has begun swelling like the sweet fruit she is and needs her mother in law." He laughed excitedly. "Kitt said that I couldn't build a bronze ship to rival that dirty corroding iron vessel he admires so much. But not only will I build a greater ship than the Birlinn Yehan, but I'll also do it in just nine days."

Chapter 28
The Return of the Prodigal Son

The peaks of an island rose above the water, and the Birlinn Yehan steered towards it with a steady western wind. The skies were clear.

"Isenkliff," Captain Lodemar announced. "That was a smooth passage. They say," here his voice dropped: "Arrival depends on the lady Aslaug's liking. I am glad that I appear to have been welcome always. Some captains have been lost in these waters for months and had to turn about without sighting Brynnir's island."

"Then I shall hope that the lady never objects to my presence," Flannan said.

"You should, King Flannan," Lodemar replied with unusual seriousness.

In the west-south-west of the island, the mountain sloped down into a fan-shaped deep bay, open to the west wind but sheltered from the strong winds out of north and north-west by a ridge which ran into the sea. Flannan wondered if it was a natural harbour, or perhaps a Sea God had created this perfect anchoring ground. Here those landed who came to Isenkliff for Aurora steel, Lodemar told him. There was no ship moored there now. The Birlinn Yehan came sailing towards the coast, took down her sails, and with a churn of one propeller, turned to present her backboard side. Aft and fore, anchors were lowered. Lodemar's younger brother Karnatz was in command of the manoeuvre. Flannan was glad that the brothers were on his side in his plight. Since Gasda's rescue, they even gave him his royal title.

Kitt was standing on the foreship, in his smithy with the tools stowed and the forge battened down. All he possessed he wore on his body, weapons, tools, medicines and trophies. Flannan was extraordinarily glad that he had won that boy's respect.

The prince – the young king - wore the Bethrek pelt for the occasion; the sailmaker had turned out to have a sense of fashion and had quite ingeniously attached the fur to the blue brocade coat. The paws lay over the shoulders and the head as a collar on the broad back.

The cutter went over the side, with the aid of a crane.

They were watched by a tall, broad-shouldered red-bearded man in a leather apron who had come down from the hill as the ship manoeuvred and was now standing on the shore. Long white hair shot with red strands streamed in the wind. Even from a distance, his eyes were bright blue. The Smith of Isenkliff himself, Lodemar muttered, as if the man might hear over the wind.

The cutter came alongside a long stone jetty, and again Flannan wondered if this was a natural formation. Iron rings were set into the stone, for the fastening of boats. Lodemar was the first to leave the cutter via a gangway, made of metal as was everything on his ship. Steps led down to the pebble beach, which were all visible at low water.

Lodemar fell back for the express purpose of ceding precedence to Flannan; that also was something new. Flannan, in turn, motioned to Kitt; surely the boy should be the first to disembark on his home island.

Kitt had left in spring and returned with the first autumn rains, seven months later. To him, it felt like seven years. His father was standing on the shore. Eckehart had never done that when a ship came in. He looked older than when Kitt had seen him last, and the white strands in his red hair had become broader.

"There you are Kitt," Eckehart said. "We were expecting you earlier." This seemed quite an understatement and boded ill.

"I was cut off in the Murkowydir," Kitt ventured.

"Yes, you never listen. We were worried out of our wits." Eckehart said in the same incongruously placid tone. Suddenly, he slapped Kitt in the face, something he had never done before. He had to reach up to do that. "Did you have to grow so much!" he accused. Kitt looked at him numbly, and Eckehart threw his arms around him and hugged hard. "Your mother will be glad, though what she will say I don't know," he said.

After introductions were made, they walked up the path, Lodemar and Flannan beside Eckehart. Walking behind the young king in his new cloak, Kitt thought he still saw the green, gleaming eyes of the Dodlak. Four men at arms were carrying Gasda's stretcher. Lord Bonyd, Brodi and Neilo brought up the rear.

The hall came into sight. In Aslaug's garden the peach tree had been flowering when Kitt left; now yellow and red peaches shone from the dark green foliage.

"We can bring all the men in here," Brodi said, surprised at the dimension of the blacksmith's hall.

Aslaug was standing before the long table. She wore a silk dress thickly embroidered with gold thread. Her blond hair was held back by a net of silver and pearls. The white strands had returned and were thicker now. Freshly baked bread, a great joint of roasted meat, a golden jug and goblets stood ready on the table, covered by the tablecloth embroidered with blue Auga blossoms. All that showed Kitt that his mother had expected the royal visitor. How she always knew these things he never knew, only that she had many skills beyond the preparation of medicines.

His little sister Swantje came running on short legs, falling over, getting up. Her hair was buttercup yellow and had grown into ringlets, and her eyes sparkled sea blue.

Kitt scooped her up. "Birla!"

Seven months collapsed as she put her two small hands to his face and burbled with delight.

Prince Flannan bowed deeply to Aslaug. "My lady, here is one of my men for whom I am most anxious to ask your help." He made way for the men carrying in the stretcher. "This is my servant and friend Lord Gasda. Your son saved him from certain death and tended to his wounds. He has suffered much and is very weak."

Aslaug handed the tablet with the goblets to Eckehart and led the way to the room beside the kitchen, which was her sick room and dispensary. There, Kitt transferred the Dog of Rilante from the stretcher to the bed and set aside Flannan's fur-trimmed blanket. His mother pressed her lips together at the sight of the tortured body with the ribs visible in a ring from breastbone to back. Kitt didn't tell what had led to Gasda's bad state and Aslaug didn't ask. Both knew better than to discuss this in front of the hurt man. He reported the application of the death-defying purple blossom to prevent the inflammation of the wounds and gangrene and of duck broth to restore strength. The wounds were clean, no sign of the much-feared suppuration. Aslaug touched the arrow wounds and found no heat.

"I didn't have enough poppy to stitch him up, and I didn't dare to use too much Uskeva spirits in case it weakened him more."

"We had a big poppy harvest. You missed seeing all the poppy blossoms," Aslaug said.

When the poppy tincture was working and Gasda dimly conscious, they stitched up the arrow wounds and changed the dressings on the superficial cuts, bruises and burns. After they finished, Kitt repositioned the fur-lined blanket and Gasda's gaunt hands clung to it.

When they returned from the sickroom, Aslaug sat down at the table with the men, instead of retiring to her seat by the window on the gallery, as she usually did when warriors came to Isenkliff.

"He will live, and he won't be a cripple," Aslaug answered Flannan's question. "He is exhausted, has no strength left. He must rest absolutely for ten days. After that, he may be moved provided that he frequently rests for another thirty days."

"You and your men are welcome to stay the duration," Eckehart invited.

"I am most grateful to you, my lady, for the care of my friend, and to you, my lord, for your offer of hospitality," Flannan said. "As I am grateful to your son for saving Gasda at great danger to himself. The Red Death he has risked does not bear contemplating." He shook his head with emotion. "It was the Murder Bear himself who held Gasda captive, after he had trapped his host of a thousand men in the Bacenis."

"The Murder Bear?" Eckehart asked tonelessly.

"The meanest mother – savage Woodstalker," Brodi said helpfully.

"Even we here on Isenkliff have heard about the mindless cruelty of the Woodstalkers of the Murkowydir and this most implacable of their warriors," Eckehart said.

"Are the Woodstalkers so dangerous then?" Aslaug asked almost absently, but her straight back belied her negligent tone.

"Yes, Lady Aslaug," Flannan said. "The only ones who dare go into the Bacenis are desperate men. And the woodsrunners, from outside the society of Rilante, many of them of mixed blood. A man who crosses the Struenfoly is considered dead, and his affairs are handled as such until he returns. Which he likely never will. Not even the woodsrunners will go into the Bacenis now. Trade in fur and ores has stopped on the border because of that same Woodstalker called Murder Bear, infamous for his bloody deeds against the hunters, settlers and soldiers."

"You never told us anything about the Murder Bear, Kitt." Eckehart had gone so pale, that it was noticeable even in the firelight.

Kitt shrugged. "A war leader of the Feen, one of the people living in the Murkowydir, which the Rilante call the Bacenis. Along the Struenfoly they call him Canaras Muntrer, Mad Bear, or Murder Bear, but his real name is Mangan Sorkera, that means Singing Bear. He's hunted me for years, and he's challenged me, but I'm always running from him and his warriors."

"Lucky for him," Brodi said. "The Bethreks weren't so lucky though because you didn't run from them."

Drawing a deep breath, Eckehart gave vent to his feelings. "Damn it, son! Why? Why do you keep going there?"

"But father, how could I not go into the Murkowydir! Animals live there that long disappeared from other parts of the world. I have seen a basilisk and the White Serpent! In the Murkowydir grow trees with red trunks that twenty men cannot span, and more than two hundred feet high, and there are others only as big as a hand, but a thousand years old and medicine plants that grow nowhere else, like the purple flowers that can stop gangrene."

Aslaug smiled, nodding slightly. "Yes, it was very clever of you to recognise their power. One of the most useful things you ever did, and you saved lord Gasda's leg with it."

Encouraged by that, Kitt continued. "Winter is not so long and hard in the Murkowydir; there are green plants and fresh meat, when here on Isenkliff everything is frozen!"

Eckehart's fist crashed on the table. "Never mind the game and the plants which you went to gather in spring and didn't bring back in autumn!"

"Instead you brought a bad conscience, again," Aslaug said, her light-blue eyes lighting on Kitt.

Kitt fell silent and turned his head away to look into the fire, a deep dusky flush creeping up his cheek. He had never told his parents of the encounter with a Woodstalker four years ago, the first time he had killed another human being to survive himself. Now it was as if the body was lying on the table, for Aslaug to see. And the bodies of the Creatures of the Mist had joined him. Not much space left.

"Please do not chide your brave son," Flannan said. "Nobody but he could have saved my friend Gasda."

"Your son is a bloody...he's a hero," Brodi added. "And a healer too. Just when I thought he couldn't surprise us anymore."

"That's what I'm saying," Lodemar said.

"The wound treatment you did very well with what you had," Aslaug said.

Kitt knew he wasn't off the hook.

"We have come in search of you, Lord Eckehart," Flannan said, and Kitt was grateful for the shift of attention back to the king of Rilante.

"Not for your sword though? You already have yours, I see." Eckehart pointed to Kitt's seven-star-sign visible between the hilt and the lip of the sheath of Flannan's sword. "I thought Rilante swore by bronze. No smith on Isenkliff made a sword for a Rilante-man before, and now the crown prince himself carries a steel blade. How do you find the handling? May I see?"

Kitt watched his father looking at the sword, the third he had made alone without Eckehart's advice.

"Best I ever had. Kitt persuaded me to a longer blade, and the balance is such that I don't notice it."

"Your son made a sword for the King of Rilante, Master Eckehart," Lord Bonyd remarked. "Through circumstances beyond his influence which he didn't want to come about Nolan Ri is king now."

"I should feel best if you condescended to just calling me Flannan, Master Eckehart. I have a great boon to ask. My father, King Tirnmas, has sent me to learn about iron and to equip my men with it if you accept."

"You are planning a radical change, Flannan? And your father consents?"

"He does." Flannan nodded. "All the bronze Rilante needs for arms and tools is made by the Cryssumha people of the eastern province. They are different from us, in looks, in customs, despising us as upstarts, forgetting that without Rilante the trees would soon grow down to the shore of the sea again. There are...bad feelings. There are attempts at secession. It is not good for Rilante to be so dependent on Cryssumha bronze and so exposed to Cryssumha Donadroch magic. For there are few in Rilante born to the white Dredorocht magic, I have no knowledge of anyone, though the tales of the past tell of such men and women. But in Cryssumha, the dark Donadroch magic runs in many veins. Steel can be worked entirely without magic, your son assures me. Knowing the metal is all the magic, that is what he says."

"Bronze can be worked without magic also," Kitt said, as one who was willing to be just.

Flannan smiled grimly. "Yes, but Donadroch magic sticks to it so. Bells, mirrors, I know whereof I speak."

"Yes," Kitt said. His face had darkened so much that not for the first time Flannan wondered what exactly had happened to this boy in Cryssumha.

337

Chapter 29
The Truth Will Out

The autumn days were mild and sunny. The tents for the men stood in the place below the smithy, protected from the west wind, and the cattle and sheep were grazing by the creek, watched in turn by sailors so that they should not stray into Aslaug's garden.

Flannan inspected the smelting ovens and the forge in the company of the young and the old Master-smiths, taking notes and making sketches. He now saw the beauty of steel, and even began to appreciate the stark, bare rawness of iron. He wondered where the stacks of iron bars came from that suddenly appeared, and whether it was indiscreet to ask. Now and again the smiths allowed him to fetch and carry and hand things to them and once to hammer on a glowing iron. Sometimes he thought he saw things, gnarled faces and hands where there was only rock.

Every day he visited Lord Gasda, who was healing, but depressed and monosyllabic. Flannan's heart ached for him, and the thousand Rilante soldiers, dead in the Bacenis.

At the end of a long workday, a sail appeared on the horizon. Flannan saw it first through the gap in the rocks by the smelting ovens. "The Golden Hind is coming," he said. "I know her rigging from any distance," he answered Kitt's questioning look.

Driven by the steady west wind, the ship was coming in fast. As the workers were walking on the cliff path towards the hall, they watched the Golden Hind slide in beside the Birlinn Yehan with the dash and precision Tomme Der, her First Officer, was fond of displaying.

Warmed to his heart, Flannan entered the hall where the long table was already laid for dinner. Two ships. He had a fleet now.

A tall, blond, young sailor with an attractive open face came into the hall, Tomme Der, the First of the Golden Hind. In his wake followed a stocky Rilante soldier in scruffy regulation garb and mail tunic. He had bright-red hair and beard cropped short, with indifferent freckled features, and sharp, light-blue eyes.

"I seem to know that lovely face!" Brodi exclaimed.

"Glad to see you, Tomme Der!" Flannan called out. "I see you brought the Hind! And you, my dear Gilroy. How glad I am to see you both!"

"The damage is repaired." The First Officer shot a reproachful look at Captain Lodemar, who grinned unrepentantly.

"Do you have news from Iwerdonn?"

"None of it good my lord," Gilroy answered.

Flannan's face fell.

"I heard that King Tirnmas was alive," Gilroy said hastily, "at least he is not dead but..."

"Is he a captive?"

"Worse. His mind...destroyed by Donadrocht Cryssumha magic."

"We really know nothing definite," Tomme Der said with a little frown marring his smooth forehead.

"Before you tell me more, allow me to introduce you to our hosts." Manners, Flannan thought, were such a good crutch, when you were bleeding inside.

Eckehart filled their wine goblets to the brim, and Flannan drank deeply from his. He looked briefly to Kitt, who had not taken his place at the table. Instead, he had retreated to his corner by the fireplace where he was trying to make himself invisible and startlingly succeeding. So absolutely still he sat, that it took Flannan a mental effort to pick out the contours of his shoulders and arms neigh indistinguishable from the wooden beams of the house, and the pale hair blending into the granite of the walls.

"I have more bad news," Gilroy was saying. "Lord Gasda and the Thousand..."

"We know," Flannan said.

"I was saved on the Struenfoly..."

"We know."

"I beg your pardon, my prince...my king. I thought I was the only survivor."

339

"You almost were," Flannan said. "So, tell me what happened to you after you returned to Dundingin, for that I do not know."

"I escaped with the help of the bronze smith Gobin. A friend of...a friend. He coloured my hair with the soot from his forge. But much as I tried, I was unable to overtake Ardri on the road to Iwerdonn. He advanced with a speed I am unable to comprehend, while the countryside was boiling with Cryssumha people crawling out of holes in the ground. Nobody had known that there were so many of them! They massacred the people of Iwerdonn...I wasn't in time to warn them...I heard about King Tirnmas turned into a mindless puppet dancing on a string...I couldn't have done anything..."

"I know my dear Gilroy," Flannan said.

"I made it to Bilawini. The Golden Hind was still in port, and Tomme Der was ready to follow you."

"I was indeed," the young, blond man said. "We took on more men from Bilawini and we ferried several families north to Akla where it seemed safer, though I don't know where in Rilante is still safe. We made the run three times, or I would have been earlier."

"Of course, you had to take them. They weren't prepared to go when we passed."

"Is that?" Gilroy's mouth fell open. "I beg your pardon my Lord Gasda, I thought..."

"I thought the same." Lord Gasda was standing in the door of the sickroom, leaning on Aslaug's arm. His face was haggard, and the memory of pain nested in the corners of his mouth and in his eyes. He was wearing a linen shirt and hose of Eckehart's which hung from his gaunt frame.

Kitt rose to assist, and Flannan anticipated him.

It was then that Gilroy spotted Kitt. "I don't believe it," he said and stared. "Kitt! You here!"

"Gilroy. You here," Kitt responded without enthusiasm.

"My dear Lord Gasda, so good to see you on your feet." Flannan led him to the table, sat him down in his chair, and wrapped him in a blanket handed to him by Aslaug.

There was a shuffling of men making room for Flannan to sit beside Gasda.

"I heard voices, and this time, it wasn't the echo of dead men. How glad I am to see you, Gilroy. Were there more survivors?" Gasda's pathetic tone of hope was terrible to Flannan, as was the way he slumped down in the chair when he realised the truth.

"Kitt here, he saved my life. Picked me up in the Struenfoly."

"He saved my life too," Gasda said dully.

"Nobody survived in the Bacenis but those he saved," Gilroy said. "Unfortunately, he also saved Prince Ardri, that traitorous snake."

He should defend his brother, Flannan thought, but he couldn't he really, seeing Gasda's broken body and the hunted look in Gilroy's eyes. "He's still my brother and a Prince of Rilante," he said as gently as he could. It came out weak and was met with the silence this remark deserved.

"What haven't you told us?" Eckehart demanded.

"Oh, several things," Flannan said grimly. He looked at Kitt in his corner and spread his hands.

Kitt shrugged and leant back, resigned.

"That was another reason why I investigated you in Dundingin," Gilroy continued relentlessly. "Found out that you have a name with the savage Woodstalkers. Which made me even more suspicious. There are about a handful men on the whole of the frontier who have that doubtful honour. Translates into something like Feilan, wolf cub."

"Feilan, I like that. Since you object to kiddo." Brodi grinned.

"Luckily, you didn't hold it against me, or I wouldn't be here," Gilroy pursued. "You didn't mean no harm, that much is established now. Unless it's all part of the plot. I see you have reached a position where you can..." Gilroy shook his head. "No, I don't believe that. Such a plot? But if you had seen the streets ripped open, and the holes disgorging...things...you would believe anything. I can do nothing about it."

"Won't you tell all of it?" Eckehart asked. "The whole story?"

"I rather wouldn't," Flannan said, "and it is a damn long-winded tale."

"We will hear the whole story," Aslaug said, and somehow Flannan didn't think of contradicting her. After taking a deep breath, he began to speak. "My father, King Tirnmas, loved my mother, the queen Murine, so much, that when she died, he wanted no other wife."

"The Mother of Thirteen bless and rest her," the Rilante men muttered.

Flannan plodded on. "But after several years he gave in to political necessity and contracted a marriage to Serenaiba, a young noblewoman from the ancient royal family of Cryssumha. It was done to overcome the division of Rilante." He looked round defiantly. "Little did he know then that most of the members of the royal family of Cryssumha are Dredorocht-born, nay worse, dark Donadroch magicians, and have always delved into the ancient star alchemy. Serenaiba used her dark arts to ensnare the king."

"Why did she do that?" Aslaug asked.

"It has been Serenaiba who ruled Rilante, not the king. Her Cryssumha creatures crept through the palace in Iwerdonn, and my father changed from a powerful warrior king into a bauble hanging from Serenaiba's girdle." Flannan's face was white like the knuckles of his hand, gripping the wine goblet.

"You said she was young. Is she beautiful?" Aslaug continued probing.

Flannan smiled bitterly and shrugged. "Oh, yes. Very beautiful. And she gave Tirnmas three more sons."

"Then that would be all the sorcery she needs? And if something happens to you, then one of Serenaiba's sons will inherit the throne and favour the Cryssumha people over Rilante?" Eckehart shrugged. "Same old story. Holds no interest to me. You don't need to go on."

"Sir! You are speaking to the King of Rilante!" Pushing back his seat, Gilroy sprung up, and so did Kitt, but much faster, more silently, and almost unnoticed.

"Sit down and shut up, Gilroy!" Flannan snapped angrily. "Have you gone quite mad?"

Scowling, Gilroy sat down, and Kitt relaxed again on his place by the fire.

"We will have the whole story from beginning to end," Aslaug repeated.

"You are precipitate to discount my motivation, master Eckehart," Flannan said. "I assure you that I would not bother you with something as trivial as that. I cannot expect you to believe that I

342

loved my little brothers and that I am not overly keen on the throne, although that is nothing but the truth. Ridevin, the eldest of Serenaiba's sons, disappeared five years ago, Kuranori, the second, three years ago, both never to be seen again. Then, this spring, my youngest brother, Ardri, disappeared. Now, what do you say to that?"

Eckehart surveyed Flannan shrewdly. "We live here a long way from the kingdoms, but my guess would be the prince who did not disappear."

Gilroy stirred, opened his mouth and closed it. Kitt was watching him narrowly.

"Do be careful, Gilroy," Flannan admonished. He grinned hardily. "Seems so obvious that I would be inclined to suspect myself. Same old story, yes?" Flannan shook his fiery head quietly. "But maybe you reconsider when you hear that there is a prophecy that when the Wandering Stars come right, lost Cryssumha can be resurrected by a king of the Old Blood. Cryssumha blood."

"Ardri was always watching the stars," Lord Bonyd said. "Somehow I didn't connect that to the prophecy which I took for an ancient fairytale, didn't take it seriously. I am to blame." He looked shocked by the sudden realisation. "It was a long way coming, but I only began to suspect when Ardri also disappeared. I asked an astronomer, and he told me that in fact, the Wandering Stars come right every two or three years. Not a rare constellation at all. Then I wondered how there would ever be peace in Rilante."

"Never," Gasda said, his voice was still weak. "I thought if we had Kione Lonnir...suddenly there was hope...and it is there, it was the last I saw before..." He coughed painfully.

"There was a chance," Flannan said and replaced the fallen blanket.

"Ultimately, it was all about the white bronze crown Fenifindrune, which was once worn by the ancient kings," Lord Bonyd pursued. "It has been lost since the day, long ago, when Cryssumha fell under the stone axes of the wild woods savages, when the ancient city of Rivin Claghini was swallowed by the trees of the Bacenis. But it is still there, and then we heard that traitors searched for it."

"That was my task," Gilroy took up the tale. "With your permission, Lord Bonyd. In Dundingin, I found out that all three of

Serenaiba's sons went into the Bacenis to search for Fenifindrune, one after the other. The first two never returned."

"Shut up, Gilroy!" Flannan demanded just as Aslaug said, "Continue, Gilroy!"

Somehow Gilroy seemed to have heard only Aslaug's command. "Your son Kitt brought Prince Ardri out of the Bacenis and with him Fenifindrune. Then back in Dundingin, Kitt foiled all our attempts to...stop Ardri and his Cryssumha conspiracy. Your son is one devastating mother...obstacle to come up against."

Suddenly Aslaug turned around on her seat towards Kitt, and her uncompromising light-blue eyes fixed him. "Your interference has done much damage in Rilante. Learn from that to never interfere, if you are not sure about the consequences. And I advise you, never to be sure because you just don't know enough."

"Yes, mother."

Kitt met Aslaug's gaze fully, with such a strange mixture of courage and humility in his grey eyes, that the men averted their eyes and made a show of taking up their goblets and drinking. It was suddenly very quiet in the hall. "You took the fate of a whole kingdom into your incapable hands," Aslaug continued. "Through your fault, people died, as surely as if you had slain them yourself. And it isn't over even now."

"Yes," Kitt said. "I know."

"Remember it always!" Aslaug finished in a brittle voice.

There was a deep intake of breath from Flannan. "No, my lady Aslaug, your permission to contradict most vehemently. In justice to Kitt, he saved a man in the wood who was in trouble and unable to defend himself. Saved him from this," he stood up and spread the pelt of his cloak."

"Green God of the Woods!" Tomme Der was heard to exclaim.

"Is that...?" Gilroy asked.

"You better believe it," Brodi said grimly.

"Preserving a life can never be wrong, never," Flannan insisted. "At no time had your son any way of judging the possible consequences of saving my brother. It would have been so much easier for him to just walk away, and yet he decided that it was better that a man lived, and that is a commendable decision, no matter what the consequences."

"He just saved everybody who needed saving," Captain Lodemar added. "Nobody can hold that against him. I believe he'd save the Murder Bear if that Woodstalker were in a tight spot."

Kitt had in fact once rescued Mangan Sorkera from being torn apart by the Shakro Shork, the Black Thorn in the heart of the Murkowydir wood. He had never told anyone about that and never would. Silence was golden, of that he was more and more convinced.

"My brothers Ridevin and Kuranori had nobody to save them," Flannan said sadly. "I fear that they died a terrible death. If I can forgive Kitt for having preserved my ambitious little brother from the same fate, surely you can too, lady Aslaug."

At last, Kitt was released from the Aslaug's gaze, and the blue eyes bent on Flannan now. "What is a natural and good feeling in the common man may be irresponsible in royal blood. You stand above the crowd, but for your exalted position, you must pay the price, King Flannan. And the price is to forego all the sentimentalities lesser men are entitled to."

"Wasn't I telling you just now? I care nothing for my exalted position. I am just a warrior, really." Flannan spread his hands, with the pronounced knuckles and callused insides characteristic for a fighting man. "At least in war, you know who the enemy is. I prefer ship planks and open battle to court intrigues. Iwerdonn may be built of rough stone, but the betrayal and the hunger for power are the same as at the great golden courts of Daguilaria, Tolosa and Cladith Culuris. Ardri always wanted to be king, and I was even thinking of giving up my birthright in his favour."

At that, there was a protest from all Rilante-men.

"Those who want to rule should never be allowed to, King Flannan," Aslaug said.

"I couldn't agree with you more," Flannan retorted, drank down his wine and set the goblet down hard. He was feeling exhausted, and his heart was sinking as Aslaug persisted in calling him king. That wise woman of power thought his father lost, despite hearing that his body was alive. He looked over to Kitt who was doing his invisibility trick again. Flannan wished he could do that.

"Why did you leave your capital, King Flannan, before your rebellious brother reached Iwerdonn?" Eckehart asked.

345

"You mean, did I run away?" Flannan swallowed hard. "Because my father, King Tirnmas, has sent me to you, Eckehart before...before...it was in one of his lucid moments and my father knew precisely what would happen. We have no chance against the dark Donadroch magic, as long as the strength of Rilante relies on the bronze of Cryssumha. We have no counter-magic, and so we need steel!" Flannan emptied his beaker again as if it contained plain water, and not strong, red wine from Tolosa, and looked Eckehart straight in the eye. "If my father was mistaken in sending me here, at this moment, my Lord Eckehart, I'm never going to forgive myself, nor you."

Everybody at the table sat very still.

"It's not about the lost throne I mind," Flannan continued, "not even the way my little brother took it from under me, though frankly, at first, it did gall me. What matters is that Ardri wants to turn back the time, to wipe Rilante off the face of the earth, like paint off a wall, so that the underlying dark pattern of old Cryssumha comes to light again, the Cryssumha of bronze and blood sacrifice and Donadroch star sorcery. I can't stand by and let that happen. I'm still hoping to save my father, King Tirnmas. They won't murder him until they can be secure in their power. Until then they'll use him as a puppet. Will you make me the iron weapons I ask, blacksmith?"

The disapproving fire of Aslaug's eyes was bent on Eckehart now. "Interfere again?"

Eckehart met Aslaug's scornful gaze fully. "Whether I make the iron weapons for Rilante or not, each way I will be interfering," he said. "Remember Kitt, I said I was making weapons for men, not their choices? "

Kitt nodded. "You did father. I did not entirely understand you then."

"You mean you thought that I was just making excuses to do the things I wanted to do." Eckehart smiled. "But really it is like the man's life you saved. The man's deeds after that are his own responsibility. Not yours."

"It's three lives he saved, even five if you count Neilo and me, seeing as he didn't bash in our heads when we attacked him," Brodi said. "How will you keep track of whether we behave or not, Feilan?

You can't, so don't beat yourself up. By the Judges, how confused you are!"

Aslaug turned upon Kitt again. "And what are you thinking of, sitting there without food after working all day?" She scolded, heaping a plate with enormous cuts of meat.

"I'm not hungry," Kitt muttered.

"Nonsense!" Aslaug snapped, smearing butter thickly on a fresh loaf of bread with her hands dancing with irritation. "As if your not eating would make anything better. It doesn't, don't you think it."

She pushed the plate under Kitt's nose and stood over him with her arms stemmed on her hips, until the youth had eaten a reluctant bite, and suddenly realising how hungry he was, ate every last crumb of it.

Chapter 30
The Black Galley

On the evening of the twelfth day of Edrin, the ninth moon after Winter Solstice, a sunset like a burning city set the western sky on fire, and out of the blaze sailed a ship like a black swan.

The smiths had just finished their work at the smelting oven, assisted by Flannan and Gero.

"Another customer for your Aurora blades?" Flannan asked. "Somehow it looks – ominous. Do you get raids for your gold? Many must know you have it."

"Gold?" Eckehart said. "If anyone wants it they can take it. We don't care. We don't work for gold."

"I see where you get your disregard for gold, Kitt."

"It's a fine material for jewellery. Women like it."

Ardri smiled at Kitt's grown-up manner which didn't impress the older men, who all smirked a little, but the boy, so attentive usually, fortunately didn't catch this.

"That is a valid reason to work it," Eckehart said, his blue eyes twinkling merrily. "See Flannan, nobody comes to Isenkliff to raid. What can they rob here? They are welcome to the gold. But nobody will take it. They all want our work more than gold. We blacksmiths, we have no need to fight."

As they walked along the cliff path details were becoming visible of the arriving ship.

"It's a galley," Flannan said with amazement. "Three decks of oars. Who uses a ship like that on the open ocean?"

"A ship from Kemitraim?" Kitt wondered. "They also prefer bronze. I read in a book..."

"He reads so many books," Eckehart said in an aside to Flannan.

"Reading is a habit which you can pick up without rightly realising," Flannan replied seriously. "Before you know it you're addicted and searching for new things to read."

348

The galley neared Isenkliff resembling a black centipede running on the water. They still couldn't see any men. When the ship was near, a black banner broke out. A nine-cornered star blazed green, red and white. The pattern was familiar to Kitt. Gobin, the bronze-smith, had drawn it once in Dundingin. It symbolised the union of copper and tin, and that was hardly a coincidence.

"Damn it! And I looking at the thing coming on like a bloody halfwit!" Flannan shouted, as he was breaking into a run, calling for his armour and his weapons.

"This time, we need to fight. Hide with Birla and mother," Kitt told his father before he also ran to arm himself.

With flashing oars, the black menace of the galley bore down upon Isenkliff in the face of a stiff, unusually cold north-eastern wind.

Flannan stood above the high waterline ready for the fight, Lodemar and Kitt beside him. Men came running to form up behind.

"I wish we had more shields," Flannan muttered under his breath.

"We'll make them, after this battle!"

"My dear Kitt, you are the stuff a war leader is made of!" Flannan said gratefully.

Without reducing speed, the galley bore down on the Golden Hind and ran through her, splitting her hull with the knife-sharp elongated keel, spilling timber and screaming men. The men on the shore also screamed.

Cordage and entrails dangled from the bloodspattered, pointed ramming spur as the galley came on. The metal hull scraped along the Birlinn Yehan, with a sound like two bells crashing into each other, one iron and one bronze. The iron ship danced crazily at her mooring, the decks tilting and throwing sailors back and forth.

The galley did not slow down as it drove past the mole into the little harbour steadily, inexorably, heedless of its bottom scraping over the ground. The bronze armoured keel buried into the pebble beach and the beat of the oars stopped.

A black-clad figure sprang onto the beach from the upper deck, the whole fifty feet or so, the voluminous fur coat, coal-black with silvery spots, floating around him like a giant wing, as he floated down.

349

The men stood rooted to the spot. A mutter of dread and hatred rose as in the newcomer they recognised Ardri, once Prince of Rilante. Now he was the proclaimed king of the reborn ancient kingdom of Cryssumha. The secret that Kitt had guarded so long was now in the open.

A broad, silvery ring, studded with green and blue gems, sat on Ardri's straight black hair, that despite his youth was already shot through with fine white strands. The ancient crown Fenifindrune gave his regular features an alien, remote aspect. His eyes were blazing in a black light, but when Kitt had known Ardri, his eyes had been vividly blue, like Flannan's.

In his left hand, he held a great sword, sheath and hilt thickly ornamented with globular figures, which gleamed rose-red in the sinking sun. At the sight of that sword, an ice-cold dread trickled down Kitt's spine.

With a smile, Ardri faced the men on the shore. "Almost like Torin Daraval, eh big brother?"

"How are you going to get that floating coffin free again, little brother?" Flannan's voice was calm.

"I'll make you row, Crown Prince of Rilante." Ardri laughed out wildly, exultantly. But almost immediately, another emotion crossed his face, and he said quickly: "No, no, I won't harm you Flannan. No pain, do you hear? Not for you brother, never for you. Oh, why didn't you take your ship and sail away when you still could. Why did you have to seek out Mavors' steel? Now you leave me no choice. But there will never again be any pain for you. You will be happy, big brother, I will see to it, and protect you, as you always protected me, when I was the despised Cryssumha bastard in the filth of Rilante. I have not forgotten, Flannan."

"You can't protect yourself, little brother."

"I see." The black, burning eyes looked past Flannan. "I commend you, brother, you have succeeded in finding the one man in the whole world I was ever afraid of. Good to see you, Kitt! I'd almost forgotten how big you are. I am glad that you got out of Cryssumha alive."

"Not your fault," Kitt said grimly.

"It was the Master of Mirrors who tampered with the ship," Ardri said with an indescribable expression. "It doesn't matter anymore, but even so, I want you to believe me. Glic Tusil needed you dead, even before you burned his tower, because he thought that you were a creature of Mavors...which of course you are. Sometimes he seemed to think that he's the ruler of Cryssumha."

"But he is, little brother, or more likely Serenaiba," Flannan said.

"No, they aren't." Ardri shook his head with a slow pleased smile. "Nor is Lord Morrik, who also was mistaken on that account. None of them truly reckoned with this, brother." He drew the bronze sword from the sheath and turned it over, letting the fiery light of the sunset run along its length like spilt blood. "The sword Slatynrigan makes me the true ruler of Cryssumha. Glic Tusil didn't know, because he is a mage, but no warrior. And Morrik didn't know, because he is a warrior, but no mage. I am both."

"Very, very careful now," Kitt murmured in an aside to Flannan. He had seen a man forget who he was at a touch of that blade, without a drop of blood spilt.

Flannan paled a little, the long humorous mouth twisting in disgust. "The foul Donadroch magic of Cryssumha."

Ardri smiled. "Slatynrigan will give both of you to me. You will forget past and future, to live only in the now, like animals. Splendid docile animals. But there won't be pain, no pain. Nothing can touch you after the Sword of Cryssumha. I'll take care of you, Kitt, just as I will care for Flannan. This I swear by the souls of Ridevin and Kuranori." Ardri raised the rosy blade and came towards his brother and Kitt.

Something moved on the galley. Stunted, dark-haired men began to swarm down from the ship on ropes; they came boiling over the rails like black froth, twitching pale faces and trembling limbs, each movement jerky and twisted and yet ultimately purposeful. Stumbling past Ardri, they threw themselves at the men on the shore, carrying them back by the sheer pressure of human bodies. The thick throng of the Cryssumha people blocked Ardri's way towards Flannan and Kitt. They heard him curse.

Flannan and his men began to hack at the Cryssumha-men as if they were chopping weed. The black men clawed at them with bare hands. All faces were distorted with age-old loathing.

351

Using all his strength, Kitt began to throw Cryssumha and Rilante men sprawling right and left until he came clear of the melee. Then, he drew his sword and confronted the King of Cryssumha.

Ardri stepped towards him with a strange smile, affectionate and ruthless at the same time.

Kitt threw down his sword.

Before he could check the impulse, Ardri's eyes flickered towards the steel blade lying on the ground. Kitt sprang.

They fell together, Kitt's hand closing around Ardri's sword hand; he pressed very hard and released, and the ornate hilt fell from Ardri's numbed hand.

Kitt snatched up the bronze sword, rose and took back a step. Again, he felt the alien magic of Slatynrigan tingling in his hand like a metal bug. Bile rose into his mouth, and he fought the overwhelming urge to drop the evil thing.

Dazed, Ardri got up on one knee and raised his head to see the rose-red blade hanging above him.

"No! Kitt! Don't!" Flannan struggled desperately to get through the press, his sword mowing down a man with each swing. "Don't kill him!" he shouted. "Don't! Don't! Please!"

"No pain," Kitt said softly.

In that last moment, Ardri made no futile attempt to escape his fate. Kneeling in the sand, his eyes were on the sword Slatynrigan as it came down in a rosy arc.

Kitt touched Ardri's forehead lightly with the tip of the blade, and he seemed to freeze up. From the point where the bronze touched the skin, a wave ran over his face, and blotted out all expression. He fell back loose-limbed, a black rag doll flung onto pebbles of the beach.

Flannan had finally hacked his way through the Cryssumha rowers and sank down on his knees beside Ardri to raise him in his arms. "Little brother!"

Ardri opened his eyes. They were not black any more, but blue, the same vivid blue as those of his brother. "Flannan," he said and smiled broadly. "Here you are. Mother is waiting to teach me the secrets of the black lead and the white lead. But I'd rather come and sail on your ship."

Kitt sheathed the sword Slatynrigan, feeling a profound relief that increased with every inch that the rose-red blade disappeared from sight. Holding it by the sheath in his left, he wiped his sword-hand on his clothes again and again.

The Cryssumha rowers slacked their attack and were instantly cut down by the Rilante men. A gory carpet of dead bodies covered the pebble beach, their twitching hands and faces still at last.

Kitt saw Eckehart approach, watched as his father was coming nearer, circling the bodies, looking at each of them. When he came up with Kitt, he shook his head. "All dead. Nothing for mother to heal."

"I didn't kill any of them. That is," Kitt hesitated. "Not with my own hands. But it's my fault all the same."

"No, it's not your fault, son!" Eckehart shouted. He glared at Kitt. "Who the hell do you imagine you are, that you feel responsible for the fate of all these people? The Three Weavers? The Angel of the Host? The Heavenly Dicer? The One-Eyed God? The conceit of you! You are strong, son, no doubt about that, but it's just muscle, and not at all the kind of power that shapes the destiny of men. You better get some humility into your thick skull, before you go crazy."

"But if I hadn't gone to Rilante..."

"Oh, right!" Eckehart said exasperated. "Then don't go anywhere ever again. Go to bed and sleep until you die. Then there won't be any consequences from your actions." He cocked an eye at Kitt whimsically. "Only from the things you don't do."

Kitt laughed, it was like the cough of a tiger ending in the yip of a wolf cub. "I can't win then father?"

"No, you can't. Because nobody can. So, will you stop trying to be all-knowing and all-powerful? As I told you before, a hundred times, you can only do your best. And that my son, you do remarkably well. You saved a lot of people and gave this wretch Ardri every chance to take the right road, and you did well for Flannan. You saved us too. You saved our little Birla. Don't expect your mother to say it, but she knows."

Without me, she wouldn't have needed saving, Kitt thought. He met his father's eye and refrained from saying so.

Eckehart turned his back on the ugly picture of the carnage, and went towards the house.

The surviving Rilante-men were all able to walk up the valley by their own volition.

Kitt took the path to the smelting ovens, as he had done so often rather than face Aslaug's sharp disapproval. Not that it had ever been any good. Although Eckehart's words never failed to comfort Kitt, he could not really believe in them. His mother would not agree with what his father had said. And deep down he always believed Aslaug, who told him all the things that he beat himself up with. Most of all he didn't want to see what the sword Slatynrigan had done to Ardri. He was still holding the thing in his hands like the leash of a rabid beast. But, he was not little anymore, so he squared his shoulders, turned about and went to the hall. He knew that he could not hide from the consequences of his actions, and he had to help the wounded.

By the tents, Aslaug was tending to the wounded Rilante-men with Eckehart assisting her. Without a word, Kitt laid down Slatynrigan and joined them, to clean scratches and bites and set broken bones.

When his mother spoke, it concerned specifics of the treatment. "Bites are the worst," she remarked.

"The spoilt oranges medicine?" Kitt suggested.

"I'll prepare it," she said and went to the hall.

Kitt knew that there would be no infection of the wounds. There never had been, in anything which his mother treated.

The wounded were comfortable, and Kitt went to the hall.

When he opened the door, he heard the incongruous sound of laughter, and saw that Ardri was sitting at the table with a set of round, polished, coloured stones, agates, amethysts, opals and rose crystals and malachite, lapis lazuli, azurite and chrysoprase, and many more gems in all the colours of the earth. They had once been gifted to Kitt by Liane, the gladiator, and were his dearest childhood possession. Now they belonged to Birla who was rolling the spheres across the length of the table to Ardri, the colours flashing in the candle-light. A fire-opal ball escaped towards Flannan, who rolled it back. Ardri looked up at his brother with a smile so open and happy, as Kitt had never seen in the brilliant, charming, cold-hearted King of Cryssumha.

354

For a moment, it seemed as if Flannan would burst into tears. "He is a child again, the little brother who loved me before he changed. But I don't think he's an idiot, do you, lady Aslaug?" he murmured anxiously.

Aslaug didn't answer.

"Will he ever grow up again?" Flannan insisted.

"He will have another chance," Aslaug said, her face growing stern behind Ardri's back. "But the price in death and misery has been high."

"Then all will be well," Flannan said, having clearly paid attention to the first part of the sentence alone, and began to shove the playing stones across the table with a will.

Ardri smiled at Kitt who stood with his back pressed to the doorframe, the sword Slatynrigan dangling in his hand, never to be entirely forgotten.

"I remember you," he said. "You are my friend."

"The best you ever had," Flannan said. "I'm your brother, I must love you. But a friend just does you good for no reason at all."

Ardri looked uncertain, so Kitt smiled tentatively, and not very convincing, he thought.

Ardri laughed.

Kitt wondered if Lord Gasda heard that laughter as he rested in the adjacent sickroom.

"Go to your men, King Flannan," Eckehart admonished. "You should be with them now. We will care for your brother."

"You are right." Flanna went out without a glance for the Sword of Cryssumha in Kitt's hand.

"Come and play too," Birla invited.

Kitt shook his head. "I have something to do. You entertain the guest in the meantime."

She nodded her blonde curls gravely.

Kitt carried Slatynrigan past the table, and swiped the crown Fenifindrune and the Mooncat cloak, which lay where the former King of Cryssumha had taken it off in the heat of the play. He didn't notice.

Kitt wondered if he envied Ardri, so free of all the death and grief he had wrought in his few days or reign. Free of doubt, free of guilt. That was what Ardri had wanted for him. *Would it be so bad?*

He had to put the Sword of Cryssumha somewhere safe, if ever there could be a safe place for the murder weapon of the mind. Kitt lit a candle, went to the back of the hall and opened the door that led into the mountain. Behind another door was a dark chamber, the floor covered with heaps of gold in coins, bars and magnificent things made from the precious metal. From there, he went into another identical room, and through four more. In the last chamber, deep in the mountain, he laid Slatynrigan on top of the heap of gold and Fenifindrune beside it, and covered both with the Mooncat cloak. Gold had once before proven to reign in the evil magic of Cryssumha. When the Birlinn Yehan had left, he would find a safer hiding place for the insignia of Cryssumha.

Chapter 31
The Turning Tide

The next morning only the churned beach told of the battle.

The dead bodies had disappeared; not a bone or shred of skin was left, or a spot of blood on a pebble. The dark galley resembled a gigantic swimming coffin, her oars dancing up and down in the waves as if moved by skeletal hands. The Rilante men muttered uneasily. There had been two dead of their number, torn apart by the bare hands of the Cryssumha men, and the dead from the Golden Hind washed onto the shore, ten sailors. Their bodies also had disappeared without a trace.

Kitt could have told them that the Lütte Jotun folk who lived in the rocks and hills of Isenkliff ate any meat that couldn't outrun them, alive or dead, and that they never wasted a carcass. But he didn't. The one good thing was that the cattle and sheep would not be needed to pay for this iron. They could stay on Isenkliff to graze and chew the cud a little bit longer. That thought consoled him a little.

The unhappy muttering rose to an angry pitch, and Kitt saw that Ardri was standing in the door of the hall.

"Listen up!" Flannan shouted. "My brother Ardri is not the King of Cryssumha anymore. He was touched by the sword Slatynrigan and has forgotten all about it."

"Why then it didn't happen," Brodi muttered.

"Treat him like you would a child without a past," Flannan pleaded. "For my sake."

"We love you, Flannan, but you are asking much," Gilroy muttered.

"You did that to Ardri, Kitt? With his own Donadroch magic sword? Called Slatynrigan?" Lodemar asked.

"Yes."

"It is true that he is a halfwit now?"

"Yes."

357

"And he did this same thing to his father, King Tirnmas, turning him into an idiot?"

"By all accounts."

"Where is Slatynrigan now?"

"Hidden."

"Hm," Lodemar said. "A pretty kettle of fish."

"Why didn't you kill him?" Cathmor, one of Flannan's men at arms demanded.

"Because Flannan would never forgive me."

"True, he wouldn't," Coil, another man at arms said. "We can none of us understand it."

"We're not required to understand it," a man named Esmond said.

The three men at arms stood together in a little group. Kitt had often seen them together. He thought that Flannan had better watch out for his brother at all times.

By midday, Lord Gasda was seen to leave the hall for the first time since he had been carried inside. Several men ran to attend to him. At his request, they took him to the tent Gilroy shared with Brodi and Neilo.

"I wonder if you have a free space," Gasda said. "Prince Ardri may have forgotten the treason he committed, but I cannot be under the same roof, even for my love of Flannan, who is my king and will always be."

"He'll always be our king," Gilroy said, "As truly as we cannot forget either."

*

Flannan saw the black looks, and he knew that none of his men understood his unwavering attachment to the brother who betrayed him and their father, King Tirnmas of Rilante.

Whenever he couldn't find his brother at once, he feared the worst. The formality of his men answering his questions hurt. Seeing Lord Gasda looking so pale also hurt. He had moved out of the hall's sickroom, but his manner to Flannan remained faultless. "Forgive, my king," he said. "Do not think me ungrateful. I will always be in your debt. But I cannot listen to the voice that told me about Kione Lonnir."

"Speak no more, my friend," Flannan said sadly, "I understand. But be assured that he doesn't remember it. He is like a child, helpless. I could not abandon him now."

"You could not, my king," Gasda said, his voice surprisingly steady. "You did not abandon a man who lost a thousand soldiers."

"How can he compare that?" Gilroy commented, keeping his voice low in the neighbouring tent because every louder word could be overheard in the camp. "It was a noble undertaking to go for Kione Lonnir, and it didn't cease to be noble because it failed. This time."

He, Brodi and Neilo had moved in with Cathmor, Esmond and Coil to provide Lord Gasda with a private tent, as befitted his position.

"He can compare it," Brodi said. "Flannan won't abandon anyone, just like our Feilan will save everybody. Much the same."

"It does them honour," Esmond said. "It is our job to do our best for Flannan."

"That is so," Cathmor agreed, and Coil nodded.

"What is on your mind?" Gilroy inquired.

*

To his relief, Flannan found his brother at the work place up in the cliff, his hands smeared with clay to the elbows, helping to close the oven, while Kitt explained patiently about the smelting of iron.

Flannan smiled at the irony. "If the witch Serenaiba could see her son like that!" he chuckled. "Working the lowly iron, the slave metal, the corruptible dirt."

Kitt made a face at hearing the Cryssumha epithets on the iron again.

"Kitt teaches me the blade!" Ardri shouted, "Did you know, brother, that he is the best sword fighter in the whole, wide world?" He waved dirty hands, indicating the width of the world.

"Yes, I know," Flannan said. "Don't bother with that humble speech of yours, Kitt. The child doesn't understand this sort of nicety."

"Nor does his brother, who is old enough," Kitt muttered, and jammed the bellows into the nozzles.

"I get that from a boy, what age are you, Kitt, sixteen?"

"Seventeen. Soon."

"A sixteen-year-old boy bullied by his mother. Until you're not, and then, we'll see something."

"You did see something of that and didn't like the result," Kitt muttered, and worked the bellows furiously.

Ardri tugged at Flannan's velvet sleeve enthusiastically with his clay smeared hands. "Kitt has promised to make a sword for me so that I can protect you. You will be a good king, just as our father is, and I will be the man who walks behind you. That's what younger brothers are for. Together we'll be invincible, brother."

"Yes, invincible. And extremely grubby." Flannan looked ruefully at the soiled blue velvet of his sleeve but made no move to free it from his brother's dirty hands. He dearly hoped that the iron weapons would be ready soon. Get it over with the whole nasty Cryssumha business to never need to think about it again - if that dream was ever possible, as long as the stars reformed their patterns, over and over.

*

The following morning, the black ship was gone - not an oar or nail was left. The high tide washed away all traces on the beach. Only the inhabitants of Isenkliff knew that the galley had also gone into the mountain, piece by piece. The black ship had become part of the bargain Eckehart made with the Jarnmantsjes, the Lütte Jotun folk of Isenkliff.

Eckehart and Kitt brought iron swords out of the smithy, and piled up mail, shield buckles and fittings, and lance blades.

"When did they make all that?" Gilroy muttered. "And where did Eckehart keep it all? When I looked into the smithy yesterday, there were only a couple of swords inside, nothing like this number. How I long for a world without any kind of magic, and be it white Dredorocht!"

"There is no such world," Cathmor said.

Flannan's blue eyes lightened up at the sight of a hundred new iron blades that were gleaming coldly in the morning sun. "Iron is a beautiful metal, after all." He took a hilt, raised the sword and looked at his own reflection in the polished surface. "I know that, like your son, you don't care for gold either, master smith," he pursued." You didn't name your price yet and now that you fulfilled your side in

360

full, I wonder what you will have of me? That which is at home and I don't know about? I did tell you that I'm not married, Eckehart."

Eckehart chuckled. "Just give me the old bronze swords that you don't need any more. You can use the sheaths; remember to keep them dry inside."

"I take that as another good omen for the battle ahead, Eckehart. Pay up then, lads!" Flannan ordered cheerfully. Hands reached for sword hilts, and while the grey iron mound diminished, another of red bronze rose beside it.

A sudden suspicion darkened Flannan's face. "All the bronze blades, every one of them? Is it really the sword Slatynrigan you want, Eckehart?"

Arms folded across his leather apron, Eckehart looked the Flannan up and down from pale-blue old eyes. "What if I do, King Nolan Ri of Rilante?"

Flannan hesitated a moment. "I'd call it good riddance," he said finally. "I don't care for Slatynrigan's power. I would not want it to fall into the wrong hands. But you, I trust, smith of Minit Houarn. If you want the sword Slatynrigan, it shall be yours."

Eckehart shook his head. "Slatynrigan can never be mine. But I will keep it safe and never let it loose upon the world."

A different man, radiant with hope, Flannan went into the smithy where Kitt was working at the forge.

"I finished Ardri's sword this morning. Making a knife for him now." Kitt drew a glowing blade from the forge with a pair of tongs and began hammering the red-hot steel with one hand, flipping it over on the anvil with the other.

Flannan watched Kitt's hands moving. "Bronze smithing is witchcraft, but I can see iron smithing is an art, clean and precise."

"So is bronze work, all a matter of ore, fire and skill."

"So you always say, Kitt. But how can you explain the sword Slatynrigan?"

"That I can't," Kitt admitted. "Though I watched it being made, every step."

"Anyway, I'm done with bronze. Forever," Flannan said fervently. "My men are armed with steel, and I feel the tide to be turning at last. Or maybe it's just that infernal star gathering

361

dissolving. Your father says that the last swords will be ready tomorrow. When do you think the Birlinn Yehan can sail?"

Kitt calculated in his head. "My father has gone to open the smelting ovens with the batch of steel for the last repairs. Two days, if you are in a hurry."

"I am, and I am not. I like it here, but I'm in a hurry to use the iron of Isenkliff to cut the bronze chains that tied us to Cryssumha. I must make the best use of the fact that Cryssumha lost her king. So, the day after tomorrow we will sail for Rilante." Flannan looked around searchingly. "Where is Ardri?"

"I thought he was with you."

"And I thought he was here." Flannan frowned. "Maybe he's gone to the ovens with your father. He likes it there. Difficult to keep an eye on him, as on any ten-year-old. Put an edge on that new blade of his?"

"Yes, of course. He hasn't lost any of his sword skills. Only his dishonesty...his cunning."

"Strange, the way Slatynrigan blots out the memory and leaves intact all the body has ever learned. That's what he intended for us. I'm trying to think how it would have been if he had succeeded?"

"We wouldn't have ever known that anything had happened to us."

"I gladly ceded Slatynrigan to your father. You already hid it, didn't you?"

"Yes." Kitt held a hand above the knife blade, to probe the temperature.

"I had better find Ardri," Flannan said. "I don't like the way my men look at him. I understand how they feel. Nearly every one of them has lost a comrade or relative in Dundingin, and now they're worried to death about the fate of those we left behind in Rilante. Civil wars are so hideously ugly."

The blade had taken on a dull grey colour, and Kitt put it into the forge again and heaped glowing coals on it.

Flannan turned in the door. "You know, Kitt, all is going to end well after all. Thanks to you, Ardri has another chance."

"Don't thank me." Kitt shook his head. "If something were saved from this wreck, it would give me," he hesitated, "hope."

362

"What a way to talk, Kitt," Flannan said kindly. "You think far too much."

Kitt looked at the king of Rilante standing there, smiling, the thick gold embroidery of his tunic glittering. "You are in the sun always." He wished he could walk through the world as easily as Flannan did.

"And you are power incarnate." Flannan looked at Kitt as if he saw him for the first time. "I wish I could stand up to the world like you can. You don't know it yet, Kitt, but you are one of those men who can impose their law on any piece of the world they happen to stand upon. The power of kings is nothing by comparison." With a flourish of his blue cloak, Flannan was gone.

"I'm just a blacksmith." Kitt drew the knife blade from the hearth and began hammering again.

At the first blow, the blade broke, cracked in the middle.

Kitt stared at it in disgust. "Not even a good blacksmith," he muttered.

Chapter 32
No redemption

It was Cathmor who spotted Prince Ardri in a patch of pine trees on the hill above the smelting ovens - he was picking bluebells.

Holding his breath, Cathmor watched as Ardri drew uphill, farther and farther away from the ovens, well out of sight from the men who worked there, all the time picking his flowers.

"Where is he?" whispered a voice beside him.

Gilroy and two more comrades, Esmond and Coil, had silently caught up with Cathmor. Cathmor pointed.

Gilroy drew in his breath sharply. "Is he really alone at last?" His lips pulled back in a mirthless smile.

"Be careful. He always was a good fighter, and Kitt has been teaching him the blade," Esmond warned.

"Where is Kitt?"

"Still at the forge. Brodi is watching the path to the ovens."

"He's Kitt's friend."

"We all are. Just don't see eye to eye on this one matter. Brodi can distract him; hold him up if he comes up or Flannan."

"Good," Gilroy said. "First blood for the new iron blades. Cryssumha blood!"

The four men surrounded Prince Ardri, who turned around his axis once on his heel, holding the bunch of bluebells in his hands, and smiling at them. His movements were as lithe and elegant as ever. He didn't seem to remember the new iron sword hanging from his left side. That, together with the open smile and sunny blue eyes, gave the men an eerie sensation.

"Curse it, that's weird," Esmond muttered uncomfortably.

For a moment, the soldiers hesitated. Ardri's smile became questioning because the men did not smile back.

"He's the next in the succession, isn't he?" Coil said. "As Flannan is King of Rilante and not married?"

"You just made up my mind," Gilroy said. He drew his sword and ran the Prince through from behind, just above the pelvis.

With childlike surprise, Ardri looked at the man before him. His mouth opened, but no scream came, only a sigh. The bluebells spilt from his hands.

Cathmor drew his blade and drove it in below the ribs.

Ardri's knees buckled.

The two soldiers withdrew their blades at the same time. Blood gushed out and Ardri fell among the bluebells. His blue eyes snapped open and shut like a bird's.

"Damn it!" Cathmor muttered hoarsely. "I had always thought that I would enjoy doing this."

"Good blade. Goes in like a hot knife into butter." Gilroy looked at the two others in turn. "Esmond, Coil, try it. We're all in on this. Baptise your steel in remembrance of the Rilante blood spilt in Dundingin."

*

Kitt looked down at the body that lay among the bluebells, bloody and torn. "No redemption," he whispered.

From long habit, he scanned the tracks, four men, regulation leather boots with cut soles. They had patiently watched Ardri until he was out of sight from the smelting ovens, and then closed in.

They had been standing around their victim for some moments; one boot had left a deep, clear imprint in the moss. From the way Ardri's arms lay, he hadn't touched his sword-hilt, the sword Kitt had forged for him. They had run him through from all sides, nearly cutting him in two at the waist, aiming to destroy kidneys, stomach and liver, one violent stab under the ribs splitting the heart.

Flannan was coming up from the smelting ovens talking to Gilroy; Kitt heard their voices and a moment later caught sight of Flannan's burnished copper head.

They stood still. The tension of Gilroy shoulders and the studied turn of his head told Kitt everything. He did not call or signal to them. Instead, he went south along a path his feet had trodden over the years.

Chapter 33
A Sword with a Soul

The path led up and up to the bare plateau of the highest peak of Isenkliff. From here, all of the island could be seen, and the white back of Wittewal across the water to the south, and the rock needle of Erzturm to south-east.

Kitt passed a big grey boulder, with a dark opening at the base. A Jarnmantsje was sitting there; his grey fur-like hair blended into grey rags, round yellow eyes scintillated in all that grey.

"Hello, Gullo," Kitt greeted him.

The Jarnmantsje smiled so that his long, yellow tusks showed. "A good hunter Kitt is. Best meat."

"I didn't hunt that meat."

"You bring much meat here," Gullo said. "Comes across the sea on two legs with ship. Gullo only needs to eat, eat,eat. That is the great way to hunt and you did."

"Maybe I did," Kitt said, "But I didn't want to do it and I won't do again."

"Good hunter," Gullo said to his back, "Get better. Thrymthralli eat too much."

From the top of the mountain the path went down to the southern promontory. Facing the sea was a ledge with a recess carved out by wind and rain. In the back on a rock shelf lay a pair of slim, curved swords in a double sheath. Not the smallest speck of rust showed although the steel blades had been lying there for more than a year. They would be lying there for many years longer because they were not safe for a human hand to pick up. One sword held the Silver Girl, the Lady of the Moonlight Sword, the other her lover, the Golden Warrior Malan Jian.

Kitt reached behind the two swords and took a knife with a blade of black stone; it was as long as a man's hand, and shaped like a willow leaf, with fine, sharp edges of dusky light and rainbow colours - Kaulra Gooth, the blade that could take the dead across the Shadow Walls. Kitt himself had brought that blade from the Dark Wood Murkowydir; he had used it to help his friend to join his lover, and he still did not know how he had done that. He knew that he had succeeded.

Ardri's body had been brought to the smithy and laid on the table in the storeroom.

Flannan was sitting in the forge. "I can't bear looking at him, and I can't go away," he whispered. "Did you see the footprints up there? Of course, you did. I'm finding myself looking at my men's boots, their sizes, have the soles been cleaned today, is there blood on the uppers? Who do you think did it, Kitt?"

"I don't know," Kitt said, though he had a good idea, having done the same, looked at boots. "Don't turn against your men, Flannan."

"If I knew who it was..."

"You'd lose the others too."

"I shouldn't blame them; they have suffered so much. But I do. I'm not blaming you, either."

Kitt thought that he began hating to hear that. For a moment, he considered telling the griefstricken brother what he would try to do, but decided against it, in case that it didn't work as it had with his friend Malan Jian. Not to mention, that he didn't want his mother to somehow find out what he was up to, if he waited too long. He went through into the storeroom, where he opened the shutters of one window wide, and carefully closed the other.

He unsheathed Ardri's sword and laid it beside the bloody body. Then he passed the black stone blade Kaulra Gooth along the blade. The same thing happened as it had with another sword; an opening appeared that led into the blade, and yet was wider than its width. The metal began to glow.

Next, Kitt passed Kaulra Gooth over the bloody body, from the left temple to the right foot, then crosswise, just as he had done before, and again, the same thing happened. Piece by piece, the corpse disappeared. No blood flowed.

A sunray from the window lay on the table, and Kitt put the sword onto the square of light. Suddenly Ardri stood there holding the sword. He appeared as solid and whole as the living man; the clothing was without a tear. Kitt watched him warily, until he would know which Ardri had returned in this spectre, the one before or after being touched with Slatynrigan - until he knew if he had he made it better, or worse.

Ardri lashed out with the sword, once, twice. Kitt evaded him, each time increasing his distance, careful not to be herded away from the open window.

Ardri stopped. "You are my friend. The best friend I have. Flannan said so. Where is my big brother?" His voice was boyish.

Kitt closed the shutter, shut out the sun. Ardri's spectre disappeared, and the sword clattered down.

The noise brought Flannan from the forge. Speechlessly, he stared at the table, where only the sword lay. "Where...?

"He wanted to protect you with this sword." Kitt opened the shutter for the sunlight to stream in, and touch the sword.

Again, Ardri appeared, the sword in his hand, and executed a full turn with the blade extended.

"Little brother!" Flannan cried.

"Big brother!" Ardri dropped to one knee. "I will walk behind you, my king, because that is what brothers do."

Kitt closed the window, making Ardri disappear, leaving the sword on the table. He sheathed the blade and handed the sword to Flannan, who took it, as if in a dream.

"Dredorocht," he said. "I never thought that you too, Kitt...you always said that steel needed no magic."

"Steel doesn't, but I thought that you did."

"I only want my little brother," Flannan said.

*

A stony-faced King Nolan Ri of Rilante embarked on the repaired Birlinn Yehan and left Isenkliff. He never prosecuted anyone for the violent death of his brother, Prince Ardri. Nobody called him Flannan any more, not even behind his back. He always carried two iron swords.

Crazy

Kitt was dreaming, and in this dream, he saw the world with a clarity that showed everything surrounding him and that he didn't see in the waking time. What he didn't see nevertheless existed.

Something huge, black and thorny was nosing about to find his track. Its darkness was something alien and malignant, sprung from a cosmic seed.

Kitt's track was very easy to find, a deep spoor. In his dream, he was leaving footprints all over the ground, handprints on everything he touched, bites in everything he had eaten. With dismay, he looked at these obvious traces. His whole life he had been hiding his tracks, had thought that he was good at it.

Suddenly, he saw that an ancient man was walking behind him. He stooped to pick up every one of the signs of Kitt's presence. Kitt recognised him, it was Shangar Shaark Ayen, Nine Serpents.

"Gree Meder. Shakro-Shork. Kaulra Gooth," the Ludoshini of the Kra-Tini Feen said.

Kitt remembered those words too.

He saw a coal-black bear standing guard, a long-legged sinewy animal, swaying in the blue grass like a plant moved by water, and singing to itself. Kitt knew that bear, it was the same that had attacked him once. Nine serpents writhed beside the bear in a knot of black and white.

The Gree Meder sniffed for the spoor; he was the cosmic, black, thorny monster with paws ending in innumerable talons, and a long snout studded with spiky black teeth. From time to time, it made a noise between a scream and a snarl. Dark gore dribbled from two gashes in its side.

In his dream, Kitt knew clearly that the Gree Meder must recover the black stone knife Kaulra Gooth, or the gigantic black thornbush Shakro-Shork could not grow in this world. And he must avenge the wounds in his side, to quench the rage inside him.

Kitt had what the Gree Meder wanted, Kaulra Gooth. He looked down at his hands and saw that he was holding the black stone knife.

When Kitt awoke, the dream was still with him and didn't fade when the sun came up. He kept seeing the old man who was gathering his tracks, and the black bear, singing and watching and swaying. Above all towered the Shakro-Shork, the black thornbush thing that wanted to grow and devour the Murkowydir wood.

Still caught in his dream, he stumbled into the kitchen, leaving footprints and handprints everywhere.

His mother was sitting at the kitchen table. "Wake up, Kitt!" she said sharply.

Kitt woke. The black stone knife was in his hand, and he thought it had to be the cause that he dreamed like this. He had taken it from its hiding place in the southern promontory to restore a murdered man to his brother, and had not yet brought it back.

· "You must take this knife back to where it came from," his mother said and sighed.

"You want me to go back to the Murkowydir?"

"You used it twice. The monster that is searching for it; soon, it will know where it is. I don't want this monster here."

"No!" The Gree Meder must not be on the same island as Swantje Birla, Kitt thought.

"You know who you must give it to?"

"Yes, I know."

He had to give Kaulra Gooth to Shangar Shaark Ayen, the Ludshini of the Kra-Tini Fihen who had told Kitt that he must die, and decreed for him the Mik Shini, the shameful death. Kitt had never told his parents how he had stood at the Fihen torture stake. He might stand there again because he had made the wrong decision and not destroyed the alien black growth in the heart of the Murkowydir, the Shakro-Shork, when he could. That decision he had made rationally because the Meder people lived among its thorny branches. He didn't know if they were real people; he knew that they were cruel. Even so, he had decided not to destroy their thorny home and leave them exposed to the elements and the arrows and clubs of the

Fihen. Mangan Sorkera would not be beset by these doubts. With Kaulra Gooth in his hands, he would finish what Kitt had not done. He could have told all that to his mother. But he didn't.

Then, to his surprise, his mother began to tell him something, as she put lime tea and bread and butter on the table. "This black stone knife is a sliver from the oldest thing there is. This thing was hot and heavy, beyond imagination. The universe formed like a raspberry, with this thing as its core, and around it, from it, many worlds swelled like the drupelets."

"Many worlds!" Kitt said, his eyes shining as if he said Magatama, or Kush or the West Lands, the places farthest away on earth. He thought how many drupelets there were in a raspberry, a hundred, maybe more.

"Ours is just one of these many worlds," Aslaug continued. "The core cooled and sprang into many pieces which were flung throughout all the worlds. Each of these pieces is a key to every one of the other worlds, a lock-pick, a crowbar even."

"With it, it is possible to...to pass...to other worlds?"

"We even may exist in more than one of these worlds."

"We do?" Kitt said. "Wouldn't we know?"

"Perhaps we realise, some time. If the Snow Queen finds her other selves...she must never lay her hands on this key."

"She didn't come last winter."

"And for that, we must give thanks. But there are others, equally malignant. And now..."

"I used the black knife Kaulra Gooth for the second time."

Aslaug nodded. "You understand."

***

Shangar Shaark Ayen's eyes returned from the real world Nyedasya-Dyarve to the fire in his hut in Mukine-Kad-Nidyas.

Across from him sat Mangan Sorkera. The war leader's eyes became aware at once. He walked between the worlds with the same ease as the Ludoshini himself did.

Soon the wise man of the Kra-Tini Feen would be gone from the dream world Nyedasya-Aurayskahan-Ashyalish, that for those who could not see was the only world that existed. Munitera of the Zoyamizoyi, who was now lurking outside the door, always forbidden to enter, would try to be the Ludoshini of the Kra-Tini

371

Feen. If he succeeded, he would have a war leader immensely more powerful than him in both worlds - if the war leader lived.

Shangar Shaark Ayen laughed, deep and booming, like a young man. "Gree Meder come. Gita come bring Kaulra Gooth. Mangan Sorkera destroy Shakro-Shork Gree Meder. Kill Gita."

***

Kitt hid his bundle in a hollow tree, managing to do this without the slightest metallic clanking of the contents.

He moved again even more stealthily than he had before. Soon he would come into the area of the Jays, the guards posted around the Feen village. It took Kitt some time until he spotted the first Jay. Finally, he found him, high up in an oak tree. The foliage had thinned this late in autumn, or he would have been invisible. There was not much this Jay could overlook from his perch; if there were to be an incursion into the village, it would not be past him.

Kitt retreated to approach to the Feen village from another angle, which was not easy as he had to stay upwind. The Kra-Tini had dogs now, he knew. The other Jays were less tough and intelligent in the choice of their lookout, but they were nervous, and there were more of them than during Kitt's last visit. It was already the dark hour before the dawn when he was finally on the perimeter of the village, behind the hut which stood apart from the houses, before it a bent stick with nine serpent's skins hanging from the tip, rustling slightly.

From his previous run-ins with the Feen Kitt knew a lot about the houses and their inhabitants. This was the hut of the Ludoshini, the wise man of the Feen, Shangar Shaark Ayen.

The village did not sleep. Firelight spilt from inside the houses onto the circular stone-paved central place, and there were groups of warriors congregating between the two stakes, one charred, one carved with depictions of animals glowing red with a knot of nine serpents on top.

From inside the solitary hut came the muttering of a drum. This side of the village lay in darkness. Kitt slipped around to the entrance, and pushed aside the skin that hung in the doorway. Inside the hut it was dark, full of shadows. In the red light of the dying fire he could barely make out a solitary figure hunched over the drum that filled the hut with a deep rough sound.

Like a shadow, Kitt moved into the drummer's back.

"Shangar!"

The drummer did not seem to hear.

***

In Nyedasya-Dyarve, the Real World, the black bear sang and watched, and guarded the Ska Muni shadow wall of shimmering air, behind which the distorted outlines of the Feen houses were visible.

From his throat came a deep, rolling grumble, and the gaunt animal swayed in the rhythm for a long time. The nine serpents did not return.

Soon the bear would go on the trail, and there would be nobody left to guard the village.

Then he felt that he was not alone any more. An outline was just beginning to form, wolfish and feline at the same time, full of power and grace, light grey and tan, and inside something fragile, so bright that the bear could not see it well.

The Ska Muni shadow wall tore open and the lion Mooankayit stepped onto the plain. "Shangar!" the young lion Mooankayit said, but Shangar Shaark Ayen had not come back over the horizon.

***

"Shangar!" Kitt repeated louder.

The drumming stopped, and the figure stirred and stretch out a hand towards a pile of wood.

"No put wood on fire, Shangar!" Kitt spoke in the Feen language mixed with Rilante where the Feen had no word. "No move. Listen." The figure sat motionless again.

"Shangar cunning. Lie and truth at the same time. Trick Gawthrin Lye. Poisonwood. Speak truth about Meder and Shakro-Shork and Kaulra Gooth. Gree Meder is the stem of Shakro-Shork. Steel not cut Shakro-Shork. Kaulra Gooth, black stone knife, can cut. Gawthrin Lye bring Kaulra Gooth Shangar."

The figure stretched out a hand again, slowly, deliberately, to lay a bundle of thin, dry branches upon the fire. In the dim light, Kitt could see that these were willow wands. "Shangar no trick!" he warned.

"No trick." The drummer's voice sounded deep, strong and young.

The flames leapt up and lit the hut. The drummer's long hair shone blue-black and fell over broad shoulders with rolling muscles;

373

his arms were criss-crossed with long white scars. It was the Feen war leader. Mangan Sorkera rose to his full height slowly, turning around to face Kitt.

"Shangar Shaark Ayen go no return. Gawthrin Lye give Kaulra Gooth to Mangan Sorkera." He spoke the language of Rilante with a strong accent. The way he met Kitt's eye made it clear that the war leader was ready to fight.

Kitt had not come to fight. He held out the black stone knife to the Feen leader with both his hands, as he had seen the Feen do when they gave something.

Mangan Sorkera took it in the same manner, and relaxed very slightly. "Mangan will go to Shakro-Shork. Mangan owes Gawthrin Lye for bringing Kaulra Gooth. Gawthrin Lye is safe to leave the Sreedok. Mangan says he is safe. Gawthrin Lye return, Gawthrin Lye die."

"Gawthrin Lye goes to Shakro-Shork," Kitt said in the Rilante language.

The war leader did not reply. The way he stood there indicated that he was waiting for Kitt to give his reasons and that he did not expect to accept them.

Kitt squared his shoulders. "Gawthrin Lye took Kaulra Gooth from Meder. Gawthrin Lye was first to cut the black stem of Shakro-Shork. Gawthrin Lye goes to Shakro-Shork. Feen go or Feen not go." He did his best to match the arrogance of the war leader in every way.

Mangan Sorkera nodded briefly. He ducked out of the hut, motioning Kitt to follow.

Again, Kitt stood on the circular, stone-paved village place not far from the charred stake. The people who a year ago had been on the other side of the fires were quiet; there were no questions, no exclamations, just covert glances directed towards the giant, fair-haired, grey-eyed youth who stood one step behind their war leader. More and more Feen arrived, none went away, all were waiting. They would wait a day and a night and longer if they had to. Kitt saw the little woodstalker-girl, all grown up now. She was tall and straight in a tan coloured dress with red stitching and beige embroidery, and her face was round with a pointed chin, cat-like, her

374

deer eyes black and deep in the fire-light. Kitt had grown another eight inches himself since they had run across each other for the first time.

Mangan Sorkera spoke loud and clear into the silence, "Shangar Shaark Ayen go Shakro-Shork three Sun Circles. No return. Mangan Sorkera go Shakro-Shork."

A slight movement went through the crowd. A young warrior stepped forward, followed on his heel by another. Kitt knew both from the night of the Mik Shini and then from their visit to Dundingin.

"Shaluwa go Shakro-Shork."

"Tadir go."

The two young warriors spoke as if their accompanying the war leader was a matter of course.

More Feen warriors came forward, all of them young, little more than Kitt's age, and all wore necklaces of bear or lion claws or human teeth which showed that they were to be reckoned with.

"Reki go."

"Fitcher go."

"Kutcher go." Kitt also remembered these young men from his ordeal at the torture stake. The first two had kept to the background. The third was the young warrior who had burned Kitt with his own sword, made glowing in the Mik Shini fires. Kitt had broken his bonds, taken the sword away from the young warrior and knocked him down with it. Kutcher must bear Kitt a grudge for that humiliation, even more so as it had been the young warrior's own fault, for poor judgement and carelessness.

"Kutcher stay," Mangan Sorkera said in a final tone.

Kutcher jerked as if hit and glared at Kitt with trembling lips. "Djanadir Thomiat Dshooka, enemy."

"Shakro-Shork good place take enemy," Kitt retorted.

Shaluwa gave a short laugh, it sounded like the bark of a lynx. Tadir grinned broadly. A flicker of laughter ran across the village place. Even Mangan's mouth twitched a little.

Pure hatred blazed from Kutcher's eyes as he retreated back into the crowd.

More young warriors stepped forward; five more were selected. Kitt tried to memorise their names. The rejects did their best to hide their mortification, but Kitt could see it even in the greying morning light.

"Srisit lead warriors." A slightly older warrior nodded briefly; the name meant Three Arrows, Kitt understood with his hard-won knowledge of the Feen language.

Each young warrior who had been picked then went to his house, where the women handed them provisions for the way.

The little woodstalker-girl, who was not little now, came to tug at Kitt's hand. She held out a leather square with a paste of dried meat, fruits and nuts caked together in wisent fat, that the Feen called Biltis. She pulled the corners across, wrapped the whole with a leather band stitched with red and beige threads and held the package out to him. Kitt took it. She smiled at him, laid her hand on her left breast and said, "Moshonalak."

"I'm Kitt."

"Kitt. Gawthrin Lye. Djanadir Thomiat. Kitt."

Kitt thought her very beautiful.

The ten Feen warriors and Kitt set out south in a mile-eating, silent trot. By the hollow willow tree, Kitt paused briefly to recover the bundle he had hidden before he entered the Feen village.

The war leader directed a withering look at a mortified Jay in the willow thicket. "Gawthrin Lye come go want Sreedok," he remarked in a colourless voice.

"Only when Mangan Sorkera play drums," Kitt replied politely. From the look the Jay shot at him, he knew that he had made yet another enemy.

They ran on Mangan's own painful old track, only briefly paused to eat their Biltis, washing it down with water from a brook. Occasionally a rabbit crossed their way, and they ate the tender meat raw, sharing out the bloody bits. After three days of marching, they came to the place where Mangan Sorkera had been taken captive by the Meder. From then onwards, they moved as if they were in Graykhol Rere territory.

*

Inside the Shakro-Shork, the black growth at the heart of the Sreedok wood, the Gree Meder opened his eyes and sniffed. Dark liquid trickled down his left side, where eighteen poison teeth stuck in his flesh; pain and rage and nameless thirst blazed in his coal-black eyes.

The Gree Meder rose to his feet and with him rose all Meder, their noses quivering. Enemies were approaching, blood and meat for the black thorn-tree Shakro-Shork.

*

Although Kitt and Mangan Sorkera had already seen the Shakro-Shork before, they were as awed as the others at the sight of the black thorn-bush hanging above the highest trees of the wood like a smoky wave, ready to crash down to choke and devour everything green.

Kitt opened his pack. Under the sardonic eyes of the young Feen warriors, who were almost naked, he donned a mail tunic made of steel scales which gripped into each other with many links, offering a smooth surface, a helmet with neck protection like the tunic and a nose guard, steel arm and leg protection. Heavy boots and iron-studded leather gloves completed his armour.

"Gawthrin Lye like wear tree?" Tadir earnestly pointed to a hollow willow tree, his eyes alight with mockery. "Gawthrin Lye safe hollow tree."

"Gawthrin Lye build Dshooka coward high walls, wait grow Shakro-Shork." Reki opined.

"Call coward Djanadir Thomiat dead Shakro-Shork," Kitt retorted amiably.

The young warriors seemed to understand his Feen words correctly. Reki flushed with shame and fury. Not only had Kitt rebuked him for picking the wrong time for a quarrel. Also, by mentioning the other name the Feen had given him, he reminded them of his contemptuous treatment of several of their warriors. "Shakro-Shork uprooted Djanadir Thomiat answer Reki, Tadir," Kitt added for good measure.

Reki drew a sharp breath, and so did Tadir. Kitt's offer to take on both at the same time after the battle was won was another deadly insult.

Shaluwa's laughter was abrasive. The young warriors could not expect any support from their older companion, all to the contrary. "Warrior wield word knife," Shaluwa said.

"Djanadir Thomiat wield word fist." The war leader smiled. "Enough talk. Gawthrin Lye protect back Mangan Sorkera."

Kitt nodded consent.

"Tadir, Shaluwa help Gawthrin Lye obey Gawthrin Lye," the war leader continued, both in Rilante and Feen language.

Both young warriors jumped as if stung, but one look at their leader's face made them bite back their protests.

"Yes," Shaluwa said, and Tadir nodded reluctantly.

Kitt began to think well of them.

The war leader spoke to the young warriors; from what Kitt could make out he explained the Meder weapons and style of fighting. "Fitcher, Reki kill all Meder see," he completed his instruction.

The pale, patterned Meder waited before the Sharkro-Shork, male or female, he couldn't distinguish. It was difficult to count them because the black patterns on their skin blended into the thorny branches so much and they were so silent that it seemed the black thorn-bush itself was watching out with hatred. Kitt estimated there were at least forty Meder with slings that ended in sharp thorns dangled from their fingers that ended in black curved talons. There would be no surprise moment. Neither the Fihen nor Kitt were inclined to waste time for analysis. If there had to be a pitched battle with odds of four to one, or more, they would fight it.

The Fihen warriors and Kitt took the positions they had agreed upon. Reki, Fitcher and the other five opened the battle by assaulting the Meder host with a volley of arrows, and each missile hit a vital spot.

Mangan Sorkera attacked the Shakro-Shork on the side opposite the melee, and began to cut into it with Kaulra Gooth.

Kitt followed with a blade in each hand.

The black thorn-branches quailed at the approach of the black stone knife in Mangan Sorkera's hand. He began to slash methodically at the creepers and a lashing fury broke loose like decapitated serpents, drenching skin and hair in purple gore that immediately began to stink of unnatural decay. The sword in Kitt's right and the long knife in his left whirled to keep away the thorns from Mangan's naked skin.

378

The Shakro-Shork was fighting for its life fleeing away from Kaulra Gooth, the black stone blade, the merest touch of which broke open stems and branches in a spray of gore. The tunnels contracted to protect the innermost that held the Gree Meder. Creepers began worrying the thick leather of Kitt's boots and breeches like dogs. He felt the creepers hit his armour, the thorns seeking hold in the smallest opening, to wrench the small rings apart with the inexorable force of growing plants, but much faster. A link snapped, and he felt the first sting in his flesh. He could do nothing about that, not daring to cease his protection for Mangan Sorkera for a moment. Just one hit with a thorny whip would flay off the unprotected skin.

Soon Tadir's shout told Kitt that the Meder had become aware of the real attack. Suddenly Meder were before as well as behind them. The war leader had cut into a tunnel. Kitt bludgeoned a face with the pommel of his sword, the dagger sliced through a claw, immediately following each movement through to protect Mangan Sorkera, and his own face.

The creepers took hold of Kitt's mail, wrapped themselves around his legs, broke as he tore free, others latched on in their place. More links of his mail broke, thorns burrowed through to his flesh. Battling the thorny creepers, Kitt had no time for the Meder. He could only hope that Tadir and Shaluwa would deal with all of them, and as he was fending off several thorny whips at a time, he realised that his and Mangan Sorkera's survival depended on the young Fihen's ability to keep the main Meder host at bay. Having to rely on others was a new experience for, him and he did not like it at all. More Meder came through the tunnels Mangan Sorkera cut into on his way towards the heart of the Shakro-Shork. Just once Kitt could spare a moment to look over his shoulder to see a mask of red blood and purple gore.

"Leave Meder Shaluwa!" the mask said and grinned.

At last Mangan Sorkera and Kitt reached the centre of the Shakro-Shork. The black twisted stem was before them in the thorny dome. Nine serpent's skeletons hung from it, the teeth buried in the purplish skin, and around the serpents' heads, the trunk had rotted.

Meder were coming in from all sides and the lashing creepers and contracting tunnels tore them apart. The Shakro-Shork was now flailing at everything like a wounded Dodlak.

Standing before the black trunk of the Shakro-Shork, the war leader raised the black knife and plunged it into the purplish skin. The trunk split open like swollen flesh, and purple gore splashed to the ground with a smell like rotten blood.

Mangan slashed at the black trunk again and again, reaching into the widening wound up to his shoulder, until he had severed it completely. The upper chunk hung from the interlocking branches, and greyness spread as the purple liquid flowed out and added to the pool that formed around the lower severed half; here the greyness also spread. A scream tore through the Shakro-Shork that was taken up by all, Meder, Feen and Kitt.

By then, Kitt was wrapped in creepers head to foot, unable to move, the thorns tearing at him like a dying Dodlak. In the brief moment their eyes met, Kitt wondered just how far the Feen's code of honour might differ from his. Then the war leader began to slice at the creepers that were holding Kitt. As the purple gore was running away, they turned dry and rustling, making it easy to break them off. He pulled the dry thorns from his flesh. It hurt. Mangan Sorkera helped him. That hurt more.

Tadir and Shaluwa came bounding across the thorns, smeared all over with purple Meder gore and their own red blood running from countless scratches, elated. Fitcher and the other young warriors emerged from the dead Shakro-Shork, scratched even worse than Tadir and Shaluwa.

"All Meder dead!" Shaluwa laughed, and Fitcher nodded grinning.

Then very slowly, a figure with the skin hanging down in bloody strips came towards them stumbling over the dry thorns. That had to be Reki. But Reki did not complain.

Of the Feen, only Mangan Sorkera had not a scratch.

"Shangar Shaark Ayen dead," the war leader said.

"Munitera Ludoshini?" Shaluwa asked.

The young warriors looked unenthusiastic. In their opinion, the Ludoshini of the Zoyamizoyi Feen was no good, or the Zoyamizoyi families would not have had to seek refuge with the Kra-Tini.

"Better ludishini no," Mangan said, meaning that it was better than to have no Ludoshini at all. But he was not convinced of that himself.

Kitt threw off the last dry thorn creepers. They stood facing each other, Gawthrin Lye and the Feen. There was a pause.

"Gawthrin Lye bring Kaulra Gooth Mangan Sorkera," the Feen leader said slowly. "Gawthrin Lye fight Shakro-Shork."

"Gawthrin Lye no like hunt Feen game in thornbush," Kitt replied haughtily.

The young Feen warriors relaxed imperceptibly. Djanadir Thomiat was a worthy enemy, Djanadir Thomiat had manners. The battle lines were clear again.

"Djanadir hunt Feen game, Feen hunt Djanadir," Fitcher said cheerfully.

"Djanadir Thomiat die Tini tree stake," Tadir seconded. "Mik Thomiat, great warrior death," he added politely, and Shaluwa indicated his approval of the compliment.

But their war leader did not seem willing to accept Kitt's offer to take up the old feud just where they had left it. "Gawthrin Lye save life Mangan Sorkera Shakro-Shork."

The warriors tensed again. This time the atmosphere changed at the admission of debt from their revered leader. How they must hate to be beholden to him, a non-Feen outsider. Kitt could almost understand that, if ever he could understand anything of the Feen way of thinking.

"Mangan Sorkera save Gawthrin Lye from Mik Shini." Mangan Sorkera had allowed Kitt to escape the torture stake when Shangar Shaark Ayen had decreed the Shameful Death for him.

To judge by the way the war leaders deep, black eyes blazed at Kitt's words, it had been the wrong thing to say, too obvious a gift, and thus a deadly insult. The war leader looked at Kitt fully. "Mangan Sorkera challenge Gawthrin Lye death fight two times. Gawthrin Lye no fight."

This was like an eerie repetition of another day when Kitt had met the first human being whose life he had taken. He had had no choice then, and he had none now, but now as then it all ultimately came down to one thing - he intended to survive. Since then, he had learned much about the Feen and knew that there was only one way to answer the challenge. Kitt met the war leader's gaze squarely. "Mangan Sorkera fight Gawthrin Lye now?"

Mangan Sorkera smiled happily.

The nine bloodied Feen warriors drew apart in a loose circle, to leave the war leader and Kitt to face each other. For a moment nobody spoke. Just when the tension had mounted to the point when both adversaries should reach for their weapons and clash, Kitt broke the silence.

"Wait!" With the left hand, he reached up to the chin strap, loosed it, and took off the helmet. Then he opened the other straps, one after the other.

The young Feen warriors stared at Kitt in his torn, bloody leather clothing, and then at each other in bewilderment. The armour had made Gawthrin Lye almost invulnerable to Feen weapons, but their code of honour did not demand of him to divest himself of this advantage. Instead, it was just another proof of the valour of the war leader, to take on these odds.

For a moment the Feen did not know how to behave, unable to make up their minds whether Gawthrin Lye's offer to meet Mangan Sorkera on equal terms was an insult, bravado, or just one of those strange things non-Feen did. The battle tension was broken. Shaken by Gawthrin Lye's second refusal to avail himself of the upper hand luck had given him, Mangan Sorkera's fierce animal eyes met the quiet gaze of Kitt's grey ones.

"Mangan Sorkera say Gawthrin Lye Mer Moz." The war leader tipped his forehead. "Tuzakzak, beryalasur," he added in the Rilante language, that of Cryssumha, and again in the Nordmann language. "Gall, crazy."

Kitt thought that the war leader had made his meaning quite clear now in four languages.

Shaluwa nodded vigorously in agreement. "Mer Moz."

"Mer Moz!" each of other young warriors muttered. Suddenly, the Feen turned on their heels, sprang over a heap of dry thorn branches, and disappeared into the woods, leaving Kitt to stand among the remains of the dead Shakro-Shork.

"Mer Moz," he said, and looked down at his ripped mail, the torn leather; he pulled another long thorn out of his sleeve and looked at the red tip. "They're right."

A few years ago, Kitt would have taken that to be just a simple insult, typical for the Feen who did not accept any ways different from their own. But now he remembered that somebody, was it Faibur of Dundingin, or Gweronell of the iron ship Birlinn Yehan, or possibly Cynan Concen who had died the Red Death -that someone had told him that the Fihen thought those of deranged mind touched by different worlds, and considered it unlucky to harm them. By calling him Mer Moz, Mangan Sorkera had done more than merely dismissing Kitt as crazy – he had made him an untouchable for all the Feen of the Murkowydir.

Kitt could now go openly to the Zinnfluss where his boat lay. Before he went, he wanted a closer look at the dead Meder, better than had been possible when they flitted through the thorns, blending in. He still didn't know what they were, if they even belonged to this world, and most importantly, if the Meder been human. He could take his time too, as there was no more hurry for him to escape the Feen.

The Meders' pale, white and clammy skin was deeply scarred by the charcoal- black patterns that turned their faces into masks – if those lines could be tattoos. Kitt began to think that they were something the Meder were born with. That brought him to the next question, if they were born like humans, or were the fruit of the Shakro-Shork. He couldn't even ascertain if there were males and females.

The short hair that covered their round heads was thick like mink fur and of a deep, velvety black. Their fingers ended in black claws that were curved like those of cats. The teeth revealed by the thin black lips pushed back were white, sharp seams, like scissor blades. The pupils of their dark eyes without white were horizontal slits.

Meder means devils, Shangar Shaark Ayen had said, and Kitt could see nothing human about them and neither did they seem to belong to the cats. His examination did not answer his questions and only brought up new mysteries. He considered, if he wanted their claws and teeth and skin as trophies, as he had taken those of the Dodlak.

He did not want them.

On the way back to his boat, Kitt did not hide any more. The Feen knew he was there.

He still avoided approaching any of the settlements, to offer no provocation. All might not yet be aware of the war leader's pronunciation.But it seemed that they were, because he began to find small gifts of food in his path, which he interpreted as the wish to hurry his passage through the territory, tolerated, but a stranger.

When he came upon a party of women who collected hazelnuts he gave them a wide berth, but not wide enough to not hear them say, "Gawthrin Lye. Mer Moz." They tacitly continued their work without paying more attention to him than to any other inedible animal. The Jay watches and scouts also ignored him, but one did advise him of a bear in the vicinity.

A column of warriors passed without looking at him. He was just the crazy Gawthrin Lye. They meant no offence, but an absence of a challenge. It felt strange to walk beneath the bronze leafed beeches, elderberries and red bird-berry-trees, through clearings thick with blackberries and red currants, past the remains of cities swallowed by the woods, Aestwik, Vordayorn, an ancient Cryssumha city of six and eight cornered ruins with no known name – all without the certainty that each smallest mistake, be it a careless imprint in the fallen leaves or a startled crow's outrage, would be punished with death.

Even so, Kitt could not shed his second nature to move as silently as sunlight and shadow, leaving as many traces. There still was the Dodlak to be careful of, bears jealous of honey and nuts, Kalonek, Archantel lion, the coal-black and silver Sheh Ri, shy, but deadly, and most dangerous of all, the Hunters in the Mist.

Kitt had hidden his boat on a rocky peninsula that reached far into the Zinnfluss outfall into the Graumeer.

Moored neatly beside it he found his old whalebone frame boat covered in walrus skin, which he had given for lost after the debacle of Bear Mountain. It contained all his belongings and the violet blossoms, still dry in their wooden container. The fresh meat had been replaced with Biltis and the green leek of spring with red and white onions. He also found a freshly hunted and partitioned hare wrapped in its own skin. New also were a bark container of dried elderberry blossoms and a bag with nuts: chestnuts, walnuts, beechnuts, hazelnuts. The bag with the nuts, and also the leather square, in which the Biltis was wrapped, had a red and beige stitched pattern.

The girl Moshonalak.

She appeared from behind the willow-tree where she had been so well hidden, that Kitt had not known she was there. Was he getting careless because he was Mer Moz? Or was the girl a very good hunter?

She approached him with a slight smile on her beautiful mouth and in her deer eyes without the white showing, coming nearer, not stopping. She stretched out her hand and slipped it into his leather tunic. Then her other hand – and then her hands were everywhere. Kitt's body reacted, and it felt so good to that he just let her do with him what she wanted.

She wanted them both to be naked.

She wanted to straddle him rocking back and forth, her smooth legs muscles contracting while he stroked the sleek line of her hips and her swaying breasts. In the end, he flipped her over and pinned her down.

Then they swam in the river.

Then she threw her arms and legs around him in the water.

At first she didn't want to go out to sea in the boat, but then she wanted to try, and Kitt padded it with reeds so they could lie in it together, as it gently rocked on the waves of the bay.

They spent four days together. On the fifth day, she told Kitt that now she would be able to prove her value. At least he thought that was what she said, but he could be mistaken, as she spoke entirely in the Feen language. She said she would leave for her village that he now knew was named Mukine-Kad-Nidyas and that he should return in spring for violet blossoms.

When she had left him, Kitt set sail for the western wind to take him home to Isenkliff.

Leaving Isenkliff

The grey mountains of Isenkliff rose steeply from the grey waters of Graumeer. On the west side, the rise of the land was gentler where the green valley of a creek sloped down to a protected bay with a beach of sand and pebbles. In this little natural harbour bay lay a serpent ship with the high keel drawn up onto the beach.

A sailing boat that was approaching from the west, changed course towards the southern side of the island. There, the rugged coast allowed the only access via a rock called Brynnir's Anvil. The more fearful and superstitious of the northern people spoke of this landing place as the Devil's Anvil.

Fifteen feet long, the boat had a whalebone frame with walrus skin stretched over it double. The young man who sailed it was well over six and a half feet tall and powerfully built with broad shoulders, slim hips, and long legs. The shoulder-long reed-coloured mane whipped in the western wind. Near the shore, the wind subsided a little. He dragged the boat up to Brynnir's Anvil.

Then he stood on the rocky beach looking up the top of the cliff, and as he stood there, he was uneasy, tense, both hands not far from sword hilt and knife, the grey eyes troubled. When he finally moved up the steep path, it was with the deliberate grace of a great cat.

A serpent ship was in the harbour, Nordmänner from Asringholm or the Blauochsland.

Kitt's experience with such visitors had been mixed; the Nordmänner warriors often seemed to take his very presence as a challenge. That was why he landed on the southern side of the island, at Brynnir's Anvil. The Ferys people from the opposite shore used this rock outcrop when they wanted hoes, ploughs and swords mended. Suddenly he had the feeling that they would never again come.

Something was not right on Isenkliff. He could he not shake this feeling of strangeness; it was as if he had landed for the first time on an uninhabited island. But this was his home, and he had been gone only twenty days -twenty days to return the Black Knife Kaulra Gooth to the Murkowydir wood, that its inhabitants called the Sreedok, and others called it the Great Wood Bacenis. He had returned from there often before, and it had never felt like this. His habitual bad conscience was catching up with him; that was nothing new, though. This time he hadn't killed anybody, not even the Meder, whatever those murderous creatures had been, people or cats or something else entirely. But lately, somehow, he could never get rid of a guilty feeling.

As Kitt went up the cliff path through the familiar terrain, his sense of unease did not abate. He came over the ridge and looked down into the valley where the house stood. In his mother's walled garden, the leaves were red and thinned out, and the trees had shed their fruit because Aslaug had not gathered the apples and pears. The fallen fruit spoiled on the ground. The cattle weren't in their meadow by the creek.

Kitt watched for some time and didn't see his father, mother or little Swantje Birla. That was not unusual this late in autumn when fruit and crops were harvested – except that they were not, he could see that the turnips stood in their plot with their wilted leaves soggy with rain. The cattle, a veritable herd since the departure of the Birlinn Yehan, was nowhere to be seen. Neither was a whole crew of Nordmänner, thirty or forty men. They had to be somewhere.

Kitt donned his mail before he approached. The broken links reminded him of the struggle in the Shakro-Shork and snagged in his leather tunic.

On his way to the house Kitt saw nobody. The neglected garden lay in the sun. The doors of the house were closed, the windows shuttered. Suddenly he was overwhelmed with an inexplicable, desolate feeling of loss. Afraid to open the door, he stood motionless.

At last, he stirred, reluctantly stretched out the left hand and slowly opened the scullery door. His right hand flew the short distance to the sword hilt. Inside, nothing was in its old place. The table was shoved aside; pots, logs, ashes and shards of crockery lay on the floor.

Unaccountably, his bows were still hanging on the wall, the Kirgis and the ash bow, together with the quivers full of arrows. The kitchen next door was the same, the familiar cups and plates smashed on the floor.

Kitt listened for noises from inside the house.

Nothing.

Although all his instincts urged him to run, to storm, to throw open all the doors, he moved with caution.

In the hall, the floor was strewn with books and parchments. A look upwards showed the empty shelves, as if somebody had dragged down everything and thrown all over the balustrade. He couldn't be sure if some books were missing or just buried in the heaps of paper, parchment, wood leaves and papyrus.

Each time before he opened a door, he hesitated, afraid what he might find behind it, relieved when the next room revealed only more of the disorder he had seen in the hall.

He should not have left, Kitt thought again and again. He should have been here to protect his family. This had to happen one day. For years, men whose way of life was violence had come to Isenkliff to buy his father's steel, men whose profession was death, for whom the lives of other people counted for nothing.

He ascended the stairs to the first storey and first, he went to his little sister's room, and he gripped his sword hilt, more to hold on to it, than anything else, as he reached out and pushed the door open. Her room was as empty and in a shambles, like the rest of the house. He leaned against the doorpost for a moment, uncertain what to do next, but with a horrible sense of urgency.

Just where were they, had their bodies been thrown into the sea, or down the well, or had they been abducted – he could think of too many horrible possibilities. Swantje Birla's favourite blanket wasn't there. Her game set of gemstones was also missing and the little bear of rabbit fur. The search of the rooms Aslaug and Eckehart had inhabited was inconclusive; it seemed to him that all their personal things were there, on the floor.

His own room Kitt found untouched, to his surprise, his bed, his few clothes including the black silk cloak of the Red Lily Knights, and some books he had been reading the eternity of a month ago. There was a sense of abandonment as if the things belonged to another youth, who would never come back.

Kitt went down into the hall again. He opened the door of the last room built into the cliff that led to a flight of chambers, where the floor used to be covered with the gold the warriors paid for their blades. The gold was gone; not a single coin had been left in a dark corner.

Perhaps somebody looked for the royal insignia of Cryssumha, foremost the sword Slatynrigan, that dangerous, mind-destroying weapon. His father had promised to find a safe hiding place, and Kitt hoped that he had done that in time, but that preoccupation was marginal before the disappearance of his family.

Kitt ran out of the house towards the smithy. At first, he had the weird illusion that the smithy was not there. He shook his head energetically, to clear his sight from the sudden tears that blurred his eyes, and saw the stone shed where it had always been, built half into the rock, like the house.

He threw open the door and found the forge empty, undisturbed; here there was no disorder. Eckehart's tools lay neatly in their places.

Kitt's swords and lances were in their weapons racks; a new mail tunic of incorruptible steel lay on the shelf. It was his size, and he took the time to doff the broken mail and don the new.

And then Kitt caught his breath. For some unaccountable reason he saw only now that there on the anvil lay a sword. It was a thing of deadly beauty, a cold, steely gleam that drew Kitt's eyes and lit a desire. The straight blade was unusually long and broad, heavy enough to cut plate armour into metallic shreds, sharp enough to slice through flesh and bone with scientific precision. The grip was wrapped with plain leather, and the cross-guard a simple steel bar; the pommel was a slightly egg-shaped ball designed to crack skulls.

Drawn body and soul, Kitt reached to seize this sword, and the hilt seemed to spring into his hands. From the mirror of the polished steel, his grey eyes looked back at him. He lifted the blade and found it balanced so finely that it could be thrown like a knife or javelin.

"A door!" said a subdued man's voice outside the smithy.

"Must be the smith's workshop," said another voice, amazed. "It wasn't here before!"

"The Zaubar magic of Isenkliff!" the third voice wavered a little. "We should have listened!"

"Quiet!" This voice had authority.

Nordmänner. Through the small windows in the thick wall, Kitt saw a branch of the elderberry stir; he heard the light footfall of men who were taking position around the smithy.

Noiselessly, he withdrew into the storeroom. Both windows were shuttered. A quick look around showed him that this room also was untouched, the stacks of steel-bars complete.

Grimly, he waited.

Here, at last, were the men from the serpent ship. They had plundered the house and were responsible for the disappearance of his parents and his little sister. Or their death, that was a possibility. If they were captive, then Kitt's one chance was to disable the attackers as quickly and decisively as possible. Kill them all, then free little Swantje Birla and his parents wherever they were kept. Perhaps leave alive one Nordmann, make him speak, to shorten the search.

Outside nothing moved, the silence lasted.

Suddenly the door splintered under the impact of a tall, fair-haired, leather-clad warrior, who landed on the floor; crouching, he turned on his heels, his sword ready in both hands, and his eyes raked the room. The light from the window was in his eyes, and he did not yet see Kitt lurking in the storeroom.

"Nobody here." The Nordmann straightened up and lowered his sword a little.

"Coming in." Another man followed the first, bare blade in hand.

Kitt stepped out. The intruders' eyes widened at the sight of the powerful figure with the long flaxen mane suddenly materialising out of the shadows with the fluid movement of a cave lion. Before their swords could come up, a glittering arc moved across the first man's neck, another flowing step, and the sword tip stuck in the throat of the second man. They fell without a cry.

As the new sword drank first blood, something broke inside Kitt, the chrysalis of his upbringing, to leave only a warrior, a hard will

390

and a sharp intelligence governing a system of excellent muscles and sinews, of fast-reacting senses and nerves - a killer, nothing else, intent only on massacring single-handed a whole ship's crew.

"Is the gold there?" called the imperious voice from outside.

"No gold," Kitt replied. "Iron."

Through the broken door, he saw four warriors armed with swords and axes stand before the smithy in a loose semicircle. They were Nordmänner like those who lay on the floor in their blood. He saw a fifth Nordmann who stood beside the door to the left, motionless, with his sword uplifted, and a sixth warrior farther away; he had a bow trained on the door.

Kitt stayed just inside, careful that the man with the bow should not catch sight of him. For some moments, nothing happened. When it became clear to the men outside, that Kitt would not come out, the man beside the door stepped into full view slowly, big and broad in full armour. From the way he held his head and shoulders, it was clear that he was the leader. He had ice-blue eyes.

"Iron, is it," the Nordmann said flatly.

Kitt took one step across the threshold to meet him.

The leader saw the sword in Kitt's hand, and the same flame that was in the grey eyes sprang up in the blue.

"I came to have a sword made," he said slowly. "It is this one."

"You can't hold this one."

"Can't I, boy? I say that I will cut your throat with it."

The other men began to move in, and the archer changed position because the leader's mailed shoulders were between his bow and Kitt.

"Hold it!" said the leader, and raised his sword. "I'll take him." His blue eyes looked into Kitt's grey, recognising what he saw there, a cold, bright hardness. He smiled. "Tell me your name, boy so that you shall not die nameless."

"I won't die." In Kitt's head, there a white silence narrowing his perception, and only the Nordmänner stood out sharply like black silhouettes before the white.

"Feilan. A wolf cub." The thin lips drew back in a cold smile over strong white teeth. "You are brave Feilan, but your misfortune is that you meet Starri Sköldarson of Orkneyjar."

The fire of battle madness was in Starri's eye, mirroring Kitt's; he laughed when the blades engaged in a shower of sparks. Like weightless lightning, the heavy blades warred too fast for the eyes to follow.

The fighters could not keep up that flailing whirlwind forever; arms would tire, the wind give out, eyes and brain slip. One would falter first. It was Starri who first slowed down for a fraction of a moment, and Kitt's sword struck through armour and heart. Looking straight into Kitt's eyes, the big man stood still, with the mad smile still on his lips.

Then he fell.

Kitt wrenched his sword free. With one hard stroke, he slew the Nordmann who reached him first, and ran the next man through, fast and unemotional. He evaded another Nordmann's axe, took it away and smashed it between neck and shoulder. He heard the archer shout because he could get no free shot at Kitt. Two Nordmänner were attacking him with axes and swords. The archer threw down his useless bow and quiver to join his remaining comrades in the melee.

At once, Kitt separated the bowman from the others and split his head to the teeth with the axe.

Thirty Nordmänner formed up back to back. Kitt just smiled and picked up the strung bow of the fallen archer.

Three men tried to reach him at a run; Kitt cut them down.

The others reformed.

Kitt began to shoot; his arrows found the men's faces and gaps in their armour with fearful accuracy.

The formation broke again.

The last fight was bitter and ranged over the whole valley. Again and again, it was Kitt who attacked, and drew blood with each sword stroke. He had already learned that numbers didn't matter if he could have a moment alone with each man. He was stronger than they, faster, his endurance longer. His face was a mask.

The two remaining Nordmänner turned to flee towards the shore. Kitt followed them, the pounding of the death race like a bridge over the spreading numbness in his heart.

With their backs against their ship, the two made a stand. One was bleeding from the side and leg, the other from a deep gash across his face. Kitt's sword sheared through the hand that held the axe and blocked the sword-stroke of the last Nordmann left. They stared at each other across their engaged swords.

Kitt pushed the other's blade away with his, stepped back, and swung his sword high. The Nordmann brought up his blade in time to block Kitt's blow, the force of which struck the hilt from nerveless hands, and he fell against the boat.

Kitt's blade was at his throat. "What did you do with the little girl? And the smith and the healer?" It was a wolf's growl.

Beside them, the man with the severed arm was still standing, swaying. Looking at the blood spurting from the stump, he sat down heavily by the boat, his lips moving. Kitt ignored him.

"There was nobody here, when we came," the Nordmann croaked.

"You must tell the truth," Kitt said in that low growl and leaned on the sword a little.

Blood ran from the Nordmann's neck; he choked and tried to grab the blade with his hands. His eyes were defiant, and he tried to spit. "Why should I lie to you, Feilan? I'm not afraid of you. You are flesh and blood."

Now that the battle was over, the cold, bright, hard thing sank to the bottom of Kitt's soul again, and a little sanity flowed back into his eyes. His voice was still a wolf's growl. "You say nobody was here?"

"I say nobody was here for months! This place has been sacked a time ago and not by us."

The Nordmann's words tallied with the impression of desertion that Kitt himself had, before his fear for his family's fate had driven everything else out of his mind. Now that he thought clearly again, he remembered specific details in the house that had spoken the same language.

"Months? I've been gone from here only twenty days." Kitt sounded as unsure now as he suddenly felt.

The Nordmann gave him a peculiar look. "That may well be. And yet it is as I say. Kill me and then go and see for yourself."

Kitt searched the serpent ship and found nothing. No captives. No gold. No Slatynrigan. The Nordmänner's shields were there. If they had carried those, they could have formed a shield-wall and it might have been harder to kill them all.

Kitt left the last surviving Nordmann leaning against the ship, both hands pressed to his side, red trickling over his fingers, his dead comrade at his feet. He went up to the house again, trying to keep his panic in check.

Rectangles on the table showed where books and parchments had lain in the gathering dust before the Nordmänner had thrown them to the floor in their frustrated search for gold.

A liquid had dried in Aslaug's kettle.

There was a dead starling in a corner.

Again, he had the disturbing feeling that the house had been deserted for months, even for years. There was no sign at all of little Swantje Birla, that she had ever been here, that she existed.

"We took no little girl," the Nordmann said; he stood in the hall door. "I would not lie to you now. We never killed any child." He slowly sagged down on the doorstep, leaving a thick smear of blood on the doorframe.

Kitt went into the room beside the kitchen where Aslaug kept her medicines. They were untouched, neatly in their caskets and linen bags in the cupboard with the many drawers, overlooked by the plundering Nordmänner by a miracle such as Aslaug was able to arrange. He was sure that she had drawn a sign on the doors of the cupboard, invisible lines that made the eye slide over and past it. He could not see it, because Aslaug had never taught him, but he guessed that she had done the same with the smithy, and his room. He had found the doors only because he knew they were there.

The familiar smell of the herbs and barks poured out as Kitt opened the drawers, and for a moment it was as if Aslaug was standing there, saying that it was easy to wound and hard to heal. Kitt thought how he had saddened his mother with his weapons training, while she had tried to teach him to be a healer.

Why didn't I ask about Swantje Birla first? It hadn't even occurred to him to just ask.

Swallowing the lumps that kept rising in his throat, Kitt gathered Aslaug's wound medicine and clean linen bandages, and returned to the surviving Nordmann. He drew away the bloody hands clutching his side, cut away the clothing, and revealed the profuse bleeding. Kitt staunched the blood, cleaned the wound, closed it with five stitches, applied Aslaug's wound medicine and bound it up. Then he attended to the leg wound. His hands moved quickly and lightly.

"Nobody would even look sideways at the Smith of Isenkliff or the Mount Lyfja woman, let alone kill them," the Nordmann said. "They must have gone away and taken everything of value with them. That is what it looked like. A deserted place. No sign of any attack but somebody must have gone through it before us."

Why would they have gone? That made no sense, no matter what the Nordmann said. *Unless something had happened? But what? How to find out why they had left, where to find them now?* And if they returned, they would come back to bloody corpses strewn all over the valley. He had been tested, and he had failed.

Kitt left the house to look into each dead face in the pale golden light of the sun sinking in the south-west. Longest, he looked into the proud, ruthless face of the leader. Even in death, Starri's eyes were startlingly blue.

How could I have been so sure, and at the same time so wrong? How couldn't I have spotted the signs of departure? "I killed them for nothing."

"Don't you think twice about that, Feilan," said the Nordmann by his side. "When we land on any shore, riches await or death. Both are good. It was a good day, a good fight. You fought a great battle, as in the heroes' tales. When you cross the Rainbow Bridge, you'll find us all there, waiting to fight you again."

"I'll bury them."

"The ship. Fire," the Nordmann said. "If you will do that for us, Feilan, then we shall drink your health in the Hall of Valaskjalf."

The sun stood low above the western sea as a glowing orange and rose-coloured sphere. Smoke wreathed the deck of the serpent ship.

The Nordmann was sitting on a rock, exhausted. "You should kill me and put me with them," he said.

Kitt shook his head. "I treated your wounds, so I can't kill you."

"If you think that to be kindness, you are wrong," the Nordmann said bitterly.

The fire caught on the sail and roared into a great blaze.

When the serpent ship had burned down, darkness had fallen. Kitt half led, half carried the Nordmann back to the house. He settled him on the bed in the sick-room with rugs and blankets. The Swordmaster Diorlin of Eliberre had healed in that room and Lord Gasda, the Dog of Rilante. From the medicine cupboard, he took a glass bottle containing a mixture of Bilsenkraut and poppy extracts, measured some into a glass of water and carried it to the Nordmann.

"What's this?"

"Against the pain and to help you sleep."

"Sleep? In this place?"

Kitt put the draught it beside him. "If you change your mind."

When he turned to leave the room, the Nordmann's stolid mask cracked. Desperately his hands scrabbled over the cover, trying to get up, sinking back again. "Don't leave me here alone, man! Rather cut my throat!"

"Be still, or you'll bleed again." Kitt held the desperate man down until he gave up the struggle. "You are safe in the house."

The Nordmann shook his head feebly, his eyes closed. Kitt managed to get the draught inside him before he fully realised, and left him to an exhausted doze. He went out of the hall; he could not bear to lay down to sleep in his room, where everything was as he had left it, while nothing else was. As he took the cliff path to the smelting ovens, he thought with a sudden mad hope, that his family might be there all the time.

At the ovens, there was no sign of his father Eckehart's recent presence. The grass seemed to have grown fast around the stone anvil where Kitt had forged his first blade. The pine trees were singing their endless song in the constant west wind.

Kitt sat there all night, as he had after his first confrontation with the Nordmänner, with Harmar Saesorgison of Asringholm, who was also dead. As he had then, he thought about true courage, and back to the day when, for the first time in his life, he had killed another human being -and when he had killed again, always in defence, to survive. Today he had attacked.

In that darkest moment before dawn, Kitt slept, and he dreamed of the Bloodswamp.

The giant Kri warrior was the epicentre of something that had left a widely flung circle of dead Theusten warriors. Blood welling out of countless wounds showed that he was still alive. The broad chest fell and rose slightly with his fading breath.

More than one of the wounds was mortal. His steel-grey eyes were beginning to break. With fading senses, he heard voices. The world darkened around him, and he hoped with a mad hope that the sun would go down before the scavengers arrived.

Steps came in his direction, they drew nearer. He more felt than saw somebody bending over him, and he waited for hands to touch him roughly, intent on making bitter the last moments of one they feared and hated so much.

It would not have mattered to him, now that she was dead, his mate of so many days and nights, so many battles. They could not have touched him if it had not been for the child, the last spark left of her and him.

The boy lay very still behind him, like a young animal sensing the hunter. The dying Kri warrior spent his last strength trying to raise his defenceless body towards the shadow of the enemy above him, offering an easy triumph, so that they might overlook the boy.

A face swam into his narrowing view, a woman's, hard and white as if carved from bone with the knife of suffering. Her blue eyes were deep wells of something the dying Kri had never seen before.

The woman's strange eyes saw the child.

Powerless, he watched her hands taking him away.

Then the woman spoke, and with uncomprehending hope, the Kri saw that it was life that was on her mind.

He said only one word and that was the first time anyone heard a Kri beg. "Kitt."

Kitt woke with his name in his ears.

The sun rose in the south-east. He walked towards the house, seeing every rock and tree as if for the first time. Out of somewhere within him came images and sounds -he heard deep shouts, saw steel flash in the sun, blood so red spilling on grass so green, the sternness in the face of a warrior wavering for a moment, as his companion fell beside him.

When he entered the house, the metallic smell of drying blood was strong. The Nordmann lay in the hall; his cheek rested in the sticky dark pool of blood that had spread on the floor and run under the long table. He had cut his throat with Aslaug's kitchen knife. Kitt stared down at him mutely. That this fearless man had been so afraid of what he had thought the night of Isenkliff held that was worse than death - Kitt had not reckoned with such terror, although he knew that the Ferys were reluctant to set foot on the shore of Isenkliff; he remembered the reverence many Nordheim warriors had shown Eckehart and Aslaug because they thought they dealt with the Lütte Jotun. It had been the truth that he had told the Nordmann. The Jarnmantsjes didn't come into the hall uninvited. He had not taken this man's fear seriously, and so he had died.

As he stood by the dead body, suddenly, Kitt saw the letters, in the middle of the table. They had been lying there, undisturbed, all the time. There were two.

The first letter was scribbled with a piece of charcoal on the white rice paper that a golden warrior had once brought all the way from Luxin Shoo. The runes sprawled over the whole sheet.

My son, for that is what you will always be in my heart, I did not make the sword you find in the smithy, although I wish that I had. Your father carried this sword. It never failed him. If you don't neglect it, it won't neglect you. Name it Inoar.

Kitt stared at the letter uncomprehending; with hands suddenly unsteady, he turned it around and found nothing on the reverse, only a smear of charcoal and a thumbprint.

The second letter was parchment, written in fluent black ink lines by somebody to whom the runes were a natural means of expression. It had been written some time ago and been unfolded to place upon the table. The creases from storing it were visible with tiny ink flakes collecting in them.

Seventeen years ago, a deadly weapon came to Nordheim and cut our lives through into a time before and after.
This weapon was no sword, bow, lance or axe, and it was not made from bronze, iron, stone or wood. It was a weapon of human flesh and bone, a people of warriors, for sale to anyone prepared to pay their price.

The Kri.

Nobody knows from whence they came to pitch their leather tents on Kullen Tor in Tridden Moor - that today is known as the Bloodswamp.

More deadly than common mercenaries, stronger and wilder than all the warriors of Nordheim, the Kri knew no compromise. They did not parley, took no prisoners, and had no mercy. For them, only victory or defeat mattered.

After the first of the warring lords of Burgenland had taken Kri mercenaries into service, no lord could keep his stronghold and lands, who did not hire them. And in Daguilaria, the Eternal Emperor, forever hungry for land and slaves, turned his calculating eyes towards Burgenland, and also the Evil Men exiled from Thule, hungry for power over the bodies and souls of men.

As the unfeeling weapon in the hands of greedy men, the Kri were about to bring down the North, the whole world, in a spiral of destruction. Then, for the first time after the battle of Kalkhorst, Svalinir's spear was cast once more. All the tribes of Nordheim were united, and the hundred thousand came from Nordheim to Lalland. King Grimwolf of the Theusten was our Heerking.

I, Aslaug of Lyfya Mountain was there in Tridden Moor, to help where I could.

Surrounded by all the warriors of Nordheim, the Kri fought until their last remains were wiped out in one soul-destroying battle, all the warriors, both men and women. On the white heads fell the sword and the children were hunted and killed like wolf cubs.

There was no mercy left in the world.

When it was over, at last, I walked among the dead for a long time, without coming upon a single living soul in the bloody mud of the battlefield. With me was Eckehart, the Smith of Stargard.

We found the wounded Kri warrior, the only one alive on this battlefield. He lay in a circle of dead Theusten, all the men of Grimwolf's following. In heaps, they lay around him; so many that I did not want to count.

Bleeding from many wounds the Kri was dying. Another warrior was beside him, a woman. She was dead. There between them, I saw a boy child. I asked the dying Kri what his name was, and he said: Kitt.

We came to Isenkliff, Eckehart and I and the child.

The last paragraph was newly written by the same hand.

In the eyes of the world, you were our son. But you are a Kri, the last of these deadliest, these ultimate warriors. I have tried to make you into something else, and I have failed.
Blood cannot be cheated.

The letter ended as in the same abrupt manner as it had begun and the life Kitt had known broke into a million shards.

He tried to reread the parchment, with single words jumping out at him that transformed his world into something new and alien, staring numbly at Aslaug's clear, precise handwriting until his eyes stung and the letters swam before them, to see if he had overlooked something, a kinder word to him, who had thought himself her son for all the seventeen years of his life.

There was nothing, only her admission of failure.

Eckehart and Aslaug had left him. *And why not*, he thought, as word after word hit home like a club, *I'm not their family, not even their own kind.*

There was nobody who was his kind because his race had been exterminated like raving wolves. He too was a killer by birth. That was why Aslaug had been so adamantly opposed to his weapons training, while she had tried to teach him not to be a monster, that one day would have to be hunted down and killed.

But all her efforts were useless because it was in his blood, so she had refused to teach him any of her magic and now left him.

Haven't I proved her right? Perhaps not with the dead Feen warrior, and then the Hunters in the Mist, when he had only defended himself. But now, he had set out to kill, and Isenkliff had become a graveyard for thirty-nine Nordmänner, who had only wanted gold.

Kitt folded up the parchment to store it in his tunic above his chest. His face had hardened into the mask of the warrior, he could feel it.

He carried the dead Nordmann down to the shoreline. There was enough charred wood left of the serpent ship to build a pyre.

Things fell into perspective with the logs he piled up. Kitt's family hadn't been killed or abducted. His parents – foster parents - had left and taken little Birla with them after his mother had sent Kitt to the Murkowydir wood on the errand to return the black stone knife Kaulra Gooth. They had not waited for his return. That was the truth. The reason glowed before him, burning flesh and bones. His mother had foreseen these fires, he was sure.

Kitt would leave also. It was late in the year to begin a journey when the winter storms could overtake the wanderer.

That didn't matter.

West and south-west lay the Murkowydir, full of wonders, savage beasts, and wild people, some familiar to Kitt, others were muted murmurs, or shadows faintly glimpsed. Kitt was Mer Moz, crazy, free now of the wood the Feen called Sreedok. But he would not go back there for a girl with deer eyes, because she had asked him to return only when the violets blossomed.

Kitt's mind ranged beyond the Murkowydir, beyond Nordheim. In the ports of the Northern Circle ships from all lands lay, their bellies filled with strange wealth from the Lands under the Sunset.

South, the glittering courts of Daguilaria and Bohemia ruled over fertile, soft lands. Knights duelled in the vineyards of Tolosa, to mix their heart-blood into the red wine.

East, the golden mailed knights of Khartweli rode into battle on golden horses. Caravans, strings of black dots before a sky of brass, threaded the Mawaranarian deserts.

Farther south, the god-ridden Meira-valley was populated by sorcerous priests and their resigned victims and there were legends of celestial metal.

Under the horizons of myth dreamed savage Kush and unfathomable Luxin Shoo. Cities' names went through his head like shooting stars, Hartberg, the metropole that was reaching out to take the world, and needle spired Chrasten, ruled by philosophic emperors, sophisticated Lutetia, and Peleset and Quartingis, Queens of the Seas, Nurkande the Beautiful and Binkat the Rich, the twin stars of sin and soft living in the Golden Necklace, alabaster and golden Dolavira. He would go to all these lands, see all these places.

With the funeral blazing behind him, Kitt went back up to the hall, thinking about weapons, medicines and equipment, which to take, which to leave for some more Nordmänner to loot.

One blocky shape beside the path was not a rock. The Jarnmantsje tilted his shaggy head aside to look at Kitt quizzically with eyes sparkling like yellow rock-crystal.

"Why burn all good meat?" he demanded. "Kitt good hunt. Why not give for Gullo to eat?"

"They wouldn't have liked that, Gullo. The Shiplords from Asringholm and Orkneyjar need their ship funerals."

The Jarnmantsje snorted.

"Gullo, where have they gone?"

"They come and go, the Smith and the Healer, yes, they do. I see. I know. Sometimes there is only one, sometimes they are both here. They want things their own way, yes they do. Must let them have their own way. Gullo can do nothing."

"Will they come again?"

"Restless, the ones with the power. Gullo is always here in the mountain, doesn't go away. Good place, the mountain. Iron, coal, not too damn much space, not too damn much light, no, very good."

"I will go away to see the world."

"The world, too damn much space. You won't like it, no," the Jarnmantsje said morosely. "There always is a smith on Isenkliff."

"Yes, but I will go. Goodbye, Gullo."

"You are a good boy Kitt, yes. Don't you worry none, boy, no, don't you worry," Gullo said after him, and it sounded as if two rocks were rubbed against each other.

*

There always is a smith on Isenkliff. Take up Brynnir's Hammer, never leave. One came, one was free to go.

Eckehart had retaken the hammer, deep inside the cliff in Brynnir's forge. He held it in his hand, didn't let go, even when he slept.

A twist had been caused in the fabric of the universe, a knot, caused by the influence of the nameless black thing from the beginning of time. Kaulra Gooth, black stone tooth, the Woodstalkers called it, Kitt had told him. What bottomless foolishness. This thing came from when there were no names, no words, no shapes at all. Kitt had brought it to Isenkliff and used it, once from the goodness of his heart, the second time in the desperate attempt to undo the consequences of what he saw as his fault. He knew no better; Aslaug would not teach him the Seidar magic that showed what lay hidden beneath everything.

The twist caused by the black thing had opened the possibility of a gap in the age-old succession of the Smiths on Isenkliff.

This gap Aslaug wanted to use as a trap.

Eckehart would not have it.

He held Brynnir's hammer in his hand, not letting go. He wanted there to be no slip at all.

Aslaug had left Isenkliff with her daughter Swantje. She had a Queen's chair waiting for her in Theustenland. Grimwolf the Heerking would have no other wife. Her leave-taking had been acrimonious, full of reproach. She had wanted him to come also. Had demanded it.

Eckehart had nothing waiting for him on the mainland, but that was not the reason he stayed. He stayed so that Kitt could leave.

Aslaug knew his plan, as she always knew everything. That was the reason for the way she had spoken before she left. And why Eckehart had a sense of victory, at last.

*

Everything was different on Isenkliff, as if separated by a membrane from the life he knew. Kitt would not spend another night in his old home. He was going away in his boat across the sea towards the mainland, and did not look back in the darkness.

✶✶✶

For illustrations, relevant documents and maps see the
Illustrated Series Companion Book with Library

✶✶✶

The Bloody Hand

Wandering Blacksmith 3

The Red Lily Knights taught Kitt about their code, to Help, Save, and Serve. Visiting with them resulted in Kitt becoming embroiled in the Tolosan Troubles. To escape, he stows away on a Kossean trading ship, the Mariella. This sea journey lasts far longer than he thought. A pirate ship with purple sails appears on the horizon, the Orokun of the Bloody Hand. While the pirates board the Mariella, Kitt boards their ship. He becomes armourer on the Orokun, which soon sails by his rules. In the leaking four-master and riddled with contrary magic, he faces a Sea Witch, the Kraken, Mermen, and monster-storms, and celebrates his twentieth birthday in the main mast. The search for a safe port leads to the hidden island of Satanazes, where treasures wait, and ghosts.

The Star Song

Wandering Blacksmith 4

Kitt's success as a pirate is matched by the bounty on his head, and not all pirates are happy how their armourer runs the ship.

The Orokun of the purple sails makes fast in the wild port of Khattom, far away from kingdoms and empires. There, a stranger drugs Kitt and steals his sword. The hunt for the thief leads Kitt to the lost city of Yoamihassidasse, in the thrall of a cosmic predator, which catches humans in a net of stellar music. Falling to the lure of the Star Song himself, Kitt can only survive by destroying the demon. His enjoyment of the millennia old library is short lived because an army of a hundred bounty hunters has followed him into the mountain. Finding gold, the mercenaries begin to steal the riches of an old empire and slaughter the defenceless people. Kitt must save the city again.

Road of Dragons

Wandering Blacksmith 5

Part I

Kitt finds that his ability to fight is more prized than his craft. By now he is twenty four years old and has killed hundreds of men in hundreds of battles. He wonders if perhaps he only met the wrong people, and always hopes to find a market for Aurora steel.

Kitt comes to Nurkande, a caravan town of the Golden Necklace, on the border of the red desert Kisil Kora. Trade on the caravan roads has come to a standstill because the Dragon-Lord has risen and loosed the Dragon-Sons to steal, torture and murder. Dragons don't exist – do they?

Kitt meets the crime lord Salawar and his gentlemen of fortune. He finds out about the Dragon-Sons and enters the wondrous city of Varakhsha, which is above the desert sands for only one day and one night.

Part II

The descendants of the old dragon Mundarcho Ashdar are prominent in Binkat, another city of the Golden Necklace, and they search for the Rosary of Varakhsha, a string of rose-coloured pearls taken from the heads of Golden Dragons. Kitt comes to Binkat to apprehend the Dragon-Lord and avenge a murdered poet, whose ghost is haunting him.

Then, the old dragon Mundarcho Ashdar is found asleep in the Mountain Under the Moon, a dry river flows again, and suddenly, dragons are everywhere.

Meteor Iron

Wandering Blacksmith 6

Kitt is done with fighting and decides that from now on, he will work as a smith. People would respect him more, if he were still a warrior, but being a humble workman is good enough for him, and safer - for others. A secret of steel sleeps in Taumeiryale, the legends tell, and he wants to uncover it. When Kitt comes to the city by the river Meira, he finds that he is the only blacksmith there.

Maiat, the Higher Order of things rules in the person of the Sunlord, a ten-year-old boy. Tempted by the dark secrets, the boy befriends Kitt and brings them both into open conflict with the priests of the Temple of Eternal Light. Soon, the great, winged serpents slither through the streets to devour who they find, and not even the golden palace is safe.

Two great secrets of steel surface, a fallen star and iron from distant shores. Magic comes within Kitt's reach as it never has before. For the first time, a water woman weeps, and a dark angel schemes from beyond the world divides. From the fallen star, Kitt forges the Dream Cup, the Mirror of the Invisible, the Dividing Sickle, the Kettle of Mutability, the Wand of Wenmut, and last, the Shield of Heaven and the Star Sword, to end all evil, once and forever. The latter transports him to the world of the Diamond Star, where justice is not what Kitt thought, ending in a soul-destroying catastrophe.

As the Star Sword's maker, he must hide the dangerous weapon to never be found again, and for this, he travels far south. There, he meets an old friend, Sogolon Ogidigan, and together they face a serpent-monster, absolute evil and the dead roaming the kingdom of Akan.

Other books by Mark B. Gilgam

Wandering Blacksmith Series:

Wandering Blacksmith 1   Hardening the Steel

Wandering Blacksmith 2   Heavy Metals

Wandering Blacksmith 3   The Bloody Hand

Wandering Blacksmith 4   The Star Song

Wandering Blacksmith 5   Road of Dragons I + II

Wandering Blacksmith 6   Meteor Iron

Connect with Mark B. Gilgam

I really appreciate you reading my book!
Readers' feedback is essential for authors.
If you liked this book, tell the world, and give it five stars!
If you have comments or questions, here are my social media coordinates:

Amazon Autor page: https://www.amazon.com/-/de/Mark-B-Gilgam/e/B0842V712P/
Facebook:
https://www.facebook.com/profile.php?id=100045878844332
Quora: https://www.quora.com/profile/Mark-B-Gilgam
Smashwords Autorenseite:
https://www.smashwords.com/profile/view/MarkBGilgam
LinkedIn: https://www.linkedin.com/in/mark-b-gilgam-1aa509221/
Medium: https://medium.com/@markbgilgam
E-mail: mark_b.gilgam@yahoo.com

Impressum

Mark B. Gilgam
c/o Block Services, 4th Floor, Silverstream House
45 Fitzroy Street, Fitzrovia
London, W1T 6EB
Great Britain